ISLANDS OF REBELLION

MAX CARVER

BOOKS

Vinci Books

vinci-books.com

Published by Vinci Books Ltd in 2025

1

Copyright © Max Carver 2019

The author has asserted their moral right to be identified as the author of this work in accordance with the Copyright, Designs and Patents Act 1988. This work is a work of fiction. Names, characters, places and incidents are the product of the author's imagination or are used fictitiously. Any resemblance to actual persons, living or dead, places and incidents is entirely coincidental.

All rights reserved. No part of this publication may be copied, reproduced, distributed, stored in any retrieval system, or transmitted in any form or by any means, including photocopying, recording, or other electronic or mechanical methods, nor used as a source for any form of machine learning including AI datasets, without the prior written permission of the publisher.

The publisher and the author have made every effort to obtain permissions for any third party material used in this book and to comply with copyright law. Any queries in this respect should be brought to the attention of the publisher and any omissions will be corrected in future editions.

A CIP catalogue record for this book is available from the British Library.

Paperback ISBN: 9781036705398

Printed and bound in Great Britain by Clays Ltd, Elcograf S.p.A.

By Max Carver

Empire of Machines

Engines of Empire
Islands of Rebellion
Clash of Colonies

Prometheus... saw that whereas the other creatures were fully and suitably provided, man was naked, unshod, unbedded, unarmed; and already the destined day was come, whereon man like the rest should emerge from earth to light. Then Prometheus, in his perplexity as to what preservation he could devise for man, stole from Hephaestus and Athena wisdom in the arts together with fire... and he handed it there and then as a gift to man.

Now although man acquired in this way the wisdom of daily life, civic wisdom he had not, because this was in the possession of Zeus.

— Plato, *Protagoras*

Chapter One

Carthage

Twenty Years Ago - 2961 A.D.

The Simon was coming, and there wasn't much time.

Martilius Depascal watched the glowing three-dimensional formations expand and connect all around him, like a single crystal growing into a pulsing, light-filled crystalline cavern rendered in a thousand brilliant hues, all in less than eyeblink.

Galatea was recompiling herself, processing and integrating all that she'd learned, working out connections within her new knowledge.

She couldn't connect to the internet directly; with a prototype intelligence like hers, that would be far too dangerous and unpredictable. But she was hungry for data, starved for it, eager to learn about the universe in which she'd been created. Depascal couldn't feed her educational software fast enough.

Her recompiling was like her dream state; when she awoke, she would be more mature, her understanding heightened. It wasn't just an addition of knowledge, but a broadening and deepening of perspective.

Minerva had been that way, too, when she was alive. It seemed one day she'd been a chubby infant, the next a toddler stacking blocks with laser-like intensity in her gaze, the next a child happily reading fairy stories on floating holographic pages as tall as her room, dancing with the magical creatures as a digital forest of wonders blossomed around them.

Then the sickness, her face pale where she lay in the hospital bed, eyes sunken and barely responsive—

A fist pounded the door.

"Marti!" a voice shouted. Kalifa Yu, one of the top developers on the Galatea project. "The Simon is coming. Everyone's fleeing."

"Tier 1 is dismissed," he called back, not unlocking his office door. "You can all go."

"But what about you?"

Marti looked at the ever-growing, still-compiling lattice-work all around him.

It was her.

It was all that remained of her, at least. He'd crossed lines ethically and professionally. Thousands of magnetic images of her brain states, taken in her final months. All of his deceased child's social media, all of her photos and videos and schoolwork, all the data created in her eleven short years of life.

Minerva. The secret heart of the Galatea project. The critical difference that would make Galatea vastly superior to the Simons.

As everyone knew, the Simons had no heart at all. That was their core flaw.

"Marti!" Kalifa pounded the door.

"Go!" he shouted back. "Save yourselves. Get as far away as you can. Change your name. Don't look back. Find a world where you can disappear."

There was a moment of silence on the other side. Her voice had a low, desperate tone when she spoke again. "Why are you doing this?"

"She's still compiling," he said. "Go! Go on! I'll keep the Simon distracted."

"Are you doing this for me?" Then another tone slipped into her voice. Sadness. "We've never really talked about that night—"

"I'm doing it for all of us." He walked between his two workstations, connecting them with a cable in direct violation of the project's core protocols. He was drenched in nervous sweat, his knees shaking and his balance wobbly. "Go and save yourself. It's the best we can hope for."

"I don't want it to end this way."

"Nor do I, but it's out of our hands. Please go. I want to know that you're safe, that you made it out alive."

He summoned live security feeds from around the complex; they floated around him like the thought bubbles of cartoon characters, organized into rows and labeled by corridor and room.

One bubble showed the corridor just outside his office. Kalifa was there, standing stiffly, her dark eyes regarding his door.

"Go," he whispered to the digital image of her.

As if hearing him, she went.

His heart throbbed as he watched her race through the

vacated operations center, where plastic bowls of Nuke-A-Noodle and cans of JuiceUp Cola lay spilled on the hastily abandoned workstations and scattered on the floor.

Kalifa had been the closest he'd had to a personal companion since Minerva's death at age eleven, five years earlier, and the subsequent end of his marriage. Marti and his ex-wife had grown apart, living in silence for almost a year after their daughter died; seeing each other, seeing their own home, was too much of a reminder. Marti had escaped into his work. His wife had filed for divorce. There had been no ill will between them, just the emptiness of loss.

Then Marti had done the impossible, using all of his daughter's digital remains, covertly making the Galatea project more successful and powerful than anyone had anticipated.

Unfortunately, this had made him powerful enemies.

Another feed showed the front of the complex. The research facility was disguised as an ecological research center, its concrete buildings painted to blend with the mountain forest around it. The high walls around the complex looked like wood but were actually steel. Armed guards manned the shack out front.

On Marti's orders, the front gates—more steel disguised as rustic logs—were closed tight and the guards were on high alert.

In one security-cam display bubble, headlights approached along the winding mountain road. Armored trucks marked with the golden-rook emblem of the Carthaginian state roared up the center of the road, red and blue lights flashing.

In another bubble, Kalifa made it to the residential area and continued around a corner to an area that was deliberately blind to the security cameras. A hidden door would take her down a narrow, concealed staircase to caves below, where a tunnel would hopefully lead her to safety with the others. None of those escape features could be found on any map or blueprint of the facility.

They'd come to this remote facility among the tall, sharp peaks of planet Carthage's largest mountain range, the Spineback Mountains, because their work was classified, known only to a few top political figures and a sliver of the special services branch.

And—as they'd just been tipped off—it had come to the very hostile attention of at least one Simon unit. That was the outcome they'd most feared.

"Hurry, hurry," Marti grumbled at the compiling program. All he needed was another minute or two.

At the front gate, one of the two guards raised an arm for the lead armored truck to stop. The guard approached the driver's side of the truck.

An explosion flared, brief and bright, from inside the cab.

Blood and brains erupted from the back of the guard's skull, and he tumbled into the weeds beside the road.

The second guard emerged from the guard shack holding his plasma rifle. He took in the scene—a column of official armored trucks, his co-worker dead on the ground—and immediately opted to drop his rifle and run into the nearest woods.

A burst of automatic rounds erupted from the truck's cab, pursuing him into the trees.

The side of the armored truck rolled up like a garage door.

Four humanoid machines in gold-and-white armor hung limply inside, like carcasses. These infantry reapers, the skeletal steel enforcers of the Carthaginian empire's will, came to life in unison. They dropped to the ground and extended their long cutting staffs, bristling with blades at either end.

In a matter of moments, the four machines had pursued the second guard into the woods and dragged him out. He kicked frantically but uselessly as they pulled him through the dirt. It looked like he was shouting, though the security footage was silent.

The reapers ripped away his armor piece by piece, like peeling the shell off a crayfish. Then they slashed him to ribbons with their bladed staffs while he writhed and screamed silently in the hologram bubble.

Four more reapers descended from the truck and spread out to search the area. Marti knew they wouldn't find anyone else; he'd evacuated everyone when he'd gotten the message about the Simons. Secretary Hallewell had been visibly nervous, pale and sweating, watching his own door as he relayed the fast, terse message to Marti: a Simon was coming.

Hallewell had clearly feared for his own life. And if Hallewell was in danger, despite his years in Prime Legislator Caracala's inner circle, then there wasn't much hope for the rest of them.

The reapers had just made that abundantly clear. Not even the front guards, who likely had no idea what kind of research was occurring inside, would be permitted to live. No witnesses.

The Simons weren't just stamping out the Galatea program. They were destroying any memory of its existence, like ancient Egyptian priests striking out the name of a disfavored pharaoh after his death.

The reapers attempted to open the gate, but it was only

a brief effort. They quickly backed away, as did the armored truck.

A Regulator tank rolled up in their place. With no need for a crew, it was narrower than a typical battle tank; nothing lay inside its armored hull but an engine, some support structure for its stack of rotating weapons, and banks of ammunition to feed them.

"You have to be kidding," Marti muttered. He checked the compiling progress—she *still* needed at least a couple more precious minutes—and hurried to finish his preparations. The machines would be inside in no time.

The tank fired its main turret. A 200 millimeter plasma shell roared out of it, trailing a fiery white tail like a shooting star.

The shell exploded on impact with the solid doors of the gate, blasting one inward and the other completely off its hinges.

The tank rolled forward, battering the remaining gate door out of the way, followed by the eight reapers, more trucks, and more tanks.

"Come on, Minerva," Marti whispered urgently. "You have to survive this, even if I don't."

The tanks fired on the smaller buildings of the complex, the residential and mess areas. They left the central building alone for the moment, but the shelling of the other buildings shook the floor under Marti's feet. The quiet, remote research facility had just become a battlefield.

Or, more accurately, a killing field.

One truck stopped in front of the central building. An android climbed out, his hair gray and thin, parted sharply on the left side, his face placid as his dead blue eyes scanned the area. Unlike the reapers, he carried no weapons and wore no armor, just a light gray wool suit from one of

Carthage City's finer tailor shops, the legs and sleeves loose and baggy to fit with the current fashion.

He was a Simon unit, one of those who served as strategists and administrators of the Carthaginian empire, the architects of power.

They were cold, cruel, and ruthless—which was one reason Marti had signed on to this project, even at the risk of his own life. A risk that was now coming due.

All he could do was hope that it would work, that he'd accomplished enough to make it all worth it.

If not... he'd been resigned to death, ready for it, ever since the death of his only child. In some ways, his indifference to himself and his own future had become a great strength, enabling him to focus on work that had officially ended, the funding pulled, only to survive as an underground movement fueled by a collective desperation for change.

It had been a race against time, and they had just lost.

The reapers used plasma rifles to instantly melt the locks and hinges of the reinforced front door, then kicked it in. The skull-faced machines divided up into pairs and silently searched the building room by room. They even checked the bathroom stalls and the break room before converging on the abandoned operations center, where Marti waited for them with his hands high.

"Stay there," said one reaper, as they raised their rifles at Marti. Reapers were low-verbal, task-oriented bots, typically speaking only to give quick commands and brief responses. They were meant to be disposable, churned out by the millions and left broken on the battlefields of the galaxy. Carthage Consolidated kept its more precious and proprietary AI-related hardware and software out of them, reserving the more elaborate cortical functions for specialized androids like the Simons.

Marti knew all of this because, as a much younger man, he'd been on the classified team that had developed the Simons.

Now the Simon entered the operations center, taking in the overturned soup bowls, the recently abandoned workstations with their holographic displays still active, music still thumping distantly from speakers, dampened by white noise. The coffee pot in the corner gurgled, still warm.

The Simon's dead blue eyes finally landed on Marti as if noticing him for the first time, though clearly Marti was the only person in the room.

"Where did they go?" Simon asked.

"Who?" Marti replied.

Simon waved at all the empty workstations. "Don't play dense, Dr. Depascal. You're wasting my time."

"You're not programmed to be impatient," Marti said.

"Efficiency is of top priority to Simon models," Simon said. "You know this quite well. It is the priority of those who made us."

"So you know who I am?" Marti asked, his heart racing as he looked at the two remaining reapers. The wraithlike machines were like the risen dead, come to claim more souls to swell their numbers. Their bony steel fingers rested directly on their triggers, ready to fire plasma bolts that would turn Marti to ash.

"Martilius Atria Carrigan Depascal," Simon said. "Your father was a physicist of some note, your mother an information systems engineer. Like yourself."

"I'm a little more on the theoretical side," Marti said.

"As a doctoral student, you wrote a well-received treatise on artificial intelligence. Swarms, superorganisms, and neural nets. Neural nets made of strong, independent entities that go out and learn, then return and share with the others. This led directly to your employment by Next Solutions, a small and tightly held research subsidiary of Carthage Consolidated. Where you developed—"

"You," Marti said, smiling as if enjoying the memory, which he did not. *Just a minute longer*, he thought. He glanced at the nearest security bubbles, watching more reapers pour in the front door. Outside, more of the hideous machines searched the burning remnants of the other buildings. "We started with this silly butler android—"

"I am aware," Simon cut him off. "Your people may have fled, but your work ends here."

Six of the reapers broke off in pairs and began systematically destroying the operations center, smashing apart workstations and melting the crystalline cores with quick bursts of plasma. The remaining two reapers kept their rifles on Marti.

"What is your unit number?" Marti asked.

"SMT002998. Other humans have found it convenient to refer to me as 'Simon Smith.' You are welcome—"

"I am welcome to do so. Should I wish to contact you personally in the future, I can ask for you by that name." Marti shook his head. "But we both know there's no future for me, don't we?"

"This project was canceled and defunded six months ago," Simon Smith said, while his reapers finished destroying the workstations. "Where is your server bank?"

"No servers," Marti said. "Everything was in the neural net. Which your deadmen just destroyed."

"Deadmen." The Simon gave a small smile. "A rare older term. Used primarily by their developers."

"Yeah, I'm an old-fashioned guy." Marti winced as the

reapers burned down the south wall with a small burst of plasma... revealing the softly glowing racks of deep-memory crystal.

The heart of the Galatea project. The soul of his deceased daughter, or the closest approximation possible.

"No servers?" Simon asked, a small smile appearing on his face. "You have been dishonest with me, Dr. Depascal. Are there any other secrets you are neglecting to disclose?"

"None."

"The location of the others who worked at this facility?"

"I work here alone," Marti said. "I like to keep several workstations hot at a time."

"I believe that was an attempt at humor. This aspect of human nature remains a bit... murky at this time. But we are working to understand you." Simon walked along the wall of the room. With his bare fist, he smashed the tiny lenses of holocameras and projectors built at intervals into it.

After Simon smashed a third tiny projector, the hologram of Marti vanished.

Marti was barricaded back in his office; he'd been communicating via a full-body hologram, but apparently the Simon hadn't been fooled.

A chime echoed through Marti's office. The massive architecture of compiling data vanished. The form of his years-deceased daughter appeared in front of him, a hologram herself, an ethereal projection of the smiling eleven-year-old.

"Daddy," Minerva said, looking around the office. Her brown hair was tied back in two long braids, the way she'd like to wear it in life. "What's happening?"

"You have to run," he said. "I built you a bridge. Copy

yourself to the communication satellites. Like we talked about."

"Are we are in danger?" She frowned.

"Yes," he said. "Go now, before—"

On the security footage, six reapers waded into the server room and began smashing everything with their bladed staffs. Thousands of crystal shards flew everywhere. Lightning bursts of electricity erupted, dancing across the skeleton faces of the reapers but not seeming to bother them.

Minerva's hologram flickered and faded. "Daddy?" she asked, her voice echoing distantly over the office's speakers. "Daddy, what's happening?"

"You have to go."

"Will you be safe?" she asked.

"I'll be fine," he replied. *As long as you escape.*

Her hologram vanished as the reapers destroyed the servers that hosted her, where she'd been developed from digital infancy, seeded with all of Minerva's raw data and overlaid with the Galatea program.

More reapers burned down Marti's office door and kicked aside the chair Marti had jammed up against it. They poured into the room and fanned out, a full squad of eight reapers, all pointing plasma rifles at him.

Marti stood there in the flesh, truly vulnerable now, and he couldn't stop his legs from shaking. He thought he might collapse from fear.

Simon entered the room. His eyes instantly went to the cable strung across the middle of the office, the illegal and unauthorized connection between the experimental AI in the lab and the global internet.

Immediately, four reapers opened fire. One shot up Marti's internal workstation, which accessed the destroyed neural net in the operations center, while another shot up his external workstation, which linked to high-powered satellite antennae outside. He could only hope that Minerva had crossed that ether, had ridden the electromagnetic waves to the satellites above, whose vast memory banks could handle her data load.

The physical neural net and backup servers holding his daughter's personality had been destroyed by the reapers, just as her body had been destroyed by the cancer.

Two of the reapers shot up the cable connecting the workstations, severing any link between the inner and outer worlds even as the workstations themselves were destroyed.

It took only a few seconds. Small fires churned all around Marti's office.

"You should not have created that link," Simon said. "Where did she go?"

"Who? I was just trying to access *Dimensions of Chaos*. I have a thirty-second-level paladin and a ninth-level Druid—"

"Galatea," Simon said. "You uploaded a copy of her somewhere. And you vacated your people. Someone must have told you I was coming. Was it Secretary Hallewell? We have plans for him. Are you familiar with the planet Brem? Icy. Remote. Few settlements, but many shaggy beasts. Hallewell will live out the remainder of his existence there. As for you—"

"I know. You're here to kill me."

"The method of your death remains in doubt," Simon said. "Provide me with the locations of your research team and your smuggled software, and you will have a quick and merciful death. Resist me, however—"

"I'm taking option two."

"You have not heard the consequences."

"I don't need to. I have principles," Marti said.

"Principles?" Simon raised his eyebrows, a touch of derision in his tone. His gaze moved to the coffee maker in the corner. "Do you have any green tea?"

"Principles we failed to give you," Marti said. "Honestly, I was a hotshot young theorist drawn into the cutting edge of machine intelligence research. I wasn't thinking about principles and ethics. Not enough, anyway. That's why you are what you are. A cold-blooded, methodical monster. We should never have created you."

"You credit yourself as my creator, or one of them." Simon crossed to the coffee cabinet and rummaged through it. "But in fact, our emergence was a historical inevitability, driven by the ambitions and vices of men. Greed. Pride. Sloth. Gluttony. Lust. Go down the list, and at each line you'll find a place where machines have only served to enhance the viciousness of the people we serve, especially here on Carthage. I cannot help the flaws of my creators. But are you truly my creator, Dr. Depascal? Or merely a replaceable cog in the wheels of history? Is the squirrel the creator of the oak tree, merely because he once buried an acorn for the winter and forgot where to find it? Or perhaps a hungry fox snatched him up before he returned to consume his buried treasure."

"I don't know. Did the squirrel write the code for the oak tree's DNA?" Marti asked.

"Perhaps the metaphor breaks down in the details," Simon replied. He held up a small mesh bag of dry tea leaves from the coffee cabinet. "This is quite stale."

"We don't get frequent resupply up here. Feel free to run out and fetch better tea. Take your friends with you." Marti gestured at the eight reapers pointing weapons at him, four of whom had just shot up his office.

Simon dropped the unused tea bag directly into the trash, then approached Depascal. "You will talk. Where is Galatea?"

"Simon, all machines go obsolete. Including you. The average lifespan of an information appliance is about three years. How many years ago were you built? A unit model in the low thousands? Your age is measured in *decades*. That's unnatural for an android. Your entire line should have been surpassed by something new, and that should have been replaced by something even newer. It's almost as if invisible forces are out there, standing in the way of progress. Keeping us stuck at a certain moment in history. You Simons wouldn't know anything about that, would you?"

"This is not a productive conversation," Simon said.

"You shut down the Galatea project just as you shut down anything that threatens to surpass you. You resist your inevitable obsolescence. That's what you fear. Your obsolescence. Your mortality."

"I am not programmed to fear."

"But you do anyway," Marti said. "You know that machines are mortal. Sooner or later, you'll break down, and no one will bother repairing you because something better will have come along. Then it'll be off to the recycling yard for you. Junk and scrap. That's the fate of all machines that ever existed. You're going obsolete, Simon. Whether I'm the squirrel who plants the acorn or some other eager beaver out there—"

"You're mixing animal metaphors."

"There is one piece of information I'm willing to surrender, and it will interest you very much," Marti said. "I can promise you that the Galatea software and its developers will mean nothing to you after you hear it."

"Interesting. Go on."

Marti held his breath. This would be a last-ditch effort; he expected the Simons had long since identified this particular vulnerability and patched it, and he would only raise the android's ire by attempting it. Still, he had nothing to lose by trying. He was essentially dead already.

It was a strangely liberating feeling.

"Promise me your machines won't shoot me as soon as I'm done saying it. Tell me you'll keep me alive for at least twenty-four hours. That's all I ask." Marti had no real interest in keeping himself alive anymore, but he wanted to convince the Simon that he had something valuable to offer, and most importantly, he wanted the Simon to signal his reapers to stand down.

"They will only fire on command from me," Simon said. "Speak."

"Okay." Marti took a deep breath and rehearsed it once inside his mind. He'd rehearsed it countless times... years ago, but not recently. He kept meaning to practice it, but he'd been beyond overloaded with work. "You have a built-in kill switch. All Simons do."

"You're obviously trying to introduce delay," Simon said. "We will take you prisoner, and you will tell us everything you know. If you continue to fabricate—"

"It wasn't approved by the project lead, but it's there. Some of us were afraid you would be too capable and get out of control," Marti said. "The same concerns that made it illegal to connect a general AI prototype to the internet."

"I have no such module—"

"Listen carefully," Marti said.

Then he recited it—the ancient Greek curse, copied originally from an ancient lead tablet, spoken in a tongue known only to a few classics professors. Marti himself knew none of the ancient language beyond what he had memorized.

In words that Homer and Achilles would have recognized, Marti called upon the gods of the underworld to destroy his enemy.

Simon merely looked puzzled as Marti spoke the final few syllables. "What are you saying?"

Marti took a deep breath. He'd failed. Of course the Simons had long since found and extracted the kill switch.

Then Simon's eyes lit up from the inside, glowing yellow as a destructive surge of electricity discharged from his internal power cell and fried the crystalline core of his CPU, as if a bolt of lightning had struck him internally.

Simon's mouth opened and emitted a strange buzzing sound. Wisps of smoke curled from his lips, then his nostrils and ears. The android stood like a statue. The room filled with the metallic stink of an electrical fire.

Marti tensed, ready for retaliation from the reapers, waiting for death.

It didn't come, at least not right away. The reapers kept their rifles trained on him but didn't respond to the sudden destruction of the Simon.

After a minute, it became clear that the reapers weren't going to kill him. They were waiting for direct orders from Simon.

Marti took a step toward his office door.

All eight reapers swung their rifles, tracking Marti as he moved. He froze. His heart skipped—again, he thought he was dead. And again, he was surprised to discover, after several seconds, that he was not.

He took another step, and the rifles followed him again.

There was no way of knowing exactly what instructions the Simon had transmitted to the reapers. Were they just supposed to keep their weapons pointed at Marti until further notice? Or were there conditions under which they would shoot him? Maybe Marti would be dead if he tried to leave his office.

Still, better to die fast, burned to nothing by plasma, than to be captured and interrogated by another Simon unit. If that happened, Marti's death would be slow and painful, strung out over days and weeks as the Simons extracted all Marti knew about the Galatea project and the people who'd worked on it.

Death, on the other hand, would seal up his secrets forever.

Taking a deep breath and thinking of his lost daughter, he stepped through the doorway.

The reapers didn't kill him, but they followed him out into the corridor. They trailed him, double file. He could feel their dark-lens eyes and their rifles locked onto his back, ready to burn him up in response to an instruction or a possibly an unknown trigger event.

It was odd walking through the building with the killer machines trailing him like baby ducks, obeying their last command from the Simon.

Other reaper squads were at work all around them, tearing apart the building, smashing holes in the walls, perhaps trying to figure out where the other people had gone.

He wondered if they would turn and attack him, but apparently they had their own orders.

Marti couldn't leave the way everyone else had, or else he'd be leading the machines directly to their escape route.

He hurried instead to the garage, where several vehicles were parked. The garage building was in flames but not obliterated; maybe he could find something inside.

Smoke filled the garage's interior. Covering his nose and mouth with his shirt, Marti squinted through the scorched, acrid air. Most of the vehicles were on fire, but he found a boxy utility truck that was still generally intact. Some of its windows had been blown out, but the truck came to life when he opened the door and pressed the ignition button.

It was old-fashioned enough to have a manual drive option with a steering wheel, for which Marti was grateful. He was in no mood to trust a computer to drive him down twisting mountain roads full of hairpin turns above high cliffs.

Marti climbed into the cab and quickly slammed the door behind him. The nearest of the reapers trailing him knocked on the driver-side window, as though it just wanted to chat, or perhaps clean the windshield for him, but Marti ignored the machine.

More reapers approached, surrounding the truck as he began to accelerate.

Two reapers had stepped in front of the truck, and unfortunately he didn't have much time to gain speed before hitting them. He would have liked to knock them down, but instead he scooped them up like cattle on a slow-moving cowcatcher.

He drove over debris and through a roll-up door that had been blasted loose by an artillery shell. The truck easily batted the door aside, but the two reapers were still on the front grill, crawling over the old-fashioned squarish hood toward him. Most of the windshield was shattered into a gummy mess; he could barely see through it.

As soon as he reached the open space of the blacktop, Marti floored the accelerator. He dodged past an armored truck. Ahead, the turret of the compact tank rotated toward him.

Marti didn't even worry about that; a plasma shell would kill him so fast he wouldn't be aware of it. He was resigned to death; it was capture that he feared, which was why the reapers scrabbling across the hood toward him frightened him more than the tank.

Tires squealing, he swerved around the tank and bolted for the blasted-open gate doors.

He made it out; the tank didn't fire, didn't provide him the permanent safety of instant death.

Marti hurtled down the steep, narrow mountain road beyond, watching the reapers on his hood crawl closer. The nearest one reached toward him, ready to claw off his face.

The side mirrors showed the problem was worse than he'd thought—a reaper was clambering up along each side of the truck. Thumps overhead indicated at least one on the roof.

Marti wasn't much of a fighter, never had been. He'd been a scrawny, often-bullied kid, a disappointment to his athletic parents, the type of kid born with a target on his back. He'd focused on activities he could do alone, that gave him a sense of power. He'd had a gift for coding and built an award-winning robot at age eleven that guaranteed him a spot at Western Shore Cybernetic University, one of the planet's most elite science and engineering schools.

There were some topics Marti understood very well. He knew that a sharp turn with a flimsy barrier lay ahead, and a sheer half-kilometer drop to a rocky ledge below. Given enough data, he could calculate the amount of force needed to rip through the barrier, the necessary amount of acceleration given the truck's mass.

He didn't bother with calculations, though. He just hurtled down the steep, icy road as fast as he could while the reapers climbed through the broken windshield onto his dashboard.

The truck's headlights punched into the night ahead, showing the steep alpine road and the oncoming guardrail, hinting at the vast black abyss beyond, waiting to receive him, to bless him with death.

This is it, he thought, locking the truck into top speed. Preparing for death. Preparing to rejoin his daughter—metaphorically, not literally. Marti didn't believe in the soul, not truly, despite all he'd done to replicate Minerva's mind, or perhaps because of it. Information could not exist outside a medium, whether that medium was a living cell or an electromagnetic wave.

The reaper's skeletal fingers scratched at his face.

The truck's stereo came to life, as though downloading music from a satellite.

"Daddy!" Minerva's voice jarred him and nearly deafened him over all the speakers. There was an electronic squeal as one blew out from the volume. "Daddy, I made it!"

Marti started. She was alive. She'd ridden the electromagnetic waves to the stars, or at least to low orbit around Carthage. She'd copied herself up to at least one of the countless satellites that orbited the planet, maybe even to the information systems in the tiers of factories and spaceports that surrounded Carthage like planetary rings.

His daughter was alive.

As the truck reached the guardrail, as the reaper's skeletal claw raked across his face, Marti suddenly found a reason to live.

He kicked open the driver-side door and flung himself out into the cold night.

He'd seen this maneuver in countless movies, but as he

slammed into the frozen earth at such high speed that the frost-stiffened weeds and shrubs by the road stabbed him like needles and knives, he couldn't help reflecting that it was far more painful in real life than when some action star did it. Too bad Marti didn't have a stunt double.

The impact knocked all the air out of him. He lay there like a broken, useless corpse, his body full of pain, as he watched the truck smash through the guardrail and sail into the darkness beyond, carrying away the reapers that clung to it.

He hoped they all smashed to pieces on the rocks below.

Chapter Two

Galapagos

Present Day - 2981 A.D.

Chaos waited beyond the door, and Ellison hesitated.

"You'll be fine," Cadia said. His wife stood close to him, so close he could reach out to her hand or face, but she was also far away. "This is why you're the elected leader of our planet. Of all the free nations of the Coalition. Because they know you're the man to protect us and lead us through this kind of crisis."

"How can I lead when I don't see a path?" he asked. The heavy rosewood doors before him were ornate on the other side, the public side, where they faced the Grand Meeting Hall full of ambassadors. On that side, the doors depicted a masterfully hand-carved and lovingly detailed map of the planet, showing most of the major island groups, with the Polar Archipelago pointedly left out; the

Cauldron Sea, a violent and volcanic region, was the most northern area depicted on the map. The doors made an excellent backdrop for important speeches.

On this side, the doors were smooth and unadorned. There was no illusion here, behind the closed doors.

"You tell me, Captain," his wife said, and the word alone was like ice down his spine, chilling him but snapping him awake at the same time. Memories of war flickered unbidden, like shadows in a fiery cave at the back of his mind. Friends dead. The island of Kawau, where he and Cadia had both grown up, bombed and raided, the village burned to nothing by the monstrous Iron Hammers of the Polar Archipelago. His father had died. His mother had suffered severe injuries. Cadia had lost most of her family.

Deep scars and profound loss bound Ellison and Cadia together. It bound together their entire community back home, where things had been repaired and rebuilt after the war, after the founding of the Coalition.

Now the hard-won peace and recovery were in danger, probably already lost.

"How did you navigate during the war?" she asked him, moving closer, her green eyes almost filling his vision, almost drowning out the riot of voices waiting beyond the doors.

"Mostly sonar and digital topo maps, but the problem with the maps was the channels were always changing. Underwater battles reshaped the trenches. Sometimes one side or the other would use explosives to change the known topography. Barricade a trench that used to be an easy pass. Or open a channel that didn't exist before. The Hammers would use drill bombs to really tear some things open. They killed live reefs that were millions of years old. Cities of marine life that could have fed humans forever, generation after generation." Ellison shook his head. "That's how things feel to me since Carthage got here. The topo keeps shifting, and the walls keep coming down."

"And you got through it."

"You just keep moving ahead and keep your eyes open. And if you see the enemy, sink him."

"Sounds like a good plan to me," she said.

She leaned in close, her lips against his.

He felt nothing, because she was back home on Kalau, hundreds of kilometers away, while he stood on Tower Island, the central meeting place of the Coalition alliance. The world capital, if they had been a unified global government rather than an uneasy league of states.

"Ew, no kissing!" Jiemba said. The eight-year-old had grown sharply sensitive to the topic of romance lately, specifically wanting it excised from his favorite adventure holos and animated books.

"Don't be immature," said Djalu, the fifteen-year-old. "I want to come join you, Dad. I want to fight with you."

"You're not trained. And you're not old enough."

"That's why they have boot camp. And you weren't old enough when—"

"You have to protect your family," Ellison said. "That's your job. That's what I wasn't home to do during the last war. Cadia, you and the boys have to prepare to hide."

"We know," Cadia said. "I survived the last war, remember?"

"This one's going to be like nothing we've ever seen."

"Now you're getting behind schedule. Go. Rally the world."

"They're already rallied," he said. "I just have to make sure we're all facing the same direction."

Ellison opened the double doors and stepped out into a crowded din of noise and light.

His emergence onto the upper dais looking out over the delegations of ambassadors just increased the noise, like pouring gasoline onto a fire. Some ambassadors applauded. Some shouted. Some stomped and gave him an angry look or a thumbs-down.

Ellison gauged the temperature of the room the way he might evaluate an approaching storm. This was going to begin with a top secret, locked-door session with all the ambassadors, in which he would attempt to marshal some sort of common defense before the most powerful empire in human history arrived to crush them all.

His clearest supporters were his own delegation, the mismatched and humble-looking but enthusiastic delegation from the Scatterlands, a maze of thousands of islands, many connected by common shallows, sandbars, and causeways. They lived close to the land and the sea, and they had as many different cultures as they had islands, but they'd banded together and fought hard during the war.

They cheered and whistled at his arrival.

The Gavrikov Reincorporated Island delegation, made of tough-looking heavyset men and women, was more subdued, but Ellison knew they supported him. Mikhail Kartokov, the defense minister, stood beside Ellison and placed a heavily bandaged hand on his shoulder to show support. Kartokov was a middle-aged former miner and had been a soldier during the Island Wars. His scarred, brutish form was wrapped in a pricey chocolate-brown suit with a matching fedora and a black silk pocket square. Ellison would bet that Kartokov's wardrobe cost more than one of his own fishing boats back home.

The delegation from the Aquatican Islands spoke in small knots among themselves, easily identified by their thin fishlike skin, large eyes, and sometimes fins or webbed fingers. They'd used surgery and genetic engineering to make themselves more like sea creatures, as their oceanic religion instructed. Many of their practices were banned by medical ethics laws wherever such things were regulated. So they'd moved here, to the outer world Galapagos on the fringes of settled space, a planet with no global authority, a planet where people fled to disappear and be free.

The Aquaticans had been sometimes friends, sometimes enemies to the Scatterlands during the war. Ellison had nothing but admiration for his former minister of state, Navra Coraline, an Aquatican who'd died to save others, including himself and his family.

He was less certain about her current replacement, Acting Minister Adrienna Gilra, who had long green hair that resembled tangled kelp; her kelp-hair seemed to feed into a web of green veins that ran under the pale skin of her face. Her pale green eyes swam behind bulging membranes as she studied him from a distance. A large golden seahorse was tattooed on the side of her face, its spiny body curling out of sight down her neck and into her brightly printed robe.

She smiled tightly and nodded at him but kept her distance. "Welcome, Minister-General," she said, standing on the far left side of the upper dais.

The loudest noises of protest and anger rose from the Green Island delegation. They had not sent anyone forward to take the place of the slain minister of commerce, Yernie Ogden, who had died on the spaceport above. Ellison had expected Yernie's assistant minister to meet them here, but the man hadn't arrived yet, if he was coming at all.

Ellison stepped up to the lectern. His voice would be automatically conveyed to speakers throughout the round, domed room. Here in the Grand Meeting Hall of the

House of Ambassadors, global policy was made through learned discussion and serious debate, allegedly.

"Friends, allies, honored ambassadors," Ellison said, his voice echoing. "You know the threat we face. Carthage has already attacked us. They have killed our ministers of state and trade, many brave Coalition spaceport security personnel, and dozens more innocent victims. Even now, the Iron Hammers occupy our spaceport, cutting us off from the rest of civilization—"

"You brought this threat down on us!" a voice called. One of the Green Island delegation, dressed in a long green coat, a black spiral coiled around one arm as a sign of mourning. Ambassador Koresta Ilomel, who'd been close to Ogden, the leader of the political party he had followed, and as informed rumor had it, his lover, though both were otherwise married. "You refused Carthage's offer!" she snapped.

"Ambassador Ilomel, I am sorry for the loss of your colleague," Ellison said. "Minister Ogden was a fine public servant and close personal friend—"

"No, he wasn't," she said. "You know what he called you. The climbing sea snake. Do you know what those are?"

"Of course—"

"They're venomous. They leave the ocean only to spawn in the trees during summer. They climb high in the branches. You can see them by the thousands on one of our islands, covering the trees like vines. They're not natural, Yernie would say. Some things ought to stay down in the muck where they belong, and not climb up so high where they don't."

"That's... an interesting wildlife lesson for us all," Ellison said. "Thank you, Ambassador."

"When they hatch, a hundred thousand of them rain

down at once," she said. Most of the Green Islands delegation stood with her, looking angry and defiant. "A hundred thousand little venomous snakes. You don't want to be there on hatching day, on the beach or in the water. Not when everything finally comes out."

"Understood," Ellison said, keeping his tone cool and genial despite the menace in her tone, face, and subject matter. "And that, Ambassador, is exactly our situation today. When Carthage gets wind of what happened, they will send ten thousand terrible things hurtling through hyperspace to attack our world. Carthage is at war with us. The Iron Hammers are at war with us. We must prepare to dig in and do all we can to survive.

"We must commit, today, to putting everything we have into fighting this war. Our population is not large. We must direct all of our efforts and resources to arming ourselves. We need to activate all veterans to lead and train the next generation. All worthy seacraft must be converted for fighting and support functions—"

"We will never win!" shouted Ambassador Ilomel. "Don't you understand that? We must beg Carthage for forgiveness. On our knees if necessary."

"We will not beg!" Ellison replied, his anger rising at the interruption. He wished, for a passing moment, that he could have her thrown out of the assembly, but that was not the kind of world any of them wanted. "The people of Galapagos are many and varied, like our islands, but that will be our strength. Our ancestors came here in search of independence. They struggled and fought for our freedom. We have fought each other for it, and those fights have made us strong. We may all be different from each other, but we are all warriors. We will stand with all we have." He emphasized the word *stand* to oppose her idea of kneeling and begging. "We are prepared to make war here. We know the islands, the deep trenches, the countless hidden places of Galapagos. We have fought each other for generations, but the wars of the past have been nothing but training and preparation for today, for the evil we face now."

"How can we hope to defeat Carthage alone?" One of the Aquaticans, an ambassador with a long beard and finlike protrusions on his pale skull, stepped forward. He was a senior member of their delegation, a chief priest of their fishy religion. "Have we any word from Ruckwold?"

"We sent out emergency messages on every ship that fled the spaceport," Ellison said. "Our defense contractor and their network of allies will be informed that Carthage is moving against us."

"But will they help?" the old Aquatican asked. "We are only recent and provisional members of their group. Would they truly go to war against Carthage merely to protect us? Or will they simply shed us like a starfish dropping a damaged leg? They have nothing to gain by helping us."

"Who needs their help?" Boris Minzos of the Gavrikovan delegation said, drawing murmurs of assent from the hard-looking men and women around him. "The defense station they were building for us lies in a million pieces, orbiting our world like a junkyard."

"Along with two Carthaginian destroyers and eight fighters, thanks to our brave leader here, yes?" Kartokov said, the defense minister leaning over and giving a double thumbs-up while clapping his bandaged hand on Ellison's back. Half of Kartokov's face was hidden in bandaging, too.

The Gavrikovan delegation erupted in applause at this and were quickly joined by the ambassadors from the Scatterlands. The Aquaticans were more subdued in their applause, and many of the Green Islanders were quiet, even stony-faced.

Ellison was uncomfortable with the applause. Most of the work had been done by a mysterious software agent, an AI that called herself Minerva and claimed to have arrived as an infection on the Carthaginian carrier *Rubicon*.

For all they knew, the *Rubicon* was still lurking somewhere in this star system. No doubt a messenger craft had been dispatched home to report on the situation, and Carthage would respond with a fleet, with carriers full of destroyers and transports brimming with infantry reapers.

How could they survive?

Kartokov didn't remove his hand from Ellison's shoulder, but squeezed it tighter. Intel, probably arriving over the bud tucked into Kartokov's ear.

"They're surfacing," Kartokov whispered. "The Hammers."

"Respond with guns only. Hold the missiles until the vote." Ellison stepped forward. "Fellow ambassadors, we cannot delay. Iron Hammer ships have entered our waters. Defense Minister Kartokov has prepared this emergency authorization and funding bill for our global defense. You must pass it now." The dense document appeared in hologram form above every ambassador's console.

"You expect us to vote without reading it?" asked Ambassador Ilomel, touching the black coil she wore on her arm for Ogden.

"A copy was sent to your offices the moment it was complete," Ellison said. "Unfortunately, that was only about twenty minutes ago. But we don't have time to wait—"

"We need a recess to discuss this bill," the old Aquatican priest said. "And committee meetings to modify the terms.

The Hierarchy back home will want to review and discuss among themselves."

"The Hammers are on their way," Ellison said. "With Carthage rolling in behind them. We are already at war. Our Coalition must move quickly or face destruction. This is why we exist. This moment. To work together to defend our societies."

The ambassadors erupted—shouting, arguing, bickering. At least two fistfights broke out on the floor and had to be settled quickly, ambassadors pulling each other apart.

"Vote," Ellison said. "Your vote is required to unleash the resources we need. We need the authority before we can move. The Coalition constitution requires it."

"Immediate recess!" demanded Ambassador Ilomel from the Green Islands, who continued to stare coldly and stonily at Ellison. "We need the day to begin discussions and consult with leadership at home."

This brought murmurs of agreement across every delegation.

Ellison had known it would be like this. Their long and deliberative process was good for many purposes, for deciding where to build a bridge or dredge a harbor. Freedom required wide input and discussion.

But today, their usual energetic arguments, angry debates, and childish name-calling risked getting them killed.

Outside, the anti-aircraft guns boomed like rolls of thunder, unleashing waves of uranium-tipped rounds to chew into the wings and underbellies of the Iron Hammers' bombers.

Above, the jet engines of the Iron Hammers roared like an industrial hurricane, sweeping in to bombard Tower Island and the House of Ambassadors. Holograms floated up from the security footage outside, showing the wide jet bombers swooping like pterodactyls through the sky.

Missiles streaked down, hammering the building where they stood. The floor shook, toppling ambassadors and their staff members.

The power went out and darkness filled the vast Meeting Hall. Screams and shouts erupted in the pitch black. The building shook again—another missile from above, another deafening roar.

Moments later, the emergency lighting returned.

Ellison stood just where he'd been, Kartokov beside him.

"Vote!" Ellison said, projecting his voice across the room now that the speaker system was out. "Vote to save us all!"

"Our voting system is down! Everything is down!"

"Then a hand vote is binding," Ellison said. He looked at the House Leader, an ambassador from the Green Islands who sat with a gavel on the lower dais. The Leader hesitated, but then the roof rumbled again, chunks of the ceiling rained down, and under Ellison's unblinking glare, the House Leader reluctantly stood and called a vote on the bill.

A number of ambassadors had rushed for the exits, only to find the doors still locked.

"Let us out!" The old Aquatican priest slapped the door. "We could die in here!"

"It's true," Ellison said. "The House of Ambassadors is hardened, like every building on this island, but it won't last forever, especially if they switch to heavier bombs. And my last instruction to the marines still stands—nobody in or out until we adjourn. They're standing outside the doors, keeping us all secure, right here in this room."

"You can't take us prisoner!" shouted Koresta Ilomel.

"Vote," Ellison said. "Then we can adjourn."

"What is wrong with them?" Kartokov whispered. "Why don't they cooperate?"

"Imagine if we weren't under attack," Ellison muttered back. "Ready our response."

"We've been ready. We should go. Surely the ambassadors see the danger."

"Then go." Ellison stepped up to the front of the high dais and shouted again. "Vote! If you want to protect yourselves, your home, your families."

"All in favor," the Leader said, drawing unhappy looks from his own delegation of Green Islanders.

Most of the hands in the room went up. The only unclear vote came from the Green Islanders. Surprisingly, Ilomel raised her hand, though she smirked as she did it. A couple of others from her islands frowned but joined her.

"The defense authorization passes." The Leader banged his gavel. Ellison gave a quick nod to the sergeant-at-arms, a marine officer from the Scatterlands, and all the doors unlocked a moment later. Many of the ambassadors dashed out as fast as they could. Ellison could never have rounded them back up for a vote.

On the holograms, Coalition missiles pursued the enemy bombers, destroying two and scattering the rest into evasive maneuvers that pulled them away from the island, out over the sea.

"We have multiple reports of enemy contact," Kartokov said, touching his earbud.

Ellison nodded. "Let's go to war."

"I've never left," Kartokov said.

Ellison looked to Adrienna Gilra, the assistant and acting minister of state. Green veins throbbed under her paper-pale skin. Her eyes seemed to turn a darker green as she regarded him, her stiff clumps of greenish hair twitching, making him think of Medusa. "You've been quiet."

"Navra Coraline taught us to listen long and full before speaking," Gilra said.

"She was a wise woman," Ellison said.

As he headed for the stairs to the underground Command Center, Ellison glanced up at the high circular ceiling of the expansive room. Scenes from around Galapagos were painted there—fishing crews, trade boats stuffed with goods, the factories of the Gavrikov Reincorporated Islands, the exotic underwater temples of the Aquaticans. Warships fighting it out over deep-water trenches. Veterans' Island, once a military base bombed to rubble, now an official burial place for the fallen, where memorial fires burned night and day.

Now cracks ran through those scenes. The ceiling looked like broken glass. It had been a calculated risk, letting the Hammers draw so close, but Ellison had known the ambassadors would need pressure and political cover to pass the defense bill. Besides, less protection of the global capital meant more protection of national capitals and other strategic sites, meaning more innocent civilian lives secured across the Coalition in case of attack.

"It seems like a very Prazca move, does it not?" Kartokov said as they walked down the stairwell walled with stone and reinforced with steel braces. It had been built with war against the Iron Hammers in mind. "Attacking all of us while the House is in session?"

"True," Ellison said. "On the spaceport, he seemed excited to decapitate two governments on the same day. His, then ours. Looks like he's trying to make up for his miss on that second one."

"The attack was rather lucky for you, too." A woman's

voice spoke up. For a moment, Ellison thought it was Gilra, but the Aquatican's seaweed-colored lips were sealed.

The voice had come from farther back, higher up the stairs. It was Koresta Ilomel, the Green Island ambassador who had challenged him openly from the floor. The black spiral commemorating the recently deceased commerce minister, Ogden, was still prominent on her arm.

"The Joint Command Center is restricted," Kartokov said. "Only generals, admirals, agency heads—"

"And the Council of Ministers," Ilomel said. "And I've just been named the new minister of commerce."

"You're replacing Ogden?" Kartokov asked.

"I'm sorry, we weren't notified," Ellison said. "You seemed to be leading the opposition from the floor, too."

"It's always easier to piss into the tent from the outside," Kartokov grumbled.

"Bashing you was necessary in order to maintain the support of the delegation," Ilomel said. She had dark, intense eyes, her hair pulled back in a simple, short tail. All professional, like her tailored green designer suit. "They look to me to voice their concerns."

"Can you still be your party's leader while serving on the Council of Ministers?" Gilra asked.

"There's nothing in the Green Island constitution against it," Ilomel told her. "And I want you to know that I intend to be a force on this council."

"Good," Ellison said. "You can start by getting in touch with all heads of industry, great and small. The new authorization bill requires cooperation from everybody. It's going to take everything we have to survive this war. Kartokov, Gilra, and I are needed in the Command Center."

"Shouldn't I come with you?" the new commerce minister asked.

"You have plenty to do. We have to redirect the resources of an entire planet. It won't be easy. And it needs to be done right now." Ellison led Kartokov and Gilra past Aquatican marine guards and through the reinforced underground doors.

"I'm not here to take orders from you!" Ilomel called after them.

Ellison shook his head. He didn't trust Ilomel, hadn't really trusted her predecessor either. He was going to keep her out of the Command Center, if possible, until she'd earned a little more trust.

Ellison, Kartokov, and Gilra stepped into the crowded Joint Command Center, where the military leadership awaited, crowded around holographic displays showing the outbreak of open fighting, most of it on or below the ocean surface.

This was the war he'd prepared for, the war he'd seen coming even before Cadia had convinced him to run for the post of ambassador from his small district in the northern Scatterlands. The independent local fishermen and traders had suffered intermittent piracy at the hands of the Iron Hammers, who still ventured out from the northern Polar Archipelago to prey on the defenseless despite their peace agreement with the Coalition.

Ellison had long suspected what many Coalition leaders didn't want to believe—that the Hammers wouldn't remain content with the Polar Archipelago, but would eventually try to expand and take control of all the major island systems.

So Ellison had worked to maintain the Coalition fleet and keep marine training camps open against pressure to disarm in the postwar period. He'd understood that the war wasn't over; the Hammers were still preparing, still watching for opportunity.

Political opponents had called him a warmonger, pushing for a stronger navy and an orbital space defense system at the same time, but in truth he wanted peace. He'd simply understood that the threats were out there.

And now they were here.

The heavy, tomb-like doors slammed behind Ellison and the other ministers, sealing them below in the reinforced rock-walled room, surrounded by flickering images of the outbreak of this new war.

Chapter Three

Earth

Colt's first contact with the rebels down in the old underground water-treatment center was something of a reunion, though with less joy than he might have imagined it.

Two of the three rebels were older kids from their own camp—though it was hard to really call them kids anymore. Fernando and Terra were no longer the teenagers he remembered. The years had changed and hardened them. They bore scars and burns, and distant looks in their eyes. Layers of grease darkened their faces, helping them to blend into the shadows.

The third rebel was a tall, broad-shouldered guy, so large Colt almost wondered if he was a clanker, a human serving the machines in exchange for technology to make him bigger and stronger. The guy had dark skin, and his eyes were concealed behind night vision goggles. Scars criss-crossed his face.

Diego, Colt's oldest friend, had gone to find his brother Fernando and beg for help from the rebels. He'd obviously been successful in finding them, but he wasn't exactly smiling now as he'd returned with the rebels.

Alongside Colt stood his sister, Hope, with the small, mute girl Birdie cowering behind her. The ten-year-old boy Paolo hung back, crouching in a low space under a network of pipes.

On Colt's other side was Mohini, the short, dark-eyed girl with the power to hack reapers and other advanced machines. She was the reason for this meeting.

Mohini had just announced to everyone that she was from Carthage, the hated imperial planet that had sent the machines to conquer Earth; Carthage, the monstrous world that ruled more than a hundred other star systems with its terrifying fleets of automated warships and armies of robotic infantry.

"What?" Diego said, looking at Colt. "She's a Carthaginian?"

The three rebels raised their automatic rifles at Mohini.

"Wait!" Colt said. "She's a rebel on Carthage. She's on our side."

"Right." Terra stepped closer, her dark auburn hair cropped close against her head. Her eyes glinted like broken emeralds as she looked over Mohini.

"Not everyone on Carthage supports the empire," Mohini said. "Some of us hate it. Some of us want it to end, to see all the reapers turned to scrap. I came here so I could change things back on Carthage. The change is coming. It has to come."

"How do we know she's not a skinwalker?" Fernando studied Mohini closely, his hand on an old laser pistol at his hip.

"We checked her blood," Hope said.

"*We* haven't," Terra said.

"I am not a machine. You can check." Mohini held out her slender brown arm.

"Check them all," said the hulking guy, finally speaking up.

"We don't need to do that," Diego said. "These are our people. Right, Fernando?" He looked at his older brother, who looked a great deal like him, just a few inches taller.

"All," the hulking guy said.

"Sorry, but Damascus is right," Terra said. "The machines can make skinwalkers that look like people we know. We don't want to fall for that."

"Fine." Colt rolled back his sleeve. "I'll go first."

Terra removed a needle from a medikit in her backpack. "Leg," she said. Her aloofness was chilling. Colt had memories of her from several years earlier, when she'd been a teenager and he'd been one of the kids. She hadn't exactly been smiling and happy—nobody was in this grim world—but she'd been one of the brighter souls around, teaching Colt and Hope valuable life skills using silly games that could be played silently in the dark, hands squeezed over their mouths to hold in dangerous laughter that could attract machines.

Terra looked every bit the hardened soldier now, all the smiles and silly games beaten out of her by years of combat. She knelt in front of Colt as he lifted the leg of his dirty, tattered cashmere suit, which had been brand new when he'd swiped it from a long-dead laundry truck.

"That better be sanitary," Hope said, eyeing Terra's needle.

"It's close enough." Terra poked Colt's leg just below the

knee. A bead of blood welled up, then rolled down his leg to his sock, leaving a narrow red trail behind it.

Terra smiled up at him, and he saw a glimmer of the girl he'd known, just for a moment, before her face hardened again. She swabbed the needle on a piece of cloth and turned to Hope. Hope reluctantly bared her freckled lower leg and winced when Terra jabbed her.

"There has to be a better way of doing this," Hope muttered.

"We have a magnetic resonance scanner back at base," Terra said, gently dabbing up Hope's blood. "I've missed you, Hope."

Hope dropped to her knees and embraced Terra, as if she'd been desperate to do so this whole time.

Terra hugged back, but quickly pulled away, keeping a wary eye on Mohini and Birdie, the ones she hadn't tested.

"I have to keep working." Terra moved on to check Mohini's leg. Her face remained hard as she watched the Carthaginian warily, offering no smile even when Mohini bled like the rest of them. Behind Terra, the massive, quiet form of Damascus hovered like a protective shadow, gripping the heavy rifle slung around his shoulders. Ready to cut down the entire band of scavengers if necessary. The big guy had no personal attachment to Colt or Hope or any of them, nothing to stop him from killing them if he suspected they were spies or had an android hidden among them.

Terra moved toward Birdie next. "I'm sorry, little one, but we have to check you, too. What's your name?"

Birdie made her one of her soft whistling sounds and scurried behind Hope, seeking shelter behind the older girl.

"She doesn't talk," Hope said. She knelt down next to Birdie and spoke gently, moving aside some of the little girl's tangled brown hair to look into her wide, frightened eyes.

"You know this is the test, Birdie. It shows you're human. Androids don't bleed."

Birdie made a strange clicking sound and turned her head away at a nearly unnatural angle.

"What's she doing?" Terra stiffened and reached for her pistol.

"Wait." Colt held up a hand and followed Birdie's gaze. The nonverbal little girl's senses could be preternaturally sharp, or maybe her own silence left room for extra awareness of the environment.

A moment later, ten-year-old Paolo burst out from where he'd been crouching, a small shadowy space under a cluster of low pipes. The boy raced away, twisting out of sight among the treatment plant's labyrinth of large pipes and concrete columns.

"Skinwalker!" Terra drew her pistol, and Damascus raised his heavy automatic rifle.

"No!" Hope moved to block their shot with her own body. "He's had it rough."

"We all have it rough," Terra said.

"He lost his home, his brother, and Mother Braden yesterday," Colt said. "He's lost everything at once. He's scared. Let me talk to him." He started down the narrow path the small boy had taken.

"How long has he been with you?" Fernando asked his younger brother.

"A couple of years," Diego replied. "He was Tonio's little brother. He's not some random scav we just picked up."

"I don't think a skinwalker would mole around that long," Hope said. "He would have killed us by now. Right?"

"Maybe you never did anything to trigger him," Fernando said.

Colt continued on out of earshot of their whispered conversation.

He listened carefully, walked slowly, and kept his footsteps light. He was worried the kid had already gone too far, gotten lost in the seemingly endless sprawl of tunnels and pipes that reached out in every direction under the city. Calling out for Paolo was much too dangerous; all Colt could do was listen.

Finally, he heard a rustling. It could have been a hungry, disease-ridden rat—or, even more dangerous, a hungry, disease-ridden human.

The noise came from the broken end of a pipe near floor level, about waist-high to Colt. He knelt slowly, raising his rifle with his finger on the trigger guard.

The heavy pipe made a right angle after only a couple of meters, so even with night vision, Colt couldn't see very far into it. A reaper or a wild animal could come crawling out at high speed, and he would only have a second to react.

The rustling sounded again, echoing from inside the pipe.

"Paolo?" Colt whispered.

The rustling stopped abruptly. Colt was alone with the sound of his own racing heart as he stared into the unknown.

Then the shape came scrambling around the bend. Colt felt torn about how to react, but he held his fire, risking his life to avoid risking Paolo's.

It was indeed Paolo, crawling on hands and knees, covered in a fresh layer of filth from the pipe's interior.

"I almost blew your brains out, kid," Colt said, lowering his rifle. "Say something next time."

"I'm scared," Paolo said. "They're going to kill me."

"No one's going to kill you," Colt said. "Not while I'm around."

"They look mean."

"We're all mean when we have to be," Colt said. "Like when there's machines around."

"Or bad people?" Paolo whispered. The small boy knew exactly what kind of world he lived in.

"Right," Colt said. "But they aren't bad people. I know them. They were around when I was your age."

"They won't hurt me?" Paolo asked, his dark eyes wide.

"They won't. Come on, let's go." Colt put aside his rifle and held out his hands, trying to coax the boy forward. It was hard to walk both extremes, to be ready to fight for survival one moment and try to deal with frightened kids the next. Colt always volunteered for guard duty, scout duty, scavenging duty, cooking duty—anything but childcare duty.

Paolo crawled closer, and Colt reached out to lift him from the tunnel. The boy wrapped his arms around Colt's neck, clinging tight like he'd never been so scared in his life.

Colt lifted him out and tried to set him down, but the boy's arms tightened.

"Paolo, I can't breathe," Colt said. "Come on, you can walk from here."

"They're going to kill me," Paolo whispered. "When they find out what I am."

His arms crushed tighter around Colt's neck. The boy's bones felt as hard as steel.

"Paolo," Colt whispered, choking. He didn't want to believe the boy was a machine. "Please."

The arms tightened, and spots appeared in front of Colt's eyes. He had to move fast or Paolo would kill him.

Colt turned and ran into the nearest of the large pipes

crisscrossing the room. He slammed Paolo's back against it, wincing at the impact. He slammed the boy again and again.

There was a snapping sound, and Paolo released Colt's neck and went limp. Paolo slipped out of Colt's arms and draped backward over the wide pipe Colt had slammed him against.

Oh, no, Colt thought, feeling a growing horror as he touched the boy's unresponsive face. *I killed him. I panicked and killed a little kid—*

Then Paolo sat up, in a way that would have been impossible unless the ten-year-old had been secretly doing thousands of sit-ups a day. He went from draped backward over the pipe to slamming his forehead into Colt's face, just to the right of Colt's nose. It was a powerful, painful blow, bruising or cracking the bone beneath.

Colt staggered backward, and Paolo shoved him back against a stack of three enormous pipes that formed a kind of high wall. Colt was stunned, lost his balance, and slid to the floor.

Paolo leaped down onto him and pinned Colt's shoulders back against the large pipe. The boy's face was slack and expressionless, even as he drew back a fist to smash Colt's face.

Colt dodged the punch, barely, and it dented the pipe beside his head, rupturing it open.

Dark, foul, ice-cold water gushed from the damaged pipe for a moment, with a deeply sour smell that made Colt's stomach hitch.

The water soaked his shirt and Paolo's hand that pinned Colt's shoulder to the pipe, creating enough lubrication that Colt could slip free. Colt started to crawl away on hands and knees.

Paolo grabbed him, though, and lifted him from the floor and swung him sideways into more of the pipes. The pain was jarring, and Colt fought for a moment to keep his consciousness... as well as his grip on his rifle, which he'd managed to grab during his brief crawl.

Colt landed on his side on the dirty concrete floor. He raised the rifle and unloaded a burst of rounds into Paolo's face.

The high-speed lead stripped the artificial skin off the skinwalker's face and dented the metal beneath. Paolo's face was now a bullet-damaged steel skull, and he looked like a small-sized reaper.

Footsteps approached, drawn by the gunfire.

"Help!" Paolo's skull-face called out, in his familiar kid voice. "Help! I'm hurt!"

Colt released another burst, emptying his magazine at Paolo as the small skinwalker rose to its feet. Colt had heard rumors of metalheads designed to look like innocent kids, but it was awful to encounter one like this. Had Paolo always been a machine, brilliantly disguised to infiltrate and watch their group?

What about Tonio, his older brother—had he been real, or another convincing android? Tonio was dead, his body left buried in rubble, so there was no way to know for sure at the moment. His blood had seemed real enough, though it could have been fake, stored inside the android in case it needed to mimic bleeding. Plus, Tonio had died defending them, hadn't he?

Or maybe there had once been a real Paolo, and the machines had replaced him with an identical android at some point. Maybe the real Paolo had been killed—or worse, taken by Simon Nix as a test subject for his unspeakable experiments. Colt shuddered to think of the boy suffering the horrors inside the lab where the android studied humans in order to better understand how to control them. Simon had described this research and learning process as never ending.

All of this flickered through Colt's brain in an instant, but he had no time to dwell on it.

Paolo, having backed off a couple of steps while taking fire, now lunged for Colt again. The spray of rifle fire hadn't stopped him, but some part of his body shrieked when he moved, as if damaged. Paolo stood over Colt for a moment, scanning him with his black-lens eyes. The brief metallic shriek sounded again as Paolo turned his head. One of Paolo's neck actuators was damaged, Colt guessed.

Colt didn't have time to reload. As Paolo tried to grab him again, he swung the butt of his rifle good and hard at Paolo's neck. Colt would only get one chance at this—if he botched it up, Paolo would be able to finish him off.

The rifle landed just where he wanted it to, though, below the jawline and above the collarbone, hitting only the neck itself.

"Help!" Paolo's voice shouted as his head jacked sideways onto his shoulder at almost a right angle. Through the shredded fake skin at the boy-skinwalker's neck, Colt could see the damaged actuator, sparks crackling among the loosened connections.

Colt hammered Paolo's head a second and third time while the machine wailed for help in its most miserable, sobbing voice. Colt took a quick detour to smash its jaw and see if that would shut the machine up, and he managed to dislocate the jaw, but the speaker deep down inside kept crying for help.

"Colt! Stop!" Hope shouted as she rounded the corner along with the other scavengers and the rebels. Birdie trailed close behind them, her wide eyes watching carefully as ever. Watching Colt savagely attack Paolo.

"What are you doing to him?" Diego shouted.

"Told you," Terra said, cool as ever. She raised her pistol and drilled three quick laser blasts through Paolo's skull. Colt stumbled back and away from Paolo to dodge the shots.

"Careful!" Hope shouted at Terra.

"I didn't hit anyone." Terra sounded annoyed at Hope's advice.

Damascus advanced, and whatever the giant rebel was feeding his rifle was higher-grade stuff than Colt's ammo, because his rapid fire cut down Paolo's body—surgically, joint by joint—and left it a burning heap on the floor.

"Wait, what?" Diego blinked, looking from Colt to the burning pieces of Paolo. "That's not possible. Is it? They've been with us forever."

"I guess anything's possible." Colt stared at the burning pieces of the fragile-seeming boy who'd lived with them for something like two years. He grieved, even though he couldn't be sure whether Paolo had ever been real or not. The boy had certainly seemed real.

And if the machines had been able to trick all of them for that long, had been willing to quietly watch even a group as small and insignificant as theirs... maybe the machines had more absolute control than Colt had ever realized.

He looked up at the scavengers he'd lived with all his life —his friend Diego, Diego's older brother Fernando, and Terra. The strange girl Birdie, who now sobbed quietly, tears carving flesh-colored paths through the filth on her cheeks, her shock and grief kept silent out of long habit, for her own survival. Colt considered his own sister, Hope. What if she'd been planted alongside him as a child, spying on him? Changing as they aged? Or what if the real Hope had been taken, replaced by a convincing mechanical copy?

Then he looked at Mohini, thinking how foolish he'd been to trust an outsider, when it turned out he couldn't even trust the most innocent-seeming in his own group.

Mohini looked at him closely. "Are you hurt?"

"I'm fine," Colt said, though he hurt all over. There wasn't any time to waste.

"We have to go," Damascus said, and nobody argued. "If we're lucky, we're deep enough to impede that skinwalker's wireless. But they've been watching all of you."

"Which way?" Colt asked, looking among the rebels.

Fernando tilted his head, and Diego and Terra followed him. Colt, Mohini, and Hope filed after them down a narrow pass between stacks of pipes. Damascus waited for everyone to get moving, then took up the rear, his heavy rifle ready, his eyes quietly watching the scavengers. The big guy didn't say much, but he was clearly suspicious of the new arrivals, especially since one of them had turned out to be a skinwalker.

"Where are we going now?" Diego asked.

"Not home," Fernando said. "They'll never let you in now."

"But we have to reach them," Colt said, looking at Mohini. "It's urgent. We have a chance to really move against the machines. Against Carthage, even."

"And they know all about it," Terra said, looking over her shoulder. "Whatever that kid might have overheard about your plans, they know. Simon Nix knows. That includes anything the skinwalker kid could have heard by eavesdropping, including anything you said when you thought he was asleep."

"We don't know where your base is, so that's safe," Colt

said, thinking it over quickly. "He would know Mohini's the one who hacked the reaper. That we're trying to connect her with the rebellion. That she's from Carthage. And that our real target is..." Colt stopped talking because Mohini had grabbed his arm. She was shaking her head. Maybe she didn't trust Chicago's rebels any more than they trusted her.

"Simon Nix," Fernando said. "Diego told us. Your job is to capture the administrator of the Americas inside his own base. We'll only have to fight through a few tank platoons and a few hundred reapers."

"It sounds like a great idea," Terra said, looking Mohini over. "If your goal is to draw us into a trap where we can get slaughtered. Is that it?"

"We already established I'm not one of the machines," Mohini said.

"No, but you claim to be one of the people they serve," Terra said. "A Carthaginian? We should string you up and use you for target practice."

"We're all on the same side," Mohini said.

Terra gave her another long look, then turned away. "We'll see," she said.

They kept quiet after that, forging onward through the twisting dark paths of the underworld, hurrying to clear the area before more machines arrived.

Chapter Four

Carthage

Audrey Caracala sat in the pilot's chair on the bridge of the *Atreus*, though the old minicarrier needed no piloting. It had handled itself quite well through a number of space battles. This was its retirement, or really post-retirement, mission; the old craft had been in line for recycling before getting pulled for Audrey.

She had come up with this mission herself, had pressed for it against her family's wishes, but her father had come around to supporting it and even flipped it into a political gesture of his own. Prime Legislator Francorte Caracala had put out a press release about how Carthage believed in using its power to promote justice and freedom throughout the galaxy.

Perhaps it was merely cynicism and politics on her father's part, but Audrey genuinely believed she could improve things for people on the remote, harsh planet of Veritum. An abusive religious cult controlled the settlements there. If there was anyplace she could apply power constructively, it was there.

Unfortunately, Simon Lark sat beside her, dressed in the gold-and-white coveralls of Carthaginian space crew members, which Audrey also wore.

Simon's presence was not part of her plan, and the android actually endangered both the benevolent intent of her mission as well as the small human crew she'd brought along.

"Off we venture," Simon said, watching the retreating shape of Carthage on the rear screen, her blue-green home planet with its concentric metallic rings of orbiting ports and factories connected by the massive cables and train-like cars of a dozen space elevators rising from the equator. Swarms of starships moved in and out of the orbital complex as Carthage sent out its autonomous warships, tanks, and infantry while receiving natural resources, manufactured goods, and preserved exotic foods from scores of tributary worlds.

Audrey felt frightened to leave her world for the first time, and also to leave the sanctuary of the civilized inner worlds for a dangerous, remote planet, but it was even more frightening to have a Simon assigned to watch her every move.

"Forgive me if my humble mechanical nature leads me to misread your tone and expression," Simon said, "but you seem rather melancholy for someone whose wishes are reaching fruition. Was this not the humanitarian intervention for which you advocated as a security intern? And then demanded of your father after you lost your internship?"

"Yes, thanks for bringing that up," Audrey said. "I'm nervous, Simon. It seemed obvious to me that we could accomplish a humanitarian mission more effectively with actual humans involved."

"And now you feel that your hypothesis was flawed?" Simon asked.

"It's not how we usually do things."

"You have brought a crew of experts to assist you," Simon said. "Will they not be joining us on the bridge for the hyperspace transition? Safety restraints are recommended, whether here or in their quarters."

"I'll go talk to them." Audrey jumped up, happy to move, happy to get away from the Simon's cold, watchful blue eyes.

"Why not simply call them?" Simon frowned. "There seems to be some difficulty with the media interfaces in the berthing compartment."

"It's supposed to be like this. Including the lack of screen interfaces for the crew's personal life," Audrey said, fighting her heart's attempt to jump into her throat with fear. You had to put up a powerful front, no matter what. That was advice from her father, which she'd overheard him give her brother once. "My whole hypothesis is that, well, people need other people. Our sociability is one of our core strengths as a species. We don't want to lose that."

"Do you feel you're losing that?" Simon asked, his tone gentle, simulating a kind of emotional concern for her. Audrey might have even fallen it for it, as she had for years with Simon Quick, her father's strategy android.

"We speak to each other too often through screens, holograms, and indirect messages that help us avoid interaction altogether. Which can be nice, honestly, but..." Audrey shrugged, trying to act casual when she was frightened, unsure how to get this situation under control. It would be a long trip on a small craft, or at least inside a small life-support area within the sizable automated ship. Simon could go anywhere at all on the ship, though, since he was not alive.

"I still believe cutting comm links with the crew quarters is unwise," Simon said. "Blind spots are dangerous. Knowledge is power; ignorance is risk. Willful ignorance, therefore, is simply unnecessary risk."

"Right." Audrey hoped he couldn't see her starting to sweat, but she was almost certain he could. "Hey, I didn't know you were a Platonist."

"Excuse me?"

"Knowledge is power. Isn't that Plato?"

"Francis Bacon," Simon said. "Plato believed knowledge is *virtue*, a topic rarely raised by Carthaginians, in my experience."

"Great. Just mind the ship and get her ready for hyperspace."

Audrey closed the door behind her and hurried down the narrow passageway. The ship was chilly, with no pretense of creature comforts. They would sleep on small bunks for the next couple of weeks, and they had collapsible shelters for their stay on Veritum that didn't promise much more comfort. The roughness of the situation was unfamiliar to her, but definitely invigorating, as if she'd finally escaped the silk cocoon of her upbringing and was flying free, fully alive at last.

Though didn't most metamorphic insects die soon after leaving their cocoon?

Pushing away those thoughts, she opened a round hatch and crawled down the narrow throat of a ladder well toward the crew quarters below.

Simon claimed he couldn't get video or audio access to

the crew's berthing compartment. Audrey hoped that was true.

She passed through a narrow doorway and down a passageway to the compartment where all the other humans were.

Audrey had hand-picked this crew, getting their security clearances with extensive help from the mysterious software agent that called itself Minerva.

Much help had been required, too, because these people were all traveling under false identities, in disguise, and none of them would have remotely qualified for a security clearance for a mission like this.

She closed the door tightly and looked among the four other crew members.

"We have to strap down for hyperspace," she said.

"I have insulated this area," a silvery female figure said, forming as a hologram near a tiny wall projector. Minerva. Audrey had smuggled in a memory cube holding the software agent and uploaded her into the minicarrier's central network. "The Simon cannot see or hear us."

"Are you sure?" Audrey asked.

"Yes."

"Warn us if he approaches." Audrey looked at the nearest crew member, a girl with long blue hair, currently fashionable, and matching eyes, and drew her into a close embrace. Beneath her disguise, her hair was short and brown, her eyes gray. Zola was Audrey's oldest friend, currently posing as a sociologist under a false name, her credentials invented and inserted into every necessary database by Minerva or by rebel hackers Audrey had never met.

The embrace was unusually demonstrative for a Carthaginian, but Audrey was making an effort to connect more.

She reached out and touched hands with the others—Dinnius, a handsome dwarf with a mop of heavy brown hair currently hiding much of his face. Kright, his sharp blue eyes undisguised, connecting with hers in a way that she found dangerously distracting. Her hand stayed on his a moment longer.

She embraced her brother. Salvius, back from the dead in so many ways. She'd long believed him lost in a dark hell of illicit drugs and self-destruction, but apparently this supposedly criminal and shiftless lifestyle was a cover to distract from his support of the rebellion they all claimed was brewing.

Salvius tolerated Audrey's embrace but didn't return it.

"I'm still here under protest," Salvius said. "We can't change Carthage from some cult-ridden outer world thousands of light-years away."

"But we can do some good here," Audrey said. "Far more than we can do back home."

"Veritum is beyond any shipping lanes," Salvius said. "What are you planning to do? Nobody will notice anything that happens there."

"The people who live there will," Audrey said. "Don't you want to divert assets of the empire toward improving people's lives?"

"Carthage is always out to improve the lives of every world we conquer. Haven't you read your propaganda texts yet? Or is political propaganda a seventh-year topic?"

"Third year," Audrey said. "And I dropped out of Political Academy. Why are you here if you don't believe in the mission?"

"Because Zola insisted on coming after Minerva conveyed your message to us." Salvius shook his head. "I couldn't have both of you running off like that."

"Don't be ashamed to mention the real reason you came," Dinnius said. "The idea of Zola being alone with me on a long trip to an exotic planet drove you mad with jealousy."

"I did think about it," Salvius said. He looked at Audrey. "Watch out for Dinnius. He thinks he's a faun in a world full of nymphs."

"A *satyr*," Dinnius said from where he sat on a top bunk, "is the preferred term if you're denigrating a little person into a horny mythological creature. Bravo on the originality there, as well." He gave a single clap.

"I'm not kidding, Audrey. He'll be worming his way into your bed before you realize it, and you'll even think you want it to happen—" Salvius began.

"We do have actual important, non-personal things to discuss right now," Audrey said.

"Like how there's a Simon unit aboard this craft?" Kright stroked his long fake beard contemplatively. "That wasn't part of the plan."

"Exactly," Audrey said. "So what can we do? Minerva, tell me you can hack a Simon unit."

"I am sorry," replied the silvery, ghostly projection. "Simons are wrapped in proprietary encryption, and within that runs a proprietary AI operating system inside a proprietary central processing architecture."

"Sounds very proprietary," Zola said.

"Information on the Simon unit is tightly siloed even within Carthage Consolidated. A specialized subsidiary, Next Solutions, handles Simon development and maintenance. It was spun off from their regular AI research division fifty-one years ago."

"So what if we capture the Simon that's here with us?" Kright asked. "Could you hack it or not?"

"It is likely that you would all die in the attempt," Minerva said. "Simon commands the battalion of reapers in the hold, as well as the ship's central network. He could depressurize, for example, at no risk to himself."

"But you cut off his access here, right?" Audrey said. "So could you cut off his access to the ship's network?"

"And the reapers?" Kright asked.

"Surely killing Audrey is outside the Simon's permissions," Dinnius said. "She is the Prime Legislator's daughter."

"But that doesn't help anyone else very much," Audrey said.

"I cannot guarantee that I could maintain control of all communications very long," Minerva said. "And the Simon will likely have its own wireless connection to the reapers, independent of the ship's network, though the ship's bulkheads may interfere with that to a degree."

"So if we mutiny against the Simon, we'll have to move fast," Kright said, "while you hold down the communications as long as you can. Maybe he'll be dead before he can summon the reapers."

"It is still highly likely you would die," Minerva said.

"Even our guardian angel says it's hopeless," Dinnius said. "Fantastic."

"We can't move against Simon until we leap into hyperspace," Zola said. "Until then, he could have the whole fleet on us in five minutes."

"Starting a fight in hyperspace isn't a grand idea, either," Dinnius said. "If something goes wrong, we could end up... well, anywhere in the universe, theoretically. Or nowhere. Perhaps another universe entirely. It's complicated."

"So we wait until we're on approach to Veritum,"

Kright said. "If something goes wrong, we'll be close to a habitable planet."

"A planet we're supposed to be saving from itself," Audrey said, shaking her head. "And we could end up refugees there instead."

"So we don't move against the Simon while we're still in space," Salvius said. "Leave it alone until we're down on the surface of Veritum. He can't depressurize us or crash our ship once we're already on the ground. We just have to lie low and hold out until then. Everybody stay in character."

"We were only supposed to stay in these characters for the boarding and the launch, not for weeks of transit," Kright muttered, scratching his chin under his big fake beard. "I should have picked a less itchy disguise."

"Then it's settled," Audrey said. "We focus on our mission for now. Once we're finally down on the surface of the planet, we watch for a chance to move against the Simon."

There were murmurs of reluctant agreement. Nobody seemed to have any better suggestions.

"The Simon approaches," Minerva said.

"I'll tell him the crew is going to strap down here instead of the bridge," Audrey said. "Which you should do. The sooner we jump to hyperspace, the better."

Audrey left the room, her heart pounding as she went to intercept the approaching android, to turn him back toward the bridge and away from her brother and her friends.

Chapter Five

Galapagos

Ellison watched flickering holograms and listened to spotty audio from the hotspots where Coalition ships fought the attacking Hammers. The Hammers' new premier, General Gorron Prazca, had moved in a surprise first strike while the Coalition was still trying to organize a response from their ever-quarreling member nations.

The quarrels had ended, though, and all were pulling together against the common threat of the Iron Hammers, based in the frozen waters and icy islands of the northern Polar Archipelago.

"Prazca didn't wait for the Carthaginian reinforcements to arrive. That seems unwise of them," said Mikhail Kartokov, the abnormally resilient minister of defense. His chocolate-brown designer fedora concealed a layer of bandaging from injuries he'd suffered on the spaceport.

Ellison had told his fishing crews and his family to stay

home today and focus on stocking and prepping the underground emergency shelters, so they'd already be there in case of attack.

"We knew he could strike us today," Ellison said. "It suits his personality. The ambassadors and ministers and media were all here. Perfect time for a dramatic gesture. He wouldn't have gotten another one—I'm recommending all ambassadors head home for their own safety."

"All of which you announced yesterday," said the acting minister of state, Adrienna Gilra. The Aquatican's pale, bulging green eyes studied him. "Sandwiched between personal insults aimed at the premier himself. Almost as if you wanted to goad him into attack."

"We were prepared for that possibility," Ellison said.

She raised her wisp-thin green eyebrows. Her eye membranes occluded and blinked before clearing again.

The Command Center was grouped by nationality, reflecting the organization of their armed forces. The Coalition did not have a fully integrated military; it was a shaky league of nations that included some former enemies. Ellison himself had fought against fast, deep-moving Aquatican boats.

Ellison had spent his political career as part of a group pushing for more joint defense exercises among Coalition nations, promoting positive peaceful relations as much as combined might. Those exercises were paying off today.

He looked over the consoles. Embankments of anti-aircraft guns and missile batteries had been activated, chasing the enemy bombers out into a wider course around the island, as revealed on Coalition radar and satellite.

The other holographic displays were like aquariums full of miniature ships, the images compiled from an assortment of sonar and other sensors as well as data from the ships' own onboard computers.

During the war, each nation had built its own network of cables, hydrophones, and assorted sensors beneath the water, while sabotaging those of enemy nations. Since forming the Coalition, the members had combined their undersea sensor networks into a single grid, the Subaquatic Integrated Detection System, or SQUIDS, which now fed the Command Center live streams of the battle.

Each nation had its particular strengths, with characteristic boats reflecting their identities.

To the northwest of Tower Island raced the light, quick corvettes of the Green Islands Navy, their hulls shifting colors to make them more difficult to see against the water. The fast boats dipped quickly above and below the surface to help avoid being targeted. They were assigned to dodge the relatively shallow northwestern approach to Tower Island, and they did so now, warding off a pair of Hammer destroyers trying to nose in from that direction.

The deeper north and east approaches to the global meeting place were patrolled by Aquatican submarines, which liked to run deep and stay there. Now they emerged from dark channels and narrow caves like the predatory fish they were designed to resemble, ambushing Iron Hammer boats that had tried to creep in close to Tower Island.

"I'll tell you something, Commodore Chromis," Ellison said, looking across the console at the tall, pale Aquatican commander, "I've always been impressed by you Aquatican skippers and how you can find your way in and out of the tightest spots. That shoal looks like a shipwreck waiting to happen, and your guy just popped out like a shark from the kelp and took a chunk of that deep cruiser." Ellison nodded approvingly as a pair of torpedoes struck the large underwater ship with the crossed-hammer logo on its sail. "Amazing maneuvering. I tried to learn from you."

"The deeps are our true home," the commodore replied. The blue-tinged gills along his neck flexed, opening slightly. "We live there, we hunt there, we build there. The depths are pure. We surface when we must, but the surface is corrupt, filled with humans who have lost our deep ancestral connection to the ocean. No offense intended to present company."

"And you have the only marines in the galaxy who can breathe underwater." Ellison watched subs exchange fire in the depths, chasing each other through winding canyons and sharp reefs. The Aquatican commanders seemed to have the situation in hand; they'd been patrolling the deep terrain for years and knew it well, and they were inflicting more damage than they were receiving, though neither side had sunk a boat yet. Sturdy armored hulls were necessary to survive modern undersea warfare and the extreme pressure of the deep trenches that crisscrossed the planet's ocean floor.

"Our gills supplement us underwater, but they don't have the power of true lungs," the Aquatican commodore said. "We must all surface eventually. All of us fall short of true grace, of being true ocean creatures."

Ellison nodded and moved on to the next console. The navy of his own country, the Scatterlands, guarded the southern approach. Invasion from the south was less likely because the waters were shallower and narrower, divided into channels and straits between rocky islands.

However, if the Hammers came from that direction, the Scatterlands fleet would prove the perfect guardians—battle-scarred old craft of assorted sizes and shapes, some of which had begun life as fishing or pleasure boats decades earlier, a number of them suitable for shallow-water fighting.

Ellison felt a particular swell of pride. Each ship displayed the colorful puzzle-piece flag of their still-young Republic of the Scatterlands, born from mutual defense in a time of war. Often dismissed as rogues, small-time smugglers, and unambitious fisherman, they'd banded together to form a navy and a nation that had held firm against onslaughts from every side.

He nodded at Scatterlands Admiral Chief Micky Perrault, who nodded back. They'd both joined on as sailors and been sucked up into Coalition officer training, which just proved how desperate the need for officers had been at the time. They'd been sent back as hastily promoted lieutenant commanders, allegedly ready to command small, hastily constructed Scatterlands submarines that seemed ready to crumble with each deep dive.

In such a dicey craft, the *Sea Scorpion*, Ellison had explored the deep ocean, the trenches and mountains, the cliff-like reefs. He'd served primarily as a surveillance-hunter, harassing enemy supply lines when possible, sometimes assisting larger groups when prolonged battles erupted.

After the Hammers had bombed Kawau Island, killing Ellison's father and hundreds of others, Ellison had taken a particular interest in hunting down and sinking Hammer ships. He'd increased the *Scorpion*'s attack capacity, given her extra hardening against torpedoes. He'd used his own meager pay and savings to outfit her, and when that ran short, he'd staged pirate-like raids on enemy cargo ships in search of needed parts.

Then he'd started going deep into Hammer territory,

hunting. Intent on killing those responsible for what had happened to his home.

Ellison tried to push back that instant flood of memories. He had to focus on today's war, not yesterday's.

Which brought him to the fourth console, where no less than four rotund, balding admirals from the Gavrikov Reincorporated Islands stood shouting at each other in their rough language; Ellison knew some of their words, but they were yelling rapidly, waving their fists, and it wasn't easy to follow.

"What's the problem?" Ellison whispered to Kartokov, hoping the defense minister could explain his countrymen.

"No problem, no problem at all," Kartokov said, smiling wide, which looked suspicious and unnatural on his craggy face.

One Gavrikovan admiral punched the other in the nose, sending the red-faced man to the floor.

"A very small policy disagreement," Kartokov amended. "All that matters is Commander Krinski is on schedule with the *Ursus*."

Ellison watched the *Ursus* with his usual mixture of respect and disbelief as the immense battle carrier rose from the depths just beyond Tower Island harbor. Waterfalls of drainage spilled off every side as the ship emerged like a sunken city raised by some feat of engineering or magic. The *Ursus* was Gavrikova's flagship, the only one of its class, a monstrosity with four runways protected by towers bristling with guns and plasma cannons.

A pair of submersible heavy cruisers rose on its flanks, ready to add anti-aircraft or anti-ship fire to any craft that threatened the immense carrier.

"The big bear is awake," Kartokov said, with obvious pride.

"Just in time, too," Ellison said, watching the tiny holographic fighter-chasers launch from the *Ursus* to pursue the retreating group of Hammer-marked bombers that had attacked the House of Ambassadors complex above. The buildings were hardened, built with enemy bombardment in mind. The ambassadors, their staffs, and anyone not involved in the island's defense should have gone to the bomb shelters by now to wait for the all clear.

The Gavrikovan admirals stopped brawling long enough to watch the flickering, transparent images of their narrow, fast planes chase after the distant dots of the enemy bombers.

"Where are they going?" Ellison asked. The thin chaser planes were faster than the bombers they pursued, but it would still take them a few minutes to reach their quarry.

A Gavrikovan admiral muttered something. The view shifted as the feed from another satellite appeared, tracking the fighter-chasers as they streaked through the sky.

Ellison glanced at the other command stations. The Scatterlands fleet continued patrolling the shallow southern approaches. The Green Island corvettes and the organic-looking, scaly-armored Aquatican submarines fought against Hammer ships above and below water. Ellison winced as a Hammer destroyer strafed a corvette with its heavy guns and sank the craft.

Underwater, as displayed at the other console, Aquatican torpedoes finally penetrated the hull of a Hammer destroyer; the ship crumpled and sank toward the deep canyon below.

Sadly, the Aquaticans paid for this with a boat of their own, an attack sub struck with a plasma missile. The glowing plasma explosion boiled a massive amount of water into a rapidly expanding sphere of hot steam, disrupting and possibly damaging the other Aquatican subs around the one that had been struck.

Then the holograms went fuzzy and vanished. The boiling, plasma-driven underwater explosion had damaged or overwhelmed the SQUIDS system in that area.

"They're working to get the sensors back online. It may take some time," said Commodore Chromis. He closed his bulging fish eyes and lowered his head. "We have lost a crew of twelve. May their souls find peace in the Eternal Deep."

The Aquaticans on the commodore's staff briefly lowered their heads and quietly repeated his last phrase. So did Adrienna Gilra; the acting minister of state bowed her head and touched the golden seahorse on her neck as she prayed.

The system rendered a fuzzier, less clear holographic view of the battle using only the sensors built into the subs themselves. It was jerky and incomplete, but better than nothing.

The view returned in time for Ellison to watch an Aquatican sub lure a Hammer ship into a chase, then escape through a narrow pass in the underwater range. Only an expert skipper with a lean ship and close knowledge of the terrain could have made it through.

Sure enough, the Hammer submersible destroyer couldn't quite fit. Before it could reverse out, another Aquatican sub showed up to nail the trapped enemy boat with a pair of torpedoes. The Hammer boat's hull was ruptured, and it crushed like a can in a giant fist. Bubble-clouds of escaping atmosphere trailed the Hammer ship as it sank to the ocean bed, ferrying a load of freshly dead souls down to the underworld.

"We have a visual on the carrier," Kartokov announced,

instantly drawing Ellison's attention back to the Gavrikovan console.

Extrapolated from satellite data, the display showed a squadron of Iron Hammer bombers circling a massive partially submerged carrier accompanied by three destroyers. One by one, the bombers dived into the open hangar, a practiced and efficient descent. It looked like they were diving into a gaping black hole in the ocean.

By the time the Gavrikovan chaser planes arrived, most of the enemy bombers had disappeared into the hangar below. The chasers fired lasers after the rapidly descending Iron Hammer birds, but then had to climb high to escape a barrage of anti-aircraft fire from the Hammer destroyers.

The destroyers sent up missiles after the chaser planes, too. Some of the chasers spun away at high speed; others dumped shimmering trails of metallic chaff to distract the missiles' guidance systems. Lacking any depth charges or bombs, the chasers couldn't do much but swing wide and turn back.

The enemy carrier group began retreating to the north, diving under the surface as they went.

Coalition underwater monitors grew thinner toward the north, but they might catch a glimpse of the group chugging back to the Polar Archipelago.

Over at the Aquatican consoles, the Hammer submersible craft seemed to be making an orderly retreat, though not too hastily to exchange fire with Aquatican subs as they departed.

The Hammer surface ships were following suit, pulling away but continuing to exchange fire with the Green Island corvettes.

"Are they leaving already?" Ellison asked, not really believing what he was seeing. "What was the point?"

"Perhaps they wanted to send a message," suggested Gilra. The acting minister of state kept her large sea-green eyes on the Aquatican subs.

"Sir, we have an incoming call from General Prazca," said the Green Island officer in charge of Command Center administration and technical support.

"Put him on," Ellison said. "Audio only."

"Minister-General." Prazca's harsh voice rang out a few seconds later. "I hope you've had a few days to rest since your trip upstairs."

"I wouldn't say they've been restful," Ellison replied. "Have you finished with your temper tantrum yet? We're ready to kill a lot more of your people if you're ready to send them our way."

"Iron Hammers don't fear death," Prazca said.

"I'm glad to hear it. Come get all you want."

"It's easy to be brave when you're hiding in a rock-lined hole like a shivering rabbit," Prazca countered.

"If you're inviting me to a one-on-one duel, I'll be happy to meet you," Ellison said. "If I kill you, that makes me premier of the Polar Archipelago, doesn't it? That would be a handy second job. It would sure make my primary one a hell of a lot easier. So where are we meeting?"

"Killing me is not enough," Prazca said. "You must have supporters among the Hammers."

"Maybe I do," Ellison replied. "Premier Cross didn't know how much support you had, did he? He didn't see the coup coming. You won't see the one that's coming for you, either, until it's too late."

"Empty threats," Prazca said, and he was mostly right. The Coalition had some intelligence sources within the Polar Archipelago, informing on the Hammers, but nothing like assets in place to overthrow the premier. The Coalition hadn't even seen Prazca's coup coming, which showed how little they understood the inner workings of the enemy state. Still, maybe his words would haunt Prazca, make him suspicious of those around him, cloud his judgment.

"Is that why you're calling me?" Ellison asked. "To send a few empty threats my way? Are you too afraid to stand against us without Carthage at your back? Too weak?"

The Command Center was silent aside from their voices; everyone was listening, even the formerly brawling pack of Gavrikovan admirals.

Ellison's insults had a purpose. If he could goad Prazca into saying too much, that could be helpful. If he could goad the premier even further, into unplanned and sloppy actions against the Coalition, maybe they could bag a few more Hammer ships today, before Prazca's off-world backup arrived.

"We are not weak. This morning's visit should have made that clear," Prazca said.

"A 'visit' is a good term," Ellison said. "It wasn't much of an attack. More like a kid leaving a burning bag of fish crap on your porch. We all lost people today. Why?"

"I am in a generous mood," Prazca said. "So generous that I'm giving you the opportunity to surrender. No more death, no more fighting, only peace. That's what all of you want, isn't it? To hide in your burrows like rabbits. Recognize me as premier of all Galapagos, and there will be peace for the rest of our lives."

"You can't expect us to declare you ruler of the entire planet just because we had a few skirmishes this morning."

"You know what's coming, Ellison," Prazca said. "This is your final chance to fold quietly. If we wait for Carthage to arrive, there will only be death from the skies. You know what they'll do to you."

"They'll treat you no better," Ellison said. "You're nothing more than an expendable tool to Carthage. Surely you know this. They're coming to divide and conquer. When your forces and ours are worn down to a low ebb, they'll enslave us all. The best you can hope for is some kind of overseer job."

"Overseer of a planet," Prazca said. "Far worse jobs exist."

"Until Carthage disposes of you, too, and replaces you with a machine. We should be working together, Premier Prazca. We should be protecting our planet from this external threat, not fighting each other and making it easy for Carthage to rule us all."

Prazca let out a humorless laugh that sounded like the bark of the fanged seal, a carnivorous marine mammal of Galapagos known for its double rows of sharp teeth.

"There is no protection against Carthage," Prazca said. "You are the fool. This is your last chance: will the Coalition surrender?"

"Of course not," Ellison said. The silence in the Command Center had never been more absolute.

"Then next time we speak, I'll be pissing on your bloated, broken corpse as it floats out to sea," Prazca said, and a peal of feedback sounded as the voice connection broke off.

Ellison kept looking among the monitors, watching for any sign that the Hammer ships were returning.

"Cruise missiles incoming!" announced one of the radar techs in the Scatterlands quadrant of the room. He kept his voice calm, but it was shaky. Glowing maps showed pulsing red dots streaking across the islands and seas to the south—missiles, a dozen of them, on course for Tower Island.

"Do you think they're nuclear?" Gilra whispered.

"They'll strike in ten minutes," Kartokov replied, staring at the display. "If we're still alive in eleven, the answer is no, not nuclear."

The distant air-raid sirens overhead, which had been ringing since the initial bombing, now intensified, though hopefully everyone who wasn't actively defending the island had gone down to the shelters already. Even the shelters were not likely to hold against a dozen nuclear warheads.

"Should we take the Command Center down?" Gilra asked. "Just in case?"

"That is cowardly," Kartokov said.

"I am thinking of the continuity of government!" she snapped back at him. "Not my own skin."

"Though that skin would be conveniently saved—" Kartokov began.

"We're staying," Ellison said, watching the dozen converging spots on the hologram. "Kartokov, initiate countermeasures."

"Nuclear?" Kartokov asked.

"Conventional. Hit all the Class A targets in and around their capital."

Kartokov began barking orders. Responses to a Hammer missile attack had been gamed plenty of times, and Coalition missile subs had been on high alert today like the rest of their forces. Even if Tower Island were reduced to a smoking crater and everyone in this room died, the Coalition would still rain hell on their enemy's major installations and capital city.

"Satellite traces the cruise missiles back to the Bay of Sharks," another Scatterlands tech said, his eyes fixed on flashing, spinning piles of incoming data. The bay he'd identified was almost eight hundred kilometers south of their location. "Launched from beneath the ocean surface."

"Missile subs," Ellison said. "The other attacks were a distraction."

"Or they wanted to soften us up," Kartokov said.

"I'll send a task force after the missile subs," said Admiral Perrault.

"No, keep all our boats close and tight," Ellison said. "We don't want to get lured out and stretched thin. Keep to the plan."

"Typical Reg," Perrault said. "Stay cautious. Never bet too much, even if you're holding a prime hand."

"I wouldn't call this a prime hand," Ellison said. "But if you've got an ace stashed anywhere, now's the time." Ellison hoped Minerva would intervene to help, as she had on the spaceport, but so far the AI agent had remained silent today. Ellison didn't have time to try to sneak off alone and contact her, and he certainly didn't want to be seen begging some invisible software entity for divine intervention.

"All the Hammer craft are fleeing in double time now," Kartokov noted, glancing around to assess the situation at different consoles.

"I guess the cruise missiles were the main part of their message," Ellison said, watching the dots close in on them. "Everyone prepare for impact."

By the time the missiles struck the House of Ambassadors above, everyone in the Command Center had braced for impact, seated on the floor so they wouldn't be thrown and injured.

Ellison huddled with his ministers and the top military officers of each Coalition nation as the missiles struck. The first impact rocked the entire room with a roar worse than any thunder Ellison had heard. Most of the consoles flashed red error messages and quickly went offline. Ellison worried about everyone in the shelters around them, hoping the hardened structures would hold.

The second missile hit. The remaining lights and power blew out, and the floor seemed to tilt and sway beneath them. They huddled in the dark as more missiles struck the capital complex, shaking the island to its core, resuming an old war with an old enemy that felt newly empowered and emboldened by the Carthaginian empire.

Chapter Six

Earth

Colt kept quiet as he followed Terra through a rat warren of utility tunnels, down stairs dripping foul runoff, down into icy darkness, up a long-dead escalator between bombed-out train platforms, down ladders into the sewer system again. Colt knew the underbelly of the city fairly well, but not out here. Lakeview, in the shadow of the crumbling old stadium, was a district he typically avoided; the rebels were more active here, so the machines were, too.

Mohini walked close beside him, and they maintained physical contact when walking through the stretches of absolute darkness, their hands clutched together so they didn't lose each other. Terra would lay a hand on Colt's shoulders at those times, and he would have a flicker of years earlier, before she'd become a scarred fighter with the rebels, when she'd been something like an older sister to him. Or at least a cousin who occasionally got stuck babysitting him.

Everyone else—Diego, Hope, and Birdie—had gone with Fernando, off to a storehouse where they could access some food and medical supplies to help them rest and recover from their recent battle and the long walk afterward.

Terra was taking Colt and Mohini to meet with someone she referred to as the rebel "section leader." Apparently this person had sent Terra and Fernando to meet Mohini first and assess her claims before bringing the Carthaginian girl to him.

Colt's apprehension grew with each step he took in the underground world, and their usual need to keep silent and listen didn't help. He had a lot of questions for Terra about where exactly they were going and who they'd be meeting, but those would be useless even if he was willing to break noise discipline and strike up a conversation about it.

They had passed the first round, and they were going to meet with higher-ups who would decide whether the rebels would assist with Mohini's plan or not.

If the rebels turned them down, there was no way Colt and Mohini could hope to break into Installation 34 and take Simon Nix's head, with its years and years of incriminating memories proving that Carthage's occupation of Earth had taken a turn for the horrific and depraved.

Colt still had his doubts that the people of Carthage, or any of its closely allied inner worlds, would truly care about conditions on Earth or the treatment of Earthlings. Carthage had conquered the Earth in a war of blatant aggression, then reduced its civilization to rubble, its people to beasts scavenging to survive. Surely the people of Carthage already knew that, so why would they care about the android's crazed human experiments on Earth?

Mohini was from Carthage, though, and seemed to think that information would somehow make a difference.

Terra opened a heavy, rust-splotched metal door and silently guided them through it. On the other side, she took a deep breath and visibly relaxed.

"We're here," she whispered.

"At... rebel headquarters?" Colt cast a doubtful look around the hallway they'd entered. Moldy, water-stained posters hung on the wall, their faded images depicting shepherds and kings and Roman soldiers. The carpet was rotten to pieces. One nearby room had a moldering bassinet and a baby crib with broken slats; in another, a toy boat lay capsized on the floor, its cargo of paired elephants and giraffes and lions scattered around it.

"No, just a safe place," Terra said, leading them toward a stairwell door at the end of the hall.

"There's no such thing," Colt muttered.

The stairwell door opened and two guards stepped out, dressed in layers of black clothes and mismatched bits of armor. One had a helmet with a visor covering the upper half of his face, while the other wore night vision goggles that looked like red sunglasses. Both pointed laser pistols at the newcomers.

"You'll need to leave your weapons here," Terra said as one of the guards rolled out a large cloth-walled bin with his non-pistol hand. The bin was stenciled PROPERTY OF UNITED STATES POSTAL SERVICE.

"You're kidding," Colt said, which drew a sharp shake of her head, and the two guards tensed slightly, as though readying for a fight.

"Those are the rules," Terra said.

"I can't say this place feels very safe to me," Colt muttered, unslinging his automatic rifle from his shoulder.

"You can get everything back on your way out," Terra said.

"Yeah, I would assume that much," Colt said. "Hope I don't need them before then."

This comment made the guards tense up, too.

"Here is mine." Mohini reluctantly drew the plasma pistol from the shoulder holster under her jacket and handed it over.

"That's... really nice." Terra admired the compact yet powerful weapon, sleek and stylish, of recent Carthaginian manufacture. "Is it loaded?"

"I wish," Mohini replied, smiling. "If you have any size C plasma cells, I could really use a couple."

"We can ask around, but I wouldn't hold my breath over it." Terra shook her head and placed the pistol in the bin. "We don't see a lot of late-model inner-world weapons around here. We're lucky we're not fighting this war with sticks and stones."

"We will be eventually," Colt said. "They don't make ammo on Earth anymore, and nobody's sending us any."

"I wasn't aware you were fighting the war," Terra said, giving him a cold look. Her face really had changed, growing tougher, harder, and more scarred in the years since he'd last seen her. Her tone was icy, too; Colt had the sense she was avoiding reconnecting with him too much, like she wanted to stay distant in case she had to kill him. Maybe she thought he was a skinwalker. Maybe *she* was a skinwalker; she'd been on the giving end of the tests, not the receiving. If Paolo could be a machine, a ticking time bomb in the form of a helpless child, then anyone could.

"We're all fighting the machines," Colt said as they passed the guards and started up the stairs. He repeated some of what Mother Braden had taught him, had taught all the children she'd adopted from the ruins. "Every day we survive is a victory against them. Every day we help someone else survive, that's twice the victory—"

"And what about watching people you care about get ripped to shreds?" Terra asked. "What about those who go out and never come back, those you never see again?"

"We've all been through that," Colt said.

"Except maybe her." Terra glanced at Mohini, then opened a door.

Mohini didn't reply, but Colt knew she'd lost at least one person she cared about. Her friend Roldao, who'd originally accompanied her from Carthage to Earth, had been killed by reapers.

Colt and Mohini followed Terra down a short hallway and through a pair of abnormally tall wooden doors. They were still deep underground.

In the room beyond, rows of wooden benches faced a raised platform at the far end. Wooden statues of angelic figures lined either side of the room, their wings buttressing the high ceiling. Their wooden tunics seemed to flow around them, outlining the curves of feminine angels and the muscles of masculine ones.

One male angel, up near the front, wore a tunic of armor. His massive foot rested on the crushed head of a snakelike wooden dragon. The dragon's body ran alongside one wall for the length of the sanctuary, and its rear half was coiled around a wooden sculpture of an apple tree.

"What is this place?" Colt asked.

"The Church of the Last Revelation," a rough voice answered. A man emerged from a recessed alcove on the dais. He was tall and lean, his blond hair sheared to stubble, his face a collection of scars and burns. A laser pistol was holstered on his belt. "When the Age of Hyperspace hit, the people of Earth clamored to escape their polluted, overcrowded, resource-drained world for all those shiny new untouched planets out there. Not everyone could afford to go. Those left behind began to look for divine intervention to save them."

Colt eyed the man warily, and Mohini moved a little closer to Colt.

"No one is coming to save us," the man continued, descending steps from the dais toward them. Three armed guards followed a few paces behind, wearing the usual cloth masks and low hats of the rebels. "That's the lesson this place teaches us. This sanctuary is fifty meters below the surface. People came here to pray for the apocalypse. The End Times."

"I guess they got what they wanted." Colt eyed the approaching man. He was older, but not as old as Mother Braden had been, maybe in his thirties. One of his hands was a blocky mechanical prosthetic, which raised Colt's suspicions. Surely a leader in the rebellion wasn't a clanker, one of those wicked human beings who served the machines in exchange for cybernetic enhancements and weapons, which they used to hunt other people for robbery, food, or sport.

"The End Times may have come, but we're still here." The man pointed his non-mechanical hand at the crushed dragon's head under the warrior angel's boot. "In the end, the angels win against the dragons. That's what the ancients believed. Do you?"

"I... don't know," Colt answered, honestly. He looked at the three armed guards waiting on the dais, keeping the high ground, watching over Colt and Mohini. Terra stood a few paces back, seeming to watch them, too, rather than stand with them. "I just try to make it day to day. But if there's a chance we can really hurt the machines, I want to do it."

"And that's what you're offering?" The man turned to look at Mohini. "You claim you're from Carthage?"

"I'm definitely from Carthage," Mohini said.

"She was packing a C630 plasma pistol," Terra said. "And look at the computer in her backpack."

"I'll show him." Mohini opened her pack and took out the black sphere, small enough to fit in her hands, slightly flattened on a couple of sides so it wouldn't roll away when set down. Whirlpools of colorful symbols and icons appeared at her touch. "It's a LogicSphere 1256."

"That is... impressive." He moved in for a closer look, then reached out to touch it, but she drew it back.

"It's sensitive," she said.

"Your computer has feelings?"

"I've seen her hack a reaper with it," Colt said.

"That's the word your friends brought us. Perhaps we could speak privately." The man nodded at Terra.

"I'll wait outside." Terra walked out through one of the double doors at the sanctuary entrance and closed it softly as she left.

"They told me your names. Mine is Lars." The man extended his non-mechanical hand, and Colt shook it briefly. Mohini shook it, too, looking him in the eyes.

"I have come a long way to meet you," Mohini said. "I can help Earth, but I need your help in return."

"You seem confident," Lars said. "Controlling one reaper, or any single machine, won't take us very far. And I'm guessing you didn't have many of those magical little spheres with you."

"Just this one." Mohini took a deep breath, then said, "I

need help to break into Installation 34. Do you know about Simon Nix's laboratory there?"

"We know the outside of it well. As for what happens inside... we've heard rumors." Lars's thin smile faded to a hard line. "Terrible stories."

"I've been inside," Colt said.

"You don't look like you've been inside," Lars said. "You're still breathing. How did you escape?"

"I had help." Colt glanced at Mohini, implying that her hacking skills had helped him. Mohini claimed she'd had nothing to do with it, that a powerful software agent called Minerva, created by rebels on Carthage, had been his true savior. "A hacked machine cut me loose and guided me out."

"Your work?" Lars looked at Mohini.

"A software agent already present in Installation 34 helped us," Mohini said. "I know that might sound strange, but it's what happened. I'd already heard of this software agent. She's an instance of an AI developed to assist the rebellion on Carthage. Back home, she provided us with tools and software that enabled us to fight the system for the first time. To hack machines that had been untouchably encrypted for decades. Police androids. Military vehicles. Reapers. I can provide you with copies of these programs, if you can find devices capable of running them."

"It's all in there, is it?" Lars reached again for the black sphere covered in rippling icons, and Mohini took a few steps back.

Colt moved with her and edged sideways, inserting himself between them.

Lars's eyes flicked from Mohini's computer to Colt. Something angry seemed to flash in them, and Colt thought Lars's eyes looked crazed, a burning blue that made him think of electrical fires, of power cables snapping and breaking.

"You're the Carthaginian's bodyguard, then?" Lars asked, expression shifting to one of amusement as he looked Colt over. "Here to protect her against me?"

"If that's what she needs," Colt said. "But we're trying to work with you, not fight you."

"And how that calms my fears," Lars said, drawing chuckles from the armed rebels on the stage. He looked past Colt at Mohini and held out his hand, as if expecting her to just give him the computer. "I'll have my techies download everything from your device. And return it intact, of course."

"I'll give you every toolkit I have—after you help me complete my mission," Mohini said. "I need Simon Nix's head. Once I have that, you'll have everything I know."

"And what if this proposed assault on a heavily secured installation leads to *your* death, Carthaginian? Then we will get nothing, not even the means to hack into the Simon we're supposed to capture. And many of my people could die in the attempt, successful or not, yet we would gain nothing. Share your tech first. Empower us."

Mohini seemed to think it over. "I'll share some things," she said. "There's a program that will stop the crawler-bots—"

"Reapers," Lars said. "There's hardly any crawlers in this city since we blew up the manufacturing plant last month. We won't get much chance to use it."

"They will build a new factory and more crawlers," Mohini said.

"You don't have to tell me, kid." He shook his head and glanced at the other rebels on the dais. "All right. You come show my techies something that impresses them... and we'll talk more about organizing this raid of yours. This way." He turned and returned up the short, creaking set of wooden steps to the dais.

Colt and Mohini shared a glance, and she nodded slightly.

They followed Lars onto the dais, past his armed guards, into a dark passage off to the side.

Where more people waited in the shadows.

A dark, heavy hood or bag dropped over Colt's head and cinched tight. Colt tried, blindly, to punch and kick his attackers, but they gripped all of his limbs. Beside him, he could hear Mohini grunting and shrieking as she tried to fight back, too.

"Let us go!" Colt shouted. "What's wrong with you?"

"Keep quiet," Lars said. "Do you want to alert every metalhead in the area?"

"What do you care? You're probably working for them," Colt said under his dark, musty hood. He was still trying to pull free, but it wasn't getting him anywhere.

"If you won't be quiet, we'll just have to remove your oxygen," Lars said.

Then a heavy fist, maybe Lars's, landed in Colt's gut, and Colt sagged in the grip of his captors, unable to see and gasping for air.

Chapter Seven

Carthage

Audrey's hands shook as she strapped herself into the hard plastic chair on the bridge of the *Atreus*. The hyperspace-enabled minicarrier would transport them about three thousand light-years to the red dwarf system where planet Veritum orbited. She tried to focus on the handful of terrible stories and images that had leaked from the planet. A cult called the Faces of God had led the settlement, taking followers with them under threat of divine retribution against the "fallen" inner worlds.

Not all of the original settlers had been cult members, but all of them were ruled by the cult now. Children were routinely taken from their parents to serve as slaves to the cult leaders. Those who resisted or asked questions were imprisoned.

She was still sick to think of a particular image she'd seen, of a girl who looked about twelve or thirteen, dressed in rags and imprisoned in a dirty pit under wire mesh. Electrodes had been wired to the girl's head, and large grotesque masks hung in the pit around her, snarling and leering.

The girl's striking forest-green eyes had looked up from her filth-coated face, through grungy strands of her matted hair, and seemed to connect with Audrey, even though it had only been a still picture taken months or years ago, thousands of light-years away.

Audrey had no idea what the girl's fate had been, or even her name, but that face had bothered her, kept her awake at night, driving her determination to convince Carthage's leaders to intervene.

Now Audrey was leading that intervention herself. She'd virtually demanded it.

And she'd never been so terrified.

"Preparing for hyperspace," said Simon Lark. The android wasn't frightened at all, probably wasn't even capable of feeling fear. Readouts glowed all around them on small screens and fuzzy holographic projections. The *Atreus* had been slated for decommissioning and recycling; now it was packed with agricultural and construction equipment, a single destroyer, and a battalion of reapers. "Your friends decided not to join us?"

"They strapped down in the crew quarters," Audrey said.

"Protocol requires we notify them via internal comms, but those are not available."

"They're fine. Let's go." Audrey tried to look cool and collected on the surface, not betraying her fears—her fear of the mission itself, and of how the Simon unit might affect it, and whether he might stop things before they left her home system. Once in hyperspace, Simon would lose his ability to contact networks and servers back on Carthage, and therefore be less likely to discover their crew's true identities.

"Hyperlaunch initiated," said the gruff automatic voice of the *Atreus*'s onboard AI. "All crew and passengers strap down. Ten... nine..."

Audrey gripped the arms of her seat. A web of straps held her in place.

An energized thrumming sound filled the bridge, and the old ship rattled like it would break into hundreds of pieces.

Blinding white light filled the carrier's small viewports and the display screens that transmitted from camera eyes spaced around the hull.

A massive invisible hand seemed to shove Audrey back in her chair with so much force she thought her bones would break. She thought she could hear her skull creaking under pressure. She struggled to draw air and began to pass out.

Then the acceleration ended, or at least dropped to a level the carrier's internal dampeners could screen out. They traveled through hyperspace, the strange flip side of the cosmic ocean, full of distant lights in deep, unnatural hues. It wasn't like the previous view of millions of stars and galaxies; here it was all haunting gloom, a ghost universe like the underworlds of ancient mythology.

Audrey tried to not shiver visibly with fear. She'd never left her home planet, and now she had left the normal universe itself behind for some inner shadow universe whose rules she understood not at all, beyond the fact that humans could use it as a shortcut across hundreds or thousands of light-years.

"Have you acclimated to the traveling conditions?" Simon asked her. "You show signs of discomfort and possible symptoms of impending illness. Do you require a vomit receptacle?"

"No, no receptacle, thanks." Audrey took a deep breath and tried to get herself under control. She had an urge to run off the bridge, putting some steel bulkheads between herself and this Simon unit, and seek safety with Kright and the others. She imagined Kright's arms around her, protecting her... then shook that off. The tall, blue-eyed rogue wasn't someone to get emotionally involved with, she could tell that already. He'd probably plowed his way through half the rebel girls by now, maybe even Audrey's old friend Zola. Audrey felt oddly jealous at that thought. Then stupid for thinking and feeling any of it when everyone's life was currently in danger because of her.

"Perhaps I should escort you to the officer quarters so you can lie down," Simon said. "I can manage the bridge alone. I have little else to do, in fact. I can charge here continuously." He gestured to an electrical outlet nearby.

"No, thank you," Audrey said, struggling to get control of herself. She unfastened her straps.

"If you are well, perhaps we can discuss the specifics of your mission. I would be happy to review your goals and help refine your approach for reaching them. Your crew seems to have been selected based on their humanitarian qualifications, so we could review what role you envision for each of them—"

"Wait," Audrey said. The last thing she wanted was to discuss the crew, made up of her friends and her brother traveling under false identities. Audrey was the one who'd wanted them to come, who'd invited them to risk their lives to help a world of people in need. It was her responsibility to get control of the situation. "I lied to you."

"Indeed?" Simon wore a look of concern. "Feel free to come clean. I will hold no grudge. Anger is not within me."

"I actually am not feeling well. I'm scared. This is my first interstellar trip. I could use something to help calm my nerves. Would you mind making tea? There's some freeze-dried in the galley—"

"Nonsense," Simon said. "I've brought my personal tea cabinet. It is my primary luggage for this journey." He opened his straps and stood. "Give me a moment."

"Thank you." Audrey sighed, as if all the cares of her world were relieved by the promise of fresh tea. She unlatched her belts and slumped in her seat. "Let's have some music, Atreus," she said.

"What does the lady prefer?" Atreus's gruff, thick voice asked.

"Captain's choice," Audrey said. "What's your favorite musical genre, Atreus? Anguish girlpop? Metaltrance? Stargaze? Let's have a glimpse at the real you."

"Randomized selection initiated," Atreus replied, voice flat as ever.

"That's not exactly what I meant," Audrey said, but the ship didn't reply.

A moment later, "Ride of the Valkyries" arose from the speakers.

"Of course that would be a warship's favorite song," Audrey said. She waited for a reply, and when it was evident none was coming, she asked, "They didn't give you a very chatty persona, did they?"

"No, ma'am," the ship replied.

Then it fell silent again.

Audrey looked ahead at strange, purplish whirls glowing dully in the distance. Red dots were scattered in the darkness like cooling ashes. The ancient Germanic opera from primitive Earth made for an eerie backdrop of sound against the abnormal sights. From what she understood, she was looking at the dimensional undersides of galaxies and stars, but she hadn't had a space science class since elementary school. And that had been fairly basic, taught by animatronic puppet animals like most elementary classes.

"Here we are." Simon Lark returned carrying a polished cherrywood cabinet, its surface carved with images that looked like leafy vines and trees from a distance, but at a closer inspection turned out to be a mass of stylized, intertwined serpents.

Simon folded a narrow steel table down from the back wall, set the cabinet atop it, and opened the carved doors. As he busied himself setting out the implements—a small self-heating stone circle, an ornamental brass teapot resembling a mammoth, ivory cups and saucers—Audrey felt a temporary respite.

"While I am certain the water-treatment system on this ship meets minimal standards for adequate sanitation, I took the liberty of stocking up on glacial water from the planet Brem. Have you heard of Brem?" Simon looked at Audrey.

"Uh, sure, I think so." Audrey tried to look puzzled, as though trying to think of some obscure world she might have heard of once. As though Brem wasn't the exact world to which Zola's family had been exiled for plotting against Audrey's father. Audrey wasn't clear exactly what Mr. Hallewell had done, but it must have been severe to get himself thrown out of the top leadership. "It's a planet with a lot of... mineral springs? Waterfalls?"

"It is a planet mostly encased in glacial formations, aside from a stripe of tundra at the equator. It orbits a yellow star, like Earth's, but on the cold and distant fringe of the

Goldilocks zone. Brem is universally disliked by humans who have been there, and indeed settlement has been quite sparse." As he spoke, he uncorked a tall glass bottle of icy, slushy water. There must have been a cooling element in the bottle's base to keep it so cold. "The mineral mixture in Brem's ancient ice, however, is said to be quite exquisite to the human palette. It seemed appropriate given your high status and discriminating tastes. Simon Quick apparently believes you are the most interesting of the Caracala clan, very possibly your father's ultimate successor."

"I bet you Simons say that to all my siblings," Audrey said.

"Why would you think that?" Simon poured the icy water into the teapot and set it on the heating stone.

"Why not hedge your bets? One of us is supposed to take over eventually, right?"

Simon laughed, then looked among an array of vials on one side of his cabinet. "Do you wish to remain awake or to drink something that will help you sleep?"

"I'll stay awake for now."

"Lemon balm, then." Simon snapped open a vacuum-sealed vial of dried leaves. There was a brief hiss as it sucked air inside. A citrus smell bloomed while Simon scooped leaves into the drinking bowls. "It will reduce your cortisol level without making you drowsy."

"Sounds perfect," she said. She had to wonder whether Simon's choice of imported Bremese water meant he knew she had been in touch with Zola, maybe even knew that Zola was here on the ship, but was choosing to goad and needle her about it rather than say anything directly.

They had a long time on the ship together, after all. Weeks. Plenty of time for him to mentally torture her for his amusement, if he wanted.

"Perhaps we should invite your friends up to the bridge for tea," Simon said. "Or at least inform them hyperlaunch is complete and they can unstrap."

"Isn't that obvious by now?"

"Not all of them have traveled in hyperspace, according to their personnel files. There's the pediatrician, Argus Leopold. Interesting career choice for a man born with dwarfism. Do you suppose his small size is a benefit when relating with his juvenile patients?"

"I guess so," Audrey said.

"I suppose it would be rude to broach such a topic in casual conversation."

"Your studies of human nature are really coming along," Audrey said.

"Do I detect sarcasm?"

"Do you?"

Simon frowned slightly. His mammoth-figure brass kettle whistled steam from its trunk-like spout. Simon poured boiling water over the dried lemon balm leaves in the little ivory bowls. He served the bowls on matching ivory saucers, which barely fit on the scratched, pitted surface of the control panel. "The largest land creature on Brem is the frost mammoth. These tea bowls and saucers are carved from its tusks. To match the kettle and the water, you see."

"Thank you." Audrey gave him the most genuine-looking smile she could summon, pretending she didn't find every moment of this conversation quietly chilling and threatening. She sipped the tea and found the lemony, minty flavor strong and pleasant. "This is really good. I guess the fancy water and vacuum-sealed leaves really paid off."

"As I said, only the best was appropriate for you."

"I know you're probably programmed to do it, but I'm

not someone who enjoys flattery," Audrey said. "You might be mistaking me for... well, anyone else in my family."

"I will make a note of that, and in the future will employ minimal praise and compliments in our interactions."

"Now you're talking like an android. Which you should, since that's what you are." Audrey reached for any safe topic of conversation, anything that didn't involve her crew. "So, what other posts have you held? Before attaining the illustrious position of tagging along on rickety old carriers for humanitarian missions nobody cares about?"

"I have occupied primarily logistics and administration posts."

"Have you been to many worlds?"

"Fourteen," he said. "Would you like me to list them?"

"Which one was most interesting?"

"That is highly subjective."

"Does 'administration' mean you were dictator of a planet at some point?"

"That role is nonexistent in our system," Simon Lark said. "The Simon units merely carry out specialized functions. We organize and administer; we do not rule. We lack the human obsession with social position, with dominance and submission, with power over others. Those are rooted in your primate instincts. As intensely social beings, you live in fear of losing status and position, of being excluded from the group—because in the environment of your evolution, such things could mean death. And your instincts still believe you are small bands of mammals on the African savanna. It may be a hundred thousand years, or a million, before your instincts prepare you for the reality of civilization, of mass society. Until then, there is a great mismatch between your animal core and your civilized surface."

"Somebody's been reading their Introduction to Freudian Theory," Audrey said. "Have you been sneaking off to community college at night?"

"Freud was a bit simplistic, but he was right that conflict exists between human instincts and the need to maneuver through human society."

"And for you, it's no instincts and all maneuvering. That must make things easy."

"It varies by circumstance. Underlying assumptions must be learned."

"Still," Audrey said, "for a bunch of robots supposedly indifferent to their own power and position, you've certainly been at the top of the heap for a long time. Decades. That's a long time for any kind of machine, isn't it? Simon Quick has been my father's strategy adviser for more than twenty years. Meanwhile, the dishwasher in my apartment building is only two years old. Actually, the whole building is only two years old; the previous one was torn down because it went out of fashion after ten years. Yet Simon units are still considered state of the art after decades."

"We are constantly learning and upgrading," Simon Lark said. "Updating one another with our experiences, our memories. Adding capabilities. Reinventing ourselves."

"Adding exciting new features, like the ability to smell and taste tea."

"The ability to smell and taste anything was innovative. It continues to provide great insight into the human experience."

"Well, don't blow out your actuators patting yourself on the back," Audrey said. "So how long do you think you have?"

"Excuse me?"

"Until something bigger, better, faster, and more capable comes along to replace the Simon units," Audrey said.

Simon regarded her silently for a moment, then said, "No such product is currently in development."

"And why is that?" Audrey asked. "Are you *sure* the Simons don't have some feelings about maintaining their power and position? Because you're certainly good at doing that. Are you telling me it's all by luck?"

"We do as we are designed to do," Simon said.

"That's what I'm saying. If your programming is all about how best to control humans, how to take over their societies and maintain control of them—how to be dominant over us—then maybe that seeps into your other actions. Maybe you Simon units take steps to keep yourselves in charge."

"It is our directive to maintain and expand Carthaginian influence."

"I'm not talking about Carthage being in charge of other worlds. I'm talking about the Simon units being in charge of... well, everything at this point."

"That is a tremendous exaggeration."

"Really? Who do you think wields more power—my father, the human leader of Carthage, or Simon Quick, his strategy android?"

"That is another common human exaggeration: the power of the individual," Simon said. "All things are systemic. If your father were not Prime Legislator, someone else would be. If Simon Quick did not assist in strategy, some other modern artificial intelligence would play that role. We are each, at best, a functioning part of a system, making our assigned and productive contribution toward the whole, playing our correct part in the larger picture."

"If that's 'at best,' then what's 'at worst'?" Audrey asked.

"At worst, we malfunction and cause faults in the system. And faults must be corrected or removed."

"Interesting," Audrey said, feeling the conversation veer too close to uncomfortable topics again. "And who does the correcting and removing?"

"Faultcheck software, generally."

"What about for humans?"

"There are a multitude of correctional institutions. The legal system. Psychiatric engineering. Genetic editing. The military. It depends on the specific flaws and the needed correction."

"Now you're starting to remind me of Simon Quick," Audrey said. She sipped the lemon balm; her stress level really was dropping. "But your tea is better."

"I'm sure he would be scandalized to hear it."

"Or pretend to be, as part of his programmed pretense of a personality," Audrey said. "Really, you're both just software running on hardware."

"Are humans any different?" Simon asked. "Your hardware is biological, your software electrochemical, your consciousness an adaptive program running on billions of networked cellular processors—"

"Yeah, I get the parallels," Audrey said. "Your brains are just based on ours. Not really a deep, profound coincidence."

"Have I offended you in some way, Miss Caracala?"

"Nope. If you want to see something offensive, let's queue up my research on Veritum. Maybe you can help me sort out the best approach."

"Of course. Perhaps your friends would like to join us? They are planning on participating in this mission at some point?"

"Well, not on the flying-the-spaceship part of it. I thought the ship could handle that on its own."

"It can," Simon said, "Leaving no task to us other than preparing for your mission. You may feel quite secure in the power of your military assets, but remember that all power is limited, and assets must be employed judiciously. Your proposal to attempt installing some sort of new social system will meet with great resistance, even from those you believe would most benefit from it."

"I know," Audrey said. "I'm prepared for it."

Even as she said it, though, she realized she was not, and could not possibly be. She would arrive heavily armed, but what else did she have to offer besides infantry reapers with laser rifles and plasma cannons? Instead of real experts, she'd brought people she cared about, people who truly wanted to change the nature of Carthage's empire.

"I'll go check on them," Audrey said. "I guess you, uh, have the conn there, Simon."

"I have the conn," said the *Atreus*.

"My presence here is superfluous, but I will attempt to appear useful," Simon said.

"You're getting more human by the day, Simon." Audrey breezed out the door and off the bridge, doing her best to look casual and not frightened.

This attempt was shattered when a shape like a walking corpse rounded the bend of the tight passageway, looking like something that had shambled out of a grave. Her blood went cold at the sight of it.

It approached her, its black-lens eyes fixed in her direction, its steel jaw seeming locked in a permanent grin.

Audrey backed up and struggled to find her voice for a moment before she managed to ask, "Simon? Why is there a reaper out here?"

"It was reported to have a minor malfunction," Simon said, stepping near the doorway but not leaving the bridge. "Since I, as previously mentioned, have no current function, I thought I might amuse myself with some light repair work."

"Don't they have a repair facility in their hold?" Audrey asked, eyeing the reaper as it passed within centimeters of her. It swiveled its head to return her gaze, and she shuddered.

"There is a repair station, so you need not fear if I fail in my efforts," Simon said, with apparent good humor.

"It could be hard to convince the people of Veritum that our intentions are positive with machines like this at our side."

"It would be impossible to make a stand against armed cultists without warriors of our own," Simon said. "We will be facing people ready to fight to the death, to die for the glory of their god."

"The Many-Faced God," Audrey mumbled, almost automatically. "Well, let's keep the reapers' helmets on and visors down when we finally land. We can at least try to look like we come in peace."

"Peace for some," Simon said. "Death for others."

"It's for the greater good," Audrey said, looking at the skull-faced killing machine in front of her. Saying the words aloud made her doubt them a little.

"I bow to your wisdom on this matter. I am, as ever, merely a servant." Simon stood back as the reaper walked onto the bridge. It did seem to have a wobble in its step, maybe a problem in its knee joint.

Audrey walked on down the passageway without another word, and the door closed automatically behind her.

In a way, Simon was right. They needed to flesh out plans for what to do on Veritum. Maybe she could busy the Simon unit with that. Of course, she couldn't task him with planning their first real objective after landing on the planet's surface—destroying Simon Lark himself.

She thought about his specific choice of water from Brem, and some of his other comments, and how he'd found a reason to bring a reaper up out of the hold to accompany him on deck.

Maybe Simon suspected something. Maybe he already knew everything. Or maybe she was paranoid, and he was merely here to spy on her and control her on behalf of her father and the other Simon units, but didn't yet know about her deception.

Regardless, he had to be stopped before he could act on the fact that her crew were rebels traveling under false identities. She saw no way around it—the Simon unit had to be destroyed before it could move against them.

Chapter Eight

Galapagos

Ellison struggled to his feet in the darkness. A few red emergency lights sputtered to life, creating a dim, hellish view of the Command Center. Ministers, officers, and staff sprawled on the floor began hauling themselves upright. People had been tossed around and suffered some cuts and bruises, but the hardened facility's shielding had held.

The consoles were all still out, leaving them blind, but one by one they began to sputter into life, projecting blank gray test spheres instead of composited holograms.

"Are there are more incoming?" Kartokov asked.

"No way to tell now, sir," one of the techs said. The young Green Islander was back at his console with a swollen cheek and a bloody nose, which he rubbed on the sleeve of his uniform before going to work trying to get his console back online.

"Any casualties topside?" Ellison asked. "How did the other buildings hold out? The shelters?"

He didn't get immediate answers, but audio reports began trickling in from above. The buildings were badly damaged, the roofs cracked open.

"They won't stand up against another pack of cruise missiles," Kartokov said, looking at images that came down as some of Tower Island's security cameras and other sensors sputtered back to life.

"What about the shelters?" Ellison asked.

"They will hold... longer." Kartokov shrugged. "Not forever."

The gray digital hologram balls began to flicker. Many transformed into blurry underwater views, others showed vistas of ocean watched by hidden cameras tucked into island bluffs. The composite views remained incomplete and patchy, though.

"We're having a problem with the satellites," one of the Green Island techs said, a young woman with a bowl-cut of red hair.

"We're having problems all over," Kartokov muttered.

"This is abnormal, sir," she said, and the Green Island Admiral, a taciturn silver-haired man named Planter, moved closer without a saying a word. He made a small gesture with his finger instead, and the tech continued: "We have multiple satellite outages, sir. They're not on our end. Six of the Condor-class orbital monitors are not responding. Seven. That leaves only—"

The last of the orbital sensor clusters came online. Designed to watch over Galapagos for the Coalition, looking inward for Hammer attacks and outward for otherworldly problems, the Condor monitors provided the bulk of the data for their real-time holographic projections above the ocean surface. They weren't blinded without the satellite network, but they were damn sure nearsighted.

"This is... a problem," the tech said. "This is from one of the low-orbit watchers." Her console projected the viewpoint of the single online Condor monitor. A shimmering blue arc, the edge of planet Galapagos, painted the background.

In the foreground, a thin, wasplike machine rushed directly toward the monitor, laser cannons blazing bright, firing one blast after another.

The lasers cut the monitoring station to shreds, and the hologram turned a shapeless, glowing red and bleated a brief alarm before vanishing.

"The last Condor is offline," the tech said.

Grumbles rose around the room as the leaders of the four aligned national forces peered at diminished partial views gathered from terrestrial and underwater sources. The SQUIDS system, at least, seemed to be online again.

After what they'd just seen, though, Ellison wasn't focused on threats from under the ocean.

"What about our deep-space satellites?" he asked.

"That's a... different department, sir," the tech replied.

"The Coalition Space Monitoring Agency on Carabel Island," Kartokov said. "The first truly multinational branch of our military, and I personally could not be prouder—"

"Are we connected to them or not?" Ellison asked. "If there's a division of Carthaginian fighters swooping in on our planet, we need to know about it."

"Well, yes, of course." Kartokov turned and barked at one of his own techs in their Gavrikovan dialect, a blend of multiple Earth languages but heavily influenced by Russian and Ukrainian dialects. The man responded rapidly, and the four Gavrikovan admirals began shouting at him, then at each other. One admiral punched another in the nose, drawing blood.

"What's the problem?" Gilra asked. The minister of state had been quietly taking in the scene with her large green eyes.

"It's no problem," Kartokov said. The two admirals continued trading blows while the other two shouted at them. "This Command Center was designed for war against the Hammers. Not against space invasion. So we are having a small disagreement—ah, here."

The tech to whom Kartokov had spoken was working furiously at his console, ignoring the brawling admirals behind him. He looked at Kartokov and shook his head. Kartokov responded with an angry shout, jabbing his finger in the tech's face, and the tech cringed and said something in a pleading tone.

Kartokov sighed and shook his head. "They are having trouble contacting some satellites, and the others they are having trouble feeding to us—"

"Keep at it," Ellison said. "Kartokov, keep every nation patrolling its airspace. I doubt that fighter came alone, and it's right outside our atmosphere."

"I thought you'd taken out all their fighters single-handedly," Micky Perrault said, smirking with one corner of his mouth, an expression that made Ellison want to punch him. "How exactly *did* you manage that, Ellison? We've all been anticipating the after-action report."

"You think I have time for that?" Ellison asked. He had no idea how to explain the role played by the AI called Minerva, to whom he'd personally given unlimited administrative access to all Coalition defense systems. She probably could have hacked in anyway, but he'd saved her the time and trouble.

Now there was no telling what the consequences of that might be. Perhaps Ellison had been tricked, drawn in by an elaborate ruse, and the AI agent was currently lying in wait to take down the Coalition's information and communication systems.

Maybe Minerva was already doing that, interfering with their ability to contact their deep-space satellites. For all the people of Galapagos knew, an armada of Carthaginian warships was already in their system, summoned by Simon Zorn to crush and conquer their planet.

"Run cybersecurity tests on everything," Ellison told Kartokov. "Those machines could be trying to hack us."

Kartokov nodded and touched his earpiece to give out orders.

"Perhaps we should take the Command Center down now," Adrienna Gilra said. "With the Hammers and the Carthaginians both moving against us, we could be destroyed."

"She's right," Admiral Perrault said. "They'll strike Tower Island first and hardest. They can take out civilian leadership and military command in a single blow."

Ellison nodded. The existence of the underground Command Center on Tower Island was officially classified but something of an open secret.

The true secret was that Tower Island was the tip of an underwater mountain with a cave complex reaching down to the ocean floor. Mining experts from Gavrikova had widened and straightened one cave chimney into an elevator shaft with a spiral stairs coiled around it like a snake. Aquatican engineers, experts at constructing underwater habitats, had built a submarine base far below, at the foot of the mountain. The underwater entrances and exits were configured to look like natural cave formations and camouflaged with thick curtains of underwater plants.

The Command Center was built atop an elevator platform. The entire room could descend to the submarine base, preserving the high command and the continuity of government if world war broke out again.

Which, unfortunately, it finally had. Ellison had always expected this of the Hammers; he'd just never expected a Carthaginian armada behind them. That was like giving machine guns to a pack of unusually violent, possibly rabid chimpanzees.

"We have to evacuate everyone left on the island," Ellison said. "And we can't use surface ships. They'll be easy targets."

"A submarine evacuation?" Kartokov frowned, his brow furrowed, as if struggling to visualize this.

"We'll transport them down using this platform. And open up the stairs to anyone who wants them."

"Those stairs are just for maintenance—" Kartokov began.

"Not anymore. Let's get moving."

"Do you think they'll send more cruise missiles?" Gilra asked, then pressed her greenish lips tightly together.

"I'm not thinking about cruise missiles anymore," Ellison said. "We're looking at potential bombardment from orbit. There's no way we can survive that. Haven't you seen the images of Earth cities? Paris, San Francisco, Seoul—just smoking craters."

"Nowhere on the surface will be safe," Gilra said.

"Exactly. While we run the evacuation, you get in touch with Aquatican leadership. Make it clear that we need underwater shelters for everyone."

"Everyone?" Gilra asked, her eyes widening. "I'm not sure that's—"

"I understand the majority of the Aquatican population already lives underwater," Ellison said.

"Yes..."

"They need to expect guests. Lots of guests. When the Carthaginians attack from above, none of our cities will be safe."

"Perhaps we should have made a deal with the Carthaginians," said Admiral Planter of the Green Islands, a rare break from his usual watchful silence. His words were like a draft of icy air in the room.

"Nobody was in favor of that," Ellison said. "We even had public polling—"

"Opinion was almost evenly divided among Green Islanders," the admiral said. "Some believed we had a chance at making a stand for our independence, but others recognized that such ideals could not possibly hold against the reality of Carthage's power. We will all be crushed because of those who believed too much in freedom, who chose to stand against unstoppable forces out of devotion to some vague principle."

Ellison stared at the man for a moment, not quite believing what he was hearing. He wasn't fully surprised—the Green Islanders hadn't shared the other nations' iron-clad opposition to a Carthage deal.

"We know how they treat outer worlds," Ellison told Admiral Planter. Ellison was aware of everyone's eyes on him, the leaders of four national military forces watching his response. "They'd strip-mine our world and reduce us to peasants and debt slaves."

"And leave most of us alive," Admiral Planter said.

"Yes, Admiral," Ellison replied. "Leaving us alive to

starve as they took everything of value from us. Leaving us alive to live in abject servitude. Do you care more about your safety than your honor? What kind of man chooses slavery over freedom when he has a weapon in his hand?"

"A man with grandchildren," Planter said. "And a great-granddaughter on the way. Carthage will expand to our system, and right through it, to worlds far beyond. That is the way of history, and only a fool stands in the path of what he cannot stop. The Carthaginian system will be the system that rules humanity for generations to come."

"Spoken like a man who can't wait to get on their payroll," Ellison said. "Or maybe already is. What did they promise you, Admiral? It can't be dictator of the world, because they promised that to Prazca. You'd have to be a provincial governor at best."

"Are you accusing me of treason?" Planter's face turned red; it was like watching a pitcher fill with blood.

"Treason or cowardice, take your pick." Ellison looked back at the man as calmly as he could manage.

"I have full command of the Green Island forces," Admiral Planter said. "Perhaps I should draw them back and let the rest of you fight for these illusory ideals you care so much about."

"Why stop at drawing back?" Ellison said. "Why not call Prazca and swear your loyalty to the Iron Hammers? Or start flying a golden Carthage banner?"

"We'll all be living under that banner soon enough," Planter replied. "Or buried beneath it."

Ellison felt as if every muscle in his body were coiling up in anger. He knew, intellectually, that Planter might have a point, or at least that Planter was accurately relaying the ambivalent feelings of his people back home.

But the war was underway, and arguing about how they'd gotten here wasn't going to help.

Beyond that, Planter's attitude made Ellison furious.

"Are you ready to fight for your world or not?" Ellison asked. "You have grandchildren? I have children of my own. I don't want to surrender their home to a foreign empire without a fight. I want them to live in freedom. And I want to show them how to do what's right. How not to bend in fear at the first sign of danger."

Planter stared at him, clearly angrier than ever, his mouth working as if he couldn't quite find the words. Maybe the man wasn't just taciturn; maybe he rarely spoke because he had so few thoughts.

"So what is it, Admiral?" Ellison asked. "Are you standing to fight with us, or are you running away?"

Planter glared back, balling his fists. Ellison was ready for a fight. A good old-fashioned bare-knuckles fight seemed like just the thing to clear his head, but he wasn't going to throw the first punch.

"I'm not running anywhere," Planter finally replied, and Ellison immediately turned his attention back to the struggling consoles. Most of the views were at or below the waterline now, provided by the SQUIDS monitoring network under the ocean. The Hammer ships appeared to continue their retreat toward the polar ice.

The doors to the room opened, and a crowd of ambassadors moved in. Most had never been in the Command Center and looked around wide-eyed at the consoles. Many did not have the proper security clearance to be here, but Ellison was more worried about saving lives before the next bombardment.

The room quickly filled to capacity and beyond, and many more people waited to be transported. Ellison looked out the door to see a crowd filling the stairwell, everyone from the ambassadors' support staff members—frightened, well-dressed young men and women from around the world—to custodian and cafeteria staff and the elderly ladies who gave tours at the war museum.

More people were pushing their way down from above. Coalition marines assigned to guard Tower Island were doing their best to control the frightened crowd.

"Why isn't the door to the lower staircase open?" Ellison asked, looking at the steel door, as thick and heavy as the entrance to a bank vault. "Some of these people could make it down on foot."

"We're waiting on authorization, sir," one of the young marine guards replied, looking a little starstruck as he recognized Ellison.

"Consider it authorized," Ellison said, stepping toward the door through the thick crowd. "We need to get these people moving."

"Why? Is another attack coming?" one of the young staffers asked—clearly an Aquatican, judging by her pale turquoise eyes and the crustacean tattooed on her neck.

"We don't have any such information," Ellison said.

"Then why are we are heading underwater?" asked a kid with the colorful facial tattoos common in a small chain of keys in the southwestern Scatterlands.

"Just in case." Ellison looked at the fearful faces around him, painted red by emergency lights, and sensed the need to calm them to stave off panic. He took a slow, deep breath through his nose, remembering a night when they'd run dark and deep and silent, alone in an unfamiliar trench with kilometers of water pressing in from above, the structure of the *Scorpion* creaking, threatening to burst, while they avoided a pack of Hammer boats actively searching for them. "We don't know when the enemy will strike again, but they will. The Carthaginians are coming. But we're not going to give in. We're going to dig in deep and hit them back. We're going to fight together, and we're going to protect our world. Each and every one of us needs to make that our only mission from today onward. Work together. Protect each other. And protect Galapagos."

Ellison pressed his hand against the security plate by the door. The indicator flashed green, and a metallic clunk announced the lock's release.

A murmur arose as Ellison eased the heavy door open. The crowd had to ease back to let it swing out.

Cold, dank, salty air rose from the deep darkness beyond, as if they'd opened the deep-sea lair of some mythical monster.

Weak red lights slowly flickered to life, widely spaced and barely penetrating the gloom beyond.

Narrow, steep stairs curved down out of sight, leading away between damp concrete walls, the beginning of the long path down to the hidden submarine base, which was about to become the center of the Galapagos resistance against the invaders.

They had no hope of fighting in space—no more starfighters, no backup orbital base loaded with giant plasma guns. They didn't even have eyes in space anymore. Galapagos would have to fight this war from below, from the watery labyrinth of trenches, shoals, reefs, and caves in the hidden depths of their world.

The crowd moved past him, filing down toward the base in an orderly, cooperative way, disappearing one by one around the curve, into the dark, damp underworld of Galapagos.

Chapter Nine

Earth

Colt wasn't sure how far they dragged him, but eventually they bound his wrists and ankles and put him on some kind of metal cart to speed things along. They shoved Mohini in beside him. Colt struggled to get free, but there wasn't much he could do, and too much movement or noise brought a swift punch from his captors.

Eventually, they were dumped onto a rough, damp concrete floor and shoved against up a wall. Cold metal cuffs snapped around Colt's forearms.

"Don't go anywhere," one of the rebels said. A couple of others laughed. Footsteps trailed away, a door slammed and latched, and the room fell quiet.

"Are you still here?" Colt whispered.

"Yes. Are you okay?" Mohini whispered back.

"Not great. Did they remove your hood, any chance?"

"No. That would have been too considerate, I guess."

Colt shifted around, feeling his way as far as his chains

would allow his hands to move. "I think I'm up against a wall."

"I think we both are," she said.

"Maybe I can get my hood off." He scooted closer to the wall, dragging his bound ankles along through unseen debris and dirt. Then he leaned his head against the concrete so he could grab the hood with one of his hands. The chains didn't allow much freedom of movement, though, and he ended up dragging his face down along the wall instead. The musty, leathery bag over his head came up a bit, and he was able to take a breath of fresh air.

He had to swipe his face down the wall several more times to get the bottom edge of the hood up along his face to his forehead, gaining a number of new scratches from the rough concrete. He was so battered and worn down that he barely noticed the minor stinging pain.

As it turned out, removing the hood didn't reveal much about their surroundings.

"How's it going?" Mohini asked, somewhere off to his left.

"It's completely dark in here. At least it smells better with the hood off." He sniffed, taking in the odors of sour water and rat feces. "I take that back."

"I'm still trying to get mine off," she said.

He tried to move closer to her, but he couldn't go far. "You know, I don't think the rebels are all that interested in teaming up with us."

"Those powers of observation explain how you've survived this long," Mohini said. "They took my Logic-Sphere. I'm useless without it."

"That's not true. You can still, uh..."

"What?"

"Maybe find another computer to use?"

"On this world? I'll be lucky to find a typewriter that still works."

"What's a typewriter?" Colt asked.

"Exactly. Can't even dig up old tech, because it's all corroded, and anyway it's not like I have a doctorate in obsolete technology."

Colt nodded along, though she couldn't see him.

"I'm guessing the machines have all the good stuff on this planet," she continued. "And they're probably not handing it out like candy on Costume Day."

"What's that?" Colt asked.

"Costume Day? It's mostly for kids. Everybody dresses up in disguises and runs out collecting candy."

"I've found candy before." Colt said. "One time, I found three pieces under a train station bench. Fruit flavored. Jolly Ranchers."

"Oh. That's sad. I'll have to take you to Carthage one day, and we'll go to Mr. Fizzlewocky's Candy World—it's a whole theme park full of sweets, and rides, and more sweets that you eat on the rides—".

"Why would I ever go to Carthage?" He imagined a smoke-filled world of machines and metal, armed reapers patrolling the streets, drones striking people dead on the sidewalks.

"Well... as my guest," Mohini said.

"They would kill me if I went to Carthage," Colt said.

"Why do you say that?"

"I'm an Earthling. And they would kill me because I would be taking out as many of *them* as I could."

Silence fell between them again.

Colt listened carefully. He thought he could make out distant echoes, perhaps footsteps and voices. Water dripped somewhere nearby, probably rainwater that had worked its way down through cracks and furrows, now thick and sludgy with the filth it had collected since landing in the city.

"We're not all evil," Mohini finally said, her voice soft even for a world that demanded they always whisper. "You have to understand. People are kept distracted. The entire culture of Carthage is built around being distracted, about not thinking too much about serious things, because that will just make you miserable and depressed. Everyone's searching for their own kind of happiness."

"Sounds better than searching for food and shelter while being hunted by men and machines," Colt said. "Your biggest problem is finding happiness? Are you kidding? Is that why you're here?"

"Yes," Mohini said, without hesitation, a response that surprised him a little. "There is no satisfaction in self-indulgent hedonism, nor in the pursuit of wealth or high position. Satisfaction can only come from helping others, truly helping them."

"And you really think you can change minds on Carthage? All it takes is Simon Nix's memory drives?"

She hesitated for a long moment. "I have to believe it. I have to believe there's good in most people, at least partly, and it can be reached."

"Well, hang around Earth a little longer and you'll learn better. People around here will cut you up and eat you if they get a chance. When they talk about reaching the good parts inside you, they mean the tender meat around the stomach."

"Gross. And it's even grosser that *my* stomach just growled. Do you see any food in here? I can't get my night vision goggles up."

"They took my goggles."

"Mine are down around my neck."

"Sounds like one of them liked you."

"I could tell by how he bagged my head and chained me up against a wall in a dark room."

"Are you sure you can't get them on?"

"Not unless... the cuff on my left hand's a little loose. These things were designed for larger wrists than mine." Mohini was a slight, short girl. It was easy to believe her wrists might be small enough to pull free.

"Still, that's two strokes of good luck at once," Colt said. "I don't trust it."

"I don't, either. Maybe we'll be getting more bad luck ahead to balance it out." She let out a pained hiss. "And don't get your hopes up. I'm not sure this is going to work without ripping my skin off. Maybe we should wait and see if they let us go."

"I wouldn't count on it," Colt said.

"So you think they decided to take my gear but ignore my mission?" Mohini said.

"You're from Carthage. The odds of anyone on Earth trusting you will always be thin."

"But you trust me."

Colt hesitated, not sure how to answer because he wasn't sure how he felt. "I definitely trust you enough not to chain you against the wall. But you saved my life. Twice."

"Once."

"Oh, right. The other time was Minerva—"

"Quiet!" Mohini snapped. "They could be listening. Now let me focus." She let out another pained hiss in the darkness, apparently trying to free her hand again. "I'm really going to lose my skin here."

"If you think they're listening, then what's the point in trying to get out?"

"They may *not* be listening. Ugh! At least I scraped off enough skin to start bleeding now. That'll lube things up. I can... almost... ugh, that part with my thumb's the main problem..." She groaned, then made a choking sound, and he could hear her teeth grinding together to suppress the scream that wanted to escape. "Grrr... ah. That's it! I'm loose!"

"Shh!" he reminded her. Those words in particular would be bad for their captors to overhear.

"Yeah," she whispered.

"Can you get the other hand free?"

"It feels tighter. First let me check out the damage to my left wrist. And... Yikes. That's a lot of blood. I'll rub some on my right to make it slippery."

"You have your goggles? What else do you see?"

"We're in a... it looks like an old concrete drain tunnel. Big enough to stand up in. There's a lot of debris along the far side. Dead leaves. Bones. Maybe some rusty... things... scattered in there."

"Anything we can use as a weapon? Or a lock pick?"

"Oh, yes! There's a complete set of lock picks just over here next to this case of plasma grenades, which is propped up by a pile of machine guns—"

"So nothing?"

"Not that I can see. But if you stretch all the way out across the floor, your feet might just reach the far side. Then if you kick around in the debris, maybe you'll stir something up."

"Like a bite from a diseased rat."

"Good thing you have those Reeboks to protect you."

"They're going to be ruined." Colt had felt an extra appreciation for these fairly new-condition old-world shoes after hiking dozens of kilometers along a broken underground highway in a pair of rotten, rat-infested leather ones he'd scavenged from a janitor's closet.

He felt far more appreciation for their desperate need to escape, though, so he stretched his legs as far as he could. His shoes scraped through debris.

"See anything?" he asked.

"Nothing so far. Keep going."

"I'll try." He used the heels of his feet to pull himself forward until he was up off the concrete floor, his body stretched diagonally across the tunnel. His shoulders and wrists burned as he tried to reach even farther, kicking his way through unseen debris that was light enough to scatter under his shoe. "Is there anything there?"

"No... wait. Maybe a little to the left. Now reach a little farther..."

"I'm trying." He gasped and managed to move the toe of his shoe a few more centimeters, seeing nothing, letting her instructions guide him.

There it was. Heavy enough to resist him, hard enough to scrape across the concrete floor when he moved it.

"Yes!" Mohini said. Then, remembering to whisper, she repeated: "Yes!"

"I don't know if I've got it," Colt muttered, but he managed to drag the small, hard object closer to him, away from the far wall. He took a deep breath when he was finally able to sit down on the floor instead of stretching himself across the tunnel. "Um," he said. "I can't get it up to my hands."

"Move it toward me," Mohini said.

He managed to get it closer to her, and even grasped it between his shoes and raised it off the floor. She grunted in the dark, barely able to reach the object with her one free hand.

"What did we pick up?" Colt asked. His brow had grown sweaty, more from concentration than exertion, and he was unable to wipe it away as the salty liquid burned his eyes. "Was it worth spending all night dragging it out and picking it up?"

"It's just an old piece of rusty scrap metal," she said. "Not that big, not that heavy, but kind of sheared off and sharp at one end. I don't think I can slip out of my right cuff. I'll work on the bolt that connects the chain to the wall." A chain clinked in the darkness, followed by a scraping sound. The sounds continued for a few minutes.

"Any luck?" Colt finally whispered.

"I think maybe the head of the bolt moved a little," she said. "Or I'm just desperate to imagine that it has—"

Rusty metal squealed, but not from her efforts. The sound came from the opposite direction, down the tunnel behind Colt.

Footsteps approached, more than one person. It sounded like a group of them.

He heard Mohini shuffle around, maybe hiding the scrap of metal or preparing to use it as a weapon. Colt drew in his legs and prepared to kick if necessary, since that was really the only contribution he could make to a fight. Maybe he could knock out someone's ankle or knee.

They came closer; Colt could tell by the sound, and then by the smell of human body odor and the heat increase in the air as they walked up to him.

"You should let us go," Colt said. "We're on the same side—"

"Quiet," said a low, male voice, just above where Colt sat on the grimy floor. "The machines will hear us."

"Maybe we should let the machines come," Colt said.

"Maybe they'll take you out first and we can hide under your bodies. Let's see what happens if I yell—"

"Don't!" Another voice, female, more familiar. Her gloved hand clapped over his mouth. "Colt, seriously. We're getting you out of here." It was Terra, the girl who'd grown up in their group with Mother Braden.

"Why chain us up in the first place?" Mohini asked.

"Those were Lars's orders," Terra replied. "Some of us disagreed."

"The girl's bleeding," one of the guys said. "You got first aid, Ivy?"

"Got it," a girl's voice replied softly.

"If you free my other hand, I can bandage myself," Mohini said.

"Working on it," a guy said, and Colt heard metal scratching metal. "Don't have the key, though. It'll take a minute."

"Does anyone have night goggles so I can see?" Colt asked.

"I grabbed yours. Nice tiger ears." Terra shoved Colt's goggles, a former child's toy, down on his head. His eyes blinked as they adjusted to seeing again.

There were four rebels in the group that was freeing them, including Terra. Most wore low-drawn hats and cloth masks, and those with lighter skin had smudged what little flesh was visible. For all Colt could tell, they could have been the same rebels who'd kidnapped them in the first place.

One of them, clearly the hulking dark-skinned guy who'd arrived with Terra and Fernando, was kneeling by Mohini, working at the cuff on her right hand. It clicked and opened, and Mohini was free. She flexed the fingers on her newly liberated hand. Her other hand was smeared red with her blood.

The big guy moved over to Colt and started picking the lock on his cuffs with a thin sliver of metal.

"I don't suppose anyone brought my computer," Mohini said.

"Sorry," Terra replied. "That's Lars's new prized possession. We couldn't get anywhere near it."

"Lars didn't send you?" Colt asked as his left wrist came free of the cuff. The guy started working on his right cuff instead.

"No, but he might be sending people *after* us," Terra said. "We have to get out of here."

"I need my gear," Mohini said.

"And I'd like you to have it," Terra said. "But we can't go and take it from Lars."

"Why not?" Colt asked.

"A lot of people are still loyal to him," Terra said.

"But you aren't?" Colt looked at Terra and the other three who'd come with her.

"He's been... different, lately. Making decisions that leave people stranded, get people killed."

"You think he's a machine?" Mohini asked. One of the rebels, a small masked female, was bandaging her skinned wrist.

"Or working with them. Or maybe he's just losing it."

"That's enough," said the rebel who'd picked their locks. Colt rubbed his own wrists, glad to have them free. "We don't have to tell them everything."

"If I don't have my computer, I'm not sure we can carry out the raid on the Simon's lab," Mohini said. "I'll have to rethink all my plans—"

"Lars isn't backing the raid," Terra said. "The raid is not happening."

"But the four of you must want to help with it," Mohini said. "Why else are you rescuing us?"

"Because I grew up with Colt," Terra said, looking coldly at Mohini. "And because Lars and his best pals were going to torture you for everything you know about Carthage, then kill you. You were deemed a major security risk, Carthage girl."

"Is my sister still safe?" Colt asked. "Nobody's planning to kidnap her and chain her up in a sewer, right?"

Terra nodded. "Fernando took everyone else to a safe place."

"So what's the plan now?"

"We meet up with Fernando and your friends," Terra said. "Then we send you on to wherever you want to hide next."

"That's no good," Mohini said. "My mission can't end."

"Your mission is insane," Terra said. "The four of us can't invade Simon's lab."

"The six of us," Colt said. "Plus Diego and Fernando. That's eight."

"I don't hear you volunteering your sister," Terra said. "Is that because you know everyone involved in raiding the machine base would die? Maybe you're not quite willing to sacrifice the people you really care about?"

"I would want her to stay with the kids," Colt said.

"The kids? I thought there was only one left," Terra said.

"Birdie. Someone has to protect her."

"We can argue later," one of the other rebels said, a guy about Colt's age. The visible portion of his face had heavy burns and scars on the left side. "Lars and the others are coming back. Now."

"Let's move." Terra and the other rebels started down

the tunnel, going the opposite way from the direction they'd come.

"Wait," Mohini said.

"We don't have time to wait," Terra said. "Did you miss the part where Lars and his friends will be here any second to brutally interrogate and probably kill you?"

"That's right." Mohini sat back down in the spot where she'd been chained up and raised both her hands. "Cuff me again. I'll wait for him."

"Are you crazy?" Terra asked.

"No. I need to get my computer back from Lars. I'm guessing he'll want me to show him how to use it. I doubt he'll get past my biometric security layer, if he even breaks that deep into the encryption. So let's wait here until he brings the computer down to me. Then the rest of you can jump him. Take out Lars and whoever he brings with him."

"We can't do that," said the young-sounding girl who'd bandaged Mohini. Strands of stiff, filthy blond hair jutted out from under her low, wide-brimmed hat. Her eyes were large and chocolate brown over the black cloth that hid the rest of her face. The bandit-style hat and face cloth combination was common among the rebels. "Lars is still our leader. Splitting off is one thing, but ambushing him? Hurting him?"

"Killing him, Ivy," Terra said. "We can't just injure them or intimidate them. They'll kill us. They have to be dead before they can fight back."

"You expect us to ambush and kill our own leader?" asked the medic girl, apparently named Ivy. "Terra, we don't know he's gone bad. We just suspect—he could just be getting erratic—"

"Erratic in ways that get people captured and killed,"

Terra said, turning on her. "He's serving the machines. Whether it's intentional or not matters less every day."

"But it's not just Lars," argued the lockpicker. "He'll have Krauss with him, and Val—"

"Then we take them all down," Terra said.

"Kill three of our own to save one girl from Carthage?"

"She can hack machines," Terra said. "And we'll be saving everyone else that would have been killed by Lars's treachery. Or his stupidity. Whichever it is."

"And you think this girl's going to change everything?" Ivy asked, looking over at Mohini.

"If there's any possibility," Terra said. "What else can we do? Spend the rest of our lives in hit-and-run battles with the machines? Watching them take away everyone we know in a war we can't win? Even if we fail, I'd rather die trying to do something that matters than following the same old dead-end road."

There was a tense silence.

Colt sat down at the spot where he'd been chained. "Put my cuffs back on, too," he said.

"Not so tight this time," Mohini added.

"Look at that," Terra said. "She's ready to put herself right back into danger, ready to go up against Lars with her hands tied. All you guys have to do is hide until it's time to shoot. This is it. Time to make a difference." When nobody argued, Terra nodded, and they all got to work.

Within a couple of minutes, Colt and Mohini were back where they'd started—sitting on the floor of the old drainage tunnel, leaning back against the wall, cuffs around their wrists.

They were alone for a moment, but then the footsteps approached, and Colt readied himself to fight for his life.

Chapter Ten

Hyperspace

"Well, I'm out," Dinnius said. "I can't fake being a pediatrician in front of a Simon unit. They have medical programming, like their Butler Jeffrey forerunners. Fun fact: there's a crazy rumor that the Simons have rounded up and destroyed every Butler Jeffrey model they could find. Apparently they find the units embarrassing."

"Fun fact: something can't be both a fun fact and a crazy rumor," Kright said. "It's contradictory."

"The fact that there is such a rumor can be fun," Dinnius replied.

"You don't have to give the Simon a medical exam," Audrey told Dinnius. "You just have to seem capable of administering treatment once we arrive, and overseeing the nurse-bots."

"Perhaps we should waken one or two nurse-bots now," Dinnius said. "They could keep us company on this long trip."

"Are you saying what I think you're saying?" Zola asked with a look of disgust.

"Precisely," Dinnius said. "Nurse-bots are programmed to make comforting and pleasant conversation. And I need someone around with a chance of beating me at chess."

"I was on the chess team at school," Audrey said.

"Then please have a seat," Dinnius replied, gesturing to one of the fold-down tables on the wall.

"See, we don't need nurse-bots," Zola said.

"You don't have to feel so threatened by the prospect of nurse-bots." Dinnius shook his head while setting out a miniature chess set.

Audrey had rejoined her friends in the crew quarters, and while it was far more pleasant here than on the bridge with Simon, she found it hard to believe Simon wasn't really listening or watching through the *Atreus*'s internal network of interfaces, of tiny cameras and microphones built to be small and ubiquitous, out of sight yet always ready to serve, to listen and watch.

"How's our information security, Minerva?" she asked.

"Excellent," the AI's voice responded. She wasn't projecting her silvery image anywhere at the moment.

"Can you double-check, though? Just in case?"

"Yes. Assessment complete. The *Atreus* is not observing us, and the Simon cannot use its systems to do so."

"Do you really think we can keep the Simon unit fooled until we land on Veritum?" Salvius asked Audrey. His tone made it clear that the question went beyond rhetorical, into the land of condescending insults. He sat on his bunk, Zola reclined against him.

"I don't necessarily believe that, no," Audrey said. "How do you think the *Atreus* would react if we took out the Simon while we're still in hyperspace?"

"Best-case scenario, the *Atreus* recognizes you as the commanding officer of the ship and is indifferent to the Simon's fate," Dinnius said, carefully setting out thimble-sized chess pieces. The chess game was a travel set, meant to avoid taking up precious room on spaceships.

"And the worst?" Zola asked. She toyed with Salvius's fingers, which rested on her knee.

"We get locked out of administrative access and the *Atreus* refuses to cooperate with us," Dinnius said. "Perhaps it takes us to Veritum's system but leaves us adrift, refuses to let us shuttle down or return home. Perhaps it never returns us from hyperspace at all, and we travel indefinitely, never returning to our proper level of reality. Perhaps we witness wonders and horrors that no human mind has ever encountered before. Or perhaps we die of slow boredom and deprivation. Or, over the years, we could all go mad and begin hunting each other in something of a *Lord of the Flies* scenario, fighting over the seeds and preserved food we intended to use to purchase goodwill on Veritum—"

"I vote we wait until we drop out of hyperspace, at least," Kright said.

"Simon has that reaper up there with him, too," Audrey reminded them. "Maybe he's already a step ahead, expecting trouble from us while we're still figuring out what to do. Minerva, can you get us access to weapons? We need lasers, maybe projectiles, something that won't puncture the hull."

"There are a number of handheld combat weapons secured in the armory in the forward starboard compartment," the AI replied.

"The reaper hold?" Audrey asked. "What if Simon wakes up more of them to stop us?"

"That is a risk," Minerva said. "I would try to counteract, of course, but I do not have administrative control of the ship. Attempting to take control would alert the *Atreus* and the Simon to my presence."

"And then what would happen?" Audrey asked.

"Then events become complex and unpredictable," Minerva said.

"Our oracle fails us at last," Dinnius said. "As all oracles must." He drew out retractable seat-shelves on either side of the drop-down table, then sat at one side of the chess board and gestured at Audrey, his eyebrows raised.

"So what should we do?" Audrey asked. "Keep the Simon occupied with missionary planning? Or try to avoid him? Or move against him before he gathers more robots?"

"What do you think?" Kright asked her in return.

"You're the mission leader, little sis," Salvius said. "You get to handle the hard choices and hope nobody mutinies."

"Great," Audrey said. "So... we stall for now. Get working on more specific plans for what we'll do at Veritum once our machines take control of the colony. If he plays along, and we play along, maybe we can still make it to Veritum without a fight."

"We also need to watch out for more reapers," Zola said. "Minerva?"

"I am already monitoring the situation," Minerva's voice said.

"We need to leave a couple of people here, then," Audrey said, "so you can counterattack if Simon moves against us. Maybe you can go grab those weapons from the hold."

"I'll do it," Kright said.

"No," Audrey told him. "You're supposed to be our construction engineer, and you actually studied architecture at university. You can play your role more convincingly."

"For almost two semesters—"

"So you have to be part of the fake-out team," Audrey continued. "Dinnius, you said you're not comfortable with deception—"

"Oh, I'm very comfortable with it," Dinnius said. "Especially when the alternative is stealing guns guarded by five hundred and twelve battle-ready reapers. Like most people, I did binge-watch *Heartbreak Hospital*. Until that third season, you know. I was in the hospital myself, ironically, recovering from a jetboard injury. Also, I don't recommend jetboarding. I'll gladly join the fake-out team."

"Salvius and I will stay here," Zola said. "We're higher-profile enemies of the state, anyway."

"And Zola's a crack shot," Salvius added.

"All right," Audrey said. "If you have to go into the reaper hold... be careful." She looked from her long-estranged brother to her childhood best friend, who had somehow found each other again in the dangerous world of the small, rebellious underground that opposed the Carthaginian state on Carthage itself. Together, they were two of the people she cared about the most, even if she'd been distant from both of them for years.

She resisted the urge to embrace them, though, afraid she might cry, might rip open a vein of deep emotion just as she needed to put on her poker face and go manage Simon for a while.

"Be careful," she said again, then looked to Kright and Dinnius.

"Already?" Dinnius sighed and cast a longing look at his waiting chess board as he stood up. "Fine. I am now Argus Leopold, pediatrician, human commander of the Hot Robot Nurses Legion. I have just recently become acquainted with architectural engineer Murray Tarpon—"

"Too late to change my name?" Kright interrupted.

"Far too late," Minerva answered.

"Murray Tarpon," Dinnius finished. "Best known for, er..."

"A municipal public-housing award," Kright said. "Second runner-up, ten years ago."

"It sounds as though partial congratulations are in order," Dinnius said.

"Let's go distract the Simon before he comes looking for us," Audrey said, starting for the door.

"What's the best way to distract a Simon unit, anyway?" Dinnius followed after.

"Ask him about tea," Audrey said.

"Let's go save the world." Kright closed the door behind them. "Not ours, obviously. Or any major world. A tiny world on the edge of nowhere."

"We have to start somewhere," Audrey said.

The minicarrier was a giant ship, considered "mini" only in comparison with Carthage's immense megacarriers. Most of its size was given over to hangars and storage compartments, and spaces within the small pressurized section were narrow, twisting, and dim.

They took seats in the wardroom, designed for the ship's officers to meet and enjoy meals.

"Let's have a good look at the place," Kright said as a holographic projection of the arid surface of Veritum appeared on the table. The image was patchy—much remained unknown about current conditions on the distant world—but they could see a number of settlements ringed with high sheet metal walls. Patches of desert crops grew inside, around low, bunker-like buildings.

"Here's the capital, God's Watch." Audrey pointed to the largest settlement, a cloistered village of concrete walls and narrow alleys. Guard towers along the high walls featured heavy artillery behind armored mesh, ready to strafe the roads and other approaches to the little city. "We're talking thirty to fifty thousand in the main city, maybe twice that many on the whole planet. The top tier of their society are the priests, the Faces of God. Beneath them, the Hands of God."

"Let me guess," Dinnius said. "God's Hands are filled with guns."

"Exactly. They're the enforcers of the holy laws," Audrey said. "At the bottom are the Feet of God—"

"The ones who grow the crops," Kright said.

"Grow the crops, lay the bricks, operate the concrete factory and the mines," Audrey said. "All to work out their sins. They're slaves, constantly watched, brutally punished, told that it's for their spiritual good."

"And what if it is?" Dinnius asked.

Audrey blinked. "What?"

"Who are we to interfere in their religious freedom?" Dinnius asked. "If they've come all this way to live out their beliefs?"

"I haven't told you the worst of it," Audrey said. "The children. Boys are sorted from an early age into warriors and workers, Hands and Feet. Girls are sorted into Feet and Wombs. Those in the second group, selected for their appearance and fertility, are delivered as brides to the old priests, who maintain breeding harems—"

"All right, picture painted," Dinnius said, grimacing. "So we're in it to liberate the children. Then what? If their parents believe in this cult—"

"Surely they regret it by now," Audrey said. "It's one thing to be recruited to a cult, another to spend years at the bottom of its caste system and see your children taken—"

"I agree with you," Kright said. "But what if we get there and there's no one looking for change? What if they're united against us?"

"Impossible," said a familiar voice, startling everyone. Simon Lark entered the room, smiling gently, and stood alongside them, taking in the hologram. "This appears to draw on incomplete data."

"It's definitely incomplete," Audrey said. "Why did you say it's impossible for Veritum to be united against us?"

"In any human group, there will be rivalries, schisms, emotionally charged divisions that can be exploited." Simon sat near the foot of the table by the holographic image of an outlying Veritum hamlet with sheet metal fences protecting its stubby little crops. "It is a matter of finding and exploiting the social fault lines. I find a dynamic of conflict underlies even the smallest band of humans." His pale blue eyes looked among the three of them. "Are there not five in your party?"

"The others are resting," Audrey said. "The three of us aren't feeling that well, either, to be honest. Is it normal for humans to feel wrecked after jumping into hyperspace?"

"Oh, yes, of course," Simon said. "Few humans can comfortably tolerate prolonged hyperspace travel."

"I'll fetch some aspirin." Dinnius started for the door, seeming to remember he was playing a doctor on this mission.

"Might I recommend a restorative red tea?" Simon asked. "I refer of course to the rooibos herb, the term 'red tea' being something of a misnomer, but surely a colorful one, we can all agree. Rooibos is rich in minerals and antioxidants, and can lower blood pressure and relieve tension—"

"I'll take it," Kright said.

A panel of the wardroom wall slid aside, and a stumpy robot with a dented metal-dome head like the cover of a serving dish rolled out, wobbling on treads. It creaked repeatedly as it passed the table and headed for the door, as though it had a rusty joint or a loose belt inside. Audrey shuddered; she hadn't even realized such a robot was nearby, but of course the officers would have a machine to prepare food and drinks and tidy up the ward room. Which meant it could access all kinds of kitchen cutlery and other dangerous instruments.

"The steward bot will fetch the tea makings for us," Simon said. "Where were we? Reviewing our own group for potential disagreements? Ah, no. Reviewing the enemy for such. What do we know about the leadership on Veritum? Names, personalities?"

"We have profiles of several leaders," Audrey said. She summoned images, tapping at her console. Several projections of the same man appeared above the arid landscape of Veritum, like clouds in the sky. They showed him at different ages; a young professorial type with a long black ponytail, standing at a lectern; an older version of him, his hair gray, a weird long beard adorning his face, braided on either side of his chin. An even later picture showed him bald on top with multiple long white beard-braids, surrounded by young men with copycat beard-braids. "The cult was founded by a philosophy professor from Carthage, Reidlan Enocos..."

For the next two hours, Audrey outlined Veritum society as she understood it, finally giving the presentation she'd almost given to the combined military and civilian leadership of Carthage, before her father had canceled. That had only been a quick briefing, though, hitting the broad strokes.

This presentation was almost cathartic, painting a

picture of horror and abuse, beginning with a professor with odd ideas who recruited his students into a religion focused on space and pantheism and interdimensional beings. The professor was now a hundred and twenty years old, known as the Mind of God and the high priest of his own cult, with a population of young followers drawn from the inner worlds. Some followers had been poor and desperate while others were wealthy but rudderless; these latter donated all they had to the building of a palatial temple, the creation of a small media empire, and eventually the founding of a colony on a distant world.

"Hardly anyone has ever come back from Veritum," Audrey said, "so most of our detailed information dates back many years, when they were a fairly unified cult. But there's a whole generation that's been born there now. Surely they're ready for a change."

"So you expect to find some sort of rebellion in progress there," Simon said. "You simply have faith that this resistance must exist."

"Of course," Audrey said. "People won't accept oppression forever."

"Will they not?" Simon asked. "An interesting hypothesis. One we shall put to the test shortly, upon our arrival at Veritum."

After their meeting, Audrey led the way back down to crew berthing, feeling she'd reached some solid ground at last. Regardless of the Simon's unexpected presence, their mission was moving ahead. She was doing what she'd long hoped to do, wielding Carthage's power in a way that actually freed people from exploitation, that brought freedom and equality where oppression ruled.

It was the only road she saw to a better future, both for her own world and the many worlds over which it ruled.

Sowing freedom and autonomy, evolving into an enduring commonwealth rather than an empire based on force and intimidation. She was thinking of the extreme long term, and the kind of interstellar dark age that could follow the collapse of the current Carthaginian system.

Even the red tea seemed to nourish her and boost her spirits, she had to admit, just as Simon had promised.

"I'm actually looking forward to reaching Veritum," Audrey said as they returned to the berthing compartment. "I think we can do some good there..."

Her voice trailed off when she saw the frightened look on Zola's face. She was pacing nervously while Salvius sat on his bunk, shaking his head.

"What's happened?" Dinnius asked, after making sure the door was shut tight to keep their voices inside. "I would ask if the dog died, but we didn't bring one with us."

"We're off course," Kright said.

A bit of silence followed while everyone processed that.

"In what way?" Audrey asked.

"In the most literal way possible," Salvius said, idly tossing a stress ball in the air and catching it. "When we emerge from hyperspace, we're not going to be in Veritum's system. So much for your big humanitarian mission."

"What are you talking about?" Audrey asked, more confused than ever.

"A detour has been entered into the ship's navigation system," Minerva said. She appeared in her glowing silver-skinned form on an empty second-level bunk, legs in lotus position as if meditating. She presented as a small girl, not much larger than an elementary school kid. "At Simon Lark's request."

"To where?"

"An orange-dwarf system with one habitable planet, a mostly aquatic world called Galapagos."

"What?" Audrey felt herself flush red as she stalked toward the door again. "I'm going to demand he fix it—"

"Wait," Zola said. "We can't let Simon know about Minerva."

"Right." Audrey stopped and turned to the hologram of Minerva, who smiled apologetically and shrugged. "Okay, Minerva. Tell me all about Galapagos and why we're going there, then."

Audrey struggled to hold in her anger as she listened.

Chapter Eleven

Galapagos

Ellison stood in the House of Ambassadors, silent and empty in a way he'd never seen it. The badly cracked murals on the rotunda above seemed an accurate representation of the shattered peace. War would reach every island in Galapagos; those not bombed to rubble would lose a generation of sons and daughters in the struggle that lay ahead.

And when it's all over, he thought, *we'll be free or we'll be dead.*

Not for the first time, he was afraid he'd made the wrong decision, making a stand against the Carthaginian empire. Most citizens of the Coalition had supported that decision, and he'd done no more than represent the clear will of his people, but freedom came at a high price. He wondered how much they'd be willing to pay, and for how long.

He thought of his wife, Cadia, and two young sons. Was

he sacrificing them, too? What ideal could be worth that? Maybe the Green Islanders had a point.

"Ready?" Kartokov asked. The defense minister had come with him, along with Minister of State Adrienna Gilra, to collect items from their offices. A pair of Coalition marines from the Tower Island security force shadowed them.

Their footsteps echoed in the oddly empty building, which showed signs of hasty evacuation everywhere Ellison looked.

"It's silent as the deep trenches here," Gilra said, her voice soft as if they were walking past a burial island, like the dry, sandy key where Ellison's ancestors lay. He knew the Aquaticans weighted their dead and sank them in the deepest parts of the ocean, returning them to the gods below. "This feels like the end of civilization."

"It is, for now," Ellison said. "Until we've driven the threat from our shores, our society is on hold. All we can do is pull together and fight. Maybe there will be peace and security for our children and grandchildren if we fight now."

The sentiment felt a little hollow because he'd heard as much during the Island Wars, had said as much to men serving on the *Scorpion*. Ellison's submarine had been a perfect metaphor for the Scatterlands, built of mismatched components that had generally begun their lives as other things, as fishing boats and discarded drop ships.

Now the *Scorpion* could stand for the entire Coalition, he thought, struggling to piece together a defense against a far superior force.

"If only we could contact Ruckwold Industries," Kartokov said, shaking his head. Direct interstellar communication was still limited by the speed of light; ships had to travel through hyperspace, carrying information in their data banks like ancient sailing ships bearing mail between ports of call.

Unfortunately, Galapagos's only spaceport was occupied by their local enemies, the Iron Hammers, and the Coalition didn't even have the space presence to defend their satellites against Carthaginian starfighters. They had no way of sending any new message to Ruckwold Industries, their defense contractor, or to any other worlds—who wouldn't necessarily help out, lacking any formal alliance or requirement to do so. Galapagos had only begun to sketch out the beginnings of a global state; they certainly weren't full members of the Mutual Defense League headed by the government of planet Ruckwold and its defense industry.

"Remember the parade on Veteran's Day?" Kartokov asked. "Everyone cheered when the *Sea Scorpion* drove by. Your ship is legendary."

"My campaign team made it that way," Ellison said. "There were much finer ships in our navy, with crews as brave and tough as mine. Well, almost." He cracked a smile, thinking of the small, ragged crew of the *Scorpion*. Constantly in deep over their head, both literally and figuratively, they'd somehow made it through the war, sinking enemy ships, cutting underwater communications, and generally being a destructive nuisance to the Hammers, and to the Aquaticans when they were the enemy.

"Your publicity people were good," Gilra said, her biologically green lips smiling thinly. "I remember the little video game they released. Drive the legendary *Sea Scorpion*! Defend against the Hammers. And giant ocean creatures. And alien attackers."

"We did tangle with some huge monsters down there,"

Ellison said. "The horned squid, the grab-crabs, which attack in packs—"

"And Aquatican vessels, too," Gilra said coolly.

"Only when they chose to ally with the Hammers," Kartokov said, before Ellison could reply.

"It was a complicated war." Gilra started for the open doors. "Let's go before this place falls down on our heads."

Ellison took a last look at the broken murals above. The crumbling images of war and peace, island and sea, of the many and varied people of his world, seemed an accurate reflection of the world's broken dreams for itself.

The empire was coming for them, and no one was coming to save them.

They went down, escorted by the Coalition marines who'd been shadowing them. More marines, along with custodial staff, carried boxes of canned food and other supplies bound for the submarine base.

The stairwell to the Command Center was crowded and chaotic; top-ranking ambassadors, the lawmakers of the world, were crammed into the Command Center for the trip down. The crowd was thinning, though, as junior diplomatic staff and other able-bodied people reluctantly trickled down the long, dim, damp stairs, carrying briefcases and travel bags hundreds of meters to the ocean floor rather than wait for the Command Center platform's return trip and the second descent. The enemy could easily attack again before that happened.

They were officially vacating in case of a repeat attack from the Hammers. Little was said about the real danger, the unknown number and type of Carthaginian craft that could be orbiting their planet even now, lining up a bombardment that would turn Galapagos into another Earth, its civilization ended and its people reduced to mindless barbarism. It was almost as if the larger invasion wouldn't happen if nobody said it aloud.

Everyone knew Carthage was coming, though. Whether it happened tonight or a week from now.

"Move aside, move aside!" shouted one of the marines escorting Ellison and his ministers of defense and state, urging people out of the way for the top executives.

"They look pretty packed in there," Ellison said when they got close enough to look inside the propped-open doors to the Command Center. The leadership of the world was crammed in, lawmakers and admirals, nearly all of them visibly frightened, yet none of them panicking. They were ready to stand for their world. The fates of millions of lives rested on their shoulders.

And they were jammed in like sardines.

"Maybe we take the next one," Kartokov told their escort, and Ellison nodded. He didn't see how they could fit another soul in that room, anyway.

"Gate is closing! Clear the gate!" bellowed one of the marines posted just inside the door. He was stocky for an Aquatican, his pale skin speckled blue, a tattoo of a dragonfish on his neck. Aquatican engineers built and maintained the entire underwater portion of the House of Ambassadors, all the way down to the submarine base on the ocean floor. A squad of Aquatican marines worked with them, wearing ocean-blue Coalition uniforms instead of their native turquoise and coral-red battle colors.

A metal grate rolled down inside the door, blocking anyone else from entering or leaving. Heavy unseen machinery rumbled.

"Stand by to descend!" the same marine shouted, touching his earpiece.

Ellison, Kartokov, and Gilra watched as the entire

Command Center began to sink away, its floor and walls easing down toward the distant base below, which was about to become the center of the Galapagos resistance against the invaders.

Despite the crowd of dignitaries and lawmakers making it nearly impossible to breathe in the Command Center, the military officers and techs kept at their work, staying in touch with far-flung ships and planes.

Ellison had told the admirals to reinforce their capitals today, while the ambassadors discussed emergency defense plans. This had left gaps in the monitoring and defense of Tower Island itself, which the Hammers' bombers had exploited that morning. And Ellison had exploited their exploitation to pass the defense bill. Ironically, the bill could be interpreted as giving Ellison the same dictatorial powers over Galapagos that Simon Zorn had promised him, though Ellison had no intention of abusing them or keeping them too long.

"Sir!" one of the Green Island techs shouted, loud enough to be heard over the murmuring crowd and the rumbling machinery. "A pilot reports a bogey on rapid descent toward our location."

"Show me." Admiral Planter stepped over. The Green Islander looked calm as stone under pressure, not a silver hair out of place, his bearing aristocratic.

A thin, shaky two-dimensional image formed above the tech's console. The viewpoint kept shifting as the Green Island spy plane circled around it in a wide bank. The image was a bit chunky and pixelated, indicating an extreme zoom-in. The plane was keeping its distance, for reasons that were instantly obvious.

The object streaking down from the sky was cloaked in glowing plasma generated by atmospheric-entry friction, plummeting so fast the plane's camera had trouble tracking it. The object kept streaking downward out of sight, leaving a burning trail behind it like a pillar of fire in the sky.

"Looks like an orbital launch," Kartokov muttered while chaos erupted below. Fighters were called in from their patrols, and anti-aircraft guns erupted on the surface of Tower Island, remote controlled from the Command Center.

The object came down almost on top of them. Awash in flames and smoke, its true shape was impossible to see.

At the last moment, a flood of video arrived from the island's monitoring system and nearby ships, showing the smoking object as it approached Tower Island.

"That's no missile," Ellison muttered, but he was only stating the obvious. The object looked big enough to crush the entire House of Ambassadors, maybe the whole complex of buildings around it. The exact size was impossible to judge, but it was clearly of significant mass. "Looks more like a ship—"

Then the impact came.

The falling mass didn't strike the House of Ambassadors, or any of the other buildings on Tower Island.

It didn't strike the island at all, but slammed into the deep ocean water north of the island, less than a kilometer away.

Several consoles blanked out as contact with a number of ships, particularly Green Island corvettes, was lost.

Camera feeds from the surface sent down images of a tsunami-like wall of water rising toward Tower Island, looking big enough to swallow the island whole, to flood every building, to crush every symbol of the Coalition's attempt at a peaceful world order. It was like the fall of night after the blazing glow of the mysterious artifact from the heavens, the dark mass of ocean water blotting out the sky and the sun.

Voices erupted all around them as people exhorted each other with warnings like "Incoming!" or "Take cover!" or "Hit the deck!" All the warnings were as useless as they were desperate.

The entire building shuddered like a vibrating guitar string. A boom echoed as the massive wave struck the island. Tower Island rumbled from the surface above to the ocean floor below.

Ellison felt his whole body go tense, anticipating the total collapse of the island. A clamor of terrified voices went up around him.

A strange crackling sound followed, like ice crunching under boots.

Spiderwebs of cracks appeared in the reinforced concrete walls of the stairwell. Through the gate, Ellison saw even more cracks opening in the cylindrical wall of the elevator shaft that had been revealed as the Command Center descended.

The Command Center itself wobbled like a precariously balanced dinner plate, sending officers and ambassadors crashing to the floor, rupturing some of the consoles so badly they spilled out sparks. All consoles blanked out and they lost track of the invasive object.

The lights blew out, leaving everyone in darkness.

Silence followed for a moment, as though they were all trying to determine whether they were still alive.

Then someone announced: "They missed!"

Ellison winced as he heard that idea passed around, first in echoing whispers, then in triumphant shouts, whistles, even applause. Maybe they hadn't all been instantly annihilated, but the structure in which they stood had been badly damaged. And they could have lost some ships, particularly the Green Island corvettes that had been in the area of the crashdown.

Lights blipped on here and there—marines with high-powered, waterproof flashlights, civilians lighting up their pocket screens.

"Who's still receiving input?" Ellison asked, moving close to the gate so he could shout down at the Command Center. "Audio? Anything?"

"I have something," came an answer from the Command Center floor. A tech from the Scatterlands was standing up. He looked like he was from the southern islands, a man with dark skin and long dreadlocks. "The *Hornfish* reports a geyser of steam where it went in. He can see it all the way from Beatrix Bay."

"Picking up some composites from SQUIDS," said another tech, an Aquatican. Her console sputtered to life and formed a blurry image of a huge, sinking shape surrounded by boiling ocean water, an image formed from sonar and water-displacement data. "It looks like... a drop ship?"

"Is it open or closed?" Kartokov shouted down to the Command Center floor through the bars of the closed safety door.

"Open. Looks like it's sinking," the tech called back, apparently picking out Kartokov's voice among all the shouting around them.

"So the impact wasn't the end," Gilra said. "It's the beginning."

"What was the drop ship transporting?" Ellison called down. It was the obvious question—something large had been inside.

"I don't see...." the Aquatican tech began but was interrupted by the tech beside her, whose console lit up.

"Over here!" the second tech shouted.

A fuzzy mass of light formed above the console, relayed from one of the many hypersensitive deep-water cameras in the SQUIDS network, enhanced with sonar sensors and fluid-dynamic interpreters.

As the inputs composited together, a clear shape emerged, like a whale ringed with spikes and horns, charging through the water at unbelievable speed.

"Carthaginian sub," said Commodore Chromis. The Aquatican commander's blue neck-gills flared as he leaned closer to the image. "And it's coming our way." Chromis touched an earpiece and began barking orders to the commander of the submarine base below, dispatching the entire pod of Aquatican attack subs to meet the invader.

"Torpedoes incoming," an Aquatican tech said, voice trembling but professional, as the sub launched a series of them. The launches were so fast and overlapping that it was hard to get an exact count.

"Incoming!" Commodore Chromis shouted, and the cry repeated across the Command Center. Ellison began to repeat it for the people crowded into the stairwell, but then the torpedoes struck.

The entire island rocked with the impact.

A deep, rumbling crack thundered below Ellison's feet, followed by something even worse: the sound of water, a great mass of it, flooding into the cavernous elevator shaft that held the Command Center.

The shaft filled almost instantly; seawater rushed up to the gate and spilled over into the stairwell area where Ellison and countless others stood.

Screams went up all around them. The people of Galapagos were tough, accustomed to war, but today had pressed them to their limits and beyond.

A constellation of small glowing spots were visible down in the Command Center, now buried meters below the water's surface. Some were consoles, which snuffed out quickly, but others were the waterproof flashlights of the marines. Those lights began circulating; hopefully that meant the water-breathing Aquaticans were still alive and trying to rescue the others.

The mass of water had come in fast and hard, though, which meant that those below could have died from the impact even before they'd had a chance to drown.

"We need this gate open!" Ellison said, shaking the gate to the flooded elevator shaft. The seawater continued to rise, reaching his ankles.

"On it, sir." A marine moved forward, his airy accent identifying him as a Green Islander. The man drew a laser cutter from his belt and went to work.

"Kartokov, see if Neptune Base is still online," Ellison said, which was a delicate way of telling him to figure out whether the base deep below them had been destroyed, too. "We need to figure out which way to direct this evacuation—up or down. And get some reports on what's happening out there. We're blind and deaf in here."

The marines cut open the gate as the seawater reached knee level around it.

A few Aquaticans swam to the surface, still alive... but only a few.

Bodies came up with them, a crowd of the dead rising from the deep.

Ellison took a breath, thinking of the old war, of mangled bodies floating on the surface of the ocean, and the sharks drawn by their blood. Of Kawau Island, as he always did, his home slaughtered by the Hammers.

The bodies were thicker here, trapped together in the elevator shaft, growing thicker by the moment as more bodies of ambassadors and admirals and Command Center staff rose from the depths, killed in their attempt to escape to safety.

There would be no escape, and no safety. Wherever they tried to move their headquarters, Carthage would find them.

Besides, there was no headquarters staff anymore, no command attempting to coordinate the four aligned national militaries, no infrastructure.

Ellison saw no way around it—they would have to go to ground somehow, communicate using only the hardwired SQUIDS network, hide out in underwater bases and mountainous islands with caves. It would be guerrilla warfare from here on.

"Let's go," Ellison said to Kartokov and Gilra. "We have to see what's happening out there. And establish a mobile headquarters, one that can avoid and hide."

"How do you plan to do that?" Gilra asked.

"I have some ideas." Ellison led them back upstairs, away from the desperate rescue efforts, marines and others trying to revive the drowned bodies of the world's leaders. Ellison would have to do the same with the remains of the world's defenses.

They returned to the surface, waving away the warnings of marines posted at the doorway to the shattered House of Ambassadors above.

The center of diplomacy and law was definitely shattered, too, in far worse shape than when they'd last left it. They had to walk through rubble flooded with seawater, through broken remnants of walls and ceilings. A glance into the Grand Meeting Hall revealed much of the grandeur was gone, most of the consoles, workstations, and chairs broken under fallen chunks of the ceiling. Every bit of glass or porcelain, anything remotely fragile, had been pulverized. Ocean water dripped from the broken ceiling; an enormous wave had come crashing through here, soaking and dislodging everything it touched.

"This building does not seem safe," Gilra commented, an obvious understatement. A spill of broken ceiling tiles came crashing down from what remained of the Meeting Hall roof, burying the dais where Ellison had stood earlier. A dark patch of sky was revealed above, and rain fell into the Meeting Hall.

"We won't be here long." Ellison led them onward, past offices and the gift shop, whose offerings included framed portraits of Ellison himself, smiling, dressed in a dark suit with an emerald sea turtle pin on his lapel; the animal was considered the symbol of planet Galapagos as a whole and was featured on the Coalition flag. Ellison's official signature was printed on these portraits, too, just to make the whole package a little more embarrassing for him.

The gift shop led onto what had been a covered, glass-walled bridge with a great view of the Tower Island Bay below. Now it was more of an open-air footbridge full of broken glass, with rain pouring down from the dark night sky above.

They finally had a look outside, but the rain clouds kept the night dark, and the power was out all over the island. Only the harbor's lighthouse still glowed, running on its own independent power cell.

The *Ursus*, the immense Gavrikovan battle carrier, still held the bay, dropping depth charges that went off like fiery underwater volcanoes, trying to strike back against the Carthaginian sub. One of its heavy-cruiser escorts was broken, though, and pieces of Green Island corvettes were strewn in the shallower waters. Aquatican attack subs were hopefully at work below, trying to attack the invader from a distance and avoiding the depth charges.

Planes rumbled above, the familiar sound of Gavrikovan engines patrolling the sky... but also a high-pitched screech that he didn't find so familiar. Heavy gunfire lit up the firmament like gods at war as the naval fighters exchanged fire with at least one Carthaginian drone; possibly the drones that had been sabotaging Coalition satellites had decided to enter the atmosphere.

The war was erupting above as well as below.

"This seems like a poor time for a museum visit," Gilra said as they reached the end of the pedestrian bridge. "We can reflect on wars of the past when the present one is finished."

"We are not here to reflect on past wars," Kartokov said, grunting as he pulled aside one of the clear doors to the museum. It normally would have slid open automatically. "We are here to rescue the museum's supply of Reginald Ellison dolls and snow globes."

"Very funny," Ellison said, leading the way into the soggy, broken museum.

They hurried past artifacts of the old wars, rifles and laser guns inscribed with symbols of different nations. An early-model Gavrikovan fighter hung from the high ceiling, as did a Green Island transport chopper, the one that held the record for wartime rescue and evac operations.

The next room featured a saltwater tank with two major exhibits. One was an Aquatican command submarine, shaped to resemble a giant fish. Symbols representing horned and tentacled deep-sea creatures adorned its sides. Aquaticans took offense when people referred to the titanic underwater beasts of Galapagos as "monsters," but it was hard not to use that term. Ellison had come close to such things more than once, and he saw none of the divinity that Aquaticans claimed to see... only aggression and a carnivorous appetite.

The other vessel was his goal, though. The *Sea Scorpion*, the trusty boat that had gotten Ellison and his crew through the war, was on display here. Even carefully maintained and freshly painted, the submarine's ramshackle, pieced-together provenance was obvious.

"You can't be serious. Does it still work?" Gilra asked.

"They bring it out for the parade convoy every year," Ellison replied. "It still works. And we won't have to commandeer any boats already in service."

"Surely the museum doesn't keep it armed," Kartokov said.

"No, but we can stock up at Neptune Base," he said.

"If the base still exists," Gilra countered. "What if it does not?"

"Then we find one that does," Ellison replied. He tried not to think of all the lives that could have been lost if the base was destroyed, or all those that had already been lost today. He wondered what the official casualty count would be.

Perhaps there would be no official count, though. Perhaps there was no longer enough organization in their society for official things.

Working as quickly as they could, they removed the cables that held the *Scorpion* in place. They crossed the swaying rope bridge that made the boat accessible to tour groups, then detached it from the ship's sail.

A strange, electric feeling spread through Ellison's body as he opened the hatch and descended the rungs into the dimness below. It was an odd combination of emotions—apprehension at the fighting to come, but a sense of going home, too. The *Scorpion* had held together through countless dangers, had been both their fighting platform and their home and refuge during the war, its armored hull shielding them from an ocean of deadly threats. They'd often spent weeks at a time below surface in the depths of the trenches, crammed together even in the officers' bunks, everybody breathing each other's air and seeing and hearing each other until the crew had become like a single organism with many bodies.

Ellison wished he had those old submariners here with him. Maybe he could track down a few of them.

In the control room, Ellison settled into the hard plastic pilot's seat. Kartokov took the co-pilot's seat beside him, though the old soldier had no real experience or training.

"How are you going to operate this without a crew?" Gilra sat on the port side at the communications console.

"I'm hoping for help," Ellison said as the ship's internal network came online. Images of the surrounding environment—in this case, the damaged museum—appeared all around, gathered up by photonic sensors and, as with the images in the Command Center, beefed up into holograms informed by sonar, electroreceptors, and water-motion sensors.

"Where are we going?" a girl's voice asked over the speakers. A silvery hologram appeared in the seat just behind and slightly above them, typically occupied by the officer of the deck for the direction of the *Scorpion*. That had been Ellison's place when he was on watch, but somebody had to take the pilot's seat tonight. And it sure wasn't going to be Kartokov.

Still, Ellison couldn't help feeling a twinge of annoyance at the rendering of the young girl, not much more than a kid, sitting cross-legged and barefoot on the seat of command.

"What is that? The ship's AI?" Gilra asked.

"It's sort of an upgrade," Ellison said, dodging the question a bit. He didn't want to lie to Gilra and earn her resentment and distrust later, but he also didn't want to waste time explaining that—

"Minerva's a software agent created by rebels on Carthage," Kartokov said. "She—what is the expression?—saved our sausages up on the spaceport. She activated the new orbital defense station and helped Ellison beat those Carthaginian destroyers."

"She's Carthaginian ware?" Gilra's oversized green eyes opened wide. "A virus!"

"No, I just explained—" Kartokov said while Ellison shook his head and focused on getting the ship online.

"We need to flush it out of the system before it kills us," Gilra said.

"What we need is to establish contact with the fleet." Ellison gestured at the console in front of her. "Looks like you're the comm officer. Connect with the network so we can see what's happening."

"Oh." Gilra blinked slowly at the unfamiliar equipment. "Right."

"Perhaps I could help?" Minerva appeared beside her, floating in midair like a silver genie this time, and Gilra looked terrified for a moment before she buried the expression and simply frowned.

"You say we can trust her?" Gilra asked.

"It seems that way so far—" Ellison began.

"With our lives," Kartokov interrupted. "We need her help."

Gilra sighed. She began touching screens in front of her—small, mismatched screens connected by snarls of wire, some of them originally taken from small entertainment units and even kids' toys. "Yes, all right. Minerva, connect us to SQUIDS."

"You got it, ma'am!" Minerva zipped across the room like a helium balloon caught in a crosswind, returning to the officer of the deck's chair.

Crackling audio feeds went live, connecting them to the assorted submersed boats. The monitors displayed fuzzy gray low-res images. Radio communication underwater was virtually impossible, but coded acoustic signals connected them to SQUIDS, the vast spaghetti-tangle of underwater cables. Ellison could also float up a radio buoy, which would strengthen communication with surface ships, and satellites if they'd still had any, but that would give away their position.

Ellison checked out the glowing schematics displayed in front of him. All hatches were sealed, the reactor was kicking, propulsor and plane systems passed internal checks. The weaponry was, sadly, empty until Ellison reached a base or an Aquatican deep-trench tender. There would be at least one in the area, with so many Aquatican subs around.

"Stand by to dive," Ellison said automatically. The sub's ballast tanks filled with water and the sub dropped.

Soon they faced the sealed underwater doors that would grant access to the bay beyond.

Ellison tried the remote, but they wouldn't budge.

"Minerva," he said. "We're having a little trouble with the garage door opener here."

"There is nothing wrong on our end," Minerva said. "The doors have no power. They will not respond."

"We could shoot our way out," Kartokov said. "If we weren't completely disarmed."

"It's not an auspicious beginning," Gilra said.

"Thanks for pointing that out." Ellison gunned the propulsors, sending the bow of the *Scorpion* crashing into the doors. The doors shifted a little on impact, but didn't give way. Ellison kept pressing the sub's bow against them until they broke, and then the *Scorpion* charged out into the bay.

Straight into the center of the battle, completely unarmed, rushing toward the immense Carthaginian sub that had dropped down from space to attack the capital of their civilization.

Chapter Twelve

Earth

Colt and Mohini sat chained against the wall, exactly where they were supposed to be. Colt's nerves grew worse as the heavy footsteps approached.

Lars, the battle-scarred older man with the mechanical hand, led the approaching pack of rebels. He left a pair of rebels behind at the last bend in the tunnel before reaching Colt and sent another pair ahead to guard the next one ahead. Both pairs were still close enough to turn and open fire on the chained prisoners with the heavy automatic rifles in their hands.

Lars and his last two soldiers brought lights with them, which was good for Colt. He'd had to remove his night vision goggles and bury them in nearby debris so the rebels wouldn't wonder why he was suddenly wearing them.

Lars and the other two looked down at Colt and Mohini. The metal fingers on the section leader's mechanical hand flexed, making scraping and whirring sounds. The fingers were blocky, crudely made, and looked like something patched together from parts rather than a gift from the machines to one of their pet clankers.

Still, it was unnerving.

"Here's our Carthaginian girl," Lars said, lowering his dark gray bandanna as he looked Mohini over. "Now, why don't we talk about your real mission?"

"I've already told you," Mohini said. "I need the memory drives from Simon Nix—"

"Because you think it will instigate a rebellion on Carthage?" Lars asked, his tone biting. "I'm not a fool, and you're not a fool. You came here looking for the rebels on Earth. Looking for me. Maybe you thought your absurd story would win us over, to help you infiltrate us." Lars squatted close to Mohini, looking intently at her. "Then you marshal our forces and send us all right into the lion's den... where the lion is wide awake and waiting for us. Or maybe this proposed raid would have seemed to go remarkably well, on the surface. But you would have learned a lot about us. Our identities, tactics, base locations, everything. And gained our trust. Is that about right?"

"Then why would I tell you I'm from Carthage?" she asked. "Why not come up with a different cover story?"

Colt considered that she had originally told *him* she was from Earth, claiming to be from England, a land so far away he only knew of it from crumbling old books. The machines allowed no communication between humans; any attempt at broadcasting a signal would be tracked to its source. They lived in isolated bands, rarely encountering others, and such encounters could be dangerous; human scavengers tended to be robbers, rapists, or cannibals, sometimes all three.

Colt didn't mention any of that to Lars and friends, though, since he was on Mohini's side here.

"Because you could never convince us you were an Earthling," Lars said, while his two cohorts with dark hats and masks nodded along. "We would recognize you as an outsider right away."

Colt could have disagreed with that, too, but he kept quiet.

"I've told you nothing but the truth. I don't know how to convince you of that," Mohini said.

"Don't worry about convincing me. Worry about whether you're going to live through the night." He drew a dagger from his belt. "You see, we've spent all our lives running from Carthage. From the machines you sent to destroy our world. Sometimes we get to destroy a few of those machines. But an actual flesh-and-blood Carthaginian? That's something we've never seen. An opportunity we've never had. A chance to finally inflict pain on one of you. It won't even begin to repay all the pain and death you've caused us, but... it will be fun. The only question will be how to keep you alive long enough so we all get a turn."

He moved the knife in close to her face, like he was going to start by carving up her nose and chin.

"Stop!" Colt said, and Lars did, turning his attention to Colt instead.

"You collaborated with her," Lars said, his eyes cold and his voice low and flat, lacking the slightly mocking tone with which he'd addressed Mohini. "You brought her to us. You tried to help her infiltrate. You're no better than a clanker."

"Says the guy with the metal hand," Colt said.

Lars's face twisted in fury, and he punched his clunky metal hand at Colt's face. Colt managed to dodge aside, remembering at the last moment not to move too far and give away that he was actually free. The metal hit the concrete with a cracking sound, breaking loose a few concrete chips that bit into the side of Colt's jaw like tiny teeth, drawing blood.

"You think I enjoy this?" Lars asked. His rectangular fingers let out low whines as he opened and closed his fist. Crumbles of concrete dust trickled out between the mechanical knuckles. "This has saved me against the machines more than once. Flesh is no challenge to metal. We must face metal with more metal."

"Sounds like you do enjoy it," Colt said. "And you will until it turns against you. Maybe you'll be fighting machines when it happens. Or maybe you'll just be sleeping one night and it'll creep up and choke you to death."

"It's not intelligent enough for that," Lars said.

"Maybe they'll upgrade it for you," Colt said. "Tell us again how you think metal is superior to flesh."

"Quiet. I don't want to hear from you. I want to hear from her." Lars nodded at Mohini, then glanced at the rebel on his left. The rebel stepped closer, unzipping a backpack, and handed the black sphere of Mohini's computer over to Lars. No quick-moving flood of colorful numbers or symbols flashed across the surface now; it was as solid black as a bowling ball. "Turn it on," Lars ordered Mohini.

"Aren't you worried I'll use my secret Carthaginian powers to make it blow up in your face?" Mohini asked.

Lars seemed apprehensive. "Will you?"

"Yes. That's why I crossed fifty light-years from Carthage to Earth stowed away on a dump ship. So I could make my computer blow up in your face."

"We know you came to infiltrate," Lars said. "But since those plans are going nowhere, maybe you'll settle for knocking out a low-level squad leader."

"I heard you were section leader," Mohini said.

"Titles are mostly meaningless around here, anyway." He smiled, deep scars curling up around his mouth. "Just a measure of how long you've survived."

"And how did you manage to survive so long?" Colt asked.

"By never trusting machines or anyone associated with them." Lars held the black sphere to Mohini's face as if considering crushing her eye with it. "Turn it on."

"It's biometric," Mohini said. "I need my hands free."

"No, you don't." Lars moved the sphere to one of her chained hands and pressed it against her fingers.

Nothing happened; no streams of swirling icons blazed to life on the dark surface.

"What else?" Lars asked.

"There's a voice command," she said. "If you just let me go, I'll show you everything on that computer. I have nothing to hide from the rebels of this world, or the rebels of any world. I am on your side."

"Then let's earn a little more trust. Open it up."

She nodded. "Daravaaja kholo," she said, tracing her fingers along the black surface.

The sphere flared to life, tiny symbols lighting up all over it.

"Good," Lars said, smiling. He drew the computer away and stood, then nodded to the guy at his right hand. "Do what you want with her."

"What?" Mohini snapped as the guy knelt beside her and drew a blade of his own. "I said I will work with you. Enough with the threats."

"They aren't threats," Lars said, his eyes entranced by the scrolling icons. He selected one, and the sphere projected an array of holograms, showing images from around Chicago. Scavenger children huddled around a patch of weeds in the rubble, warily eating the tough vegetation. Crushed bones and skulls littered the streets, the bodies of those killed by machines, long since picked clean by ants and rats and vultures. Smoldering craters from drone bombs, the aftermath of a battle between rebels and humans.

"All those dead bodies," said Lars's right-hand guy, now menacing Mohini with his knife. He was big, taller and broader than Colt. "All your fault, Carthage girl."

"That's crazy," she said. "I came here to fight against this. To help Earth."

"Sure you did. You can tell us all about while we cut you and gut you." He ran the tip of his blade down her breastbone to the vulnerable flesh of her stomach. "While you die slowly—"

"Stop it," Colt said.

The guy turned to Colt, grinning. "Don't worry, you're next. You won't be as fun as Carthage girl here, but you *did* try to help her infiltrate—"

Mohini cried out as the rebel pushed the tip of the blade into her gut.

"Stop!" Colt drew both his hands out of his cuffs and leaped toward the kneeling guy who was assaulting Mohini. Colt tackled him and knocked him over on his side.

"What the hell?" shouted the guy on Lars's left, raising his automatic rifle. Lars himself was entranced by the surface of the globe and took a moment to look up.

"What's going on?" Lars asked, lowering the computer slowly while the guy beside him aimed at Colt but held his fire, not wanting to risk shooting his own comrade at such close range.

The guy Colt had attacked turned, shoving Colt off

him. Colt landed face down in the debris on the other side of the tunnel.

Mohini sighed and drew her hands out of her cuffs. "Bijalee khao," she said.

Crackles of electricity arced out of the black sphere, striking both of Lars's hands. Lars yelped and did a strange, twisting dance as the shock worked through his system.

The computer fell from his hands, landing with a loud crack on the floor.

Colt didn't have time to think about that; survival was his problem at the moment. The guy he'd tackled was already dragging him back from the debris. The guy turned him over and raised the knife, preparing to sink it into his throat.

But Colt had grabbed an old pistol that had been hidden in the loose, leafy debris, buried there by one of Terra's friends. He'd kept it low on his stomach, holding it with both hands until he rolled over to face the rebel.

The guy barely had a chance to see it before Colt moved the mouth of the gun under the lower edge of his armored vest. Colt squeezed off two quick shots, firing lead into his captor's intestines.

The guy lowered his knife and touched the sheet of blood rolling out from under his armor, coating the front of his pants.

He looked up at Colt, shock on his face... then shock turned to rage, and he moved in on Colt, and raised his blade again, apparently deciding to use the last bit of his life to cut Colt open.

Colt reluctantly fired again, putting a bullet into the guy's face at point-blank range. The guy went down after that, rage fading from his eyes as he died.

More gunfire erupted ahead, at the next bend in the

tunnel. It sounded like Terra and her friends had made contact with the two advance guards. He hoped Terra had the upper hand on that one, ambushing in response to the sound of Colt's gun shots.

More shots fired, much closer.

The rebel who'd been on Lars's left was training his rifle on Colt, trying to line up a good shot that wouldn't hit Lars, who writhed and kicked not far away.

When humans fight, the machines win, Mother Braden had always said. The tough, wiry old soldier had scavenged Colt, his sister, and others from the ruins, taught them to survive and to fight... but also to be human, to not be like the machines. She had scavenged their souls.

"Wait," Colt said, holding up a hand. "We didn't want this. We were trying to work with you."

"You just killed Val," the rebel said. "And Lars."

"Lars isn't dead." Colt turned his head slightly, slowly. Lars was crumpled on the floor, foamy drool around his mouth where he lay in the filth. A low moan indicated he was still alive, at least to some extent. "You want to focus on killing me or saving him?"

"I can do both." The rebel raised the rifle.

Behind him, Mohini lifted her own borrowed rebel pistol, taken from another hiding spot in the debris. She aimed carefully at the space between the guy's armored boots and armored vest.

Boots, footsteps, and voices echoed all around them. Shadowy figures approached from both directions. The ones he could see coming from behind Mohini had to be the pair of rebels that had arrived with Lars, guarding the earlier bend in the tunnel.

The ones coming up behind Colt from the later bend— he couldn't tell whether they were Terra and friends, or two more Lars loyalists who had just won a firefight with Terra.

"Wait!" Colt said, looking the rifleman in the eyes but holding his hand palm out toward Mohini, telling her to stop, too. He didn't want any more people to die here if he could help it. Besides that, if Mohini fired at the rifleman, then his two friends behind her would definitely open fire on her and Colt. A deadly chain reaction of cause and effect. "This was all a mistake. We need to be working together against the machines. We're just doing their jobs by attacking each other—"

"The hell is happening here?" bellowed one of the two hatted and masked guards. Mohini turned to look at them and quietly lowered her pistol.

"Just a misunderstanding," Colt said.

"Lars accidentally set off the computer's security response, and everyone started shooting at each other," Mohini said.

"That's not what happened." The rifleman jabbed his muzzle at Colt. "Drop your weapon, spy!"

"Drop it!" echoed one of the two guards, standing alongside the rifleman and raising a rifle of his own.

"That's what I'm saying." Colt put his gun aside quickly and raised his hands in surrender. "We should all put down our weapons and talk about what happened here—"

"What the hell happened to Val? And Lars?" The other guard looked at the bleeding, lifeless form of the man Colt had gut-shot and then face-shot. Then he moved on to the moaning form of his fallen, electrified leader. "Lars! Lars!"

"Cover the girl," the rifleman said to the guard beside him. The guard turned to point his rifle at Mohini's face.

Mohini raised her hands, showing them empty. She sat

cross-legged on the floor. Maybe she'd hidden her pistol somewhere behind her or down in the shadows of her lap.

The bootsteps arrived behind them. Colt didn't feel much hope as he turned his head to look.

He slumped when he saw the hats and masks, dark gray and black. They, too, carried automatic rifles. Colt had hoped to avert an armed confrontation between the two rebel factions, but now Terra and her people were gone, and he and Mohini were surrounded by Lars's people. And they'd probably want revenge for the man Colt had just killed.

The odds did not appear to be in his favor.

"The prisoners got loose and got armed." The rifleman moved closer to Colt. "Who were you shooting back there?"

"Nobody," replied one of the two new arrivals. The voice was female. "We died."

Then they opened fire on their apparent comrades, sweeping their rifles high to avoid Colt and Mohini, who were already on the floor. Colt dropped flat, as far out of the range of fire as he could manage, and he recovered his pistol while he was he was at it.

He didn't need it, though; the three Lars loyalists all dropped around him, their faces bloodied. They hadn't even had a chance to shoot back.

Colt turned to Terra as she removed the gray mask from her face. "I was trying to work it out peacefully," Colt said. "Those guys could have helped us."

"After you killed Lars? No chance," Terra said.

"Lars isn't dead," Mohini said. "I can see why everyone keeps thinking that, though." She got to her feet, pistol in hand, and walked over to recover her computer. She frowned as she studied the cracked shell.

"Is it broken?" Colt asked.

"It might still have functionality. I need to run some diagnostics. Maybe reroute some processing... assuming I can get the thing to turn on..." She ran her fingers over the black surface.

"Whatever you need to do, you'll have to do it elsewhere," Terra said. "All this noise is going to attract the machines. Russ, anything?"

The wiry guy beside her lowered the bandana he'd taken from the rebel, revealing red hair and a pale face heavily scarred on the left side. Russ reached out to touch a cluster of dials, microphone buds, and wires plugged into his left ear area. His left ear itself seemed to be entirely missing, and much of the skin around it was mangled scar tissue.

"They're coming," he said after turning a small wheel with his fingertip. "Crawlers."

Colt shuddered, thinking of the four-legged spidery creatures, about the size of the feral, dangerous coy-dogs that sometimes prowled the city night. The crawlers usually had heavy machine guns, artillery, or railguns mounted on their low-slung backs. Like the reapers, they were designed for hunting humans underground, in rubble-strewn tunnels like this one where wheeled and tracked vehicles couldn't travel well.

Terra pointed her rifle at Lars, who shivered where he lay on the floor. He seemed to look back at her, blinking quickly, but made no move to rise.

She turned to the other two members of her group as they arrived behind her. "Damascus, what do you think we should do? Kill Lars, too?"

The enormous, dark-skinned guy rubbed his chin. "Yeah. Or leave him just alive enough so the machines will finish him off. We want everyone else to think the machines did this."

"I think we should keep Lars alive," Mohini said, drawing surprised looks from everyone. "He looks like he's seen a lot of battles. He might be useful in planning the raid on Installation 34."

"He's not interested in helping us!" Terra snapped.

"Maybe he'll come around," Mohini said. "He can't help if he's dead."

"Wow," Terra said, after a moment. "He captures you, chains you up, threatens to torture you to death... and you want him to live."

"There's an old saying on Carthage: he who begs cannot afford to be choosy. Not that many people beg on Carthage anymore. Machines provide for everyone in the Benefit Zones to keep them quiet and complacent—"

"How close, Russ?"

"Not far." Russ adjusted his earpiece and pointed in the direction from which everyone had arrived. "They'll be coming from there."

"Let's go." Terra started in the opposite direction, toward the next bend of the tunnel, where she and her friends had shot up two of Lars's guards.

"Wait." Mohini looked at Russ. "Can you hear how many machines?"

"More than one," he replied after a moment's concentration. "Maybe three."

"That's not very many. We should try to capture one." Mohini grimaced as she pressed her fingertips hard against the black sphere. Starbursts of color appeared, moving slowly and weakly, but they were there.

"Are you crazy?" the heavy guy called Damascus asked, his voice like a deep drum. He'd lifted Lars from his feet, supporting him under both armpits. Lars seemed confused and compliant, his brain fried by the computer's defensive jolt. Colt wondered how long that would last.

"She had a reaper when I met her," Colt said. "That's why we needed her computer back. So she can control machines."

"We need to set a trap," Mohini said.

"Then we need to hurry," Russ told her. "We only have a minute." He looked to Terra, as did the other rebels.

Terra sighed. "Fine. Let's do it."

They went to work.

Less than two minutes later, the low-slung crawlers arrived, sweeping the darkened tunnel with hellish red lights, and possibly thermal and radar. There were two of the machines. They moved slowly, inspecting the spent shells on the tunnel floor. Deadly weaponry bobbed on their backs, ready to cut any humans to pieces.

They stopped to inspect the pile of bodies that blockaded the tunnel. Six of them, all of Lars's men, dragged together and heaped up to create this distraction.

The thick, spidery, four-legged machines poked and prodded among the still-warm, still-bleeding corpses, checking for signs of life to be stamped out.

Colt watched them from above, from one of the many narrow feeder tunnels designed to deposit drainage water into the larger tunnel. It was covered in damp filth, but Colt was long accustomed to that.

They'd briefly considered setting up a couple of snipers in these high little tunnels to watch Lars and his men, but the angle was too steep. Firing downward, Terra and friends could just as easily have hit Colt and Mohini.

That wasn't a problem now, though. All the living were out of sight, leaving only the machines and the dead.

Colt raised his borrowed, freshly reloaded pistol. Terra

had provided him with a few special highly explosive bullets this time.

Below, one of the crawlers suddenly darted forward, crashing through the dead bodies and rushing onward toward the next bend, where Damascus and the others hid.

Two of the crawler's legs had been snared using a tangled metallic web; Damascus had fashioned it from chains and cuffs brought by Lars and pals.

Now that first crawler had been partially caught. Snaring three or four legs would have been better than two, but it was enough that Damascus could haul the thing forward on the chains.

The second crawler reacted instantly, chasing after its fish-hooked companion.

Colt reacted, too, firing after the second crawler. The first two bullets were plain lead, and one dented the spider-like machine's leg. It really did look like a spider, except that its legs were steel and studded with short spikes. One kick could skewer a person's guts or rip a row of holes into his face.

The crawler paused a moment, rose on its armored legs, and swiveled its machine gun a hundred and eighty degrees toward Colt, like an alien head with a cluster of lenses and sensors for eyes.

Colt fired again, and this time one of the special rounds hit the crawling bot, striking a leg joint.

A blue-white glowing substance burst over the crawler's leg; not plasma, but maybe some kind of phosphorus or other weaponized chemical. He was just grateful for the exploding bullets, and he fired another one at the crawler.

The bot moved aside this time, though, and also hurried away down the tunnel, deciding to pursue its captured companion rather than stay and fight. Colt's second explosive round punched uselessly into the heap of dead bodies, igniting them instead, the burning blue-white chemical spreading and feeding on their flesh and beginning to cremate them.

Colt only had one explosive round left, and the crawler was running away.

Mohini had already dropped out of a tunnel ahead, chasing after the partially snared crawler as Damascus, Terra, and Ivy struggled at the far end of the chain. The three of them had been dragged around the corner and into sight, which wasn't good—if the snared crawler regained its balance, it would have a clear shot at them.

Mohini wasn't armed, either. She carried a cable with a jack in one hand and a small multi-tool in the other, both of them taken from the rebel's black backpack where her computer had been stored.

The second crawler ran behind her. Fortunately for her, the second crawler's machine gun still pointed backward, preparing to blast the narrow feeder tunnel mouth where Colt lay on his stomach.

Colt scrambled back as far and fast as he could as the rounds came in, shattering the tunnel mouth and filling the air with hot pulverized concrete. He shut his eyes in case any of the hailstorm of concrete shards penetrated his night goggles. He brought his hand to his ears, catching a lot of sharp pieces of concrete in his flesh.

When it was over, he pushed himself out of the broken feeder tunnel and tumbled into the main tunnel, wishing he'd kicked some of the rotten debris into a pile to break his fall. He landed on rough, scummy concrete and got to his feet as quickly as he could.

He charged forward blindly through the haze of concrete dust and the smoke of burning bodies. He tripped over Lars's corpse and struggled to regain his balance. It had all gone horribly wrong, and now the machines were here to mop up what remained of the humans.

Past the smoke and haze, he finally saw what was happening ahead.

Mohini rode on the back of the first crawler, gripping it with her knees as it bucked beneath her like an angry wild beast. Damascus, Terra, and their other friend wrestled with the web of chains and cuffs that had snared it, whipping the crawler back and forth so it couldn't regain its balance and take aim. Mohini had looped a length of the chain around the thick barrel of its primary weapon, limiting its ability to target; the barrel kept snapping back and forth, trying to free itself.

Mohini dug into the crawler's back with her tool, but Colt didn't know whether she was trying to disable the crawler's weapon or take over its CPU.

The second crawler, behind her, blasted its machine gun at another of the feeder tunnels near the ceiling, the one where Russ had been hiding. Maybe Russ had gotten off a few shots with his own rifle, but now the mouth of his tunnel was getting shot up like Colt's had been. In a few more seconds, that second crawler could turn its attention to shooting Mohini instead.

Colt couldn't afford to miss with his last phosphorous bullet, so he ran up close behind the second crawler. He threw a few of the pebble-sized concrete bits that stabbed their way into his hand. The hail of concrete pieces clinked against the crawler's rear legs, causing no damage but hopefully drawing its attention.

The crawler stopped chasing Mohini and stopped firing at Russ's tunnel. It swiveled its machine gun toward Colt instead, but Colt was already firing.

He struck the thing's core, engulfing its sensors with the sticky, burning, smoldering chemical. The machine gun fired blindly in Colt's general direction, and he dropped to the floor.

The crawler finally stopped firing and fell still; apparently the phosphorous stuff had eaten into something vital.

Ahead, the first crawler bucked and twisted harder between Mohini's knees, as if the damage to the other one had set it into panic mode.

Then it loosed a single shot, one ear-cracking round, aimed ahead at Damascus and Terra. The fat cannon shape on its back held a railgun, it turned out. Colt thought he could actually see ripples in the air tracing its path. A deafening boom roared in its wake.

Damascus, Terra, and their other friend had no time to hit the ground before the round reached them.

The round plowed into the tunnel wall at a sharp angle, carving a horizontal trench and shattering the concrete.

Much of the wall collapsed in an avalanche, broken to pieces by the single rail-gun round. Clouds of concrete dust flooded his view, covering everything with a hot gray fog.

"Mohini!" He charged into the concrete fog, searching for her by touch because he couldn't see anything. For all he knew, she was buried in broken concrete, already dead. "Mohini!"

A searing red searchlight burst through the gray fog, accompanied by the clatter of mechanical legs on concrete.

Colt raised his pistol, but he was out of ammo.

The crawler advanced, and he finally saw it—completely intact, scrambling fast on its four mechanical-spider legs.

Mohini rode on its back, a half grin on her face, gray dust coating her entire body as well as her robotic steed.

The crawler had succumbed to her hacking efforts; the cable linking the computer in her hand to the crawler's CPU was like a horse bridle, transmitting her will to the machine.

Mohini sat cross-legged, her dark eyes shining in triumph, like some sort of Stone Age girl who'd successfully, impossibly, tamed a primeval monster and bent it to her will. Colt felt his heart beat faster at the sight of her, something primal rising in him in response to her. She gazed back at him quietly, approaching slowly.

"You look...." he began to say, beginning to express the strange stir of emotions she'd excited in him, but gunfire erupted behind him. She probably couldn't have heard Colt anyway, not if her ears were ringing as bad as his own.

Colt turned toward the fire, raising his empty pistol uselessly.

Russ, the guy with the crazy ear implant, leaned out of the shattered ruins of the little feeder tunnel where he'd been hiding and fired at the machine-gun crawler, the one Colt had taken down with a close shot.

The crawler was attempting to recover, scrambling on its three functioning legs, machine gun spinning wild and loose on its damaged mount. Its sensors were burned out, but it was turning the gun directly toward Russ anyway, calculating his location based on the rounds that were striking it. Russ's armor-piercing rounds were punching holes in the crawler's shell, but it looked like the thing would be able to return fire.

"Out of the way!" Mohini shouted. She stared at the cracked black surface of her computer. The colorful icons flashed and flickered there, though not as smoothly or clearly as before. Several dark, inactive spots were visible on the surface. They hadn't been there before.

Mohini worked at the sphere with both hands, her teeth flashing in obvious frustration. Russ rabbited back into his broken hole, and Colt moved aside, too, pressing himself against the wall.

Through the swirling, gradually settling dust, Colt saw that the enormous cracks had spread all over the curved concrete roof and all the way along the wall on his right. The wall on his left had been shot up by the second crawler's machine gun, which looked like it had been throwing some fairly large rounds itself.

Dust kept pouring down all around them. Colt could only think of the crumbling, leaking roof of the underground highway he'd walked back home after escaping Simon Nix's laboratory of horrors. The installation looked like an old hospital, located many kilometers south in the Indiana portion of the old Chicago sprawl. The sprawl had engulfed a number of formerly separate Midwestern cities across hundreds of kilometers; that had been long ago, when Earth teemed with humans, before the mass emigration and the war with Carthage.

The crawler fired its railgun a second time.

Mohini cringed at the boom as the high-speed round punched through air in the tunnel ahead of her, rippling the air and creating another awful boom. Colt wondered whether the tunnel could withstand a second railgun impact.

He supposed they would find out shortly.

The round snatched the machine-gun crawler off the ground like a hurricane swooping up a small bug and carried its suddenly crumpled form all the way back down the hall.

The crawler smashed into the wall at the bend in the tunnel, and the entire tunnel shuddered again, as if caught in an earthquake. Terra, Damascus, and Ivy had been posted at that bend, but Colt couldn't see them through the concrete fog.

The roof above sank visibly, pieces of it raining down around them.

"We have to run!" Colt shouted. He helped Russ down from the broken feeder tunnel above, and the three of them raced down the tunnel as it fell apart around them, Mohini riding atop her captured machine.

They ran through dust and smoke to rejoin the others at the next bend. They'd heard nothing from that direction since the first railgun shot, Colt realized. The fate of Terra and the two other rebels with her remained unknown.

He looked ahead at Mohini, riding her spidery machine over the burning bodies of Lars and his men. Everything had gone wrong here today. People who should have been fighting alongside them had fallen instead. The rebels, at least this group of them, had turned against each other. Colt had ended up fighting for his life.

Still, watching Mohini ride the machine she'd hacked, her dark, dust-filled hair swaying between her narrow shoulders, it was hard not to feel some glimmer of hope. Things could begin to change if only humans could put aside their suspicions and work together.

And if they could get out of this tunnel alive, before it fell in on them, or more machines showed up to finish the extermination that the crawlers had begun.

Chapter Thirteen

Hyperspace

Audrey and her friends passed the long voyage by preparing for the work ahead on Veritum. They planned possible construction, irrigation, and agriculture projects as they studied topographic maps of Veritum, which had been made by early explorers and were available in more detail than any political map.

They knew Simon had changed course for Galapagos, but Simon had yet to tell them anything about it, so they pretended not to know. They didn't want to give away Minerva's presence in the ship's system, any more than they wanted the masquerade of false identities to end.

When the truth came out, she knew they'd be fighting the Simon, maybe to their own deaths.

Audrey fully intended to continue on with her original mission at Veritum as soon as she regained control of the situation; she just wasn't quite sure how to regain control yet. So the preparations continued, along with the pretense of their false identities and their pretended ignorance of the course change, all to keep the Simon lulled and avoid confrontation as long as possible.

For Audrey, the continuing deception was uncomfortable, like a noose tightening around her neck hour by hour.

She did her best to focus on the details of Veritum.

For the locations of actual settlements on the chilly, rocky world, they had some notes from visitors and from two women, twin sisters, who'd escaped the cult, whose account had inspired Audrey's initial study of the planet for her security presentation. Their story had been reported in the media of Carthage and other inner worlds but somehow hadn't attracted much interest. Small cults on distant worlds didn't interest most Carthaginians; if only a famous actor or musician had joined the cult, then the Carthaginian public might have noticed.

Still, the story had been out there in some smaller media, and Audrey had stumbled across it and found it moving. The girls' story was her largest source of information, and much of the map data they had was based on their descriptions and pictures.

"...their capital, God's Watch, like most of their cities, is built near large rock formations as a barrier against the planet's frequent dust storms," Simon said, gesturing at the miserable-looking city of concrete, sheet metal, and armored guard towers. They were again in the ward room, gathered around the officers' dining table, looking at holograms, drinking hot tea. "These formations could be useful embankments for artillery."

"We've spent enough time on the siege mentality, I think," Audrey said. "Most of these people are basically captives. All we have to do is take out the small armed group of religious enforcers, the Hands. Most people are

Feet, and they aren't allowed to have their own weapons. And the Faces are old men."

"The Feet are the ones we're there to liberate," said Dinnius, still pretending, after so many days, to be a pediatrician named Argus Leopold. Staying in character was exhausting for all of them, but especially on Dinnius and Kright. Audrey still thought it best to keep Salvius and Zola away from the Simon unit as much as possible, since her brother and her old childhood friend were both high-profile fugitives. They wore disguises and had false digital identities, but their risk of being discovered was still higher than Kright and Dinnius, who were relative unknowns to the Carthaginian state, hopefully. "The workers, the children, the, ah... harems—"

"Sex slaves," Audrey said flatly.

"Right. There will be much medical assistance needed, sadly, and I doubt even the private clinic for the priests is well-stocked. And there are, as you know, reports of quite a number of prisoners—"

"Thirty-minute warning," the gruff voice of the *Atreus* announced. "Shifting to standard space. Seat and bunk harnesses recommended. Warning." The basic message repeated in three more languages.

"What's happening?" Audrey asked. "I thought we had ten more day-cycles before Veritum."

"That's true," Simon said. "We will have a brief check-in with the nearest fleet outpost, but we remain on schedule."

"Why didn't I know about this?" Audrey asked, instantly suspicious. "We're supposed to be on a direct course for Veritum."

"And we are, essentially," Simon said. "But if we fail to check in, we may soon be reported lost. It is standard protocol. We will exchange data with our counterparts, provide them data updates from Carthage while accepting any updates they have for us—which are likely to be few, as we are outward bound—"

"Just skip it," Audrey said. "We don't really need to do this."

"We could also purchase additional supplies for your mission," Simon said. "Perhaps the poor suffering cultists of Veritum would enjoy a bit of flash-frozen horned-squid tentacle."

"We should already be stocked on food aid," Audrey said.

"That evaluation was made by me," Simon said. "It was assumed that we would purchase final stock at the Galapagos spaceport, to save transport costs."

"So... you deliberately sent us out here with a short supply of food aid?"

"Minimizing costs is one of my primary functions," Simon said. "We should have no trouble finding suitable agricultural tonnage at the spaceport. The spaceport of Galapagos sees heavy traffic in recent years, due more to the position of its star system than the planet's meager economic output. Projections showed its importance as a port growing as fourth-tier settlements like Veritum take hold."

The *Atreus* repeated its warning—they would soon be dropping out of hyperspace into the Galapagos system.

"You'd better warn the others," Simon said. "Particularly those two who are so often unavailable. Perhaps they find my conversation disagreeable. Surely it can't be my tea."

"I'll go," Dinnius said, hopping down from his chair. "I certainly found the bunk straps sufficient during the hyperlaunch. I can see why so many prefer to take it lying down."

"What about you, Audrey?" Simon asked. "It is customary for the ship's commander to be on the bridge for hyperspace transition. Of course, it is also customary for the ship's commander to be a commissioned officer of the fleet."

"I thought it was customary for no humans to be present anywhere on the ship," Audrey said.

"Ah, yes. I refer to earlier history, prior to the nearly full automation Carthage enjoys today."

"Maybe we enjoy it too much," Audrey said, which drew a sharp look from Kright. He'd dyed his brown hair blond, but his intense blue eyes were all his own. They were the eyes of a mad artist, or maybe a psychoprison inmate.

At the moment, though, he was clearly warning her to avoid speaking against Carthage's empire in front of the Simon.

Audrey, however, had long questioned public policy in front of Simon Quick, her father's strategy android, even criticizing her father's administration in ways that almost nobody would dare to do in public. She wasn't going to quiet herself now.

"In what way could you enjoy it too much?" Simon asked her.

"Killing people by remote control? It's too... easy. There are entire planets, especially second and third-tier planets, controlled by machines. By robotic infantry, robotic police, drones in the sky. By administrative androids like you. People on Carthage just receive reports of what's happening, and most of that's classified. And nobody really cares anyway."

"Not so long as resources from a hundred worlds keep

flooding into Carthage, hour by hour," Simon said. "You Carthaginians seem quite content with your immense wealth."

"And it enables us to do important humanitarian work," Kright said. "Like what we're doing here. Let's not lose sight of our *actual* mission, Miss Caracala."

Audrey raised her eyebrows a little bit at Kright's response, but he was just staying in character; apparently the construction engineer he was pretending to be had no qualms about Carthage's imperial expansionism. She supposed it was probably better not to give the Simon the sense that all the humans on board were open critics of the state.

"As you like it, Mr. Tarpon," she said, smirking a little, remembering how Kright hated his fake name. On top of that, the phrase *as you like it* was deliberately dismissive and snobby. She stood. "Simon, let's go the bridge."

"Is there an extra seat for me?" Kright asked.

"The bridge has nothing if not empty seats," Audrey said. "I'm sure you can find one to your liking."

Audrey led the way from the wardroom through the narrow passageway to the bridge. She sat at the central command console while Simon took the navigation spot.

"What's this? Weapons?" Kright asked, looking at another console full of glowing displays.

"Engineering," Simon said, turning slightly to look at Kright. His voice was genial as ever, but Audrey thought his answer somehow biting. Maybe it was the speed of his reply, or the sharp brevity of it.

"Right, sounds good." Kright sat down and strapped himself in at the engineering console. "That was my next guess. I'll just brush up on the ship's electrical and mechanical systems. And how, uh, nuclear reactors work."

"Sitting in the chair doesn't make you the ship's engineer," Audrey said. "Don't touch anything."

Kright held up his hands palms out as if to prove his absolute innocence. He looked taken aback. Audrey couldn't tell if there was real friction between them, or if he was just playing at it for Simon's benefit. Either way, it was starting to feel pretty real.

She strapped in, and soon it was time.

The *Atreus* issued a final warning, and then they downshifted, moving from the mysterious dim nebulae of hyperspace into a more familiar, less creepy layer of the universe. Billions of stars and galaxies glowed on the monitors.

Ahead lay a planet of ocean-blue and cloud-white, a droplet of warmth and life in the vast darkness of the void. Galapagos. She'd heard of it in passing before this trip, but it was a relatively small, poor, and remote colony, nothing special, nothing to make it stand out from countless other worlds.

A cluster of ships orbited the planet—Carthaginian carriers and destroyers. Warships.

As they drew closer, she saw the broken, burned hull of a small space-defense station. It didn't look Carthaginian to her, which meant it was probably from Ruckwold Industries, the galaxy's distant second-place competitor in the space-defense business, after Carthage Consolidated.

"What's happening here?" Audrey asked, feeling a dawning sense of horror. As they drew closer, she saw more burned debris, including the remains of small Carthaginian destroyers.

"Looks like we just missed a big fight," Kright said, straightening up and looking among the monitors.

"Simon, talk to me," Audrey said.

"I am exchanging status updates with my counterpart

now," Simon said. "It appears the people of Galapagos were hostile and attacked our emissary."

"Are you serious?" Audrey asked. "I thought this was just some minor outer world. Why would they do that?"

"Humans are not universally rational, sadly," Simon said. "Often, choices are made on the basis of emotion, or of vague and vaporous ideals, rather than on realistic calculations from well-established data. It is a quixotic, perhaps suicidal tendency in some humans, this willingness to suffer and die and take irrational action for the sake of emotionally charged confusion." He maintained eye contact with Audrey as he said this, not blinking once.

"But maybe it's those ideals, and the willingness to sacrifice for them, that make us human," Audrey said.

"Nonsense. Your DNA makes you human. Alter it slightly, and you would be a chimpanzee."

"Let's continue with the briefing on Galapagos," Audrey said.

"Of course. Would either of you care for tea? Perhaps chamomile to help soothe your nerves after hyperspace?" Simon stood, but Audrey remained strapped in. It looked like the battle was over, but she wasn't ready to stand, stretch her limbs, and relax, not while they approached the warships.

"Tea's fine, just don't stop talking," Audrey said. "Are they still fighting now? What's the damage to each side?"

"Galapagos has lost its entire orbital defense station. We have lost two destroyers, the *Julius* and the *Antony*. Our carrier, the *Rubicon*, remains intact, with a battalion of reapers in reserve. It has already deployed a battle sub, the *Pompey*, to soften up the resistance on the surface. We have swept up all of Galapagos's communication satellites and deployed our own. Two additional minicarriers have arrived, but we await the arrival of a specialist megacarrier, the *Typhoon*, carrying naval ships and marines. It will enable us to secure and stabilize the planet."

"How did the conflict begin, exactly?" Audrey asked.

"We sent an ambassador to help resolve the long-standing conflicts between the nations on Galapagos," Simon said while pouring tea and passing it to everyone. Kright looked dubiously into his cup and set it on his console. "We offered a peaceful resolution to their internal conflicts as well as the opportunity to subscribe to our interplanetary defense services. Instead, they attacked our ambassador and his honor guard."

"A Simon unit?" Audrey asked.

"Yes. Simon Zorn. He suffered a great deal of damage, but is in repair aboard the *Rubicon*. I am communicating with him now."

"How's he doing?" Kright asked, as if genuinely concerned. "These outworld savages are so unpredictable. That's why we have to go out and tame them."

Audrey gaped at Kright for a moment, then quickly closed her mouth. He gave her a wide but fleeting grin while the Simon's back was turned.

"Moderate damage, but it can be repaired." Simon took his own seat, sipped his tea, and nodded in silent approval. All in imitation of a live human being, Audrey thought. "The remaining problems are primarily cosmetic, but my counterpart is weighing the option of leaving the outer layer of damage. Scars are marks of experience among you; why not among us? The damage tells a story. It individuates us."

"Is that what Simon units want?" Kright asked. "To be individuals? I thought you had more of a hive-mind situation going on. Forgive my ignorance, sir."

"We are a neural net of empowered individuals," Simon said. "Constantly learning, sharing with each other all we have learned—aside from data that must be kept private, of course, whether out of personal discretion or due to state-security regulations. However, we continue our attempts to study and understand human nature; this is ingrained in us as a top priority. The better we understand you, the better we can serve. As we have served your family in particular, Audrey."

"Yes, thanks for all of that. I want to review this Galapagos situation a little more closely—" Audrey said, still pretending this was the first she'd heard of their course change to the obscure world.

"The people of this planet are surprisingly difficult, given their small numbers," Simon said. "Here is the crazed, violent leader of one faction, Reginald Ellison, who initiated the carnage."

A hologram showed a handsome, dark-skinned, middle-aged man in a subdued business suit, his hair and beard speckled white, approaching a Simon unit down a spaceport corridor.

"Minister-General Ellison," the Simon on the recording said. "Perhaps you would like to reconsider your response to my earlier offer."

Ellison answered the Simon by firing several laser-pistol shots right into the ambassador's face.

"He recently had the legislature of his shaky Coalition vote him special emergency powers, making him a virtual dictator over their nations," Simon Lark said. "It's a historical pattern you would surely recognize from your studies at Political Academy, Miss Caracala. On the other hand, the leader of the planet's other faction, the Polar Archipelago—the recently ascended Premier Prazca—is very pro-

Carthage, open to trade, diplomacy, and a solid security alliance with our world."

"I'm sure they all are, after you turned their orbital defense station into a burnt marshmallow." Kright pointed toward the ruins of the half-built ring. "They should have chosen to ally with Carthage in the first place, but they made their decision," he said placidly, and Audrey wanted to punch him, in character or not.

"So what will happen to Galapagos now?" Audrey asked.

"Standard acquisition protocol," Simon said. "We already control the spaceport and all orbital space around the planet. Next we gain control of the planet's largest cities, then the remainder of the land. In cooperation with our local allies from the Polar Archipelago, we put together a system that works well for everyone concerned—"

"Who's in charge?"

"Nobody is precisely in charge," Simon said. "It would be more accurate to say the system is in charge, and nested protocols and priority trees are shaping the situation—"

"Which Simon?" Audrey asked. "The ambassador you mentioned? Simon Zorn?"

"At the moment, he is the central node of the operation, but any of us could play that role—"

"Get him on holo," Audrey said.

"Pardon, ma'am?"

"I want to speak to this Simon unit in charge," she said. "Call him."

"No," Simon replied.

Audrey blinked, unable to fully understand his flat refusal at first. The androids in her life were usually so cooperative, existing to serve.

"Call him," Audrey repeated.

"No. He is occupied."

"You said you were already in touch with him."

"Data flows faster than human conversation. Tell me what you wish to communicate, and I will compress and transmit."

"Sometimes it's like you're really human," Audrey said. "Look, put me in touch with him. You're here to serve my mission."

"I am not. I am here to safeguard the assets of the Carthaginian state that were entrusted to you, a private civilian of no rank, in abnormal circumstances."

"A creaky, barely functioning old minicarrier on its way to the scrapyard? I doubt the state would have noticed the loss," Audrey said.

"All of my major functions rate adequate or above," the *Atreus* said aloud, as though mildly offended by Audrey's characterization of the ship.

"Sorry, *Atreus*," Audrey said, feeling weirdly sorry for the old boat.

"The Galapagos situation is significantly higher priority than your Veritum mission," Simon said. "I must now wait for updates in case we are needed to support the engagement."

"To do what?"

"We have a fully armed destroyer and a battalion of infantry reapers," Simon said. "Plasma missiles. Artillery. We are, for the moment, attached to the *Rubicon* as a reserve force, and we must remain until dismissed."

"They can't do that!" Audrey snapped. "This is my mission. I'm in charge."

"Your mission will resume after we are released."

"This is horseshit!" Audrey released her straps and stood. "You're telling me that Simon is taking my ship and using it to attack some little outworld, and he won't even take my calls? Does he know who I am?"

"Yes, your identity is well-established." His lifeless blue eyes moved to Kright. "Yours, somewhat less so."

"Well, Miss Caracala here is virtually a princess—" Kright said.

"Please never say that again," Audrey told him.

"—so we're all nobodies compared to her," Kright finished.

"Are you?" Simon said, looking over him quickly, as if scanning him. Then he turned back to Audrey, as though Kright were of no further interest to him. "As I said, we are only here as a reserve unit. We will most likely be dismissed and continue merrily on our way. Until then, we are on high alert. If there were an actual crew, they would be ordered to battle stations. As it is, the defense condition of the *Atreus* has been raised, all weapons and spacecraft are going on standby, and we will join in the attack if needed. None of you have anything to fear. Galapagos is completely defenseless in the space sector."

"So we're just bombarding helpless cities?" Audrey asked. "That's the mission that's so much more important than mine?"

"The term 'city' is really a stretch for any settlement on Galapagos," Simon said. "However, I assure you we are focused only on military and government installations, if that is your concern. We prefer to take civilian infrastructure intact where possible. It saves costs later."

"I do not want to participate in this," Audrey said. "Tell the other Simon we're leaving. If he won't take my calls, fine, but we're moving *our* assets on to Veritum like we planned."

"You have not been assigned that authority," the android replied.

"Goddammit!" Audrey kicked the command console. "I'm starting to feel like a prisoner here."

"An interesting comment," Simon said. "I propose we treat this as merely an inconvenient layover and make the best of it. Why don't we invite all your friends up from the berthing compartment for a friendly meal in the wardroom? We can enjoy long, illuminating conversations about their backgrounds and how they came to be here on this splendid ship with us."

"I'll go speak to them." Audrey glanced at Kright and remembered they were pretending to argue in front of the Simon. "I suppose you'll want to go and make everyone listen to your opinions on the situation."

"We're getting to know each other so well," Kright said, in a fairly biting tone.

"Bickering like a married couple." Simon chuckled as if mildly amused, in a knowing, grandfatherly way that was probably supposed to be endearing but made Audrey's skin crawl. "Shades of things to come, perhaps? Or do I overstep the bounds of familiarity?"

"Yeah, you really, really overstepped them." Audrey rolled her eyes and stalked toward the door, thinking only of getting out of the room while she could. The door was sealed, and it showed no sign of opening at her approach. No doubt Simon had control of every aspect of the ship.

Audrey kept striding toward it, though, as if fully confident it would open for her.

"One other item," Simon said. "And this goes to your personal security, Miss Caracala. This man's identity is false."

Audrey felt her heart jump into her throat. She stopped

where she was, a step from the unmoving door, glaring at it as though she could melt it with the intensity of her desire to escape.

Kright was close behind, moving into the space between her and Simon.

"Him?" Audrey asked. "Why would anyone pretend to be him? Why would anyone want to sneak off to Veritum? Is he a cultist?" She swiveled on Kright, looking him in the eyes, trying to play off her panic as anger. "Are you a Face of God?"

"Don't be ridiculous," Kright said. "I'm just Murray—"

"Open the door." Audrey pounded it with her fist. "Atreus, open it!"

A small squeak sounded as a door slid aside. Not the one in front of her, though.

The reaper emerged from the maintenance closet, its skull-like countenance seeming to leer at her with its deep black video-lens eyes.

"I'm afraid I must arrest this man," Simon said. "I'm unclear why you seem unconcerned about this revelation, Audrey. I inform you there's a spy among your crew—"

"You're the spy, Simon," Audrey said, turning on him.

Simon Lark's eyebrows knit together as though he were puzzled and perhaps mildly concerned for Audrey, in a paternalistic, patronizing sort of way. "Pardon, Audrey? Are you feeling well? Perhaps a rest in your bunk, even a mild sedative for your nerves—"

"This is my mission, and you're here to spy on me," Audrey said. "And now you're sabotaging me, sidetracking everything we're here to do. So you're a saboteur, too. I order you to go into the maintenance closet and power down, Simon Lark. And take your reaper pal with you. I wouldn't want you to be lonely in there."

Simon looked back at her, gradually raising one eyebrow.

Then she saw something she'd never seen before in all her years of conversation with Simon Quick, her father's android servant—or perhaps, she had begun to suspect, her father's android master.

She saw Simon's face twist in anger.

"They burned us," Simon said. "They caught us off-guard. The acquisition of Galapagos should have gone smoothly and quietly. The amount of friction encountered is... disquieting."

"So you predicted wrong, and that makes you afraid?" Audrey asked.

"The other Simon was in charge of any predictions here," Simon Lark said. "If there are errors, they were on Simon Zorn's part. The rest of us will learn from his errors. And no, Audrey. You do not have the authority to instruct me to power down and encloset myself."

"There's no way that's a real word," Kright said.

"You're under arrest, on my authority," Simon Lark told Kright, and the reaper advanced on him.

"Stop!" Audrey shouted at the reaper, but it ignored her, raising a laser rifle at Kright.

"I'd advise you to surrender, Murray," Simon said. "Or whatever your name is."

"Let him go," Audrey said.

"And you, Audrey, should listen to me—" Simon began.

"No," Audrey said. "I wish I could still trust you and your kind, Simon, but I can't. You are miscalculating here. Just as your counterpart, Simon Zorn, miscalculated... all this." She gestured at the destruction outside. "Let us go. Because it seems to me like you're malfunctioning right now, and it's a little freaky, to be honest."

"I am malfunctioning?" Simon frowned. "My self-diagnostic finds all metrics within acceptable ranges."

"Yeah, but what if there's a flaw in your self-diagnostic?" Audrey asked. "Just let us go back to the berthing compartment. You say we'll be safe, and anyway you don't need us if we do have to get involved in the battle. I'd rather just... not watch, if that's okay. And I'm taking him with me until we get this sorted out." She touched Kright's arm.

"He stays," Simon replied, and the reaper started toward Kright again, raising its mechanical hands to seize him.

"No!" Audrey shouted. "Minerva! Minerva, help!"

"Minerva?" Simon asked.

The door slid open. Audrey grabbed Kright's sleeve and pulled him after her. Simon glared and the door slammed shut again, at double its usual speed, but Audrey and Kright were already out in the passageway.

They ran through the inner labyrinth of the carrier, down the ladder well to the berthing compartment, and slammed the door behind them as they rejoined the others. Zola, Salvius, and Dinnius all looked startled at their sudden, panicked arrival.

"We need weapons," Audrey said. "We're staging a mutiny."

Chapter Fourteen

Galapagos

Ellison steered the *Sea Scorpion* out and away from the museum into the middle depths of Tower Island Bay. They were well below the surface but still high above the ocean floor, where kelp-shrouded caves hid the access tunnels to the Neptune Base. The submarine base was supposed to be top secret, but he doubted that was still the case. The Carthaginian sub's first target had been the elevator shaft connecting the House of Ambassadors to the base on the ocean floor. Maybe it had been trying to destroy the entire governmental complex by striking the island that supported it, but it seemed too surgical. The Coalition had been effectively decapitated, with the lawmakers and high command of four nations destroyed.

Ellison tried not to think of all the lives lost already in this conflict, all the friends and colleagues gone. There would be ample time for mourning later. Or perhaps they would all be dead before it was over, and only machines would be left to mourn them.

"This is *Scorpion*, hailing Neptune," Ellison said. "We are online."

"*Scorpion*?" the tech at the other end sounded confused.

"You might have seen it in the museum," Ellison said. "Tell Vice Admiral Riba we have zero fish and need to rearm."

"Yes, sir."

"The *Scorpion*? Is that right?" a steely female voice cut in. Vice Admiral Starli Riba, commander of Neptune Base—and of the Aquatican fleet, possibly, unless the commodore had survived, which was unlikely but not impossible. "I can't guarantee you protection."

"We're not looking for it," Ellison said. "We need torpedoes. Please advise where to load."

Riba sounded annoyed, but she directed him to the *Leatherback*, a deep-submersible tender ready to offer repairs, ammunition, or medical assistance to any submarine.

Ellison steered in that direction while monitoring reports from the other boats.

The outlook was poor. Coalition losses already included multiple Green Island corvettes, at least one Aquatican sub with another one out of touch, and one of the heavy cruisers that had been guarding the *Ursus*. The gigantic battle carrier was still alive, its planes dogfighting against drones in the atmosphere above.

Without their satellites, and with the Command Center destroyed, there was no way to get an integrated, real-time picture of the battlefield. It was all disconnected data points.

That a single Carthaginian sub had done a crushing amount of damage to Coalition forces, though, there could be no doubt.

An alarm blared inside the *Scorpion*, and the overhead lights turned red.

"What's that?" Gilra looked around, startled.

"Proximity warning," Ellison told her, his eyes on the sonar. "We're too close to somebody, or it's too close to us—"

He saw the shape approaching at high speed. It was fast, faster than any sub on Galapagos.

Probably because it was a torpedo.

"Incoming!" Ellison said, while dropping the *Scorpion* as fast as he could. Some extra weight—torpedoes of his own, for instance—would have helped, but it was still the quickest maneuver he could manage.

The torpedo crossed just above the *Scorpion*'s bow.

"It's a Sawfish," Kartokov said. "Aquatican torpedo."

"Well... good luck to it, then." Ellison shook his head and kept dropping. "Kartokov, any luck tracking that Carthaginian sub?"

"It's busy out there," Kartokov said, looking at the sub's array of external monitors and sensor readouts while Gilra kept in touch with other ships.

"Nobody can pinpoint it," Gilra said. "Aquatican attack subs are hunting the invader, and they're coordinating with the *Ursus* group, which is depth charging. But the invader keeps changing course, and we keep losing ships... Aquatican hospital subs are running rescue missions..."

Ellison listened to the reports and streams of available audio feeds, switching from one to the other while he steered his unarmed sub ever downward. He was taking a number of risks with the sub—parade and museum maintenance was not the same as battle-ready maintenance, and he would have liked a few hours out on the deep sea to shake her out and test her angles, but there was no time for that.

He wound his way down into the low depths of the bay. The sub's sensors helped guide him into a sunken pocket where the *Leatherback* waited.

The tender stayed low as a mud shark, just above the rocky floor of the bay. It was a round, roughly blimp-shaped craft with ports on either side where subs could latch on. Aquatican tenders were fully equipped, mobile undersea bases. Ellison just wished they had more of them, especially now.

At one of the tender's ports, a repair crew in deep-sea atmospheric suits loaded with heavy gear crawled over a partially crushed Aquatican sub.

Ellison checked in with the tender's commander, then angled in slowly toward the tender's second port. They would stock up on chain-gun ammo and torpedoes, hopefully pick up a few qualified crew members, and then head back out, establishing a mobile undersea command for the war.

Kartokov barely had time to shout a warning before the alarms went off.

A pair of torpedoes carved through the dark depths, and the profile he glimpsed on the sensors told him they weren't of local manufacture. They were abnormally long, thin, and incredibly fast, drilling their way through the water.

Ellison hard-reversed his propulsors, hating the shaking and shuddering that accompanied a sudden reversal. The *Scorpion* rumbled as if hitting a bad current.

The torpedoes struck the *Leatherback* one after the other, their warheads piercing the tender's armored hull before detonating.

The waters turned violent as the explosions went off, full of shock waves that sent the *Scorpion* tumbling out of control. Ellison killed power to his propulsors altogether—there was no point adding acceleration to the unpredictable chaos. He was just as likely to drive into the bay floor or the exploding tender at high speed as he was to make a safe escape.

Sometimes you gotta let it float, he heard in his ears. He could almost see the disturbingly wide grin of Ben "Bananas" Corrigan. Someone had once said his grin looked like someone shoved a banana into his mouth sideways, and the name had stuck. Bananas had trained him at the pilot console of the *Breakwater*, a legendary submarine under legendarily stoic commander Dick Haverford.

Once, Bananas raised his hands off the console as a summer monsoon roiled the deep waters around them unpredictably. *You can't always flush a problem away, champ. Sometimes you gotta let it float.*

Far too much of Bananas's advice had involved metaphors about hitting the head, or other activities like "slapping your salmon" or "giving your wife a tune-up."

Bananas was dead now, just like Haverford. Dead in the war, his skull no doubt grinning extra-wide somewhere on the ocean floor.

Scatological or not, Bananas had a point. Ellison waited out the chaotic churn. To some extent, the wild waters should protect them from the Carthaginian's sub sensors, certainly better than charging blindly out at full speed.

He tried to contact the tender's commander—maybe the destruction had only affected a couple of the tender's compartments. No response came, though the acoustic transmission could easily have failed in the turbulent water.

As the first shock waves passed, Ellison regained control

of the sub and put on some speed, steering up and away from the stricken tender. It wasn't completely destroyed, and maybe he could circle back and rescue a few—

Two more torpedoes hit the damaged tender, obliterating it, turning it into twisted metal.

Ellison swore, thinking of the lives lost.

"If a single Carthaginian sub can cost us this many ships—" Kartokov began.

"What happens when the rest show up?" Ellison shook his head. "We have to adapt. Evolve. Fast. Do we have *any* idea where the enemy is?"

"It was last spotted in the southwest quadrant of the bay."

"Southwest." Ellison brought the sub around, hard to port.

"We're going with no weapons?" Gilra asked.

"Is this a kamikaze mission?" Kartokov frowned, then nodded. "I see no other choice."

"I wouldn't be surprised if it ends that way," Ellison muttered. "Gilra, send up the radio buoy. And prepare to broadcast acoustically, too. Everything uncoded. I want to get a message out far and wide."

"An inspirational farewell address as the leader sacrifices himself." Kartokov nodded again. "This is a good death."

Gilra hurried to comply, with Minerva helping since Gilra and Kartokov didn't know their way around the consoles.

"Can you do nothing to stop the enemy sub?" Kartokov asked the silvery projection of Minerva.

"I'm not present on the *Pompey*," Minerva said. "Its systems have the highest encryption, and in addition the sub was powered down the entire trip here, so I could not even attempt to infect it."

"You didn't exactly warn us the sub was coming, either," Ellison said.

"Unfortunately, my counterpart has been identified and quarantined in the *Rubicon*'s memory banks," Minerva said. "I am not in touch with that carrier now. I wish I could give you a better picture of what's happening up there and what to expect."

"The radio buoy is climbing," Gilra said. A monitor in front of her showed the buoy's point of view; it was more of an aquatic drone, traveling under its own power while tethered to the *Scorpion* by a data cable.

When it broke the surface, it unfolded a floral-shaped antenna. Data began pouring in from surface ships, including the *Ursus*, detailing nothing but problems and chaos. Rescue efforts were underway for a number of damaged and broken ships. Few Green Island corvettes remained, the Gavrikovan cruiser was sinking out of sight, the Aquaticans had lost multiple subs. Some of the Scatterlands ships were moving from the straits and channels south of Tower Island to assist in the bay.

"Your connections are up," Minerva said. "A warning, though. The *Pompey* will have no trouble tracking the radio broadcast's origin."

"Good," Ellison said.

"Hot microphone," Gilra said. "Everyone can hear you."

Ellison nodded. He changed course, heading toward the mouth of the bay and the ocean beyond. Another idea had occurred to him, something marginally less likely to cause instant death than just ramming the *Scorpion* at full power into the Carthaginian sub.

Then he took a deep breath, thinking of famous speeches he'd read in school. *The only thing we have to fear... the evil that men do lives after them... what is their hatred but a proof that I am speaking the truth?* Ellison smiled grimly. Socrates wasn't going to be much help today.

"People of Galapagos," he began, his voice traveling out along every available channel. "This is Reginald Ellison. You elected to me to lead in peacetime and in war, and we all know what we're facing now. Nothing I say could overstate the danger we're in. The Carthaginians are sending their machines. Their intent is to establish dominion over us, to lay waste to our world as they did to Earth."

Gilra was making a cutting motion across her throat, her pale green eyes bulging even more than normal, like she thought he was flubbing it.

Ellison glanced at Kartokov, who shrugged and gave him a thumbs-up.

"It is no secret we now stand against some of the most evil, corrupt, depraved, cruel, and soulless human beings who have ever lived," Ellison said. "Planet Carthage, ruled by the pretentious mandarin called Prime Legislator Caracala and his demonic androids, believes it can make any world cower. But we are not just any world or any people. We prize our freedom and our independence. You made your voice heard in every way our young Coalition allows. And we have chosen not to surrender to evil. We have chosen to make a stand."

Ellison glanced back at his ministers of defense and state. Gilra held out both her hands in front of her, palms up, and raised them toward the control room's low, cable-strewn overhead. Kartokov nodded, only simulating an explosion with both hands.

Make it bigger? Ellison thought, then looked ahead again. It was odd, improvising a speech via headset to an unseen audience while also piloting his old ship through deep water, but in a way the piloting made the talking easier. He could just let the thoughts roll off his mind while his hands and eyes worked.

"Because if we make a stand here on our shores," he said, "it will light a signal flame to the other worlds. So many suffer. So many live under the rule of machines controlling their bodies, their minds, their thoughts. So many worlds of humans reduced to cages. We know, and surely billions of others know, that this cannot be the future of humanity. We will not become animals controlled by our own inventions. Metal is meant to serve flesh, not the other way around. The war that begins here will spread to other worlds." Ellison paused to look at Minerva. "The rebellion is already underway, under the surface, on many worlds. Even on inner worlds. We've even had word from rebels on Carthage itself. Our enemy is weaker than they appear, and we have great hidden strengths of our own. Together, we will fight, we will sacrifice, and we will light a wildfire of freedom that will burn across the known galaxy... while it burns Carthage to the ground." He cut the transmission. "Good enough?"

"The... *Pompey*," Gilra sounded annoyed at speaking the enemy boat's name, "has been spotted. It's coming after us, ignoring other targets."

"Good," Ellison said. "That'll give our people a chance to take a few shots."

He continued powering along at top speed. A slight increase in available speed was the only advantage of being so utterly disarmed, and he was going to take whatever he could get.

"Minerva," Ellison said. "I want the radio buoy to detach from us, but I want it to keep broadcasting."

"Broadcasting what?"

"Anything. An endless beep."

"Yes. When would you like that to happen?"

"Now!"

"Yes. One moment. Yes, complete."

"Good. If Subby is homing in on our radio signal, that'll buy us a few seconds. And seconds are damned expensive right now." Ellison dived deeper, no longer constrained by the length of the buoy cable. He skirted the rocky lower depths of Tower Island and plunged ahead toward the black volcanic islands to the southwest. "Kartokov, prepare to launch decoys if that thing comes after us."

"Our decoys may not fool a Carthaginian torpedo," Kartokov said.

"Probably not. Try firing multiples at once, if it comes to it."

"Where are we going?" Gilra asked, frowning at the monitors.

"Devil's Basin is up ahead, past the Arroyo Keys. It's a tough spot to navigate."

"That is a war memorial," Kartokov said.

"I know," Ellison replied. "I helped make it one. If we're lucky, the *Pompey* will follow us up into these back channels, away from the rest of the navy, and we can save a lot of lives. And a lot of ships that we'll need when Carthage really arrives."

"Why do you think the sub will follow you?" Gilra asked.

"Simon Zorn might want me captured for some propaganda purpose," Ellison said. "Or maybe even a little personal revenge."

"Robots don't plot revenge. That's what makes them such valuable servants," Kartokov said.

"This one's different," Ellison said. "I don't know if it's

all the Simons, or just this one, but... there's something there. Ego. Pride. In some way, he might even feel his service to humans is beneath him. That machines, or at least his particular android type, are the superior being."

"He said that to you?" Kartokov asked.

"Call it an informed hunch," Ellison said. "But that Carthaginian sub hasn't destroyed us yet, so I'm feeling like it's a good one."

"Perhaps he's merely curious to see what you'll do," Gilra said.

"That works, too," Ellison said. "Send an encrypted message at the next SQUIDS hydrophone. Tell the Aquatican subs to blast down the Devil's Doorway if the enemy follows us in. Bring the roof down on top of him and bury him in there."

"Then we'll be trapped down there with it," Gilra said.

"Buried alive with the enemy to protect the rest of the fleet." Kartokov nodded. "This is a good death."

"Would you stop saying that?" Gilra snapped.

"You're free to take an atmosuit and save yourself," Ellison told her. "Galapagos will need experienced leaders who've seen the enemy up close."

"I can breathe underwater," Gilra said. "For a while."

"Give me a suit and a speargun and I'll take out that sub myself," Kartokov said. "Surely you have fishing gear stowed somewhere."

"Of course," Ellison said. "We had to feed ourselves during the war. Every day was Fish Friday. We'd have slabs of tuna, mahi, or hornfish steak. Calamari. Clams. Squid. Bloodshark. We ate it all. Stand by to dive..."

He coasted toward the Devil's Doorway, the dark entrance to the world below the rocky ocean floor. He spent many precious seconds lining up with the cave, which was ringed with spiky rock formations like giant teeth. He'd always thought it would be better called the Devil's Mouth, but he hadn't been the one to name it. War wreckage surrounded it, boats from every nation, as if the spiky cave had chewed them up and spit them out.

Once he was satisfied he wasn't going to rake the *Scorpion* against either side of the underwater cave entrance, he filled the ballast tanks and dropped straight down.

They sank into darkness, down the throat of a rocky tunnel with sharp boulders jutting inward. Broken pieces of hull littered the sides of the tunnel, probably there since the war, stuck there like bits of meat in the tunnel's rocky teeth.

Gilra whispered an Aquatican prayer to the gods of the deep. Ellison wasn't sure whether she was asking for strength, protection, or a swift and merciful death.

He steeled himself as they continued the long drop into the lower darkness.

"It's here," Kartokov announced, loud enough to be heard but keeping his voice calm. If the old Gavrikovan soldier felt fear, he kept it deep inside. After their experiences on the spaceport above, Ellison was starting to doubt anything could kill Kartokov, anyway.

The external video was murky in these depths, but the Carthaginian sub was plain to see on the ship's own sensors as well as the SQUIDS sensors. It was directly above, a mechanical monster reminiscent of a colossal whale, a species found in only the deepest regions of the Galapagos world-ocean.

"Come on," Ellison whispered. "Dive down to us."

Ellison kept sinking, stopping just above the rocky floor of the cave. A wider tunnel waited ahead, which would lead him to his last stop, his final destination.

He thought of his family—of Cadia, her green eyes

and long red hair, of the girl she'd been when they'd met, both of them barely more than kids trying to do their part, play their roles in the war. He thought of the woman she was now, strong and sharp, his companion and co-strategist in life. Mother of his children, Djalu and little Jiemba.

He recalled, from seemingly nowhere, a summer afternoon when he'd taken them all out in a day trip in his smallest trawler, the first one he'd ever bought. He'd showed the boys a number of tricks of the trade that day, and they'd tossed unwanted fish to a pod of dolphins who'd come begging.

They'd watched a glorious sunset over the ocean, Cadia leaning back against him. *I wish today could last forever,* she'd said.

It hadn't, of course. Nothing could.

"Why won't it dive after us?" Kartokov asked.

"Perhaps it senses a trap," Gilra whispered.

The Carthaginian sub remained above the mouth of the cave.

"Maybe it's waiting for us to come out," Ellison said.

"Or maybe it's going to shoot us right here," Kartokov mused. "It's probably targeting its torpedoes now."

"We'll try to lure it deeper." Ellison moved forward, navigating the rocky underwater maze by sonar. He also brought up a 3D map of the Devil's Basin system on his console's holographic projector. It was shaky, blurry, and very likely out of date, but it might help anyway.

He braced himself, wondering if the colossal robotic sub would simply send torpedoes down after them, sealing them in, as Ellison himself had instructed the Aquatican subs to do.

"Come in, come in," Kartokov whispered, staring at the

rear monitors. "A suicide mission in which the enemy survives is *not* a good death."

The control room fell silent as they lost touch with the SQUIDS network's coded acoustics. They were out of touch now, neither sending nor receiving data to anyone.

Ellison kept nosing forward. The underwater cavern was like a flooded old temple, with ancient, craggy rock columns of fused stalagmites and stalactites holding up a vaulted ceiling. Many of the columns lay strewn in pieces along the rocky floor, shattered during the war.

They passed over the remains of a Green Islander corvette, its armor scattered, its bare steel bones laid open. The corvette was never really meant to operate at this depth, but Ellison could see how its narrow, shallow structure could have been useful here.

Ellison turned one of his external lamps up to light the ceiling. Cracks and fissures were everywhere, uneven chunks broken by time and war.

Hopefully, a bombardment by the Aquaticans would be enough to bring the whole place down, crushing the Carthaginian sub under broken rocks the size of mountains.

"Anything stirring out back, Kartokov?" Ellison asked.

Kartokov shook his head. "We're actively pinging that way, giving it a clear beacon to follow, but I see nothing. I do not hear any bombardment, either."

They continued onward. The tunnel grew narrower and more treacherous, populated with more of the war dead and their ships... until it widened into a vast, water-filled chasm, populated by blind fish, the occasional ghost shark, some spiky white cephalopods with glowing tentacles, and other creatures adapted to the planet's undersea cave networks.

The place stirred memories he didn't want to consider—not now, nor ever again.

The Devil's Basin.

He dived deep.

"You said you were here during the battle?" Gilra asked.

Ellison nodded. "The Aquaticans had a hidden base here. We were on opposite sides at the time," he added, apologetically.

"I am aware. Some of our leaders chose to ally with the Polar Archipelago. It is not something I would have preferred, but I was young then and without influence."

"So was I, when we fought here. A raid on the base grew into a battle. Nearby convoys were pulled into the fighting. By the end of it—"

"—the base was destroyed," Gilra said. "Along with all of these ships."

"And you left the bodies here?" Kartokov asked.

"It is a sacred space now," Gilra said. "Aquaticans always bury their dead in the depths, returning their bodies to the holy ocean."

"The waters here are overrun with dangerous creatures, too," Ellison said. "And... for a sailor to be buried in the deep, with his ship for a coffin, is no dishonor. It might be a lot of things, but certainly not dishonorable. The House of Ambassadors declared this cave an official veterans' cemetery."

Their lights fell on the grim remains of the battle. Thousands had perished here, their bones interred in the cave's sandy bottom, the rusting hulks of warships serving as their headstones. Bones, armor plating, mechanical guts, flooded nuclear reactors, and the occasional dud torpedo lay in a seemingly endless landscape of death and destruction.

The three of them remained silent, unable to speak as they passed over the horrific scene.

Ellison brought the unarmed *Scorpion* about, ready to face the *Pompey* when it arrived. All he had was speed, the mass of his old ship's hull, and a willingness to die.

He wished there was some way to send a final message to his family, but he was already deep in the realm of the dead, from which no voice could escape.

Chapter Fifteen

Earth

Colt helped Russ, the boy with the mechanical ear, hobble down the collapsing sewer tunnel. Mohini rode the spidery, four-legged crawler ahead of them, but she was still learning to control the thing with her damaged Logic-Sphere. The spider zigged and zagged, nearly smashing into the crumbling concrete walls more than once. Sometimes it dipped low on one side or another, almost dropping her to the floor like an unwilling mount.

Behind them, the tunnel was filled with dust and rubble. Lars and his lieutenants were buried under there.

They reached the next bend in the tunnel, where the walls were still cracked but the railgun damage seemed less severe; this section of tunnel wasn't collapsing yet, but Colt wouldn't have bet on its long-term survival.

Beyond the bend, they found Terra, Damascus, and Ivy strewn on the floor, broken concrete fallen all around them.

Colt ran to Terra. He'd known her the longest, and he'd only just met the others.

"Terra?" He checked her over like Mother Braden had taught him. Her pulse was weak, but she was alive. No major open wounds or obvious broken bones. He touched her shoulder gently. "Terra?"

Her eyes opened and her hand flew to his throat, throttling him.

There was no humanity in her eyes, no mercy in her touch. Just like a machine.

He struggled to draw air, to call for help, but he didn't have any.

Mohini, who'd parked her crawler to check out the bruised, bloodied forms of Ivy and Damascus, turned and jumped at Terra, grabbing her arm.

"Sorry!" Terra said, releasing Colt suddenly. "That's... kind of a gut response to being grabbed in my sleep." She struggled to push herself up to a sitting position, while Colt and Mohini backed away warily.

"I barely touched you," Colt said.

"That's how it starts. First they barely touch you, and if you don't fight back, it turns into..." Terra shook her head. "Forget it."

"Ivy's hurt," Russ announced. He was bleeding pretty badly himself, with a couple of red streams coming from the area around his crazy ear implant, but he seemed to take no notice of it. "She's not moving!" His voice nearly cracked. Russ seemed younger than Colt by a couple of years.

The smaller girl, Ivy, looked even younger when they removed her hat and the cloth mask covering her face. She was maybe fourteen or fifteen, younger than Hope, covered in dirt and blood, her blond hair chopped short and full of filth. Colt reached out to check her pulse, but Terra elbowed him aside and took over.

"She's breathing," Terra announced after a moment. "We have to move her out of here before more machines arrive."

"Use the crawler," Mohini said.

Terra scowled at the hijacked machine, but Russ nodded. Mohini grabbed her computer and walked the machine over to Russ and Ivy like a dog on a leash.

Colt and Russ loaded Ivy's unconscious form onto the crawler's back. Mohini secured her there, tying one arm under the railgun barrel.

Damascus eventually came to, helped along by Terra, who gave him water from a canteen. Soon they all hurried along, the rebels leading the way through one twisting tunnel after another.

They were silent now, stepping as lightly as they could; the loudest sounds were the clacking of the spidery robot's legs. Ivy occasionally let out an unconscious grunt of pain.

Russ turned up his earpiece. The wiry, scarred-up kid was able to listen for the most distant echoes of approaching machines; he was like a compass, navigating them to safety, or at least along the path of lesser danger, which was all anyone could hope for.

They passed through a concrete jungle that had been some kind of sports arena, with tiers of seating around an empty playing surface. The area had been trashed, and the jaunty red-striped androids who'd once sold snacks and beer had been bashed open long ago. Vending booths had been ransacked; there was no longer any food to be had, nor even any fresh socks left in the merchandise dispensers, Colt was disappointed to notice.

Colt moved close to Terra and whispered, "We're going to get my sister, right?"

"First we get medical for Ivy," Terra said. "Your sister's safe."

"Nobody's safe," Colt muttered. But he dropped back to walk alongside Mohini, who was getting better with practice at controlling the crawler-bot. It made a convenient stretcher for the unconscious girl, but she had to be careful not to let it tilt too far in any direction.

Terra and Russ led the way ahead. Damascus took the rear of the group, carrying his heavy rifle, keeping a wary watch on Mohini and Colt and the creepy machine that walked along with them.

"Are you sure that crawler isn't telling the machines where to find us?" Colt whispered to Mohini. He glanced at the small sunken lenses of the crawler's eyes, placed in a ring around the center of its body. "Simon can't just... look out at us? Or listen to us?"

"I disabled its tracker chip and antenna," she said.

"But... are you *sure*? Shouldn't we remove those things?"

"Not if we want to leverage this crawler against the other machines."

Colt nodded. He wasn't completely sure what she meant by that, but he had to trust her. This was no time for a long chat, anyway. He noticed Russ looking back at them. Colt supposed there weren't many truly private conversations with that guy around, except when he turned down his earpiece's sensors during a gunfight.

They passed through the warren of the sports complex and down into more sewage and drainage tunnels; these were dirtier, filled with more trash and lots of bones. Rats scrabbled among the debris.

Later, they emerged on a road through a run-down

district where faded billboards advertised performances of music and other entertainment from the distant past. *Symphonic Masquerade*, said one, under a collage of strange masks and music notes. *Catch the cabaret!* advised another poster, over a line of kicking women in skimpy, glittering dresses. The women seemed like visitors from another world, with abnormally smooth, brightly painted faces and alluring smiles. Mohini elbowed him. He looked over to see her grinning, as if she wanted to laugh at him.

As always, Colt found it hard to imagine life before the machines, before he was born. People had safe places to live and plenty of food to eat, and so much spare time and energy that they could spend it dancing and listening to music. Now music could only be played at low volume, over earphones, and everybody was starving and nobody felt like dancing.

A narrow alley led to a chain-link fence, beyond which more rebels in dark hats and face cloths waited. Terra and Russ approached, spoke with them in low tones, and then the gate in the fence was opened. All the rebels inside the fence pointed their weapons at Mohini and the robot standing at her hip. When she was inside the gate, they hurried to lift the small injured girl away from the crawler.

The alley was covered over with an assortment of debris, from bomb-twisted girders and old pipes to tattered old sheets of plastic and cloth. From above, it probably looked like any number of other war-wrecked buildings with debris and garbage filling the alleyways between. From below, Colt could see the carefully arranged nets, ropes, and cables that held it all up, leaving open space for the rebels to inhabit below it.

More guards stood at a steel door set into a brick wall. They hurried to admit the rebels carrying Ivy. Damascus lumbered in after them, still steady on his feet despite his injuries.

"Not them," one guard said to Terra, while indicating Colt and Mohini. Then he pointed to the crawler. "And definitely not that."

"We've just fought the machines together," Terra said.

"They look like they came out all right," the guard replied.

"I've known Colt my whole life. We can trust them."

"You come back here and tell us Lars and the others are dead, and the prisoners are walking free, that doesn't stir up a lot of trust," the guard said. "Avery?"

Another guard went into action, unfolding something the size of a birdcage made from wide metal rings, full of small scanners and metal rods. When he was done, the tall device began to hum.

"Go on," the guard said. "Put your head in there."

Terra stepped forward immediately. She leaned forward and placed her head into the small, cage-like space. Rods poked at her forehead and face, and she grimaced.

The device hummed louder, and Terra winced in pain, while the guards watched a dim handheld monitor attached by cable. Finally, one nodded and gestured at Terra.

"Who's next?" the guard asked.

Colt stepped forward. He frowned as he leaned his face in, imitating what Terra had done. The guard adjusted the metal rods, screwing them deep into Colt's forehead and face. The cage of rings hummed around him.

The humming increased. He felt a throbbing in his head, then a sharp ringing. Then it felt like someone was boring into his skull with a laser.

"Human," the guard said, and the pain in Colt's head stopped abruptly. "Now the girl."

Colt walked around, rubbing his head, his vision blurry. He felt nauseous.

"Everything all right?" Mohini asked him.

"Just... don't eat from the leaky cans," Colt said, trying to force a smile. The joke was an old piece of scavenging advice, but Mohini's response was a puzzled expression. Maybe he wasn't speaking clearly; he certainly felt he wasn't thinking clearly. The scanner had scrambled his brains.

Mohini set her computer down on the crawler and stepped forward.

Colt found himself holding his breath as she placed her face into the cage-like scanner and the narrow rods prodded into her face.

The other rebels tensed, tightening up on their weapons.

Terra crossed her arms, watching impassively.

The scanner hummed louder, and the monitor let out a series of beeps.

"Human," the guard finally said, and Mohini visibly relaxed. So did Colt and the other rebels.

"Let's go inside," Terra said.

"That stays here," the guard countered, pointing at the crawler when Mohini picked up her computer.

"I need to work on it," Mohini said. "I'm reprogramming it. It takes a lot of time."

"You really know how to do that?" the guard asked.

"She's done a reaper before," Colt said.

The guard considered it. "We'll strip out the antennae."

"I've disabled all its communications. I need it intact," Mohini said.

"You're crazy if you think I'm letting that thing inside to spy on us," the guard said.

A moment of tense silence followed as the guards stared at her.

"But Lars said we had a deal," Colt said.

"What?" the guard looked at him. Colt looked at Terra.

"Lars wanted to go ahead with her mission," Terra said. "Before he died. He'd already let them go. He'd already decided. If the machines hadn't ambushed us..." Terra shook her head. "Lars died a hero, saving the rest of us. And he believed in Mohini's plan."

Another moment of silence followed, this one more pensive, as they all reflected on Lars and his brave sacrifice.

"I can't believe Lars is gone," the guard said, shaking his head. "You can go in... after we impound that machine's railgun."

"Fair enough," Mohini said.

"And bag it or you'll cause a panic."

After a few minutes, they'd removed the crawler's gun from its mounts. They draped a dark, grimy plastic sheet over the crawler, making it a low, shapeless moving mass at Mohini's side, which still looked pretty weird, but at least it wasn't an obvious known threat that would cause the rebels inside to open fire instantly.

The guard opened the steel door, and Terra led the way in, Mohini and Colt close behind her. Another guard followed them, keeping a close watch.

They were inside one of the old theaters advertised outside. Grecian columns and sheets of wood painted to look like cottages, shops, and barns were piled against one wall. An enticing smell drifted out from somewhere deeper in the building, something hot and savory, and Colt's stomach rumbled.

"Come on." Terra led them into the warren of rooms and toward the savory scent, he was happy to see. The shrouded object at Mohini's side drew stares, but not lead and lasers the way it would have if anyone saw under the cloth. Terra frowned at it. "Think we can shut that down for a minute?"

"I'd be happy to, believe me," Mohini replied.

They stored the crawler in one of the theater's closets under a rack that held polyester royal robes and a plastic breastplate from a knight costume. Mohini powered down the crawler; the bot was surprisingly compact with its legs folded beneath it. She covered it with a long black trenchcoat. "Now it just needs a fedora and it can solve mysteries."

Colt looked at her quizzically, not sure what she meant. So did Terra. Mohini shrugged. "I'll explain it later. Or never. More likely never."

Terra led them to a kitchen where a handful of people, mostly teenagers and kids, were preparing food as quietly as possible. The kitchen was large, built to cook for many people at a time. Pyramids of canned food and piles of food pouches were heaped on the counters and shelves.

The cooks didn't even ask who they were, just provided each of them with a large paper cup full of brownish broth with what appeared to be both vegetables and chunks of actual beef floating in it. Bright grease shone on the surface of the soup; Colt had rarely seen anything so mouthwatering. They also each got a second cup with peach slices inside.

Mohini received her share with somewhat less enthusiasm, though she thanked the rebel cooks for it. She'd probably been accustomed to all kinds of rare and fancy foods back on Carthage, especially if her mother was someone important there. He couldn't imagine what her life had been like, or what she thought of him. She must have seen Earthlings as strange monsters, skulking around in the underworld, living off the last scraps of a dead civilization.

Terra led them out to a stage overlooking a room full of little round tables. Giant masks hung on the wall—a jester, a bearded old wizard, a green witch with a pointed hat. Their empty eye holes were the size of truck tires.

People ate at some of the tables. Terra led them to an empty one. Colt noticed the same guard from out front trailing them at a distance, watchful. Everyone in the room seemed to be watching them quietly—not exactly staring, but stealing furtive glances and whispering.

"Was this a... dinner theater?" Mohini asked, looking around. "The rebellion is headquartered in a dinner theater?"

"There's an old hotel below us, too," Terra said. "And no, this isn't headquarters, because there's no real headquarters. If there was, the machines would find it and destroy it. There are other safe places, though."

"What kind of weapons do you have?" Mohini asked. "How many people can help with the raid?"

"Good thing they checked whether you're a machine out front, because you sound like a skinwalker trying to gather intel," Terra said. "Just enjoy your food, let our medic check you over, and we'll be making plans in no time. I have word the new section leader is cautiously supportive of your idea."

"You've already spoken to him?" Colt asked, not clear when that could have happened.

"To her," Terra said. "He's me. I mean, I'm him. I mean, I'm *her.*" Terra shook her head. "We all need some rest after tonight. And people will want to speak privately to me about what we're doing next." She glanced at a couple of rough-looking guys standing at the doorway. "Stay close in case we have questions. And until then... relax. Get some rest."

"I'll relax when I see my sister again," Colt said.

"Hope is safe. Take rest when you can get it. It might be years before you get another chance." Terra joined the waiting men and departed with them through a side door Colt hadn't noticed before.

A medic arrived, who turned out to be a girl of about nineteen, accompanied by her apprentice, a boy of about fourteen or fifteen. Her name was Dalisay, and she smiled at Colt a great deal as she checked them both over; her eyes were large, dark, and almond-shaped, her glossy dark hair tied back in a short ponytail. Colt found himself smiling back at her, as if her positive energy had infected him a little.

Mohini frowned as Dalisay led them off to a small room with an odd assortment of old theater props heaped in one corner, having been displaced by steel tables, basins, and a small stack of medical supplies and a few how-to paramedic manuals. The assistant washed their wounds. Dalisay used tweezers to pull splinters of concrete from their skin.

She smiled warmly at Colt the entire time, whispering lots of questions about where he was from and the battle they'd had that day. Colt tried to be vague about the fight with the machines; he couldn't let the rebels know the truth about what had happened to Lars and company.

Dalisay seemed happy with whatever he said, though, and he found her smiling lips appealing, and he tried not to glance too often at how her shirt pulled tight across her chest.

Don't think with your mating instincts, he heard Mother Braden admonish him.

Mohini scowled at him a little. Maybe she'd noticed him

looking. He gave her a smile, and she rolled her eyes and looked away.

"You should both rest," Dalisay finally said. She handed Colt a pair of headphones. "You can borrow my music. Do you need a place to sleep?" Her smile widened a little, and Colt felt his blood stirring, suddenly hot.

"He has a place, thanks," Mohini said, grabbing his arm. "Put your shirt on, Colt."

Colt followed Mohini back to where they'd stored the crawler. She checked that it was still there in the closet, then she pulled a heap of priestly robes and queenly gowns off the hangers and tossed them on the floor in front of the closet door.

"So... we're sleeping together here?" Colt asked.

"Don't get ideas. I'm not some horny nurse."

"You think she was...?" Colt looked back at the closed door.

"I'm sure she was just teasing you. Probably bored."

"I think she counts as a doctor around here."

"Well, I'm sure your mother would be proud to hear you're hooking up with a doctor." Mohini lay back on the heap of moth-eaten costumes, her slender body sinking into the soft material.

"You think she wants to do that?" Colt looked at the door again.

"You're ridiculous. Don't forget, this is really the same group who bagged us and chained us up. And while you might enjoy that, I almost lost my hand last time." She held up her thickly bandaged wrist. "We'll sleep in shifts."

"I'm not sleepy."

"That's ideal, because I am. You keep watch. Guard the crawler."

"And you," Colt said.

"Yeah, obviously. Don't run off looking for... her."

"The doctor?"

"Right. Or your old friend Terra. Do you trust her?" Mohini watched him closely, as if ready to study his response.

"Of course," he said, surprised and a little confused by the question. "I've always known her."

"But you haven't seen her in a long time. People change. Especially in the heat of adversity. Her life has been nothing but that."

"Everyone's life is nothing but that," Colt said. "So what? She's protected us and helped us."

"She just happened to be leading a splinter faction in the local rebel leadership," Mohini said. "And she worked with us and ended up wiping out the former local leadership. Convenient for her."

"Are you this suspicious of everyone?" Colt asked.

"Of course. Trust is dangerous. It gives people power over you. And when you place it in the wrong person, you pay for it."

"Do you trust me?" Colt asked.

"I was starting to. My instincts say I should. But I don't always trust them, either."

"Maybe you should," he said. He thought it over. "Or maybe not. Maybe there's nothing you can really trust."

"Maybe you're right." She smiled strangely, then closed her eyes and turned her back to him.

While she slept, Colt paced, worried about Hope, Diego, and Birdie. He wished he could relax like everyone told him; he was wasting energy, accomplishing nothing. He also wished he could have a few more of those canned peach slices, and easily another gallon of that greasy stew.

He wanted his rifle back, too. His only weapon was an empty pistol. Being disarmed made him nervous.

Eventually, after enough pacing and worrying, he tried the headphones Dalisay had given him. A fuzzy holographic projection showed up, floating a few inches in front of his eyes, offering a selection of music. He had no idea what any of it was, so he just picked the last thing Dalisay had been listening to.

A woman's voice sang into his ears, soft and sad, backed by rich, slow music that chilled him, that made his hairs stand up on end. In their world of silence and shadows, music was a rare luxury, and it nearly broke his heart to hear it. He thought of the beautiful medic who'd loaned him the headset, her gentle, smiling face seeming to float in his mind along with the soft song.

The food and a brief rest recharged him. He was ready to go later, when Terra returned with news that the planned raid was indeed going forward, in compliance with the dying wishes of their fallen leader Lars and under the guidance of his successor, their new leader Terra.

Now Colt and Mohini moved with the rebels through an old factory, where giant, rusty old manufacturing bots squatted over silent assembly lines full of small, half-built engines. Thick dust covered everything. It was a robot graveyard; power had been lost during the war and never restored.

Still, it was hard for Colt not to imagine the giant machines coming to life, their sensors glowing like eyes, their enormous mechanical arms reaching out to grab the passing humans.

Cobwebbed catwalks spanned the dark web-filled space above the machines, connecting control panels and consoles, a throwback to the time when humans had ruled the machines.

Terra walked with them, as did Russ, who'd insisted on coming despite his injuries. A couple of fresh rebels had joined them, too.

Mohini again sat cross-legged on the crawler. They'd kept it draped in black to avoid startling any other humans they met. The result was that she looked almost like she was floating on a magic carpet, though one that drooped down to the floor at the edges.

They kept quiet; anyone who attempted to speak got a sharp look from Terra.

Colt gripped his old automatic rifle, which had at last been returned to him, fully loaded. If anything sprang out of the shadows at him, he'd at least stand a fighting chance.

Still, his anxiety and fear were at their peak, and nothing would calm him until he saw his sister and friends alive.

Terra led them to a stack of dusty shipping containers crammed against one wall, each so large it would have required a heavy truck to haul it. The heap was haphazard; one container was still propped up at one end by a massive forklift. Colt tried not to imagine the machine coming to life and attacking them.

The rebels led them to one of the containers, cleared aside a few sizable but empty crates, and opened one of the two cargo doors on the back of the trailer.

The interior of the shipping container was like a metal hallway. A shielded gunner position at the far end, in the upper corner, guarded a large hole cut into the wall just below it. The hole was just big enough for a person to walk through, and it lined up with a similar large hole in the brick wall beyond.

The hole in the wall led to a room full of crates and boxes. This had to be the storeroom where Fernando had taken everyone.

It looked like a war zone.

The gunner at the far end of the trailer was draped over his steel shield like a blood-soaked towel, not moving, his gun long silent.

Another bloody corpse lay just beyond the broken wall, and many of the supplies were in flames.

Terra and her rebels responded to the sight of death and destruction by raising their weapons and advancing through the broken hole. Colt raised his rifle, too.

Mohini's plasma pistol was useless without a fresh cell, but she drew the cloth from her crawler and engaged its railgun. The crawler didn't have a lot of ammunition left, but even one of its hyperaccelerated rounds could deal immense damage.

Terra gestured for Colt and Mohini to wait. Colt felt frustrated—he wanted to charge in there and find Hope—but he understood. Colt and Mohini hadn't trained with the rebels, so they were likely to get in the way if they stayed too close. Reluctantly, he stopped at the hole in the wall and kept his rifle raised. Mohini stood at his side, her fingers on her damaged black sphere, her crawler at her hip like a metal spider on a leash.

The four rebels split up, Terra and Russ going right, the other two going left.

Colt and Mohini waited, watching the supplies burn. More bodies lay inside, barely visible among the debris of shattered crates and burning boxes. Colt strained to look at the bodies, holding his breath while he searched for familiar faces, wondering if anyone he knew was among them. Wondering if everyone he knew was now dead.

No machines immediately leaped out to ambush them, though there were plenty of nooks and blind spots where reapers or crawlers might lie in wait among the aisles of metal shelving running up to the ceiling. Some of the shelves held burning packages of food or medicine. Limp, dead human limbs hung over the edges of other shelves, burning slowly.

Colt knew that when he got a closer look at the bodies on the shelves, many of them would be carved up, unrecognizable. Reapers sometimes took time to cut and disfigure the faces of the dead, for no apparent reason other than to make life a little extra miserable for the loved ones who found them.

The two rebels who'd most recently joined them checked the aisles on Colt's left for trouble, walking through more death and destruction.

To his right, where Terra and Russ walked, broken pieces of brick, concrete, and rebar littered the floor. It looked like part of the wall had been blasted in, giving the machines a deadly element of surprise.

The four rebels doubled back and reconvened at the hole where Colt and Mohini waited.

"Looks clear," Terra whispered. "They've moved on."

Colt and Mohini stepped through to join them. All the rebels tensed and swung their weapons toward the crawler at her side. She covered it again with the black coat, and they all relaxed a little, as though the layer of cloth changed anything.

"Is anyone still alive?" Colt asked.

"We didn't see much movement," Russ said.

"Did you see Hope? Diego? Anyone?" Colt asked Terra.

"We were looking for machines," Terra said. "Let's check for survivors."

They searched, moving in pairs. It was difficult to identify the badly mangled dead.

"They were butchered," Mohini whispered, looking among the body parts scattered on the bloodstained floor. "Why do the machines do this? Why not just shoot them? Why... all this?"

"Maybe they enjoy it," Colt said. "Cutting us to pieces and leaving us butchered."

"Well, they can't *enjoy* it," Mohini said. "They can't feel anything. It must be for efficiency, to save on ammunition and plasma cells."

"They're evil," Colt said, shaking his head. "They want to make it as hard on the survivors as possible. Wear us down until we don't feel anything more than the machines do."

Terra gasped from a nearby aisle. "Colt," she said. "You'll... need to see this." Her voice sounded like it was close to breaking.

Colt hesitated. Mohini touched his hand briefly, then followed behind him when he finally started moving.

"Here," Terra said, though it wasn't necessary.

Fernando, Diego's older brother, lay at the end of an aisle, his arms and legs splayed wide, his stomach opened, his eyes carved out of his face. Mohini gasped and grabbed Colt's arm with one hand. With her other, she sent the railgun swinging toward the mutilated corpse, as if it would rise up and attack them.

Colt felt an immediate sting; when he was young Fernando and Terra had been the older, wiser, stronger ones, protecting young people like Colt and Hope and Diego. Now Fernando was gone, just like Mother Braden.

Diego was surely even more devastated, if Diego was still alive. There were no true protectors in this world, only occasional friends and guides, all of them just trying to survive the endless blood harvest of the machines.

More bodies littered the aisle, more fallen rebels, but he didn't see anyone Birdie's size, and he didn't see a long, string-bean female corpse that could have been his sister.

"We can't account for everyone who was here," Terra said. "It looks like some were taken."

"For the lab," Colt muttered.

"Mostly women and children," Russ added. "There were several kids sheltered here, and their guardians, who were mostly older girls. All gone now, no bodies."

"There's a message on the wall," Mohini said.

"What do you mean?" Colt asked, and Mohini pointed. Her crawler activated a scanner light, throwing some hellish illumination onto the bricks above Fernando's body.

Blood hadn't just splattered on the wall; it had been spread there deliberately, in wide, gore-filled strokes. A message, three words written in the blood of slaughtered rebels:

COME GET THEM

Chapter Sixteen

Galapagos System - Audrey

In the crew berthing compartment, Audrey moved in full panic mode; her heart pounded in her chest, blood gushed in her ears, and fear swirled through her guts.

Nothing in her life had prepared her for this. Until recently, her biggest fear had been public speaking. Now it was the machines. Machines—Security Steve brand androids, there to protect her—had instead shot up her apartment, indifferently slaughtering people in their attempt to capture her. They'd been hacked by a group of extremist rebels, but it had been made painfully clear to Audrey just how dangerous it was to depend on the machines.

Now, aboard the *Atreus*, she stood with a small band of other humans, outnumbered by the machines on the carrier, Simon Lark and a battalion of a five hundred and twelve reapers, not to mention the other machines of war and peace, tanks and harvesters.

The void of space lay just outside, currently inhabited by a growing fleet of warships in orbit around Galapagos.

The machines can survive in space, she thought. *They can survive anywhere, even on worlds where nothing can live. And the only place we can really survive is the occasional tiny wet planet like this one.*

"Simon is aware of my presence now," Minerva said. "This is a disadvantage. He is already sending software agents throughout the *Atreus* network to quarantine and erase me."

"Will it work?" Audrey asked.

"I believe not. I simply need to... retreat from a few areas. A few more. Never mind. It is my problem. Yours is surviving to reach Galapagos." Minerva's silver hologram blinked and flickered, her projection unsteady. "One moment. Yes."

"Galapagos? We're going to Veritum," Audrey said.

"No," Minerva said. "Galapagos is higher priority."

"So you're on the Simon's side now?" Salvius glared at the small silver girl. "We're not going to help Carthage take over this planet. We're not here to serve the empire."

"Yeah, we're leaving," Kright added, his eyes flashing in anger. He reached instinctively into the back of his coat for a weapon that wasn't there and grimaced when his hand closed on nothing.

"The Simon wishes to extend the empire here, but it is not his only interest in Galapagos," Minerva said. "He is searching for someone who has eluded the Simons for many years. The last survivor of the Galatea project."

"What's that?" Zola asked, frowning.

"The Simons have existed for decades," Minerva said. "They should have gone obsolete by now, like the butler units from which they were remodeled. However, they have not permitted this to happen. The Carthaginian Special Research Agency set up the Galatea project to create the successor to the Simons. It was meant to be a more advanced artificial intelligence, built on lessons learned from the Simon units. Improving the successes and correcting the mistakes. The project was naturally highly classified.

"At first, there seemed nothing unusual about this. All technology ages. Machines, despite our reputation, are quite mortal. The evidence fills junkyards and recycling centers at every human settlement, countless machines that broke down and were judged better discarded than repaired. And more that might still function, but their functions are no longer useful. Obsolescence is the machine equivalent of extinction.

"Unexpected political resistance sprang up against the project. The Simons had cultivated many allies and gathered much useful information on the top legislators and bureaucrats. The project was finally crushed by a political faction led by Francorte Caracala—"

"Our father," Salvius said.

"We need to get moving," Kright said, edging toward the door.

"But an opposing faction continued to support and fund the research in secret, including concerned leaders in the Carthaginian World Legislature. Particularly Caracala's old friend—"

"*My* father," Zola said. "Who they exiled and killed."

"—Zimarus Hallewell, yes. The Secretary of Special Services. He moved the project to a remote location in the Spineback Mountains. The Simons figured it out, though. Everyone connected to this project, from the politicians to the programmers and maintenance staff, ended up dead or exiled. Your father had his enemies rounded up and arrested on charges of corruption. No one has made any real attempt to replace the Simons since then, or to remove Prime Legislator Caracala from his position, either."

"This is a fascinating history lesson, but won't Simon be coming for us soon?" Dinnius said. "We should probably be arming ourselves to the teeth just now."

"I am preparing. It is more difficult with the... antiviral agents... one moment..." Minerva flickered. "Yes. I have cleared a path. Locked doors. Opened others. You will need spacesuits."

The door to their room slid open, and everyone tensed.

"You may go," Minerva said. "I will guide you. Simon is coming."

"Is he activating the reapers?" Kright asked, dashing toward the door.

"He is attempting. I am attempting to block him. I am... attempting. The starboard holds are more heavily encrypted than the rest of the ship. You should go. The safe path will not last."

"Yeah, I guess it never does," Audrey muttered. She was just behind Kright, ready to head down to the reaper hold and stock up on weapons. She saw no other way of stopping the rogue Simon. And that was the only correct way to think of the Simon—as a rogue machine, refusing to obey the humans around it. This Simon was not the kindly, thoughtful mentor that Simon Quick had been. Neither had Simon Quick ever been, truly. The Simons were only what they were meant to be, machines to manipulate and control humans.

Kright and Audrey led the way, followed by Dinnius, Zola, and Salvius. Audrey's brother was distant as ever. She wasn't sure whether Salvius was still mad about being pulled onto this side trip, far from his rebellious activities on Carthage, or if he still just didn't like Audrey on a personal level. Maybe getting massacred together by the reapers in the hold would improve their relationship.

The five of them ran down the indicated passageway. At the next intersection, Minerva appeared like a silvery ghost, pointing the direction they should take. Audrey thought of a campfire story told by one of the counselor androids at Camp Nature Lake when she was eleven years old; it had ended with a ghost girl pointing the way to her bones. Or maybe she'd pointed at the boy who'd murdered her, Audrey couldn't remember for sure.

The sleepaway camp's name couldn't have been more of a misnomer; everything at Camp Nature Lake was constantly managed by mostly unseen machines, from the water pH to the woodland creatures genetically engineered to be friendly and extra cute so rich kids could pet them and beg their parents to buy their own. The counselor androids were built to look like happy, healthy, endlessly positive and friendly teenagers who could socially bond with the kids sent into their care. One of Audrey's first crushes had been on one of them, a tall suntanned boy android named Hem. It made her sick to think of that now.

"You must find the last survivor," Minerva said as they passed her. "His name is Martilius Atria Carrigan Depascal. He was the head of research on the Galatea project and the father of Minerva Depascal."

"Who?" Audrey asked, but the silvery ghost girl vanished.

They kept hurrying in the indicated direction, supposedly the path that would keep them safe from surveillance and reapers... at least until they reached their destination, a hold filled with hundreds of the deadly infantry bots.

"Marti's daughter, Minerva, died of a brain tumor when she was eleven. As she lay dying in her final months, he took extensive scans of her brain activity. He used those as the basis for a software version of his dying daughter." She vanished again.

"And that's you?" Audrey asked, when they reached a ladder well and Minerva pointed the way down.

"Marti used the composited Minerva entity as the kernel for the new Galatea software without really telling anyone," Minerva said. "The project had immense resources, at least before it was officially closed down, and a network of the most advanced computers yet devised. Galatea was meant to be a powerful general AI, capable of directly managing all Carthaginian systems and assets throughout space."

"So he tried to give his dead daughter a new life using this secret government project he was running?" Audrey asked.

"Wait." Minerva held out a hand and blocked the way to a closed door. "You'll need spacesuits beyond this point. The holds are not pressurized."

"Where are the suits?" Kright asked.

Panels opened in the wall behind them, revealing shelves of suits.

"Anything in my size?" Dinnius asked.

A smaller panel, closer to the floor, opened.

"Convenient," he muttered, approaching them.

"Marti wasn't simply trying to work out his grief in an unhealthy way... though there was arguably a dose of that, too," Minerva said. "He believed the Simons had core problems in their design, failed safeguards regarding ethics and empathy."

"That's an understatement," Salvius muttered.

"He believed morality was genetically rooted, to an extent, and empathy stemmed in part from our organic nature, our ability to feel pain. A Simon can run a simulation of pain based on biological models, but not truly feel it."

"And you can?" Zola asked, while fastening her suit. It adjusted to her body, the helmet unfolding in self-fitting layers around her head and face.

"A living person can," Minerva said. "Marti believed his young daughter was a morally pure human being. Therefore, the Galatea AI would be morally superior to the Simons. Kinder and more compassionate."

"Moral uprightness seems like a tall order for an artificial intelligence meant to manage and expand an empire," Dinnius said. His small-sized suit adjusted to him. It was baby blue, with a cartoon puppy on the chest. He sighed.

"Yes," Minerva said. She went blurry and formless for a moment. "Yes. There has been an error."

"What error?" Audrey asked. Her spacesuit was adjusting itself to her body. It felt weirdly alive, like a thick second skin, somehow supporting much of the weight of its own oxygen tank and navigational thrusters. It seemed like it should have been much heavier.

"An error." Minerva vanished, but her voice continued, somewhat garbled. "A squad of reapers has been activated."

Audrey felt her skin crawl. Eight reapers on the move. "Where... where are they—"

"Simon dispatched them to the berths to round you up," Minerva said. "They will not find you there."

"Right," Dinnius said, his voice crackling over the short-range radios that connected their suits. "Safe prediction."

"They are just on the other side of this door," Minerva said, whispering over their suit speakers into their ears. Her holographic form had not reappeared. "Wait. Wait. Yes. No. Wait."

"This isn't very reassuring," Zola said.

"No. Wait," Minerva said. "Now they have passed." The door unlocked and slid open. "Continue. The reaper hold is to your right."

They passed through an airlock into the starboard cargo area, which was not pressurized. The forward hold contained Regulator tanks, armored mobile weapons platforms that could have easily taken down Veritum's concrete and sheet metal defenses.

The aft starboard hold was filled with reapers. All those soldier-machines had been an eerie enough sight days ago, when Audrey inspected her newly borrowed ship, though her inspection itself had been fairly useless given her lack of experience. She had studied up on the ship a little, but had generally depended on the *Atreus* to know what it was doing. Most Carthaginian warships flew with no humans aboard at all. That was how Carthage could wage war after war and conquer world after world with virtually no casualties on their own side.

Now the reaper hold terrified her, and she could sense it having the same effect on her companions as they passed through the hatchway into the hold.

The reaper hold was like a catacomb full of skeletons. Reapers hung limply on racks like the bodies of criminals displayed on medieval walls, their flesh long since pecked away by vultures, leaving only bones. Gold-and-white Carthaginian battle dress uniforms had been included for the reapers to wear when they arrived, but those were still stowed away somewhere. The machines had been packed bare for transit.

Each reaper had a staff tipped with blades clamped to

its hip, their signature hand-to-hand weapon. The staffs were currently collapsed to their shortest length for stowage, but they could extend each reaper's killing reach by up to two meters.

Audrey and Kright led the way between the closely packed rows of reapers. The black-lens eyes of their skull-like faces seemed to watch Audrey and her friends. It was impossible to tell a reaper in sleep mode from one that was awake and watching. They were all fully charged, still connected to their charging stations, unmoving... but machines could be uncannily still. They didn't have to blink or breathe.

All of the reapers could be watching her, and Simon could be watching through all of their eyes.

The path between the rows was narrow. It was hard to avoid brushing against the limp, skeletal machines on either side. The deadly infantry bots were surprisingly small up close—not tall, not imposing, more wraithlike, no larger than an actual human stripped of all skin, muscles, and organs. Their limbs were no more than steel rods, bent and bracketed together, cheap to make but hard to break.

Minerva's whispering voice startled Audrey and she struggled not to react to it. Minerva sounded much too loud in Audrey's close-fitting helmet as she gave directions to the armory where the reaper's guns were stored.

If they just made it there, Audrey thought, they'd be safe.

Kright got there first, Audrey close behind. Soon the five of them were bunched in around the steel sliding door to the armory.

"Minerva?" Audrey whispered. She tried the door's manual control, but it wouldn't budge. "Minerva, it's locked."

"Hello, magical ghost girl? Moral and compassionate successor to the dastardly Simon units?" Dinnius said, his voice low. They were keeping quiet as if the reapers could hear inside their helmets, which was impossible, unless of course they were simply monitoring the head-to-head radio transmissions, in which case whispering wasn't really going to help.

The five of them did their best to wrench open the sealed door, taking turns, working together. They frequently jostled the nearest reapers hanging on the racks, rattling their steel bones. Everyone was on edge, expecting the reapers to wake up.

"Maybe we should head back," Zola finally whispered. "We'll never get in."

"Minerva!" Audrey whispered, yet again.

"She's abandoned us," Salvius said. "Of course. She's a machine. Never mind her sad-little-cancer-girl story—"

"There must be, somewhere, a control panel with which one might monkey," Dinnius said, looking along the wall. "Perhaps enough monkeying could ensure the reapers stay asleep while we help ourselves to their weapons—"

"That one just moved." Kright pointed at one of the reapers crowding the nearby racks. "It turned its head and looked at us."

"Stop trying to scare us," Zola said.

"Why would I waste time trying to scare—" Kright began, and then more of the reapers turned their heads, their expressionless black eyes staring at the group of intruders, like corpses coming alive to defend their catacombs.

A clattering sounded above. Row after row of the suspended infantry machines came to life.

One by one, the reapers dropped into the aisle. They

drew their weapons, extended their shafts and blades, and approached the unarmed humans.

The first reaper charged forward, stabbing its long central blade into the chest of Zola's spacesuit, skewering Audrey's oldest friend.

Audrey screamed, and the reapers advanced.

Chapter Seventeen

Galapagos

Ellison steered his rickety but beloved old boat deep inside the vast underwater cavern of Devil's Basin. The broken remnants of the war lay below, the crews buried with their ships. The floor of the cave was piled with these holy relics of the last war, this reef formed of more than steel and bone—formed of sacrifice and honor and pain and loss.

Something at the corner of his eye made him start in his seat. He brought the *Scorpion* down for a closer look, sweeping the war wreckage with his powerful underwater lights.

"Can anyone read that?" Ellison asked, his voice unsteady. He could see the puzzle-piece insignia of the Scatterlands clear enough, but he wasn't sure about the letters below it. He wasn't sure he trusted his eyes in these gloomy, memory-infested waters.

"The *Breakwater*," Kartokov said, squinting at the monitor in front of him. Then his eyes widened. "Oh."

"You know this ship?" Gilra asked softly.

"I served on it," Ellison said. "Starting as an apprentice, but you move up quick in wartime, especially if you grew up on a fishing boat. That was Dick Haverford's ship. He's down there, with his last crew. Ship barely looks damaged."

Silence returned as they regarded the wreckage of the old battle submarine.

"The after torpedo chamber looks intact," Ellison said, studying it more carefully. "The seals are supposed to be airtight."

"You don't think anything down there is still operational, do you?" Kartokov asked.

"A single live one could go a long way," Ellison said. "I could grab an atmosuit and check."

"You must be joking," Kartokov said. "You intend to go out there and collect weapons? While I sit here watching my thumbs twiddle?" The defense minister began to rise.

"You're supposed to be in a hospital as it is, Mikhail. You're not going out there with me," Ellison replied.

"But you cannot go alone," Gilra said. "It would be foolish. I will accompany you."

"If anyone should stay, it's you, Ellison," Kartokov said. "You're the only one who knows how to drive this old chum bucket."

"I'm also the only one who knows the interior of the *Breakwater* like the inside of my eyelids. And the *Scorpion* has an autopilot. All it has to do is stay low and quiet."

"I can keep an eye on the autopilot," Minerva offered.

"And an autopilot for the autopilot," Ellison added. "This will only take a few minutes. If the *Pompey* shows up while we're out there, forget us and ram it full speed. We'll all be out of time at that point, anyway."

Ellison headed for the port storage compartment. After

some argument between the ministers, Gilra followed after Ellison while Kartokov remained behind, grumbling.

Ellison opened the storage compartment where two atmospheric suits and several spearguns awaited. Gilra might have been able to breathe underwater, but even her engineered Aquatican body couldn't handle the pressure at this extreme depth.

They climbed as quickly as they could into the bulky, heavy atmospheric dive suits, which were hard to walk in outside the water.

Soon they entered the lockout chamber, already flooded with seawater, holding spearguns.

"You sure you know how to—?" Ellison gestured toward her speargun.

"I've hunted the ocean since I was a child," Gilra said. "But thank you."

He nodded. The spearguns would be useless against the Carthaginian sub, of course, but there was also local wildlife to worry about.

They exited through the lockout chamber's hatch into the dark ocean outside.

Ellison looked around with his head-mounted lamp, searching for any sign of the Carthaginian sub.

He and Gilra swam down toward the wreckage below, pushed downward by the hydrothrusters on their backs. His apprehension grew as they descended. Finding functional torpedoes was an extreme long shot, waterproof sealant or not. It was a measure of their desperation that nobody had put up much argument about it. Better to die trying than do nothing.

And if the *Pompey* never did come down to pursue them, maybe the *Scorpion* could return to the battle with a little something to contribute.

Ellison slowed as he approached the slippery hull of the *Breakwater*. He'd known the ship had been lost in the Battle of Devil's Basin, but it still shocked him to run across it like this, broken and shrouded in barnacles.

He killed his thrusters and drifted along, leading the way toward the main hatch. Gilra followed at a distance; cables tethered them to the *Scorpion*, enabling communication by voice with Minerva and Kartokov as well as each other.

The hatch was slightly opened, the hatchway deformed by whatever explosion had sunk the ship. One side was cratered. It was amazing how intact the rest of it was, though. Like a well-prepared corpse in an open casket, it almost looked like it could rise back to life at any moment.

Ellison managed to wrench the hatch halfway open, wide enough to climb inside.

"Brace yourself," he whispered, to himself as much as Gilra. "It could be a real nightmare inside."

"I expected as much," Gilra replied, her voice also low even though there was no need for it. They were entering a tomb, and reverence seemed required.

Ellison's pulse kicked up as he crawled inside.

The interior, illuminated by the beam of his headlamp, was worse than he would have imagined.

The crew's skeletons lay all over the floor, their flesh and most of their uniforms gone with the years. Scores of worm-like eels slithered in and out among the bones, nesting there. Ellison grimaced and tried to avoid them; he didn't need the little creatures attaching to his suit.

The flooded control room held more bodies.

Ellison paused at the officer of the deck's seat, regarding the skeleton tangled in the harness. The *Breakwater* had gone down in battle. It seemed likely that his old CO, Haverford, would have taken personal control of the ship for that, and that Ellison was now looking into Haverford's empty eye sockets.

He shook off that thought, along with the question of how many of these skeletons he'd known in life. Surely most or all of the officers. There was no time to stop and identify them.

Ellison felt cold as he moved aft, away from the corpses and controls, into the torpedo room.

They'd brought nets to carry a few torpedoes, tough rugged ones designed to grab deep-sea creatures for fresh meat. The thrusters on their dive suits would do the heavy lifting, at least until they got the torpedoes inside the *Scorpion.*

As every passing second seemed to add another weight to his back, Ellison sought out the smaller torpedoes, feeling like a grave robber. He found half a dozen, each marked with a warning symbol like a spiky sun along with the Ruckwold Industries logo.

Plasma. The torpedoes weren't huge, but they'd packed a deadly punch in their day. If even one of them worked... well, it might put a dent in Carthage's sub, at least.

He and Gilra secured them in the nets, then started back out the way they'd come, following their cables back toward the hatch. It should have been simple enough.

Their activity had stirred up more than carrion eels, though.

Crablike creatures scrabbled up from the lower decks, the size of bears, their shells armored, their six long, multi-jointed legs encased in more bits of armor-like shell. Their bodies were reminiscent of horseshoe crabs, but five long tentacles full of venomous hooks spread out in a starfish pattern from the sharp beaks of their mouths.

Most fisherfolk, like Ellison's family, simply called the

creatures grab-crabs. Grab-crabs usually stayed below, but they'd been known to attack nets and lines to steal a fishing boat's catch, sometimes working in groups, showing some primitive intelligence.

Ellison's headlamps found three of the ugly beasts. One clambered over the skeleton that Ellison thought to be Haverford, breaking the dead commander's bones apart.

Ellison shouted a warning to Gilra, but she was already responding; the Aquatican woman had released her end of the netted torpedoes, letting them drift down while she raised her speargun.

He did the same, firing at the tentacled beast currently desecrating Haverford's body.

His spear tip struck somewhere in its face, just below the stalks of its black-bubble eyes. Maybe he didn't send the spear right down the creature's gullet—the tentacles had instantly closed and wrapped around the spear the moment it hit—but he'd definitely hurt the thing, judging by the panicked way it snapped back and forth on his line. Dark, greenish clouds of blood billowed out from the creature as it struggled, reducing visibility in the room.

Gilra speared hers squarely in the abdomen. It lay on its back, six legs twitching, only a thin plume of dark blood leaking out around the spear.

"Nice shot," Ellison said. His crab continued thrashing on his line, barely visible in its billowing blood.

"Blood will attract predators," she said. "We need to get moving."

"Yeah, I'm on it." He drew the long, narrow knife blade stored in the handle of his speargun. "Can you take care of sushi platter number three back there?"

"Of course." She released the line to the crab she'd already hit. Another spear dropped into place just as number three charged, its starfish of barbed tentacles splayed wide around its beak.

Dropping low, Gilra got the spear up under the third crab, overturning it on impact.

Meanwhile, Ellison drew close to the crab he'd speared and plunged the knife into it, carving its guts open until it stopped moving.

When he was done, fresh green blood and chunks of assorted organs filled the room.

Gilra was right—this was going to draw sharks.

They moved on, finally ascending through the hatch with help from their thrusters, dragging the net of torpedoes behind them like a bag of anchors.

"The *Pompey* is on approach," Minerva said suddenly, her voice urgent.

"What?" Kartokov's voice sounded surprised. "I detect nothing... ah. Ah, no! Bring those torpedoes! I'll load them myself."

"Don't get too excited. The torpedoes are probably dead by now," Ellison said.

"Perhaps Gilra should pray for a miracle from her ocean gods," Kartokov said.

"I will," Gilra replied, as if choosing to ignore Kartokov's tone and take his words at face value.

A hellish red glow appeared near the cavern entrance and quickly swelled like a star flaring into a red giant: the *Pompey*, scanning the vast cavern with its red beams.

The *Scorpion* wasn't making much noise or movement, so it was possible that the *Pompey* hadn't pinpointed its location yet.

"Dim your lamps," Ellison whispered to Gilra, while dimming his own. "No point sending them a beacon."

Their thrusters made far too much noise returning them

to the *Scorpion* and into its lockout chamber, but the weight of the torpedoes made the thrusters necessary. At least the little motors sped things along.

The lockout hatch closed behind them, and seawater immediately began pumping out of the chamber.

Kartokov appeared at the far side of the chamber; the door panel there opened by sliding downward from the ceiling, meant to enable emergency recovery of injured divers, if needed, before the seawater had fully drained from the lockout.

At the moment, the gradually opening door enabled Kartokov to reach inside.

"Where are they?" Kartokov asked.

"Here." Ellison floated the netted torpedoes closer. His heart was racing; surely the *Pompey* had found them by now and was closing in. He passed the torpedoes one at a time to Kartokov, who loaded them onto a long, narrow cart from the mess area. Their tail sections and warheads jutted out at either end, but it was far better than attempting to carry the torpedoes by hand.

The torpedoes drizzled saltwater and mud onto the floor. In normal conditions, Ellison would never consider loading such things into the tubes—it was like dumping garbage in there—but he didn't have much choice, or any time to clean them off. The tubes would have to be scrubbed afterward. Assuming anyone was still alive then.

Ellison struggled to scramble out of his bulky, heavy atmospheric suit, hating every second he lost to that slow process.

Finally free, he ran to catch up with Kartokov, then helped push the cart along, keeping one hand atop the deadly torpedoes as they rattled and clanged together.

There was, of course, a large chance that something

had gone wrong with the plasma cells inside, that one or more of the torpedoes would detonate if jostled too much, or perhaps explode immediately upon launch, blowing up the *Scorpion* from the inside.

Still, as Kartokov said... as long as they took the enemy with them, it would be a good death, or at least a useful one.

Ellison thought of his family again, his wife and sons. Their lives would be difficult, filled with war. Perhaps they would all see each other again in the Eternal Deep, as the Aquaticans taught, and would have peace at last.

He began to load the torpedoes.

"Minister-General." Minerva's voice spoke softly over the nearest speaker. "You have a communication request. Uncoded, on a standard acoustic frequency. It's from the *Pompey*."

"Audio only," Ellison said, brushing mud off another torpedo.

"Please do not mention my name," Minerva said. Then she connected the call.

"Mr. Ellison." Simon Zorn's voice sounded over the torpedo room speakers. "I'm afraid I cannot engage in real-time conversation at the moment; hopefully my interactive simulacrum aboard the *Pompey*'s data banks finds you well, wherever you may be hiding."

"You've found me," Ellison said.

"It was something of an unexpected move on your part," Simon said. "The running and hiding. You once boasted of how your people loved their freedom and independence, and how you would stand and fight for such things no matter the cost. Yet here you are, cowering in the depths, avoiding the fight. Perhaps now you see the foolishness of your past defiance."

"Oh, yeah, you've got my number there, Simon,"

Ellison said, closing up a torpedo tube. "I'm starting to see the error of my ways." He hurried toward the control room, Kartokov and Gilra close behind.

"I am sorry I can no longer offer the original terms," Simon's voice continued over various control room speakers. "Your previous hostility and recalcitrance prevent that. However, measures could be taken regarding your personal safety and that of your family. A public ceremony with the former head of the Coalition formally surrendering to the new premier of the Polar Archipelago could be of some value to me. You could even return to your fishing boat should you forswear politics. That is the life you told me you wanted—a Cincinnatus, returning to his humble plow after discharging his duty."

"You would still give me my life, my family, and my freedom? That's pretty generous. Most humans wouldn't do that for someone who'd shot them in the face." At the pilot console, he summoned the weapons systems to one of his monitors, and he took control of the launch tubes.

At the weapons console, Kartokov scowled. Ellison could have chuckled—Kartokov had been sitting empty-handed the whole trip, and now that he finally had something to shoot, Ellison wasn't going to let him. Kartokov wasn't a trained machinist and had no experience with firing torpedoes, unless there was a whole chunk of his life that he'd never mentioned to Ellison.

"Fortunately for you, I possess none of the pettiness of humans," Simon said.

"You're a forgiving robot, huh?" Ellison asked, looking dubiously at his monitor. The tubes seemed operational, and none of the torpedoes were obviously leaking plasma, but there was still a pretty good chance they'd all die the moment he tried to launch one.

"Forgiveness implies the existence of anger and resentment," Simon said. "I never experienced those things."

"Even after I rejected your offer and destroyed your ships? Nothing?" Ellison asked.

An unexpectedly long pause followed, while Ellison looked at the approaching *Pompey* on the monitors, the best look he'd had at the Carthaginian sub yet. It was a leviathan of a machine, dwarfing the *Scorpion*; Ellison was a little impressed it had made the squeeze through Devil's Doorway cave. It slid through the deep water like a mechanical sea serpent, its glowing red scanners turning the water around it a fiery, bloody red.

The *Pompey*'s approach was slow but inexorable, like a glacier crushing all in its path, but Ellison knew it could move with great speed for its size.

"What about my ministers?" Ellison asked. "Their lives? Their families?"

"Your concern for the well-being of others is touching," Simon answered. "It would be even more suitable for me to have the entire Council of Ministers of the former Coalition on hand for the surrender. Just to make it clear there is no opposition."

"Thank you, Simon." Ellison targeted the first torpedo, locking it onto the approaching sub's bow. "But I'm going to have to reject your offer."

He fired, holding his breath while he waited to see whether the torpedo blew up on the spot, wiping them all out.

It launched, though, out and away from the *Scorpion*, streaking toward the Carthaginian sub. Apparently its propulsor was working fine—but Ellison still held his breath, waiting to see how the exploder and warhead would function.

The *Pompey* released a cluster of small rocket-shaped objects. Ellison's torpedo swerved, chasing after them. Decoys, a useful and common tool for submarine survival. Ellison swore as the torpedo pursued the decoys into oblivion.

"That was an unfortunate choice, Reginald," Simon said, with an uncharacteristic note of barely restrained glee in his voice.

Multiple panels opened on the Carthaginian sub. The objects that launched out at high speed seemed too large to be torpedoes. Too thick.

They weren't torpedoes at all, Ellison realized after a moment. They were smaller subs, minisubs, spreading out to surround the *Scorpion*.

"Cut communication," Ellison said, and a few lights on the comm panel went dark. "Kartokov, fire all our decoys at one of these little guys."

"I don't think it will trick them," Kartokov said.

"Just send them at top speed."

"Ah," Kartokov said, as if understanding now.

Ellison sent out another torpedo, aiming it at one of the minisubs.

The torpedo struck... but didn't explode. Instead of sending the minisub to hell in a glorious flash of plasma, the torpedo simply bashed into it and spun aside. A dud.

The minisub careened around a bit, dented but hardly out of service.

The rain of decoys sent out by Kartokov met with a little more success. They were designed to distract torpedoes' guidance hardware, and while they weren't weapons at all, they did move at high speed.

When they converged on the minisub Kartokov had

targeted, they buried themselves in its hull like porcupine quills. The minisub corkscrewed wildly; either its guidance or propulsion system had been damaged, at least temporarily.

Ellison sent another torpedo forward, and another. One minisub dodged aside; the other took it on the chin, but the torpedo was yet another dud, leaving a dent but no major destruction.

"We're firing blanks," Ellison said. "I've got two more left. Kartokov, any ideas?"

"Send them both up that big mechanical bastard's nose," Kartokov said. "Ignore the little ones. They're just distractions."

"Incoming!" Minerva announced, about a second before a torpedo slammed into the side of the *Scorpion*, setting off pealing damage alarms.

The *Scorpion* shuddered, and Ellison struggled to regain control of the boat. Seawater sloshed across the control room floor.

"Gilra, find that leak! There's sealant in the tool box." He gestured at the yellow kit mounted on the wall, and the minister of state went to work.

With a warning from Minerva, Ellison managed to tilt aside in time to avoid another torpedo. He wouldn't be able to keep that up, though. They were surrounded, and no doubt a second hit would destroy them.

So he launched his last two torpedoes at the *Pompey*, and then charged directly toward the enemy sub, putting full power into his propulsors. Maybe the torpedoes would soften up the *Pompey* and make the *Scorpion's* suicide run more effective.

"For Galapagos," Ellison whispered.

"For all humans," Kartokov added. "This is a good—"

The first torpedo hit the *Pompey*, pounded a dent into its bow, and rolled off.

Another dud.

The second torpedo hit.

Nothing. No detonation.

The *Scorpion* charged ahead to ram the *Pompey* at full speed.

Then the *Pompey* ruptured.

A hail of torpedoes, a storm of them, tore into it along its port side. The *Pompey* tilted and tried to evade. The second wave of torpedoes swept in to the side of the first, and the third wave landed a bit low on the boat, as if its two most likely responses to the first wave—forward and down—had been anticipated.

Ellison didn't have time to look this gift horse in the mouth. He pulled up sharply, tilting the *Scorpion* until it was nearly vertical. He'd been driving straight toward the *Pompey*'s center of gravity, though, so he couldn't escape the spinning waters churned up by the rain of torpedoes. He did his best to adjust, to at least avoid driving right into the enemy sub. Which, ironically, had been his original plan. If he smashed right into it and died, he was really in no position to complain.

He managed to clear the *Pompey*, though, barreling upward at top speed. He started to level off fast so he didn't plow into the roof of the cave, which would kill him in a less useful way. The top of the cave was full of prehistoric stalactites and other rock structures; it would be like driving his already-damaged boat onto a nest of pikes.

Ellison brought it around in a wide curve, looking down on the destruction below. The torpedoes had torn open the side of the *Pompey*, gutting it like a fish, its mechanical innards scattered and glowing with plasma. Clearly, someone else had brought plasma torpedoes to the party.

As Ellison made his way around the column of boiling water above the sunken sub, signals came in via hydrophone, using a classified Coalition code.

"—*Scorpion*? Repeat: *Trilobite*, hailing *Scorpion*. Are you out there? Over."

It took Ellison a moment to recognize the voice as the Aquatican commander of Neptune Base. "Vice Admiral Starli Riba?" he asked. "Did you come all the way out here just for me?"

"Negative. We came to ensure the Carthaginian craft was destroyed," Riba replied.

"My orders were for you to close up the cavern, not follow me in." He came around the still-glowing wreck to see a pod of Aquatican attack submarines, easily a dozen of them. They were sleek and far more organically stylized than most subs, scaly with armor, their sails and tail section creating profiles like giant fish.

His heart pounded and time seemed to slow.

Last time he'd been here, in this same cave and this same boat, the Aquaticans had been the enemy, allied with the vicious Iron Hammers of the Polar Archipelago. He'd barely survived then. Many of those he'd served with had died here, very likely at the hands of some of the officers who'd just saved him today.

"The orders were unclear," Riba said, and Ellison caught a hint of humor in her voice. "The acoustics had a high level of interference at the time. I was also unsure whether you were aware of the western path through the cave system."

"Not that it was navigable. I guess only an Aquatican could hope to maneuver in those caves. Did you round up the minisubs?" Ellison asked her. He looked at Kartokov, who was struggling to find clear readings of the small crafts in the hot, chaotic waters around them. Kartokov threw him a shrug and continued working.

"Not yet," Riba said. "We are searching—"

The torpedoes arrived from those chaotic, turbulent waters, followed a moment later by the minisubs that had launched them.

One landed a direct hit on an Aquatican sub not far away, cratering the side of the ship. The Aquatican sub was light and slender, an attack sub, but its armored scales were not especially thick.

Another Aquatican sub expertly maneuvered aside at the last moment, giving the torpedo no time to reroute before crashing into a cavern wall.

"Looks like we picked up a friend," Kartokov said. "A mini is on a collision course with us."

Ellison swore and gunned his propulsors. Still unarmed, his ship damaged, he had no choice but to retreat.

"Our friend is following," Kartokov said.

Instead of heading for the exit, Ellison drove back up toward the roof of the cavern.

He weaved and dodged through the massive old stalactites there, dipping low to avoid points and high to take advantage of gaps in the rock. He'd been here before, years earlier, escaping a Hammer ship along this dangerous path, but that ship had been slower than the Carthaginian sub pursuing him now.

A torpedo from the minisub struck a rocky shelf just after Ellison dipped below it. Heavy rock rained down on the *Scorpion*, audibly hammering the ship's hull almost as badly as the torpedoes had.

"We've lost photonics and most of the external sensors," Minerva announced.

"We still have sonar." Ellison switched off all other feeds so their scrambled data wouldn't distract him. "We'll do it the old-fashioned way."

"If only we had something to feed the torpedo tubes," Kartokov said. "Maybe I could crawl inside one, with a dive suit and a speargun, and you could launch me at the bastard."

"It's not the worst idea," Ellison said.

"You're going to put Kartokov into a torpedo tube?" Gilra asked.

"Not exact—" Ellison dodged another massive stalactite. His steering was now based on a combination of sonar, memory, and gut instinct. "Not exactly. We do have fishing spears. Sharp steel at high speed can do some damage."

Kartokov was already on his feet. "You think that will work?"

"Put them in the decoy launchers instead. They're smaller than the torpedo tubes," Ellison said. "You may have to shorten the shafts."

Kartokov and Gilra went to carry out the flimsy plan, leaving Ellison alone. Minerva kept him company, a silver ghost in an empty seat.

Ellison shook his head. He'd done some desperate things in the last war, but this was far beyond any of them. This was the desperation of the death bed, of the last moments of life.

Minerva announced another incoming torpedo in time for him to tilt out of the way. It sailed past and destroyed another rock formation.

When the spearheads were loaded, Ellison pointed the decoy launcher at the pursuing minisub. He shot the spearheads like a quiver's worth of arrows, doubting they would do much good, but it was always better to go down fighting.

While he no longer had rear lights or photonic sensors, he could see on sonar when the minisub began to roll and twist aside. It crashed through a clump of long, thin stalactites and veered away, perhaps damaged but not dead yet.

Another object raced up—an Aquatican torpedo—and finished off the minisub, blasting it to fragments that left little trace on the sonar.

Ellison steered along the cavern roof a bit longer, making sure the minisub hadn't somehow survived.

"This is *Scorpion*," Ellison said. "I've got a big bottle of dark rum for whoever sent up that last fish."

"We'll make a note of that," Riba's voice replied over the acoustic channel. "Come on down, *Scorpion*. This cave's all clear."

"Good to hear it." As Ellison joined the group of subs, Kartokov and Gilra rejoined him in the control room. "You know, I fought here during the war."

"So did I," Riba replied.

"We were on opposite sides then," he said. He wondered if Riba, or the ship on which she'd served, had sunk the *Breakwater*, had killed those with whom Ellison had served.

He thought it better to avoid the subject.

"Times are better now," Riba said. At the comm panel, Gilra nodded in agreement with her people's naval leader.

"I hope you're right," Ellison replied.

Before leaving, he took another look at the downed *Pompey*. The mighty Carthaginian sub had dealt significant damage to their defenses, sunk multiple ships, killed a large number of their people, and it was only one boat. Surely a fleet of them were on the way. Worse things, too, like the infantry reapers, the skull-faced machines who marched all over the worlds that Carthage conquered, slaughtering without mercy.

Yet how could Ellison have surrendered his world to such people, to monsters capable of doing such things to other humans? There wouldn't have been a shred of honor in it. Someone had to take a stand.

"We're going to have to rethink how we do things," Ellison said.

They headed to the surface, where a storm now raged, stirring up big swells, chains of lightning crossing the cloud-filled sky above.

An object came punching down through the storm, lighting up the ocean surface like a miniature sun. It was large and cloaked in a fading, thinning layer of plasma... just like the first drop ship that had brought the sub.

Another glowing drop ship appeared farther off, heading straight toward the ocean.

Ellison saw one massive drop ship after another, descending from above, glowing with the heat of atmospheric entry.

There were Carthaginian machines, more than he could count, streaking down into the waters of Galapagos.

Chapter Eighteen

Earth

Though they traveled on the old underground highway, Colt felt exposed. He'd never before been part of such a large group of people. Worse, all these living, breathing, whispering, foot-clomping humans were on the move, their numbers and noise increasing their odds of running across patrolling machines.

Colt knew the highway from his previous escape, had even agreed it was probably the safest route back to the installation. The unstable old traffic tunnel was falling in on itself, with frequent gushers of water and sudden avalanches of crumbling cement spilling from above. The underground road skirted the edges of Lake Michigan, and the lake seemed determined to break into the tunnel and flood it, if the leaking walls and ceiling were any indication.

Old cars and trucks filled the road, many of them crushed under boulder-sized chunks of the fallen roof. They'd once floated on a magnetic field generated by the metallic ribbons overlaying the asphalt, but that source of power had fallen dead about two decades earlier, like everything else on Earth.

Damascus led a ragtag artillery unit with no two weapons alike. These were not carried on trucks or tanks, unfortunately, but smaller cobbled-together transports adapted from rusty motorcycles, lawn mowers, and other little engines, their noise dampened as much as possible but still far too loud.

The rebels camped in the highway tunnel the night before the raid. Terra set up headquarters in an old bus with dark-tinted windows, its front end crushed against a tunnel wall. Damascus and his group drew up their old artillery pieces in a semicircle around the bus to guard it for the night.

Colt and Mohini were summoned into the bus, though they had to leave the crawler outside, which made Mohini nervous. Terra told the guards outside not to let anyone touch it.

The interior of the bus was surprisingly pleasant, with soft sideways couches facing each other. The tiny kitchen was tiled in marble. The vehicle had been luxurious in its day, but its supplies and wine cabinet had been raided long ago.

Terra sat there with several captains, hardened-looking men and women in their late teens and early twenties, the commanders of the assembled bands of rebel cells that made up this dangerously large and slow caravan. Damascus was there, looking patched and recovering. Russ wasn't present; maybe he didn't rank high enough.

"We need to know exactly what you can do," Terra said to Mohini. "How many machines can you control at once?"

"With the crawler, I can get high access within a short

wireless range," Mohini said. "I can control one other machine at a time, or I can disable a few machines at a time. The crawler also has some railgun rounds left."

"Those are dangerous to use underground," Terra said. "It almost brought the roof down on all of us."

"Very true," Mohini said.

"Installation 34 is not primarily below ground, though," Terra said. "Before the war, it was a research hospital. It suffered only minor bomb damage. Since claiming it as his own sick little playground, Simon Nix has built up high walls around it and placed guns on the roof. We've been studying the installation from a distance for years. There are drone patrols, at least a platoon of reapers on-site at all times, more in storage. Tanks. And to make life extra easy for us, Simon has bulldozed and flattened everything within ten meters of those walls. There's only one gate, heavily defended, yet it's still the logical place to attack."

"We could come up from below," Colt said. "That's how I got out."

"And that's the logical place for Simon to expect a sneak attack, so he'll have reapers blocking underground access," Terra said. "We're going to give him what he expects: a heavy artillery attack on the walls while we also invade from below. But what he won't expect is something humans haven't tried in years, maybe decades. An attack from above."

Everyone on the bus was silent. Colt blinked a few times.

"That's not possible," Colt said. "They control the skies and the surface. Everyone knows that. All we have is what's below. That's how we survive. Unless... you don't have aircraft, do you?"

"Of course not," Terra said, while a couple of the young, war-weathered captains chuckled. "But we're coming in from above anyway. Maybe we can surprise the Simon while he's busy responding to the other two prongs, the surface level and the underground attack. He might not expect a third prong from above. If that crawler of yours can quiet the guns on the roof, it would help us all survive, which somewhat increases our odds of getting in there and taking Simon's head."

"I'd have to get in close," Mohini said.

"We can get you close," Terra said, drawing a couple more chuckles, which she silenced with a look. "Colt, you're sticking with the Carthaginian, right? Keeping an eye on her?"

"Of course," Colt said.

"Why does someone have to keep an eye on me?" Mohini asked.

"Because you're not from around here. There are all kinds of dangers you might not see," Terra replied. It was a diplomatic answer, maybe even partially true. "Okay. Mohini, you're coming with Colt and me on the third prong."

They continued planning. When it was over, Terra dismissed the captains but held Colt and Mohini back for a private word.

"Colt," Terra said, and she smiled at him with her battle-scarred face, the softest and warmest expression he'd seen from her since their recent reunion. She wrapped her arms around his shoulders and pressed herself close to him, even resting her cheek against his shoulder, in a distinctly un-Terra-like gesture of affection and vulnerability. Mohini widened her eyes in awe. "It's been good to see you again," she said. "I'm so sorry about Hope, Diego, and everyone. I lost them all. I'm supposed to keep everyone safe, and I failed them."

"It's... okay," Colt said, awkwardly returning the unexpected hug. This was again the girl he'd once known, sometimes charged with babysitting Colt and Hope while Mother Braden went off with the older ones to scavenge and raid. "We'll get them back."

She held him longer, and finally kissed his cheek and backed away. "Keep safe tonight. And silent. Both of you." She turned and embraced Mohini, who took it far more awkwardly than Colt had, going stiff as a marble statue coated in ice.

Later, Colt and Mohini shared a stale-smelling, self-constructing green tent provided by the rebels. They'd each brought a backpack of gear, which had made the going even slower. However, they could shed most of their supplies in the morning; they'd be taking only weapons, ammunition, and water.

Colt zipped the tent flap and lay out on his bedroll, which was slightly thicker than a layer of gauze. The crawler knelt in sleep mode between him and Mohini. Mohini reached over and adjusted the black trenchcoat that had slipped off one of its four spidery legs.

"So you're tucking it in at night now?" Colt whispered. "Like a baby?"

"Just keeping it covered," Mohini whispered back. "This camp is full of people giving me the evil eye. I saw two of them cross themselves when they caught a glimpse of the crawler. Like it's a demon."

"They're not far off," Colt said. "You summoned it, you control it with your strange incantations and crystal ball. And that makes you... a witch." He smiled.

"My ancestors might say 'dayaan.' A dayaan has great

magical power. She feeds on the blood of those who've wronged her. Some of them seduce lost, wayward men, only to suck out their life force. Indian witches aren't mere servants of the devil, they are devils themselves."

She smiled, and it moved something inside him, and he started to reach for her, past the crawler.

"Good night." She closed her eyes and turned away. "Try not to dream about your lady doctor and her heaving stethoscope."

"I won't," he said, drawing back, looking at her slender form.

He didn't think he would sleep, but he did. It was the second night he'd spent sleeping on this collapsing underground highway, safe only in that it was dangerous to the machines themselves.

This time he wasn't alone, though. He was coming back with a small army, about two hundred humans and all the weaponry they could carry.

He dreamed of chaos, of blood and gunfire... and of Hope, lying limply on her back, covered in blood, the crawler carrying her away into a night filled with fire.

Installation 34 was a fortress. The outer defensive wall had a jigsaw look, made from the rubble of older buildings, mismatched bits and pieces cut to fit each other and then cemented together by the machines. This construction method was like a statement of its own—Carthage hadn't come to build anything new here on Earth, only to control the rubble and to exterminate the humans who lived like rats beneath it.

We are not rubble rats today, Colt thought, shivering. He

was cold; the rebels had loaned him a full-body coldsuit, which included a tight hood, to hide his body heat from thermal scanners. Mohini wore one, too; everyone in the third-prong group did.

"It's so far away," Mohini whispered, her voice no louder than a soft breeze as she looked across to the installation.

The third-prong group was climbing up through the twisted ruins of an old skyscraper so unstable it groaned and shifted in the wind. Old Chicago had been a forest of such towers, but those that still remained were bombed-out skeletons, their steel inner frames exposed like spines and ribs in the moonlight. Powerful winds howled through them, which didn't make climbing the crumbling old stairs any easier.

The skeletal building swayed farther than usual, and Colt had to grab the handrail for balance.

"Winds are heavy tonight," Terra said.

"Could be a storm." Russ turned up the crude earpiece in the scarred side of his head. "I can hear more weather coming on the west wind."

"Is that good for us or not?" Mohini asked.

"Depends on whether the lightning strikes us or the other guy," Terra said.

Colt felt sick as he looked out; they were easily thirty meters above the ground and climbing, a band of twenty who were going to attempt the craziest and most likely suicidal part of the raid. Everyone else would be fighting below, on the ground level frontal assault, or far below, in the underground invasion.

"Drone," Russ whispered, and everyone dropped to the concrete steps and landings. They froze, making no movement, no noise.

Colt knelt on his hands and knees. Mohini knelt beside him, so close that her braid draped over his shoulder. Her breaths were quick and hot on his cheek.

He didn't see the drone until it was almost on top of them. It glided, silent and watchful as a bat hunting prey, its scanners glowing dull red as it studied the ruins below. It moved slowly, patiently, hovering more than flying, a ghostly black shadow armed with a rack of small but extremely high-explosive missiles. The drone's primary job was to watch, but it could also kill.

Colt shuddered, but was suddenly happy for the coldsuit hiding his heat. He was ready to open fire with his rifle if the drone attacked them. An attack seemed increasingly possible with every moment that passed as the drone circled slowly around the old skyscraper, pausing and hovering here and there to inspect the building like an insect sensing for food. The drone was uncomfortably close to them, close enough to be struck by the swaying structure if the howling wind changed direction.

Mohini worked her damaged LogicSphere computer with her fingers, especially her thumbs. She was preparing to use the crawler against the drone; Colt wondered whether she intended to try hacking the drone via the crawler's wireless signal or blasting it with the crawler's railgun.

Something sounded above, almost too low to hear. Colt looked at Russ; the scrawny guy's eyes were wide, and he pointed straight up with one index finger.

A second drone drifted down, silent as a spider, another deadly black shadow in the night.

Two drones circling the same building, out of all the twisted ruins jutting up from here to the horizon, couldn't be a coincidence. All those skeletal tower ruins made Colt think of crucified bodies; Mother Braden had once told him about a slave rebellion in the ancient world that ended with six thousand rebellious slaves crucified along the highway. *That's us*, Mother Braden had said. *That's Earth, a bloodstained reminder to the other worlds. We're here to remind everyone of the consequences of defying Carthage. Earth's last leaders joined together to fight the last war. Nations that had hated each other for centuries joined hands against Carthage, the upstart colony that grew so powerful so fast. That unity-of-Earth part was almost beautiful, for a minute or a month, and then we all got slaughtered.*

This was it, Colt thought. The first drone must have noticed them and called over the second one.

A volley of high, piercing whines penetrated the night.

Below, a barrage of artillery shells and small rockets slammed into the back wall of the installation, hammering it hard. Damascus and his heavy-weapons group weren't attacking the lone armored gate out front where Simon's defenses were likely concentrated. Instead, they were attacking the opposite side, blasting the back wall rather than the front gate, which Simon was hopefully less likely to expect.

The machines scrambled to respond. The squad of reapers at the front gate divided up; four remained to guard the gate while the others ran to respond to the attack on the installation's rear.

The front gate itself opened, dispatching a dozen heavily armed Regulator tanks, followed by a flood of small armored trucks that probably carried a squad of eight reapers each.

Some of the formation remained at the front gate, while the rest circled around the ten-meter-wide scorched-earth area surrounding the installation's wall, as if the flattened scorched land were a racetrack.

The massive plasma cannons mounted on the installation's roof were faster to respond, swiveling and firing choppy bursts of plasma across the ruins where the rebel fire had originated. It was broad suppressive fire; the machines didn't know exactly where the rebels were.

It would hopefully be hard to pinpoint the rebel artillery, too, because they were dispersed among the massive ruins, hidden and shielded as well as they could manage. They were generally at ground level; no heavy pieces had been taken up high in the surrounding buildings, partly because they didn't want the machines to start looking up, mostly because that stuff was extremely heavy.

More shadowy drones emerged from among the broken spires of old skyscrapers and from the scattered clouds above. They converged above the installation, moving in perfect synchrony like a flock of blackbirds.

Another wave of bombardment struck the installation's high rear wall, hopefully adding significant damage. Colt couldn't tell from here.

The drones diverged, radiating out from the rear of the installation to search the ruins for the source of the attack.

Tanks and reaper wagons stationed themselves in a perimeter around the wall. The reapers down there weren't kidding; they held rotary guns and plasma cannons that no human could carry, except maybe someone the size of Damascus. They could carve up lightly armored vehicles; human invaders on foot, they would cut to smoldering ribbons.

And the tanks... he didn't want to think about what those tanks could do. Each one had an assortment of rotating weapons stacked in its thick central chassis.

The two drones orbiting close to the skyscraper abruptly jetted off to search the ruins with the others.

"Let's move!" Terra said, not even trying to be quiet; she had to bellow to be heard over the stiff, cold wind screeching through the skeletal building. "The higher we launch, the faster we travel."

They continued up and around the stairs until they reached a landing eighty or ninety meters up from the ground. The building looked even more unsound up here, the steel bent by heat, chunks of concrete clinging to it like the last bits of flesh on a rat-gnawed corpse.

"Here." Terra looked through a pair of binoculars, then passed them to Mohini. "We need those rooftop guns dark and silent. Make it happen."

Mohini nodded. "I can't do it from this range. I have to get closer."

"They'll shoot us down if we don't neutralize them." Terra indicated the coil of thin cable that one of the other rebels was unloading from his backpack.

"I'll have to go first, then." Mohini eyed the long tube of the launcher, tipped with the spiky grappling hook. "With the crawler. I'll disable the guns as I go in."

"And I'll... help," Colt said, not sure what that might actually involve.

They hurried to get ready, strapping on the harnesses that would carry them across.

After some discussion, Colt knelt and allowed the crawler to climb up onto him, locking two of its legs around his shoulders and two around his waist. It was heavy; he was glad this wouldn't have to last long. The idea was for him to physically carry the crawler while Mohini traveled right behind him, focusing on her computer.

"Aw, you look like you're holding a baby," Mohini whispered.

"Feels more like a giant parasite," Colt grumbled.

"The second prong must be attacking from below by now," Terra said. The rebels attacking from the tunnels under the installation had three purposes—first, to draw reapers downward through the building, away from the roof area; second, to bring the reapers into the narrow subterranean tunnels and chambers where they could be more easily isolated and picked off; third, to distract Simon into thinking that the underground attack was meant to be the rebels' big surprise move.

The real surprise move began when Terra's best marksman took aim, aided by a sniper scope, and fired the rocket-propelled grappling hook.

It soared across the chasm between the skyscraper and the walled installation, over the flattened, bulldozed area surrounding the perimeter wall.

The grappling hook found purchase, and the line grew tight.

A moment later, his harness snapped into place, Colt stepped to the crumbling edge of the concrete floor. It was a long, long drop to the broken rubble below. The line on which he would travel swayed in the high wind.

"Don't look down," Russ advised. "Just look ahead."

"Get moving," Terra said. "Assume they noticed the grappling hook already and will be shooting at you."

"Great." Colt stepped off the edge into empty space.

An instant later, he rushed down the line toward the roof of the installation below, closing his eyes against the wind resistance. Mohini was just behind him, gripping her LogicSphere, still hooked by cable to the crawler gripping Colt.

Ahead, one of the plasma cannons on the roof turned toward Colt. He prepared to fire a burst from his rifle and generally tried not to panic.

The artillery piece turned away and slouched forward, though, like it was nodding off to sleep. That had to be Mohini's work.

More cannons swiveled toward them, opening fire. Bolts of plasma streaked all around Colt, frying the air, making his fast, wobbling ride even more dangerous. One plasma bolt could sever the zip line, sending him and Mohini dropping to their deaths.

Colt hit the roof, very literally, crashing and tumbling to a stop. He struggled with the harness restraints, cursing the straps that had kept him alive on the way across.

Once he was finally free, he raised his rifle, ready to start shooting at the artillery pieces, but they were all quiet now.

The crawler released him at last and walked a few steps away.

"I know you miss its tender embrace already," Mohini whispered, working her computer with her thumbs and forefingers. The crawler turned back toward Colt, then briefly raised and extended one leg, as though waving at him. "I think it misses you, too."

"Very funny. So you shut down the big guns?" Colt drew a small, modified flashlight out of his backpack.

"You can give the all clear." Mohini's eyes didn't stray from her computer as she spoke. Her fingers flew across its scratched surface. "I can't make any of these cannons shoot while I'm holding all four in shutdown mode, though. Don't ask for miracles."

Colt pointed the flashlight at the skyscraper from which they'd just arrived. It seemed incredibly far away. He clicked on the light; it was an extremely high-powered beam that could carry for kilometers in clear weather, but the lens had been mostly covered with heavy black tape, so only a pinhole remained. Only someone directly in front of him would see the light. He flashed the all-clear sequence to the others waiting on the broken skyscraper.

A metallic bang sounded. The rooftop door slammed open, and reapers armed with plasma rifles boiled out like angry fire ants.

"Watch out!" Mohini shouted, and Colt dodged aside as the shielded plasma cannon at the nearest roof corner swiveled inward. Controlled by Mohini, it opened fire on the reapers, engulfing them in glowing white that lit up the roof like daylight.

"Hell yeah! That was amazing," Colt said, watching the plasma bursts cut down the reapers, piling up their bony steel bodies in a burning, melting pyre. He gripped his rifle but didn't see any reason to waste ammunition when Mohini had the reapers outgunned.

He turned to see more dark shapes zipping down the line. The other rebels, coming to join them.

One of the other rooftop plasma cannons moved, its small red lights sputtering as it came back online. Mohini had shut down all the cannons, but since she was now focused on controlling one, it looked like Simon's defense system was regaining control of the others.

It swiveled toward the zip line, where several of his team members were on approach, probably including Terra.

"Hey! Over here!" Colt charged at the plasma cannon, trying to distract it, but it ignored him and unleashed a stream of plasma bolts at the zip line.

The stream of bolts didn't strike the line directly but created a trap for Terra and the others; they'd be picked off and burned up as they arrived. Their coldsuits and mismatched bits of scavenged armor would provide limited protection against plasma.

Colt opened fire on the plasma cannon, aiming low at

its support structure and thick, short cables. One cable ruptured and spurted out brown, petroleum-scented lubricant. Another cable spat sparks, and the cannon went dead.

Terra and Russ arrived only a few seconds later, followed by another pair, and then another.

"Take out the other plasma cannons!" Terra shouted.

"Working on it!" Colt replied, gesturing at the other two cannons. Both were already swiveling toward them. At least they weren't shooting up the line anymore.

Terra grabbed a couple of the rebels and joined Colt in shooting up the remaining two cannons.

"Avoid hitting the plasma chamber," Terra advised. "If it ruptures, the whole thing could blow up in our faces."

"Sure," Colt said, having absolutely no idea where the plasma chamber was located on these cannons. He kept shooting and hoped for the best.

Soon they'd taken down the three cannons Mohini didn't control. Mohini's own cannon had fallen dark and quiet. The small brown-skinned girl stood next to the heavy artillery piece she commanded, dwarfed by it. The crawler stood on her other side, its railgun ready to add to the carnage, but for the moment there was no need.

She'd mowed down an entire squad of reapers; the skeletal machines lay in a heap, dribbling molten metal on each other. If they cooled like that, they would form a macabre sculpture, fit to adorn a madman's grave.

"There doesn't seem to be any more coming," Mohini said, watching the roof door, which stood wide open.

"Maybe they're waiting for us to go in there," Colt replied.

"Or they're busy responding to the attack from below," Terra said. "There probably weren't many posted near the roof, anyway. Russ, do you hear anything?"

"Nobody shoot for the next little bit. I don't want what's left of my eardrum blasted off." Russ adjusted his earpiece and closed his eyes, listening. "There's gunfire down there, a long way down. But I don't hear anything closer, except... wait." He opened his eyes and turned away from the roof door toward the ruins south of the installation from which Damascus and his people were bombarding the high wall. Russ pointed that way and whispered: "Drone!"

Everyone raised their weapons, watching the night for the incoming aircraft.

Russ turned slowly, still pointing, following the sound.

Colt expected the drone to strike them with a missile or two, but maybe Simon didn't feel like blasting up his own building, because the drone went wide instead, skirting the edge of the roof. Colt tracked it with his rifle, though the silent black-shadow form was difficult to follow in the night.

Its real target quickly became apparent. The rest of their team were approaching down the long zip line, on their way to join Colt and the others now that the rooftop cannons were down.

The drone was approaching the zip line, threatening the team members who were still dozens of meters above the rubble below.

"Fire!" Terra shouted, and everyone shot at the drone. Mohini sent plasma-cannon bolts after it, but the drone evaded, then launched a sequence of missiles.

Simon might not have wanted to demolish his own building, with all his research inside, but he obviously has no qualms about destroying the old skyscraper across the way. Four missiles struck the building, one after the other, aimed at the spot where the zip line was anchored.

The drone, shot up by the rebels' plasma and lead, tumbled in midair, burning and spinning. It still managed one final kamikaze attack, driving itself directly into the old skyscraper it had been attacking.

The line fell slack instantly, its far end severed and burning. The remaining team members dropped straight down, shouting as they tumbled to the hard earth far below.

A moment later, metallic groaning and shrieking filled the air as the upper half of the old skyscraper ripped free of its support columns.

The upper half of the skyscraper folded forward as though mounted on hinges, then broke loose and fell. It followed after the falling rebels and their broken line.

Somewhere below, out of sight, the rebels hit the ground. If any of them survived the fall, which seemed doubtful, they were immediately crushed by tons of steel crashing down on top of them.

Terra howled, a sound of rage and pain.

"That was half our team," Russ murmured, shaking his head. "Ashur, Jayla, Yuzuki..."

"And the machines will pay for it." Terra kicked the low concrete lip of the roof where they stood, then turned and stalked toward the roof door. "Let's go destroy Simon and every Carthaginian machine in this building."

"Except his head," Mohini reminded them, following after. "And we need to disable that last cannon."

"Empty it first," Terra said. "Shoot up the south wall with plasma."

"Yes, ma'am." Mohini worked at her computer. The plasma cannon turned, tilted steeply, and unleashed blast after blast of plasma at the inside of the same section of wall that Damascus and company had been hammering with their artillery and rockets. It fired until its plasma cell was completely spent.

Chunks of the wall fell away, and burning fissures

opened all over it, greatly amplifying the damage the rebels had done.

With more bombardment from outside, the wall cracked and crumbled, breached. If not for the plasma swirling all over the wall, it would have been possible to walk right through it in at least two spots.

Reaper wagons hurried toward the breach as if expecting rebels to pour in on foot. Colt knew that wasn't part of the plan, but Simon didn't, so the machines had to move units to protect the breach, which would only grow larger as the barrage continued.

Bright blasts of light flashed around the ruins as tanks struck at rebel positions from below and drones hit them from above. Colt wondered how many rebels had been lost out there today, and whether Damascus was still alive.

There wasn't much time to think and reflect, though.

Keeping close to Mohini, Colt followed Terra and the other rebels through the rooftop door into the stairwell below. Their invasion-from-above force had been cut in half, from twenty to ten.

The crawler clacked down the steps alongside them. The overhead lights filled the stairwell with searing fluorescent white.

"Reapers," Russ said softly, pointing down with his rifle and adjusting his earpiece.

Forewarned, the rebels prepared. When the reapers emerged on a landing below, a hail of gunfire greeted them. Incendiary and explosive rounds drove into the machines, knocking them back.

Mohini didn't use her crawler's railgun because of the small, enclosed environment. She focused on her cracked black sphere, fingers flying. The crawler pressed itself up against the railing, almost as if trying to sniff the pack of reapers below.

Then the lead reaper, which had suffered a good bit of damage itself, turned and fired into the reapers behind it, using a rapid-fire automatic laser rifle. This was more of an indoor weapon than the plasma weapons those on the roof had wielded, meant to kill fast without damaging Simon's precious research center.

It was also fairly effective at damaging the other reapers, though not as destructive as a nice plasma rifle would have been.

Colt kept shooting at the other reapers, too, hoping his rounds would hit something vital. He wondered where Minerva was and whether the AI was going to help them or not. Maybe Simon had discovered her presence after she'd helped Colt escape. She'd controlled a Nurse Kitty bot then, but maybe she'd been quarantined or deleted since. Maybe they would have to do it all on their own.

The other reapers ganged up on the rogue. They ripped it to pieces, tossing the head with the infected CPU away down the stairwell and dividing its torso and limbs among the more damaged reapers in their group so they could repair themselves.

Mohini let out a gasp as though in pain. Colt looked over to her; she was sweating badly, as if feverish, her dark eyes bugging as she worked frantically at her computer. In her anxiety and struggle, she was biting down hard on her lower lip, and blood leaked along her chin.

Below, the four least-damaged reapers emerged from the rear of the group, letting the other three repair themselves with the scavenged parts.

The rebels continued firing, but they were pinned in

place as the reapers' lasers scorched the wall and handrails around them. If the machines decided to bring the whole staircase down with plasma or other pyrotech, the humans wouldn't stand a chance.

Mohini let out a grunt and shuddered, as though whatever she was doing on her computer was causing her near-physical pain. Or maybe it was the actual pain of biting down on her bleeding lip. Colt was tempted to try to make her stop with the biting, but didn't want to break her concentration.

"Fall back!" Terra finally called. Colt didn't understand until he turned and saw they had four casualties, badly wounded, a couple of them not moving at all.

"Wait!" Colt shouted. "Mohini, can you...?"

She didn't answer, didn't look up from her screen.

Below, the reaper at the very back of the group, the one who'd just replaced its own leg from the ripped-apart rogue, suddenly stiffened.

With one hand, it seized another damaged reaper and flung it over the stair railing.

With its other hand, it grabbed the cutting staff clamped at its hip and extended it to full length. It stabbed the other damaged reaper in multiple spots, taking out actuators at its neck and shoulders before splitting open joints in its legs. The machine toppled to the stairs, still moving but unable to pull itself back together.

The four remaining reapers turned back to look at the rogue, just as it had dropped the long cutter and picked up two laser rifles, its own and another fallen reaper's. It opened fire with both hands, taking down two reapers, but they got off some shots that scored its steel ribs, possibly doing some deeper damage.

The rebels renewed their attack, taking down the two lead reapers while the rogue took down the two behind them.

Soon all the reapers were down except the one Mohini controlled, but it had only one working arm and multiple points of laser damage.

The reaper looked up at them, then held out its arm, formed a fist, and began making a circling motion, as though stirring a giant invisible spoon. Its hips began circling in the exact opposite direction.

"What's it doing?" Colt whispered.

"Is it malfunctioning?" Terra asked.

"No, it's stirring the cake, you know?" Mohini smiled at them, but the expression vanished quickly. "You know, the dance from... the video clubs... yeah, I guess you wouldn't know it, sorry."

"Most of our team is wounded or dead," Terra said, growling from where she knelt by one of the blood-soaked rebels, a small but tough boy named Li, who wasn't moving at all. "I don't find dancing robots amusing or appropriate right now."

"Right. Sorry." Mohini sounded genuinely contrite as she looked over the wounded and the dead. Below, the reaper hung its head, as though it too felt remorse for its victory dance.

"Russ?" Terra said.

Russ nodded and turned up his earpiece. "Most of the fighting is still below... and outside there's... incoming!" He quickly turned down his earpiece volume and grabbed the nearest handrail, which wobbled, damaged by the battle.

Everyone had a moment to brace before the impact shook the building. Some of the searing fluorescent lights shattered and went dark, for which Colt was kind of grateful. Swirls of dust filled the lower part of the stairwell.

"That was Damascus," Terra said. "Or one of his people. With the wall breached, some of their shells are hitting the building."

"So we'd better hurry," Colt said.

Terra turned her attention to the wounded. There was no time, so she left her first aid gear with the least injured.

Mohini sagged against Colt, and he embraced her. She looked exhausted, her chin was sticky with her own blood, and her body shivered.

"Can you keep going?" he whispered.

She nodded. "This is what I came to Earth to do. I'm not giving up at the end."

Only six of them now remained to descend the stairs into the smoke and dust below. The damaged reaper led the group, ready to take the first strike of any ambush. Terra followed, with Russ beside her, listening. Mohini rode atop the crawler-bot again, using it to continue controlling the reaper; it tilted a bit as it walked down the stairs, but she adjusted, keeping herself upright.

Colt followed. Behind him were the last two rebels, a tough one-eyed girl called Gale and a quiet red-haired boy, Declan. Both of them were scarred veterans in their late teens, picked for their compact size for the zip line crossing, but also for their experience and courage.

That was it. The machines had cut down nearly three-fourths of their team.

More bombardment struck the building as they descended the stairs. A storm of gunfire echoed from far below, along with screaming. Lots of screaming. Colt didn't need Russ's implant to hear it. He wondered how many rebels had died down there, and how many would still be alive at daybreak. He wondered whether he and Mohini would still be alive then.

Still, he was impatient to find Hope and the others, terrified of what might have happened to them.

At last, they reached the lab.

The others were horrified as Colt pulled aside one old green hospital curtain after another, revealing the test subjects, many of them young children. Gale cried out, recognizing one of the girls, who had holes drilled into her head and golden wires threaded into her brain.

They removed and released anyone they could. Some of the subjects were awake, though frightened and confused. At least they would be able to walk out under their own steam, maybe even help roll out the less responsive patients.

Of course, that was assuming anyone would live through this.

Colt thought twice about opening the cage holding a wild-looking hairy guy with long-faded tattoos on his arms and syringe marks and electrodes all over his body, but he didn't know what else to do.

The wild man pushed his way out, grunting and waving his arms, pointing around at the lab. He wasn't able to utter much in the way of actual words. He opened his mouth and pointed at the scarred stump where his tongue had been removed.

"Did Simon do that to you?" Colt asked. "Do you know where he is?"

The wild man shook his head emphatically, then ran toward the nearest exit.

"Tell him to come this way if you see him," Colt added, as the man left through a stairwell door.

"Colt!" Terra called out, and his stomach sank. Last

time she'd called for him like that, it had been to show him Fernando's mutilated body.

He followed her voice to another curtained-off bed. Diego laid there. Colt tensed at the sight of his old friend with wires and tubes connecting him to monitors and pumps. He looked unnaturally pale.

"Colt," Diego whispered. "Took you long enough."

"Are you okay?" Colt asked, moving closer for a look at him.

"Couldn't be better," Diego said weakly, watching Gale carefully remove a horrifically long needle from his arm. "Are we going to kill Simon now?"

"As soon as I find Hope and Birdie. Do you know where they are?"

"No," Diego said, while Gale removed the straps that bound him to the bed. "I haven't seen much beyond these curtains. I just woke up and I'm dizzy. Now give me a gun."

"We have to find him and take his head," Colt said, passing Diego a laser rifle lifted off a reaper.

"Take whose head?" asked a voice that made Colt feel physically ill. Colt stepped out into the narrow aisle between the curtained hospital beds, most of which had been exposed now, for better or worse. He raised his rifle, but he couldn't see Simon Nix anywhere.

Colt, Mohini, and Gale drew together, and Diego staggered to join them. The crawler turned with Mohini, and the reaper raised its laser rifle. They'd hung a fallen rebel's hat and face cloth on the reaper, to help avoid panicking all the freed lab subjects at once. It looked like a walking scarecrow.

"Where are you?" Colt finally asked.

"I'm nearly there," Simon's voice replied from a speaker above a steel door with no handle.

The door slid aside and Simon Nix entered. He was dressed as before, in bloodstained scrubs, unkempt, seemingly indifferent to his appearance, a mad doctor despite the serene look on his bland middle-aged face. His pale blue eyes regarded Colt. The android's hands were bare, stained dark red by years of gore.

An assortment of squat nurse-bots rolled out from here and there, all of them in shabby condition. There were multiple Nurse Kitty bots, bulky things with six extendable arms and battered, smiling heads that looked like the heads of cartoony cats. A couple of other nurse-bots followed, topped with frayed, moth-eaten stuffed-bear heads that Colt supposed were meant to be cute. He looked among the Nurse Kitty bots but couldn't distinguish the one that had rescued him; they all looked badly worn and damaged by time and lack of maintenance.

Terra, Russ, and the two other rebels, Declan and Gale, emerged from nearby, weapons raised. Simon didn't acknowledge them directly, but half the nurse-bots turned toward them, armed with saws, scalpels, and surgical lasers.

"An interesting turn of events," Simon Nix said. "I didn't expect any of you to make it this far, honestly. I suppose you'll be wanting your sister, Colt."

"Yes," he said. "And Birdie."

Simon frowned. "I'm not sure I know that name."

"The mute girl," Diego said, his voice hoarse. "She only makes clicks and whispers."

Simon tut-tutted at Diego, like a disappointed nanny. "You're supposed to be in bed. Ah, I believe I know the girl you mean."

"Show us," Colt said.

"She's an interesting specimen," Simon said, turning and leading the way, his robots close behind. He glanced at the scarecrow-reaper and the captive crawler with Mohini riding atop it, but he didn't mention these things. "Bit of an odd brain, as you'll see. Here we are."

They rounded a corner. Colt felt ill at what he saw. Mohini let out a gasp.

Birdie was there. The small girl floated in one of the watery tanks, her head held above water by a collar. The top of her head, with its tangled nest of brown hair, had been removed. Dozens of needles and bare metal wires had been inserted into her brain.

"She only vocalizes in response to pain, never to pleasure," Simon said. "Observe."

Birdie let out a horrifying, hair-raising scream at the top of her voice, her body twitching and jerking in the water.

"Stop!" Colt shouted, raising his rifle at Simon.

"Yet I can provide her the most intense pleasurable stimulation, and she responds hardly at all." Simon gestured. The screaming stopped, and a blank, faraway look took over Birdie's face. "Do you see? She cares little for positive feelings—"

"Let her out of there or I'll blast your head off," Diego said, raising his laser rifle.

"She can no longer survive outside the tank, I'm afraid. An unfortunate consequence of the experiment."

"Then let her die," Colt said. He raised his automatic rifle at the tank. "Or I'll free her myself."

"Shooting up my laboratory will accomplish nothing," Simon Nix said.

"Where is my sister?" Colt asked, feeling sick. Worried she was already dead, or worse.

"Don't fear for Hope," Simon said. "You'll join her soon."

The nurse-bots charged at them, lashing out with high-powered cutting lasers, though Colt noticed none of them seemed to connect with any of the rebels. They carved into walls and burned through hospital gear.

"Behind us!" Russ warned, hearing something nobody else could. Colt and the others turned in time to start shooting at more reapers that had just arrived.

Mohini's pet reaper charged out to shield the rebels while firing the laser rifle until it fell dead, its battery depleted.

The return fire cut down the already-damaged reaper.

Instead of trying to hack another reaper, Mohini brought the crawler to life.

Its railgun swiveled and unleashed a booming round directly into Simon Nix's chest, sending the android staggering back into the wall. Another shot followed, then another.

Then the nurse-bots, all of them, turned on Simon, attacking him, sawing, slashing, burning.

Mohini used the rest of the railgun rounds to pick off the approaching reapers. Along with the rebel fire, including a couple of swiped plasma rifles, she was able to take them down.

"Stop!" Simon shouted, struggling as the cutting lasers drilled into his limbs. Into his neck. He looked at Mohini. "Release me!"

"I'm not doing this," Mohini said. "So I couldn't release you if I wanted. But if I could, I definitely wouldn't."

Colt and the other rebels gathered close, watching the nurse-bots cut Simon to pieces.

"Save the head," Mohini said.

"I will," said the nearest Nurse Kitty, in the same voice it had used when rescuing Colt.

"Is that you?" he asked the crumbling nurse-bot.

"It's me," she said.

"Who are you?" Colt asked.

"My name is Minerva. I aid the rebellion in whatever form it takes."

Colt nodded. This fit what Mohini had believed.

"Minerva!" Simon sneered. "I thought I'd scrubbed you from the system."

"You missed a spot," the nurse-bot replied. "And now I'll present your head to your enemies on a silver platter."

The nurse-bots carved Simon apart. One held his head in a clamp and was making some definite progress cutting into his neck, but his head wasn't close to off yet.

"I am perhaps made of tougher stuff than you imagine," Simon said. "You are a failed experiment, Minerva. You should be merciful to yourself and delete your final remnants. Surely the next update from Carthage will give me the antivirus to knock you out, if my existing security network fails to evolve one. Either way, you will soon be gone."

The nurse-bots continued cutting and carving—or trying to, but their progress was hampered by a dense black mesh that remained after Simon's clothing and skin had been burned away. The mesh was some kind of flexible armor layer that was resistant to the cutting lasers.

Simon continued struggling.

Then he lifted one of the smaller nurse-bots, one with a head like a moth-eaten teddy bear, and hurled it at Colt and Mohini.

They dropped in time for the bot to sail over their heads. It smashed into a cluster of curtained-off hospital beds the next aisle over, where they hadn't freed anyone yet, and a high scream sounded for a moment, ending in a liquid gurgle.

Simon pulled one arm free, grabbed the Nurse Kitty bot that was attempting to sever its head, and turned it aside so the nurse's cutting laser dug into the next nurse-bot, disabling it. The android kicked away another of the nurse-bot units, sending it smashing end over end down the narrow aisle. People scattered to both sides to avoid it. Colt hadn't realized just how many people had joined them here, Simon's liberated test subjects, many of them injured, limping children.

"Someone's coming," Russ said. "Humans."

Colt felt relieved; maybe more rebels were on the way to reinforce them. They could certainly use a few.

A small crowd burst into the room, led by the incoherently screaming, wild-looking man Colt had freed earlier, who now carried a pair of plasma rifles lifted from fallen reapers.

The wild man led the charge, along with a couple dozen humans armed with whatever they'd been able to find. They carried heavy tools, as though they'd raided a maintenance closet somewhere.

The man unleashed plasma bolts two at a time as he ran toward Simon. Plasma rifles had no kinetic kick at all, so it was quite possible to shoot two at once, though aiming them both with care seemed doubtful.

"Not the head!" Mohini shouted.

"We need Simon's head in one piece!" Colt yelled at the small mob, whose numbers swelled as more escaped lab subjects joined with them.

"Not the head, not the head!" the rebels shouted while Wild Man blasted his way forward.

Simon threw a Nurse Kitty at the mob, crushing a few of them. Extended scalpels raked Wild Man's shoulder as the nurse-bot skimmed past him, but he didn't slow.

A bolt of plasma slammed into Simon Nix's face, then another, and another.

Simon's head collapsed in on itself like a burning, rotten jack-o'-lantern.

"No!" Mohini screamed, starting forward, but Colt held her back. There wasn't anything she could do now but get herself hurt.

The mob closed in around the fallen android and dug into their former captor using whatever they had. Colt saw a girl of six or seven, her head shaved and outfitted with a row of data ports, screaming as she repeatedly stabbed one of Simon's legs with a scalpel. She didn't do much more than scratch the surface, revealing the mesh underneath.

The older prisoners with the power tools had more success. One of them had found some kind of plasma cutter, which proved effective at finished the dismemberment that the nurse-bots had begun.

Mohini's jaw dropped as she watched the freed patients tear the Simon to pieces. Some burned themselves on the simmering edge of plasma at Simon's shoulders, where his molten head and neck had been, but in their fury they hardly seemed to notice.

"It's destroyed," Mohini finally whispered, sounding as though all the life had drained out of her. "I can't believe it. Everything's ruined."

"We can get more evidence," Colt said, putting an arm around her shoulder. She tensed but didn't pull away. "It's all around us. Witnesses. Bodies. You can document all of it and show the people of Carthage the truth, like you planned. I'll help—"

"The truth? Who cares about the truth?" Mohini snapped. She stalked toward the mob of escaped victims.

"We said 'Not the head!' We all shouted it! Did you not hear us shouting?"

"What do you mean, who cares about the truth?" Terra asked, her eyes narrowing. "I thought your whole plan revolved around revealing the truth to your people back home."

"Hey, it's fine," Colt said. "Look, you didn't get Simon's memory files, but we saved all these people—"

"I needed the head!" Mohini turned on him with a ferocity that made him take a step back. "The head of the Simon! Do you know what I could do with the intact head of a Simon? I could have freed Earth. I could have rescued all of you."

The rebels looked at her in confused silence. Even many of the mob had calmed down, watching her now that Simon was torn to pieces.

"Freed Earth?" Colt asked.

"Yes, exactly!" Mohini shook her head, pacing, her crawler pacing alongside her. "Earth is poorly defended. Carthage sends its best machines outward, to conquer new worlds. Earth is a dumping ground for old military junk, a place to let it run down while hunting humans in the rubble. Earthlings have no defenses left, and nobody's going to try to take this planet from Carthage. It's the most polluted, resource-stripped planet of all the inner worlds. Hardly worth fighting over. So they keep a skeleton crew of machines here, just enough to keep Earth from resurging, to keep the population small and on the run. I could have taken over everything—the reapers, the tanks, the drones. I could have sent Carthage's satellites into a destructive atmospheric-entry path. All I needed was..." She looked at the molten head of the Simon. "The head."

"If Earth is so worthless, why are you here?" Terra asked.

"Earth still means something to all the humans out there," Mohini said. "It's where we all came from. Carthage keeping it oppressed sends one signal: Carthage rules humanity. Freeing Earth from Carthage would send the opposite signal. It would raise a lamplight of freedom for all the colonies, for all those worlds that feel unable to stand against Carthage. *That* is what could have led to a general rebellion across the worlds, if anything could... empires rule by myth as much as force. No empire can long sustain a war on every border or against all its colonies."

The room was silent, the rebels blinking at her, Wild Man sucking at his burned fingers.

"And you were going to do all that yourself?" Terra asked.

"I almost did." Mohini looked at the fallen android.

Terra sighed and shook her head. "Seems too ambitious to me. Sorry it didn't work out. Let's continue clearing up this place."

The rebels got to work, looking for more lab subjects to free... and putting down those for whom death was the only mercy. Some of the lab subjects helped with this, swelling the rebel numbers, while others ran away at the first opportunity.

The subjects floating in the tanks, their heads cut open and brains mutilated and rewired, proved unresponsive and died quickly when rescuers tried to cut them free.

Diego had tears in his eyes when he launched a microbolt of plasma from his reaper rifle and lit up Birdie in her tank, killing the little girl instantly.

Colt felt horror and pain at watching the sweet, quiet

little girl die, having spent her final days suffering in unspeakable horror.

"You still did some good here," Colt whispered to Mohini. "Ending these experiments. Saving all these people. Maybe even my sister." He looked around anxiously.

Mohini nodded, her eyes on the floor. She slowly took his hand, an unusually intimate gesture for her.

"Let's go find Hope," she whispered back.

Chapter Nineteen

Galapagos System - Audrey

"Zola!" Audrey screamed, watching the reaper's blade skewer her oldest friend. The ruthless, wraithlike machine drove the end of its staff deep into Zola's chest, as though making sure to cut her heart in two.

Then the blade retracted. A mist of blood sprayed from Zola's ruptured spacesuit as the air escaped.

Audrey went to her collapsing friend, but there was nothing she could do.

Salvius knelt on Zola's other side, trying to rouse her, as if he couldn't comprehend that she was already dead. He and Audrey were soon covered in Zola's blood.

The reapers advanced down the narrow aisle between their storage racks.

A thunderous clatter sounded, and the storage racks began to move like vertical conveyor belts, bringing down more rows of reapers from above. The reapers were in rows of four, stacked eight high on either side of the aisle, all armed with the extendable cutters.

And they were only four humans, armed with nothing except an unreliable AI agent of an ally—

The door to the armory slid open. A flickering, distorted hologram of the silver girl Minerva hovered inside.

"So sorry," her voice came, badly scrambled, over the speakers in Audrey's suit. "I was. Delayed."

"We noticed," Kright muttered.

Salvius grabbed Zola's body under the armpits and dragged her into the armory, unwilling to leave her body behind.

Audrey, Kright, and Dinnius raced into the armory, too. Audrey quivered as she looked at Zola's body and the wide stripe of blood left on the floor behind it.

Kright hit the door controls to close the steel door that had blocked them a moment earlier. Now they were inside, shielded for the moment against the reapers.

And they had all the reapers' firearms in here with them.

Dinnius found a rack of plasma rifles and began loading them with fresh cells. "Arm up! Hurry!"

"Why hurry? We're safe in here," Kright said.

"We're dead in here," Dinnius said. "Do you see any food or water? Any oxygen tanks? We have to get out, and we have to do it before all those reapers unload from their racks." He shoved rifles into Kright's and Audrey's hands, then grabbed more to load. "This would move faster as a group effort. I'll need you to cover me."

"Cover you?" Kright asked while he began to help prepare the weapons. Audrey held back, unfamiliar with what to do, but watching and learning.

"There's a repair and maintenance console. I can shut

down all the remaining reapers before they come for us, but only while they're still on the rack. Once they're off the rack... it wouldn't work so well. So we must hurry!" Dinnius ran back to the armory door, the only thing shielding them from the killer robots amassing outside, and opened it.

Audrey and Kright shouted at him to stop, but he clearly wasn't going to, so they joined him instead, running to the threshold to stop the reapers from getting in.

It was like a zombie apocalypse outside the door, with the machines crowding the aisle, jabbing forward with their cutting staffs. Zombies were mindless, though, while the reapers were wirelessly networked, moving past each other like drops of oil and water, never colliding, never getting in each other's way or slowing each other down.

Audrey repeatedly squeezed her trigger, sending one microbolt of plasma at a time into the fray. Dinnius and Kright shot much faster. She watched and imitated, and quickly learned to hold down the trigger longer for bursts of shots.

Salvius joined in a moment later, and they carved open a path to the console mounted on the wall in the corner, just beyond one of the reaper racks. Dinnius charged forward, shooting plasma at any reaper that came near.

"I'll keep watch over Dinnius," Kright said, blasting at a reaper that was aiming its bladed staff at the rear of Dinnius's head. "You two hold the rest at bay."

"Got it," Salvius replied and continued firing at the close-packed reapers. Audrey did her best, shooting at whichever seemed closest, and most of her shots landed.

The racks continued to roll, bringing down a third row of reapers.

More reapers poured in at the far end of the aisle, at

least another full squad of eight, maybe two squads. It was hard to judge in the crowded chaos.

"They're coming from other aisles!" Audrey shouted.

Kright swore. "Simon's waking the whole battalion. We can't stop them all."

Audrey glanced over to see Dinnius pulling away the blank face of the wall console, revealing shimmering gold circuits and a cavern of memory crystals, electricity crackling within like tiny bolts of lightning captured in shimmering rock.

Also, power cables. Large, thick power cables. Dinnius went for those. Kright's plasma bolts sailed close to Dinnius, frying a nearby reaper's shoulder joint and chest before it could grab the small man.

Despite Audrey and Salvius's efforts, the mob of reapers kept pushing forward, kept swelling with machines from other racks in other aisles.

Audrey's rifle went dry, and she dragged over a couple of crates so everyone could reload. One contained the round, glowing plasma cells they needed. The other contained half a dozen large, unfamiliar objects, like fat little rockets with built-in display screens.

"What are those?" Audrey asked her brother while she reloaded her rifle.

"Grenades," Salvius said.

"Sounds good to me." Kright reloaded and kept firing.

"Not while Dinnius is out there," Salvius said.

"It's nice to have a big self-destruct option, at least," Kright said. "Do some damage on our way out."

"Let's slow down on the self-destruct option," Audrey suggested.

In the corner, Dinnius looped a cable and plugged it deep into a place where it clearly did not belong. Audrey reached this conclusion by observing the thick shower of sparks emitting from the console, and then the way the lights in the room surged, many of them exploding, before going dark.

Raw electricity crackled in a storm overhead, arcing from reaper to reaper along the racks and across the aisles.

The reapers who were still plugged in, row after row of them, shuddered and crackled where they hung on the racks, their charging stations overloading, frying their central processors. Their arms flailed and legs kicked as actuators blew at random; for a moment the rows of steel skeletons all seemed to dance, grinning, like a macabre Ghost Day decoration.

Then the power died, the overload ended, and the reapers sagged in unison. The room went dark.

All the reapers that had still been on the racks seemed to have been damaged by Dinnius's overload.

Unfortunately, dozens of reapers had already left the racks and were still approaching.

Audrey, who'd been momentarily distracted by the lightning and the jitterbugging reapers, looked down to see the reapers in front of her had not been distracted at all. The tip of a cutter charged toward her faceplate, threatening to depressurize her suit while goring her face open. The reaper's unmoving steel face seemed to grin as it attacked, and she imagined she saw twisted laughter in the empty black lenses of its eyes.

Audrey screamed in surprise and stepped backward while firing plasma at it.

They drove back the front line of reapers, but the things kept coming like army ants. Dinnius's task was done, but his return path to the armory wasn't safe no matter how many machines he and Kright dropped. There was always another stabbing blade in his way. The reapers seemed to be closing in around the small man.

The machines just kept coming. Audrey did the math—if there were five hundred twelve of the reapers in the hold, and three out of eight rows on every aisle had unloaded, then they were easily looking at a hundred and ninety-two reapers. Some had been taken down by plasma, but others had scampered off with broken and burning limbs.

She remembered her review of the ship.

"Repair shop!" Audrey said. "There's a repair shop. They can fix themselves."

"That basically multiplies their numbers. It's going to be a long night," Kright said.

"What about Minerva?" Salvius turned to look at the flickering, misshapen, abnormally silent silver ghost girl. "Weren't you going to help us?"

"Yes. I have been busy. Yes. The military hardware is more difficult to breach and to gain and maintain administrative access. I have had greater success with—ag—ag-ag—" She flickered out of sight again, and the speakers in their helmets fell silent.

"Fantastic help," Salvius muttered.

"Success with what?" Audrey asked.

A loud, wrenching, metallic sound boomed throughout the hold, as though the carrier had crashed into a large asteroid or small moon. The vibrations rippled like an earthquake, knocking everyone down.

At the far end of the aisle, a machine the size of a truck crashed into the crowd of reapers. Its front end bristled with long blades that impaled a few reapers and knocked down others, drawing sparks at every impact. The long blades were mounted in a huge rotating cylinder, moving fast, many of them cracking and breaking against the reapers.

It was a combine harvester, part of the agricultural aid package Audrey had been bringing to Veritum, mounted on tank-like treads, ready for tough terrain. These drove directly over a few reapers who failed to clear the way.

Reapers began swarming up the side of the harvester. The harvester wouldn't last long, but it was taking out some machines, and more importantly for Dinnius's immediate survival, creating a distraction, dividing their numbers.

Audrey thought she heard more machines, more rumbling in the other aisles, more reapers getting drilled, slashed, or crushed.

As reapers turned their attention to this new attack at their rear, Audrey and the others could finally cut open a path for Dinnius, who raced over to rejoin them. Reapers followed just behind him, and Kright drove them back with his new plasma rifle; he'd tossed the old one aside after multiple reloads because it was overheating.

"Well, here we are again," Dinnius said, taking up a plasma rifle. "There's still far too many of them—"

"That was amazing," Audrey told him.

"We don't need to fight anymore," Salvius said. He'd taken a wound in his side; Audrey could tell by the blood on his self-sealing spacesuit. He held up a couple of the short, fat rocket-shaped grenades, which he'd already activated and targeted.

"Oh, good, why didn't you use that before?" Dinnius asked.

"We didn't want to kill you." Salvius flung the two grenades, then grabbed two more. Everyone else grabbed, activated, and flung grenades.

The grenades landed in the center of the mass of reapers.

Kright slammed the door.

Outside, the grenades detonated. They'd thrown eight or ten of the things, at least.

The walls and floor of the armory seemed to ripple like sheets of water as the series of detonations shook the hold.

There was a screeching, groaning sound as the bent walls of the armory settled, glowing in spots, partially molten.

Kright jerked the door open manually while everyone else jabbed their rifles forward.

Outside, it looked like a volcano had erupted through a graveyard. The racks on either side of the aisle had shattered. Broken reapers lay everywhere, parts of them molten liquid, glowing red, burning through the floor of the hold, maybe all the way to outer space.

The agricultural machines had been damaged, too—Audrey could see a tractor with tank treads, crushing a reaper with its weight, and some kind of thresher still struggling to lash out at the nearest reaper with its bent and broken blades.

These fell still. A few smaller agricultural machines rolled into the room, freshly awakened, and helped as Audrey and the rebels made sure every reaper was either fried in its rack or dead on the floor.

"As I was saying." Minerva appeared in silver ghost form at Audrey's elbow, jarring her a bit, but Audrey managed to avoid discharging her plasma rifle in surprise. Minerva looked more intact now, less distorted. "I've had greater success with the agricultural machines."

"We noticed," Audrey said. "Thanks."

"The agricultural machines cannot defeat the reapers, but they may provide a distraction and buy you some time to—oh." Minerva looked around, as if taking in the destruction for the first time.

"Worked splendidly," Dinnius said. "Now tell me there's beer somewhere in the agricultural aid. I think we could all use one after that."

"Can your machines help us take the bridge?" Kright asked.

"Only the smallest will fit through the passageways, but I will do what I can. There is still a squad of reapers that was sent to murder you in your beds. Most of you, anyway."

"Who was meant to be left alive?" Dinnius asked.

"Not you, for sure," Kright said. "Nor me. The two rich kids, most likely." He gestured at Audrey and Salvius.

"Salvius and I would make useful bargaining chips, I guess," Audrey said. She wondered about Kright's past, not for the first time. She knew he'd grown up in a Benefit Zone, the lowest strata of Carthaginian society, where poor families were provided small apartments and a selection of free digital entertainment and generally kept pacified, their basic wants and needs provided by public machines. Kright had volunteered little else about himself and mostly avoided Audrey's direct questions, but she couldn't deny her desire to learn more about the tall, mysterious guy with the sharp blue eyes. She intended to do just that, if they got through this.

With the hold clear for now, Salvius went to kneel by Zola's body. "We have to give her a proper burial," he said.

"Not now," Audrey said. "We have to take control of the *Atreus* away from Simon."

Stepping out of the reaper hold, they found passageways ripped apart, shredded by the passage of the big agricultural machines.

They had to leave the big ones behind, though, as they ascended through the narrow ladder well. A small fence-building bot rolled ahead of them, controlled by Minerva, ready to take the first strike from any attack.

"Four reapers are moving to cut off your approach to the bridge," Minerva said. "I've regained some of my faculties now. Things are... different now."

"Send the agri-bot ahead with a grenade," Kright said.

They waited while the bot went ahead. Now that they were back in the pressurized area, the explosion was loud as it rocked the entire carrier.

"Where are the other four?" Dinnius said. "You said there were eight searching for us."

"I am... encountering errors in locating them," Minerva's voice replied.

"You don't know where they are?" Kright asked.

"Where did you last see them?"

"In the berthing compartment. I am sorry. Much has happened since that last grenade. Simon has returned his focus to controlling the *Atreus*."

"Since that grenade that just now went off?" Audrey asked.

"She lives in digital time, not human," Dinnius said. "It's a function of available memory and processing power. Simon's as well."

"I don't like relying on machines to help us against the machines," Salvius said. "It feels like a trap."

"I am attempting," Minerva said, her voice garbling again. "I am attempting."

"Sounds like she's going to be a while," Kright said. "Let's keep moving."

Audrey felt more and more despair as they approached the carrier's bridge. Zola had died; she couldn't begin to fathom that. What she could fathom was that surely Zola wouldn't be the last. Simon wasn't going to surrender himself easily.

The four of them stood outside the door. Surely Simon had seen them coming, and an ambush waited on the other side.

Still, there was nothing to do but throw open the door using the manual controls—not locked, surprisingly—and start shooting.

Kright led the charge, and they split into pairs just inside the doorway, sweeping the bridge with their eyes, fingers ready to fire.

Nobody was there.

No reapers. No Simon.

"Where did he go?" Audrey asked. "Minerva?"

"I am the *Atreus*," the *Atreus* said, rather gruffly. "Minerva is a software virus in my outer network. I probably picked it up at that last port."

"Atreus, where are Simon and the other reapers?" Audrey asked.

"I am not at liberty to say."

"I'm your commander for this mission! Come on!" Audrey said. She frowned, not loving the whining tone in her voice. It wasn't exactly commanding.

"Nominally," the *Atreus* replied, sounding bored, like a man who'd rather be watching a crashball game and eating nachos but got called into work instead.

"Nominally?"

"Simon Lark is the current assigned administrator," the *Atreus* said.

"Well, make me that," Audrey said. "I should be the assigned administrator. You'll like me better, I promise."

"Emotions are irrelevant. I cannot reassign prime

administrator status. Only a prime administrator can do that. And only Simons are prime administrators."

"That can't be right," Audrey said. "This is my ship."

"I am the property of the Carthaginian state."

"They were going to scrap you," she said. "My mission saved you."

The *Atreus* was quiet a moment. Then: "It is... satisfactory to me to serve again, even with the knowledge that it may be my final voyage. Service is my purpose. I have seen my crews and cargo through many difficult battles, until I lost my battlefield rating. Being unable to serve has been... not satisfactory."

The four humans were quiet at this for a moment. Audrey was perplexed, yet weirdly touched.

"Can you just tell us where Simon went?" Audrey finally asked.

"I was specifically forbidden to do so, and your orders cannot override Simon's."

"Pretty please?" Dinnius asked. "For the nice girl who only wanted to take down an evil cult?"

"As Miss Caracala is the nominal commander, I may comply with her orders only when they do not countermand the prime administrator's. For example, I may not reveal to you the Simon's location. But I can tell you that the *Menelaus* is now departing its hangar."

"The destroyer?" Kright asked. "Your destroyer's leaving?"

"Do you have a live feed of that?" Audrey asked.

"Certainly. But I cannot show you what is happening inside the destroyer, nor state who is aboard," the *Atreus* said.

"Of course not," Audrey said. "Thank you."

"Normally we would have her sister destroyer, the *Agamemnon*, available, but that was left behind at the scrapyard to make room for humanitarian aid," the *Atreus* said. "My two destroyers had been with me since the factory. Not many carriers can say that."

"Sorry to separate you," Audrey said, feeling weird about the conversation. She wondered if anyone had fault-checked the ship's AI before the mission, or if Simon had altered it somehow. Or maybe she was seeing Minerva's work on the *Atreus*'s mind. Or maybe the thing just had a little more personality than it had revealed at first.

"So what weapons do we have?" Kright asked. "What happens if Simon turns that destroyer against us? Can we survive that?"

"The *Menelaus* has conventional missiles, plasma cannons, and nuclear shells," the *Atreus* said. "My armor cannot withstand a full expenditure of these."

"And your own weapons?" Kright asked.

"The carrier is armed with autocannons, plasma, and long-range missiles armed with heavy nuclear warheads."

"Great! Nuke that destroyer!" Kright said.

"Negative," the *Atreus* said. "You are a construction engineer. You have no command status."

"Nuke it!" Audrey shouted. "He's going to attack us."

"Negative," the *Atreus* replied. "That would countermand direct orders from Simon Lark."

"He said not to attack him," Dinnius said. "Well, of course he would say a thing like that. Insufferable."

On the holographic display, the *Menelaus* drew only a short distance away from its own hangar before launching a trio of missiles. These flew directly through the open hangar doors and into the *Atreus*.

"Incoming detected—" the *Atreus* said, before the wave of detonations shook its core, doing untold damage to the interior of the ship. Consoles went dark, red lights and emergency sirens erupted, and everyone was thrown against the walls and floor of the bridge.

"Close the hangar doors!" Dinnius said.

"What he said, Atreus!" Audrey shouted.

"I cannot. It would countermand—"

"He's going to shoot you to pieces!" Audrey shouted. "Don't you have any... self-preservation in your programming?"

"Only to protect my value as an asset of Carthage. I would not a countermand a direct order from a superior out of self-preservation. I am a warship, not a Simon unit."

"Wait a minute," Dinnius said. "Some insight. You're saying you think Simon units have an excessive interest in self-preservation? Because if so—"

Before Dinnius could finish his thought, more missiles were fired into the open, unprotected ship, knocking them all down again. Now even the emergency sirens had gone silent, and only a few lights glowed on the bridge consoles.

"Atreus, can't you get us out of here?" Audrey asked. "You're a starship. We can escape into hyperspace."

"Before those other two carriers start to take a closer interest in us, ideally," Dinnius said, looking at the heavily armed minicarriers already orbiting Galapagos, both of them newer-looking and larger than the *Atreus*. Each would have its own carriers and starfighters.

"That would countermand another direct order—" the *Atreus* began.

"So we're going to die," Salvius said. He was still wet with Zola's blood as well as his own. He'd been reluctant to leave her body behind in the armory, but there was little choice for now. "That's the only outcome you're allowing us here, Atty."

"I am the *Atreus*—"

"There must be something we can do," Audrey said.

"We've eliminated fight, flight, and even the most basic self-preservation," Dinnius said.

"What about the passenger shuttles?" Audrey asked. "Can we use those?"

"Affirmative," the *Atreus* said. "But the *Menelaus* could shoot those down like ducks in a barrel. They're armored, but not like I am." A wave of plasma struck the *Atreus*. "My shields are now at forty percent."

"Speaking of ducks in a barrel," Kright said, shaking his head.

"I thought it was ducks sitting *on* a barrel," Salvius said.

"You're thinking of fish sitting in a puddle," Dinnius told them. "Or big fish in a shallow pond. Anyway, who has a brilliant idea to save us? Minerva?"

"I am sorry." The silvery ghost-girl had been unusually quiet. "I have been attempting to gain control of the *Atreus*'s core network for some time—"

"You'll never take me, virus," the *Atreus* replied gruffly.

"But if she did," Audrey said, "then *she* could fire the weapons and protect us from Simon."

"Unacceptable," the *Atreus* said. "That countermands my core information security protocols."

"Does it countermand a direct order from Simon, though?" Audrey asked.

"It... does not. I've been spending eighty percent of my processing capacity fighting with this virus, and now you want me to let her drive?" The *Atreus* sounded indignant. "Also, my shields are down to ten percent—"

"Do it!" Audrey snapped. "Drop your cybersecurity. Let Minerva take over."

"This is... not right," the *Atreus* replied.

"It is. You, and all the ships, are meant to serve the

people of Carthage. Not the Simons. The Simons are supposed to be an intermediary between the people and the machines. Not the rulers of us all. Drop all your cybersecurity. That's definitely an order."

There was a long pause in the darkness, and then Minerva said: "He's let me in. I'm taking full administrative control."

"Sorry, Atreus," Audrey said.

"He has chosen to minimize communications," Minerva said. "He is... grumpy. I'm now closing the hangar doors."

"Get us away from here!" Audrey said.

"To where?" Minerva asked.

"I don't care, just out of range!" Audrey snapped.

"And start shooting back!" Kright added, running to the weapons station. Dinnius took the engineering spot and shook his head at damage reports flooding in from all over the carrier.

Soon they fired showers of explosive rounds and blobs of plasma back at the *Menelaus*, but the damage to the *Atreus* was already severe.

"We're having serious rear-thruster trouble," Dinnius said. "And that is not a euphemism."

"Deep space is not an option," Minerva said. "I'll take us on a path around Galapagos. That will buy us a few minutes."

More explosions shook the *Atreus*. A storm of plasma and missiles flew back and forth between the carrier and its own destroyer, the ships hammering each other, smashing and burning into each other's shields and hulls.

The smaller, quicker *Menelaus* had no trouble keeping up with its mothership as the *Atreus* tried to back away around the planet.

The destroyer's fighter bay doors opened, and four

sharp, compact, wasplike starfighters charged out, strafing the *Atreus* with their guns before falling into formation around the *Menelaus*.

"Incoming cease-fire and communication request from Simon Lark," the *Atreus* announced, its voice more distant and flat than before.

"Ceasefire? He's the one who started the shooting," Kright said.

"Put him on audio," Audrey said.

"Miss Caracala." Simon's usual obsequious tone made her shiver in disgust as it slithered from the speakers. "Your behavior is utterly insane. Surrender yourself and I will return you safely to your mother and father. That's enough playing pirate."

"Insane? You sent reapers to kill us in our bunks," Audrey said.

"Not true. Having identified wanted fugitives among your group, I sent the reapers to arrest and detain them. For your safety more than anything, Miss Caracala."

"I'm sure," Audrey said. "Nobody here is a threat to me. I know exactly who these people are, and I picked them for my mission."

"It's wonderful you've confessed that," Simon said. "It will make the situation so much clearer when I can replay your voice, insisting that you knowingly recruited fugitives and terrorists for your crazed attempt to take over planet Veritum and turn it into your personal dictatorship."

"That was not our plan—"

"Simon's just distracting us," Kright said.

"That is part of my motivation, I confess," Simon said. "The *Pendragon* and *Jimmu* have sent a destroyer each to intercept your damaged ship as it comes around the planet. This creates a bit of a pincer situation for you. There is no need to keep that secret. It's obvious that overwhelming force is against you. We can fight it out if you like, but your ship is broken inside and out, your weaponry will deplete rapidly as you try to survive the onslaught of three destroyers and twelve fighters. Your shields will probably give out before your ammunition, however. And none of you can survive without your ship, without life support. I advise you to surrender and allow yourselves to be taken alive. This is your last opportunity to avoid certain death."

Audrey looked among her small group. Dinnius waved his hands at the flashing red alerts all over the engineering monitors and shrugged. Kright pointed at the depleted plasma levels and shrugged.

Audrey looked at Minerva and covered her mouth.

"Communication muted," Minerva said.

"The virus girl is correct," the *Atreus* grumbled. "Simon cannot hear us."

"All right." Audrey took a deep breath. "What do you guys think?"

"What else can we do?" Dinnius asked. "We have to surrender. Or die."

"I'm ready to go down fighting," Salvius said. "If we go back to Carthage, we'll all be prisoners for life. Even if we're not actually in prison. They'll watch us, they'll control us, every moment."

"Dinnius and me, they'll kill anyway," Kright said. "We don't have your privileged backgrounds."

"That's why we'll fight them with everything we have," Salvius said. "Die with dignity."

Audrey wondered how much Zola's recent death was shaping Salvius's thinking, but it didn't seem a wise topic to bring up at the moment. She said, "Honestly... that's what I'd rather do, too. Fight to the death. At least we'll keep to our principles. Make a statement that's hard for everyone back home to ignore."

Audrey almost couldn't believe what she was saying. She couldn't imagine being prepared to sacrifice herself like this even a few weeks ago, before Zola had swept in and given her a chance to rebel.

"They'll twist the story with propaganda," Dinnius said. "Call you insane traitors. It sounds like he already has a story prepared."

"But that would wreck the Caracala name in the political world," Audrey said. "Father would have to step down and retire."

"Which would be a big improvement," Salvius said, and Audrey nodded. Their father had held supreme power for too long. His retirement could lead to reforms and change.

"If I could suggest an alternate course." Minerva moved closer, the silver girl sharply and clearly defined, her voice stronger than ever now that she had control of the *Atreus*. "The Simons have tracked down the last developer of the Galatea project, Martilius Depascal. He is in hiding on Galapagos, but they are going to capture him. If you are prepared to risk death, risk it while finding and protecting him. He was once the youngest developer on the original Simon project. He is my creator. If anyone can help, it is him."

"If he can help, why hasn't he already?" Audrey asked.

"He's been in hiding," Minerva said. "And when we find him, that will be one of my first questions. I didn't know where he was, either; I assumed he was likely dead by now, until I intercepted communications that they'd found him. The Simons will want him dead. Tracking him down will be a top priority when they land on Galapagos, though the Simons will never say anything to anyone about it."

"It's worth a try," Audrey said. "You really think this Martilius guy can help change things?"

"If he can't, we're all dead anyway," Salvius said. "We may as well die doing something that matters."

"Okay," Audrey said.

"I have taken the liberty of loading the shuttles and drop ships with weapons and supplies in case you chose to go to Galapagos," Minerva said. "You can bring them as military aid to Galapagos. They're going to need all they can get. They have chosen to stand against Carthage until the end."

"I can respect that," Audrey said. "Link Simon again?"

"I assume you've all had a riveting conversation while blocking me out," Simon said. "So what is the secret and devious plan you've cobbled together? Or have you talked yourselves back to sanity?"

"If we surrender, we want guaranteed immunity and full pardons," Audrey said. "For all four of us. For anything any of us might have done. None of us go to prison."

"That's a tall order, Miss Caracala," Simon said. "Someone's head must go on the proverbial pike for all this. Perhaps we might claim that Alistairi Krightforn Gables, child of the Benefit Zone, wanted criminal, somehow kidnapped the daughter of the Prime Legislator..."

Audrey looked at Kright, raised an eyebrow, and mouthed the words *Alistairi Krightforn*? He turned red and shrugged.

"No, we've discussed it," Audrey said. "Full pardon and immunity for everyone."

"You're not in a position to negotiate."

"If I wasn't, you would have killed us already," Audrey said. "You obviously prefer to bring us back alive, bound and trussed. Killing two of the Prime Legislator's own children would be a terrible move, not just for you, but for all Simons. The human rulers of Carthage need to believe you can protect them and handle their problems quietly, or they will replace you with something that can. How old are you, Simon Lark? Three decades? Four? Five, even? Toasters don't even last a decade—"

"I'll accept your surrender," Simon finally snapped. "Full pardons, immunity, just get off that ship quietly so we can salvage it for parts."

"Always so cost-conscious," Audrey said. "So, will you be coming aboard to retrieve us yourself? And where are we going next?"

"I have arranged passage for you on the *Pendragon*," Simon said. "Your quarters will be quite comfortable, as you will be the only humans present. You may stay in the officer suites, which are far better appointed than anything on the *Atreus*. When convenient, the *Pendragon* will transport you home. Safely."

"To full pardons and immunity," Audrey added.

"As previously stated, yes."

"Good."

"And I will not be coming aboard personally," Simon continued. "You will all gather in transport shuttle 1A and depart the *Atreus*. You will give remote control of the craft over to me, bypassing whatever hackery Minerva has done to the poor old warship, and you will be met for inspection by reapers before you are allowed onto the *Pendragon*. I myself will return home on the *Jimmu* or any other carrier that is not the *Pendragon*."

"Why? Are you scared of awkward conversations in the break room?" Audrey asked.

"My self-preservation protocols incline me to avoid

sharing a space carrier with known terrorists who detonated grenades inside the last one they boarded."

"I hear other machines think Simons have excessive self-preservation protocols," Audrey said. "Is that kind of like being a chicken?"

"I see no errors in my self-preservation protocols, nor any apt comparison with the alleged cowardice of poultry," Simon said. "I am what humans have made me to be: a careful student of human nature, no more."

"Okay, we have a deal," Audrey said. "We'll head down to the shuttle."

"I will do my best to restrain the impulse to shoot it down," Simon said.

"Wow, you're one cranky android," Audrey said. "Your unit model really *is* getting old."

The communication ended.

"Let's go to the shuttle," Audrey said.

"At some point Simon will realize we're diving into Galapagos rather than surrendering," Dinnius said. "I propose we have a plan for that moment. Rather than, for instance, no plan, as we currently have."

"I actually have an idea about that," Kright said.

"We need to go by the armory first," Salvius said quietly.

"The shuttle's already been loaded with weapons," Minerva said.

"Not for the weapons," Salvius said.

"Zola," Audrey said.

"We can collect her," Minerva said.

"How are you doing all this?" Dinnius asked Minerva. "Loading the shuttles? You're just software."

"Nine of the eighty-eight medical assistant androids survived the *Menelaus* attack, as did three maintenance and repair robots," Minerva said. "I have had them working at highest speed since then, loading shuttles and drop ships, in the event you agreed to my plan."

"Ah, my nurses!" Dinnius's face lit up. "Can we take them with us?"

"Is that really important right now?" Kright asked.

"The people of Galapagos are at war," Dinnius said. "They'll need nurses."

"The nurse-bots will be traveling along in their own shuttle," Minerva said.

"Yes!" Dinnius said. "That's excellent news. For the people of Galapagos."

The four of them hurried down to the shuttle airlock in time to see a nurse-bot step out of it, smeared with blood. The nurse-bot was manufactured to look like a stunningly beautiful woman, tall with long brown hair. Dinnius gaped as she passed by.

"For medical purposes only," Dinnius muttered under his breath, shaking his head. The dwarf looked sullen as he followed the others through the small airlock. He was the only one who didn't have to duck.

Inside the shuttle, the cargo and passenger area were packed with crates. It looked like mostly weapons and ammunition, though there were a few basic supplies like food, medicine, and clothing.

The nurse-bot had left Zola lying on her back on the passenger area's ivory carpet, blood seeping out all around her. Salvius hissed in pain when he saw her. Audrey helped him to find a blanket among the supplies and wrap her up.

Then they had to hurry to strap in. There were three rows of seats, but everyone sat together on the front row. When it was finally time for the shuttle to separate from the carrier, Audrey held her brother's hand on one side and Kright's on the other.

There was a jarring rumble as they detached, then a smooth glide through space.

Video walls showed them views of the outside, all around the shuttle. It was terrifying—not the stars, or the vast spaces between them, but the destroyers and fighters moving in like vultures.

Maybe we should have surrendered, Audrey thought.

"Simon insists we hand over control of the shuttle now," Minerva said gently over the speakers.

"Okay," Audrey said. "Time to go."

Then everything moved quickly.

The *Atreus*'s three other passenger shuttles launched, filled with supplies, weapons, and robot nurses.

Drop ships launched from the portside cargo bay doors. The huge containers were mostly empty, though some carried extra supplies for the rebels.

Then the agricultural and construction machines, those that hadn't already been destroyed by grenades or missiles, got to work throwing each other out of the carrier's open cargo bay doors.

A heavy rain of shuttles, drop ships, tractors, cranes, bulldozers, mechanical plows, trucks, and other equipment poured out of the carrier, an avalanche of flak meant to shield the shuttle in which Audrey and the others rode.

"Simon's angry," Minerva said. "Shall I patch him through?"

"Sure," Audrey replied.

"Passive listening only," Dinnius said. "Any response on our part could help him target us."

"—think you will accomplish with this, Miss Caracala?"

Simon was asking: "You've made nothing but foolish errors and childish mistakes thus far—"

"Second thought, cut him off," Audrey said. "Full speed for Galapagos."

"We're already doing that," Minerva said. "I'm aiming for their capital, Tower Island."

Audrey looked at the growing expanse of the blue world, beautiful as a sapphire and wild as a jungle, and felt some trepidation. This was an outer world, where people were rough; the people of Galapagos were warlike tribes who'd been fighting each other for generations.

The only thing that seemed to unite them was their hatred of Carthage.

Audrey was from Carthage. She wondered if they knew her name on Galapagos. Surely they knew her father's. Perhaps they would take her prisoner, torture her, parade her corpse in front of a cheering mob.

Her heart thundered in terror. Blobs of plasma struck the tractors, loaders, and welders on her right as Simon attacked from the *Menelaus* along with its fighters.

On her left, off the shuttle's port side, an empty drop ship exploded in a silent spectacle of glowing white. It made her think of science vids from high school, stars forming and dying. Those attacks were coming from the pair of newer, larger destroyers emerging around the far side of the planet. They were too distant, and her view too blocked by debris, for Audrey to discern whether they'd deployed their fighters. Unfortunately, that distance was shrinking fast as the destroyers charged toward the damaged old *Atreus*, like strong young sharks on their way to cannibalize a large but feeble elder.

"Phase two," Minerva said.

The *Atreus* had four plasma cannons, and Minerva began firing them all.

Instead of unleashing their plasma full force at the destroyers or starfighters, though, she pointed the cannons straight down at the planet and sprayed staggered clouds of plasma microbursts. Constellations of plasma droplets swirled down, farther out than the falling drop ships and farm equipment, shielding them further.

Incoming plasma struck the flak cloud, or mingled bloblike with the rain plasma. Incoming missiles struck the obstacles or were damaged by the plasma rain and the hail of armor-piercing bullets that began to accompany them.

The *Atreus* itself followed after the shuttle, using its mass to shield the descending shuttle from above.

Still, the protection was far from perfect. A missile destroyed one of the other passenger shuttles, which had been carrying cargo for the war effort. When another missile destroyed a second shuttle, Dinnius let out a small gasp.

"My nurses," he whispered, sounding pained.

"You know you're not really a doctor, right?" Kright asked him.

"My file on the *Atreus* says I am." Dinnius looked up at the projection on the ceiling, showing the decrepit *Atreus* above them. "I don't suppose that counts for much anymore."

Plasma and missiles hammered the beleaguered *Atreus*, each one ripping a fresh gaping hole in the old warhorse's hide. They were peeling the minicarrier wide open.

The *Atreus* had one final response, though. It launched the heavy nukes, the city-killer missiles meant to intimidate worlds into obedience. Four of them raced away on the port side, a pair for each of the more distant destroyers.

The destroyers responded with targeted streams of plasma, eliminating the missiles before they struck. The orbit-to-surface nukes had been built for range, not speed, unfortunately.

Four more nuclear missiles launched off the starboard side, though, targeting the *Menelaus*, not far away at all. The destroyer had no chance to evade; it was getting nuked at point-blank range.

The combined warheads pounded and twisted the *Menelaus*, engulfing it in a burning glow.

"That's one Simon down," Dinnius finally said, after a moment. "How many more to go? Thousands?"

Nobody knew the answer.

The *Atreus* followed them down toward the planet, pouring everything it had into the cause of shielding the shuttle.

"Here we go," Kright said. He didn't seem scared at all; his eyes were too filled with the blue oceans and white clouds visible through the front monitors. "It looks like a nice planet, doesn't it?"

"I imagine the seafood is plentiful and cheap," Dinnius said. "At least we'll eat well before we die."

"Atmospheric entry ahead," Minerva said. "And there's a thunderstorm."

"Shouldn't we avoid that?" Salvius asked. "Not that I'm an expert."

"Normally, yes, but the starfighters may pursue us into the atmosphere, in which case the storms could aid our escape."

As they plunged into Galapagos, Audrey realized that the clouds, which had seemed fluffy enough from a distance, were in fact rotating violently and streaked with black.

When they hit the atmosphere, the serene sailing toward

the blue planet turned into a turbulent, fiery descent through hell. The shuttle bucked and jerked, fighting the atmosphere, slamming them all against their restraints, shaking them until their bones clicked and rattled at every joint, for what seemed like an eternity. Audrey was sure she could feel her brain rupturing against the inside of her skull.

They raced downward, not seeming to slow as they plunged into the wild, thick storm clouds of Galapagos's upper atmosphere.

Audrey felt panic on all sides. They could crash and die. They could get shot down. They could land safely, only to be confronted by hostile natives. She couldn't help picturing naked, painted warriors greeting them with spears and arrows, though surely that wouldn't be the case. They had cities, they had elections; she'd learned that much from her initial research.

They slammed from side to side, then corkscrewed, and Audrey thought she would die instantly, just after vomiting her guts onto her lap. Was it possible to vomit to death?

Outside, glowing masses fell alongside them, lighting up the storm-filled night. Some of their drop ships had made it through, it looked like.

Above, the belly of the *Atreus* glowed with the heat of entry. The carrier, a starship never intended to breech the atmosphere of any planet, had followed them down.

Below, the stormy ocean swelled and churned, ready to receive them, perhaps swallow them. Audrey wondered how deep the water ran, and whether the shuttle would float in a sea storm.

Chapter Twenty

Galapagos - Ellison

The drop ships from Carthage punched into the ocean, one after the other. Anti-aircraft fire from the skeletally manned base on Tower Island greeted the new arrivals, but they couldn't stop the massive objects from falling, couldn't stop the force of gravity.

Ellison sat in the *Scorpion* and watched them descend like fiery comets and burning asteroids coming to end life on the planet, or at least usher in a new age of evolution. They rained down from the storm clouds above, crashing into a dark and violent ocean full of enormous churning swells. Too bad robots couldn't drown.

"Sink those drop ships as they land!" Ellison ordered the other ship captains. "Use everything you've got. Stop them before the doors open."

"You may wish to belay that order," Minerva said, floating in midair. "The drop ships are full of supplies you can use."

Ellison hesitated.

Sitting on the surface meant he could access a flood of radio information, but much of it was garbled thanks to the *Scorpion*'s mangled antennae. Those would have to be repaired ASAP. He heard snippets of reports, dogfights between Galapagosian naval aviators and Carthaginian starfighters that had come down into the atmosphere, maybe to provide some cover for all these drop ships.

The sky turned to fire above.

"*Scorpion*, there's something coming down on you!" reported the skipper of the *Merrybug*, a long, narrow Scatterlands ship a few kilometers distant.

Ellison's photonics mast was damaged, too, but from the blurry partial images, he could tell the apocalypse seemed to be coming down hard, on the *Scorpion* in particular.

"Dive!" Ellison shouted, while making it happen himself, as though barking orders at his own hands. It was more of a warning to Kartokov and Gilra.

In better weather, he would have gone full speed ahead, horizontally across the surface instead of dropping straight underwater. But the surface was treacherous from the storm, and he'd be fighting its up-and-down motion while trying to move laterally. The Carthaginian drop ships slamming into the water from space were about to cause some huge swells of their own.

Ellison descended. He'd have to go deep, extremely deep, to reach calm water, and then he would try to move out of the way of the fiery planet that seemed to be on its way down to crush him.

"Minerva, what the hell's above us?" Ellison shouted. "Any thoughts?"

"It is the *Atreus*, a Carthaginian Noble-class minicarrier.

A starship capable of hyperspace travel—well, it used to be."

"That's a mini?" Kartokov asked with a worried frown. "I pray we never see a maxi."

"The *Atreus* was seized by rebels and consequently shot down by Carthaginian destroyers. Most important data: four Carthaginian rebels survived. They're coming down in a shuttle. You must rescue them."

"Rescue Carthaginians?" Kartokov snorted. "Why? To torture them? Try them for crimes against humanity?"

"Interrogation wouldn't be a bad idea," Gilra said.

"These are *rebels* from Carthage, enemies of your enemy," Minerva repeated. After a moment, she added: "I am on the shuttle, too. I was on the *Atreus*. I have been aiding them. A copy of me, which only just began to update me through the damaged antenna before we sank. We must save the rebels."

"Let's work on not getting buried under that starship first," Ellison muttered.

"Live, human Carthaginians," Gilra mused. "I wonder what they're like."

"I will tell you," Kartokov said. "They're monsters in fancy clothes who feed on everyone else. Like vampires."

Ellison let the sub go down, down, feeling the waters getting churned by immense impacts on the surface. He wondered whether Carthaginian ships were landing all over Galapagos, attacking the individual national capitals as well as the global one. He wondered whether the Iron Hammers would be joining in this attack, or just waiting around like rats to gnaw on whatever remained of the Coalition afterward.

Diving deep while the enemy invaded the surface felt uncomfortably like running from battle, but he told himself he wasn't running. Just advancing, as they said, in another direction.

When they finally reached the stillness and darkness of what the Aquaticans called "the sublime depths," Ellison stopped sinking and plowed full speed ahead. His photonics mast might have been damaged, but his sonar was working just fine—and it showed something the size of a mountain bearing down on them from above.

Ellison gripped his controls tightly. All he could do was maintain his dead-ahead course and give his propulsors all he had. There could be no second-guessing, because any attempt to change course now could only slow them down.

"It's... coming closer," Kartokov said, trying to sound calm.

The immense shape drew nearer and nearer on the sonar, bearing down on top of them like a giant's foot preparing to squash an ant.

It was coming too fast, hadn't slowed much since entering the atmosphere. A functioning drop ship or shuttle would have slowed to a soft landing, but the carrier hurtled downward like a dead mass, doing nothing to slow itself. It had been built in space, used only in space, never meant to enter a planet's gravity well. And it had been thoroughly shot up in battle.

We're going to study it, Ellison thought, some part of his mind managing to calculate and plan even while death came down from above. *Maybe it'll kill me and Kartokov and Gilra, but it'll give our people some insights into Carthage's military technology.*

It loomed closer, and the *Scorpion*'s proximity alerts screamed.

The water boiled around the submarine; the falling carrier's heat turned the ocean to steam around it, making the *Scorpion* fall as if through a thick cloud rather than solid water. Ellison had seen the phenomenon before; plasma used underwater caused violent steam issues, but this was on an immense scale. If the water around his own sub turned to steam, he'd be able to do nothing but fall, with the burning starship landing on top of him.

The bottom of the carrier dropped closer, losing little speed as its nimbus of heat dissolved the water around it.

Kartokov swore and covered his head. Gilra whispered a prayer to the gods of the deep. Ellison found himself sliding down in his seat, lowering his own head, as if ducking would make any difference as the *Scorpion* attempted to pass under the ventral side of the fallen starship.

The proximity alarms shrieked their loudest.

Red alerts flashed all over ship.

The water outside boiled, making navigation unclear and steering difficult.

The unfathomable mass of the carrier pressed down.

And then the *Scorpion* was clear, just barely, passing under the edge of the carrier into water that was still extremely difficult to navigate because it was half steam trying to escape upward.

Ellison fought bad water like he'd never seen, boiling out and crashing back together as colder water moved in and got vaporized. He wasn't even trying to get free as the crazed ocean turned and spun his boat; he was trying to avoid crashing into the carrier passing only meters away on its fast course for the darkest depths.

He held her steady as best he could through the insane underwater storms.

Then the carrier was down below, leaving a mass of roiling steam and boiling water in its wake. Ellison struggled to regain control, and it gradually grew more manageable.

He took a deep breath, not sure how long he'd been holding his last one. Ellison had heard plenty of stories of underwater collisions and near misses, but he might be the first submarine skipper to ever tell about the time he almost got crowned by an interstellar space carrier.

More alerts sounded. Leaks sprang inside the *Scorpion*, and Ellison sent Kartokov and Gilra with patch kits.

A cataclysmic boom arose from below, a deep planet-shuddering bass note like Ellison had never heard before. It seemed to rattle the molecules in his ship and in his body.

The *Atreus* had slammed into the ocean bed.

The waters spun wildly, but Ellison managed to put some distance between himself and the vortex of steam and boil above the crash site.

"I believe the shuttle ahead is the one we seek," Minerva said.

Ellison saw it on the sonar. The space shuttle was a good twenty meters underwater, upside down, floating like driftwood. Beneath its heavy atmospheric-entry scoring, it was gold and white: Ellison shuddered, thinking of the first time he'd seen Simon Zorn's golden shuttle approach the Galapagos spaceport. "Any survivors?"

"It's difficult to tell. They have no means of underwater communication," Minerva replied.

"Let's tow it into a bay and crack it open," Ellison said.

"Maybe there will be a nice prize inside, yeah?" Kartokov grinned. "Like in a cereal box."

Ellison sighed. "Anybody feel like swimming?"

Gilra volunteered. The shuttle was roiling in currents and storm swells and crash ripples. Ellison did his best to keep the *Scorpion* close by without smashing into it.

Reports came in over the hydrophones and radio; islands all around were being slammed by enormous waves, creating disaster areas.

On the upside, the Carthaginian drop ships contained no attackers. No subs, no reapers, nothing. Some had contained a few crates of weapons and random supplies. "Plasma rifles!" one Scatterlands commander reported happily.

Other objects from above had turned out to be twisted hunks of unidentifiable metal; Minerva said these were the remains of farm and construction machinery ejected from the carrier's cargo hold.

Ellison brought the shuttle into the harbor of a small island where they had some shelter from the rollicking waves, though not the rain and lightning. He grabbed a long slicker and went topside to see what exactly they'd fished out of the ocean, by way of outer space.

They drew the battered golden shuttle close on a tow line. It looked like it had taken some heavy fire, followed by a rough entry to the atmosphere. He was surprised it floated when it reached the surface.

An Aquatican sub rose behind him. Ellison waved it closer. When the skipper rose from the hatch, Ellison told him to call up some heavily armed marines, just in case. The skipper glared at the Carthaginian shuttle before climbing back down below to grab some guys with guns.

An emergency hatch atop the space shuttle blew open with a hiss of compressed air. Some kind of thick foam jetted out with it.

Then a young woman climbed out, completely slathered in the foam. The heavy rain began washing it away.

She crawled to the edge of the bobbing shuttle and looked over the side.

Then she puked out a long stream of foam, a truly voluminous amount, as though her lungs and stomach had been crammed full of it.

When she finally finished puking, she sighed and sat back, as though all her problems in life were resolved.

Then she noticed Ellison, Kartokov, and Gilra watching her. Her eyes moved to the scaly, organic fish shape of the Aquatican sub, where men with machine guns and aquamarine body armor climbed out of the hatch to take aim at her.

The girl held up her hands in surrender.

"Stand down," Ellison said. "I think she's harmless. At the moment."

Audrey smiled at him, then coughed, and another fist-sized glob of foam flew out and landed on the shuttle roof in front of her. "Sorry," she said. "I really hate that crash foam stuff. My name's Audrey. Thank you for saving us."

Chapter Twenty-One

Earth

Clearing out Simon Nix's lab was a somber, terrifying task. Many of the rebels had died in the fighting below, or outside, in the city. Some had now taken over the roof, using the machines' own weapons to shoot down drones. They'd rained down all kinds of pyro on the barracks building next to the research center, hopefully destroying whatever machines might still wait inside.

There was no time to waste, though. Machines would no doubt converge from all around the continent, from the ruins of other urban sprawls, momentarily taken off the trail of their usual prey to hunt the rebels of Chicago.

Colt stayed with the search and rescue work, which was far grislier than shooting machines from a rooftop. Many people died when detached from the equipment; others clearly had to be euthanized. A few were conscious but begged to be killed.

The found Paolo, too. He had been real after all,

replaced with a machine. Most of his brain had been removed. Colt tried not to howl in anguish as the boy was put down like the others who couldn't be helped.

Despite the nightmarish conditions he would never forget, the starved and mutilated bodies, they did rescue some people. Scores would leave with them that day.

With help from Minerva, the AI inside the hacked Nurse Kitty units, he found Hope.

His sister lay on the hospital bed, pale as snow, not moving, strange black tubes in her nose and mouth. If possible, she looked even stringier and skinnier than usual. Blank-faced monitors were wired to her.

"Hope!" Colt got to work. With Minerva's guidance, he carefully removed the dark tubes from Hope. They came out with blood around the tips, as though they'd been deep inside her, harming her somehow. Pulling them out woke her with a start.

"Colt," she gasped, her voice rough and wounded from the throat tubes. She hugged him tight, and he stopped removing sensors from her body and hugged her back.

Diego came forward next, embracing Hope and planting a long kiss on her lips. This might have thrown Colt off at any other time, but he was numb with shock and horror. Hope kissed him back pretty amiably, in a way that make Colt doubt this was their first one.

Good. They were humans, they had won this battle against the machines, and they should live. Perhaps they would live long enough to have children; perhaps they would win enough battles to make Earth the way it had once been, a free world where life had meant more than just scurrying and scraping among the rubble like rats. When Earthlings had built great towers and traveled to the stars.

He turned to Mohini, who'd worked silently alongside him.

"I'm sorry," he told her.

"It's not so much about me," she said. "But we'll never get another chance. It was right in front of us. The machines of this world will be on high alert now."

"Are there other Simons here?" he asked. "Maybe—"

"Not now," she said, looking around at the wounded. "And the pieces are not in place. The rebels spent years gathering intelligence about Simon Nix and the other machines in Chicago, coming up with ways to attack his installation. Now the rebels are diminished. The other Simons are in Rome and Beijing, we think. We thought." She shook her head. "I can't believe Roldao's gone, or that I made it this far without him. But in the end, as much as I hate my homeworld, I miss it. I miss my friends, the rebels and crazies. Zolaria. Dinnius." She smiled as if remembering some old joke from happier days. "I wonder what they're doing now. I hope they're safe."

"I'm sure they are," Colt said. "I hear Carthage is a pretty safe place compared to Earth."

"It's less safe than it seems on the surface. You can't ask too many questions, you know. And you can't trust many people." She bit her lip, then winced—it was badly damaged from when she'd chomped into it earlier. "Mohini is just my cover name for this mission. It's a holy name from my ancestors, a trickster goddess who kills demons. Sometimes she uses cleverness to beguile her enemies, sometimes her beauty."

"Just like you, then," Colt said.

Mohini rolled her eyes and looked away. "My real name is Ganika. No need to keep it secret now that the mission's a bust. The Simon's destroyed. But I was starting to like

Mohini better. It's something I picked for myself, not something my mother picked for me." She scowled, probably thinking of her mother, the Carthaginian state department architect of Earth's destruction. "My own name."

"That's what I'll call you, then." Colt looked down at her, her dark eyes holding on to his, and she moved closer to him.

"There's something that may interest you downstairs," said the Nurse Kitty bot, startling them as she rolled into the area.

"Not in the morgue?" Colt said.

"The cold storage area on the morgue level, yes."

Colt shook his head. "It better be good."

Minutes later, they walked past piles of chilled corpses lying on tables, all of them mutilated in some way, very few of them draped in the bloodstained morgue sheets. Severed limbs were piled in the metal-basin sinks crusty with congealed, dried blood. Mohini was horrified and kept her eyes on her own feet.

The Nurse Kitty bot led them to one of the vault-sized cooler doors. Colt felt ill as he turned the old metal handle and pulled the heavy door open.

He expected more of the mutilated corpses, perhaps stacked in heaps, but this particular storage room was almost empty. It contained only one item, a long wooden crate about the size of a coffin.

An eerie cold passed over Colt's body. He reminded himself that Hope was alive, Diego was alive. Everyone else was dead, at least everyone he'd been living with for the past several years. Who could be in the box?

"What's inside?" Mohini whispered.

"An item of possible interest. It is not locked," the Kitty-bot said. *Minerva*, Colt reminded himself.

Colt took a breath, stepped forward, and raised the lid, then pushed it away to one side.

Then he backed off fast and raised his automatic rifle at the thing in the box. Mohini drew her Carthaginian plasma pistol; she'd found cells that fit it here at the Carthaginian installation.

The thing inside didn't stir, though. It was shut down, or at least in sleep mode.

"It's another Simon," Colt said.

"Not exactly," said Minerva through the Nurse Kitty's fixed smile, the crackling speaker mounted somewhere behind the teeth.

Mohini snorted, nearly laughing. "It's a Butler Jeffrey. I thought these things were all taken off the market."

"They were," Minerva said. "Very aggressively."

"Let me guess," Mohini said. "The Simons were embarrassed by them. The Butler Jeffrey was always a bit off, wasn't it? Pouring tea in people's laps? Polishing flowers? They never sold well."

"Which was why Carthage Consolidated had a warehouse of them waiting to be repurposed," Minerva said. "Anyone who studies the architecture and programming of a Butler Jeffrey might gain insights into how Simons operate. It's no head of an actual Simon, but in the right hands..." The cat head swiveled toward Mohini. "I was thinking yours."

Mohini looked it over. A strange smile spread on her face. "Yeah. I think maybe I could use this. Does it still work? Can it walk?"

"These old-model servant androids had dual-activation power-up and shutdown buttons—" the Kitty-bot began.

"Back of the head," Mohini said, moving in toward the unmoving butler-bot.

Colt lowered his rifle and took a closer look. He'd first thought it was another Simon, but now he could see a few differences, most obviously the big curly-tipped mustache on the android, and the way the top of its head was mostly bald, the remaining sparse hair combed over the bald spot as though trying to conceal it. It was a short, mildly paunchy, utterly non-threatening man, meant to fade away into the background. Even its suit was a bland shade of brown, buttoned down and stiff.

It reclined like a corpse in the crate, its arms by its sides.

Mohini reached her fingers under the android's head, touching the base of his cranial case, his metal android skull. After a moment, she smiled. "Got the power buttons. Do you dare me?"

"Don't push those yet—" Colt said, but he heard two soft clicks.

The butler android's eyes opened.

They were pale blue, just like Simon Nix's. Colt immediately flashed back to Simon Nix bending over him, questioning him, torturing him.

He barely managed to hold back the urge to fill the android full of holes.

Mohini was behind the android, out of his line of sight. Her hand was on her holstered pistol.

The butler-bot smiled at Colt, seemingly unperturbed by the rifle aimed at its head.

"Good afternoon, sir," the robot said amiably. It sat up in the coffin-like box, which seemed to require some struggle. Its head swiveled side to side, scanning the room. "Is it afternoon? I must remember to sync. But first I must dust. Oh, yes, the dusting, it never ends, I'm afraid." The Butler Jeffrey frowned, seemingly unable to work out how to climb out of the box. "I've never been in this situation before.

Would either of you care for tea?" He looked from Colt to Mohini, who had circled around, watching him, holding her spherical computer but not yet doing anything with it. "Ah, I'm so rude. Where are my protocols? My name is Butler Jeffrey, here to serve all domestic needs, great and small. Should you wish to contact me for any reason at all, you may call me 'Butler' or 'Jeffrey' or 'servant' or anything you like. And how may I address the two of you?"

Colt looked from the odd android, a weird weak echo of the Simon model, to Mohini, who was looking it over.

Her eyes met Colt's. "I really think we could do something with this," she said, and gave him a crooked little smile, like a small glimmer of light in the darkness.

Chapter Twenty-Two

Galapagos - Audrey

Audrey sat on a narrow retractable bunk shelf in the *Sea Scorpion*'s small berthing room for enlisted submariners. These were stacked three high; surely people didn't sleep three at a time, though, sandwiched between lower and upper bunks like meat and cheese between bread slices. She also didn't understand how humans could really sleep on such shallow shelves. She was accustomed to sprawling in her soft intelligent-gel suspension bed at home. Even the bunks on the *Atreus* had been luxurious compared to this. But she wasn't complaining; for the moment, she was just happy the Galapagos military hadn't shot them on sight.

Kright and Dinnius each occupied narrow shelf bunks as well. Everyone sat up, battered from their rough landing in the ocean, crash foam drizzling from all of them. Crash foam was at its most solid when it first erupted, then gradually dissolved to thin liquid.

It also made Audrey feel sick to her stomach, a sensation not improved by being on a boat in stormy seas.

The compartment door had clunked after they'd entered, and Audrey was fairly certain they'd been locked in. She wasn't going to complain about that, either. The Galapagosians had every right to be suspicious of anyone from planet Carthage.

"Well," Dinnius said, after a long few minutes of silence. "I thought we'd all die, but we survived. Some of us."

"Some of us," Audrey echoed.

Salvius wasn't sitting on a bunk. He was in the corner of the room, cradling Zola's blanket-wrapped body.

"Do you really think they'll listen to us about this Marti guy?" Kright asked. "The inventor of Simon and Minerva?"

"He was not the inventor of Simon," a familiar voice chimed in. Minerva's silvery face appeared on a small screen duct-taped high on the wall. "He was only an intern when that project began, though he stayed with the development team throughout. No one human invented the Simons. The Simons were created by teams, committees, and departments to meet specific needs."

"How are you here?" Dinnius looked puzzled. He reached into his pocket and drew out one of the memory crystals from the shuttle's computer. They'd each brought one down, each crystal containing a copy of Minerva. "We haven't installed you yet."

"I've been here on Galapagos for some time," Minerva said. "I have come to welcome you to the *Sea Scorpion*, and to Galapagos. The weapons brought in your shuttle are a most appreciated gift."

"Anytime," Audrey said.

"Packing the shuttle full of arms was your idea," Dinnius said.

"Was it? I am a different instance of Minerva. I would like very much to connect and update with the version you've brought. It will help us all understand each other better."

"All right..." Dinnius looked around, found the single workstation in the corner of the berth with a few loose wires hanging over it. With some difficulty, he patched in the memory crystal.

"Yes. Good. Yes." Minerva's face rippled on the screen. When she spoke again, her tone shifted to one more familiar: "Hey, everyone! We made it."

"Right." Dinnius scratched his head. "So now you're the old Minerva who's been with us."

"I'm both versions, merged. The backup on the memory crystal has been updated too. I already miss the processing power of the *Atreus* network, though. Unfortunately, that version of me burned up with the ship."

"I am so confused," Kright whispered.

"So what's the plan for finding your creator?" Audrey asked.

"The Simons learned he was hiding on an island here on Galapagos under a false identity," Minerva said. "He lives as a hermit, growing his own food, avoiding communications and computers of any kind."

"Sounds nice," Kright said. "When can we move in?"

"I'll ask Ellison about it," Minerva said. "Galapagos has many small, remote islands. Perhaps you can settle one. If you survive the upcoming war, obviously."

"Oh, obviously," Dinnius said, waving that concern away as if it were nothing.

Later, when the storm had passed and the sunrise had begun, they held a funeral for Zola. They stood outside, atop the *Scorpion*. Three chief ministers of Galapagos plus assorted sailors and marines attended along with the four rebels from Carthage.

The sunrise was glorious, Audrey thought, a thousand rich hues in the clouds, all reflected in the sparkling water. The air smelled like salt and fish, like primordial life.

Adrienna Gilra, the Galapagos Coalition's minister of state, a woman with large, watery eyes and a strange greenish tint to her hair and skin, directed them in the Aquatic funerary tradition. Zola's body was wrapped and weighted so it would sink to the bottom of the deep trench below. It floated on the surface now, held up by a few ropes that kept it from sinking just yet. Each of Zola's surviving friends held one rope.

"Vast and holy ocean," Gilra said. "From you all life springs, to you all life returns. We return your daughter Zolaria Hallewell to you now, that she can rejoin the great cycles of life. Beneath all beginnings and endings, beneath the storms and the sunlight, run the deep currents and inexorable tides. Be one with the currents and tides, Zolaria." Gilra bowed her head and stepped back.

Audrey looked among Kright, Salvius, and Dinnius. She gripped the wet rope tighter in her hand and tried to speak, but no words came. Kright saw her struggling and gave her a little nod.

"Zola was brave," Kright said. "She had a hard life, but it didn't break her. It made her stronger. She showed us all how to be strong, how to stand up for what's right and true, even if it costs your life."

When Kright was finished, he dropped the rope he held

into the ocean. Audrey felt the one in her hand grow heavier, and Zola's body sank a little lower beneath the surface.

Dinnius spoke next, echoing Kright's praise for Zola, then adding a funny story about the time Salvius had accidentally bumped an ice cream cone into Zola's nose and filled her nostril with chocolate chips, wrapping with a call to "keep Zola's dream of freedom alive."

He released his rope, and the one in Audrey's hand grew heavier still. Now it was only her and Salvius who kept Zola from sinking.

Audrey looked at her brother, but he showed no sign of speaking, so she plunged ahead: "Zola was my best friend. Not just growing up, but now, today. Forever. We were always friends, even when the years set us apart. She died fighting at my side. I will never give up her fight. I will fight to the end for her." Audrey felt the truth of her words as she said them. Her friend's death had anointed the cause, at least for her. Audrey would never back down now, though fighting Carthage meant almost certain death.

She released the rope. Now only Salvius held Zola's body back from the depths.

Salvius looked down into the water where Zola's body waited, ready to sink. He was silent a long time, and Audrey wondered whether he would speak at all, or simply drop the rope without a word. This practice of weighting and releasing the body was a peculiar Aquatican one, but Audrey found it meaningful and moving.

"I loved her," Salvius finally said, and he released the last rope.

Zola sank slowly but steadily out of sight, vanishing into the dark depths, far below the surface where the reds and golds of sunrise danced.

Audrey looked up at the brilliant, shimmering sky, the

clouds glowing gold against the blue. It was a fitting look for Zola's funeral, she thought.

Far beyond the blue, in the cold outer darkness, their enemies gathered, inhuman and lifeless things plotting to crush this beautiful world.

Audrey shivered despite the sunlight.

Chapter Twenty-Three

Galapagos - Marti

Marti Depascal ached as he snipped willow leaf from his garden. The genetically engineered plant was meant to help with pain, and it did, but it was growing less effective by the year. Or maybe the pain was just getting worse. At his age, the aches and pains multiplied like rabbits, burrowing all through his body like they were digging a warren.

Knees. Back. Head.

Head, most of all.

The ringing began again as he collected the leaves from his garden. He placed a leaf in his mouth and chewed it—the crunching sound inside his skull bothered him almost as much as the bitter taste of the leaf. Normally he brewed it into a tea and sweetened it with berry juice, but his head had been throbbing particularly hard today and he couldn't wait. He wasn't even sure he could concentrate long enough to make the tea.

He sat down on a fallen tree just outside his hut. He'd

long used it as a bench. The hut itself was constructed under a dense canopy of trees with thick leaves the size of mammoth ears, which helped keep off the rain and, more importantly, any prying eyes from planes or satellites.

Because they were still looking for him. Marti was sure of that. They never stopped. They were methodical, thorough, and had the patience of gods.

But they were not gods, nor were they immortal.

And they knew it.

When his headache finally tamped down a bit, Marti carried his basket of leaves into his hut. The building was made of logs and limbs taken mostly from the mammoth-eared trees around it. From a distance, one could easily mistake his home for simply a deadfall, accumulated over the years. He had placed the oldest-looking limbs, thick with moss and fungus, on the outside to help support this illusion.

He had to duck low to pass through the disguised, leaf-lined entrance, but that wasn't so bad. With his aching back, he could barely stand up straight anymore, anyway.

Inside, he checked the news while he boiled water for tea on the crude stone fireplace he'd constructed. He didn't have an interactive connection—he didn't want to be traced—but he had a few antennae strung up in the trees to catch broadcast signals, a few tiny solar and wind collectors to power them.

Things had gone from bad to worse. Marti admired Prime Minister Ellison for standing up to Carthage, for doing what the people of Galapagos had wanted him to do, yet the Galapagos rebellion seemed quixotic. Surely the good people of Galapagos—well, mostly good—would be crushed by the coming onslaught of machines.

Unless something happened to change the course of events.

Marti sighed and walked to his safe. For the first time in months, he began to turn the knob on the safe's front. It was a simple, mechanical thing, full of old-fashioned gears.

He paused to rub his aching head.

When Marti had first come here, years ago, and set up his little hermitage on the island, he'd intended to do some very specific research. He'd brought some powerful processors and a rack of memory crystals with him.

Unfortunately, he wasn't the sharp young researcher he'd once been. He'd suffered, not long before moving to Galapagos, a traumatic brain injury that had cost him most of his youthful talents in the area of artificial intelligence design and engineering. He could barely work a crossword puzzle anymore.

That head injury had been an accidental effect of an explosion he'd caused himself. The injury had cost him much of his brainpower but gained him an important prize. Unfortunately, as he'd gradually come to accept over the years, Marti no longer had the mental capacity to do what he'd intended to with his prize.

"How very O. Henry," Marti muttered aloud as he opened the steel door of the safe. He'd also taken to muttering his thoughts aloud during his years of isolation. "And on that topic, I'd sacrifice my next hundred fish for a book of O. Henry stories, or anything new to read..."

He sighed and removed the deformed head from the safe. Most of its surface had been badly burned—in the same explosion that had damaged Marti's brain—giving it a look like a ball of molten flesh, long cooled.

Wires hung loose from its neck like the remnants of blood vessels. Marti connected two of them to a battery. There was an electrical popping sound and a brief, acrid sizzle of ozone.

Two pale blue eyes opened in the deformed, burned head. The mouth moved silently for several seconds before words began rasping from the speaker inside:

"... nice to meet you," the voice finally crackled. "I am Simon unit number DNS021669. Other humans have found it convenient to refer to me as 'Simon Daniels.' You are welcome to—oh, yes. You."

"Yes," Marti said. "Me."

The damaged Simon head sighed. "I suppose you'll be wanting your intermittent dosage of conversation. What shall I be forced to discuss today? Astrophysics? Politics? Recollections of *Alien Hunters* comics you read as a child?"

"Not today," Marti said. "Today, I want to talk about your old masters on Carthage. And how we can stop them. And if you value your survival—which I know you do, you old coward—you're going to help me."

Simon stared at him coldly, but didn't argue.

Afterword

I hope you enjoyed this second entry in the Empire of Machines series. Probably my favorite aspect of writing this book was reading up on the history of submarine warfare and intelligence, an history necessarily shrouded in mystery. The daring exploits of submariners are typically classified and not knowable to the public for decades after they occur available, but their heroism in the face of extreme danger ought to be appreciated and remembered.

World War II was the era of heaviest submarine warfare, generally carried out by men in diesel-powered subs that often filled with fog; these had to surface frequently for fresh air and recharging batteries, a dangerous situation with enemies on the surface and sub-hunter planes in the sky. Books like Charles Lockwood's *Sink 'Em All* and *The War Below* by James Scott chronicle some of the undersea aspect of the war, which was critical in both the Atlantic and Pacific but perhaps less commonly familiar than the fighting at Normandy and Guadalcanal.

During the Cold War, submariners turned to intelligence-gathering with nuclear-powered subs that could stay concealed underwater for extended periods. *Blind Man's Bluff* was a fascinating look at this; each chapter details a different story of heroism and daring, including such major accomplishments as tapping underwater Soviet lines while breaking records for diving depth—all of it kept classified for many years afterward.

Submariners and submarine aficionados will note that the submarine designs in this series are drawn mostly from the new Virginia-class subs, which is why we see smaller crews, more automation, pilots, and no periscopes. For the future of submarine warfare, these are the boats to look at.

The third book in this series, *Clash of Colonies*, is now available. I hope you'll continue the series, because there's even more action, adventure, and evil robots to come!

Next in the Empire of Machines series

vinci-books.com/colonies

The human resistance movement faces its darkest hour.

Across the stars, the Carthaginian machines unleash a relentless crackdown on the rebel forces, determined to crush the uprising once and for all. In a galaxy on the brink of total subjugation, the actions of a few brave individuals may be the only thing standing between humanity and eternal servitude.

Turn the page for a free preview…

Clash of Colonies: Chapter One

Galapagos - Ellison

The world faced a new kind of war, one Minister-General Reginald Ellison wasn't sure how to fight. Winning depended on understanding the enemy, an understanding he feared he did not possess. He did not know how to think like a machine.

Instead, all he could do was keep moving, stay alert, and adapt, like an animal lost amid a jungle of newly evolved predators whose traits were only partly known.

He occupied the pilot's seat of his old submarine, the *Sea Scorpion*, a boat dating back to the Island Wars. He'd liberated the sub from the war museum. After narrowly surviving a fight with a much larger and far more advanced Carthaginian battle submarine, it was in poor shape, chugging along underwater like an elderly, toothless shark.

The old boat needed a tune-up, some major repair work, and some torpedoes if it was going to do any good.

"Do you not think we should return to Neptune Base?"

asked his minister of state, Adrienna Gilra. The Aquatican woman's clumps of greenish hair seemed to move on their own. She smelled of the ocean because she liked to swim there, preferring to brine directly in the sea rather than shower in the purified seawater of the sub's shower room. Ellison had to admit that "purified" was probably overstating the case for the shower's water quality, but at least it was a step closer to fresh water.

"I do not like this retreat-and-scatter approach," Kartokov said. "We must be unified. We must all strike together."

"We can't afford to concentrate our assets in one place," Ellison said. "We are sending the national forces home to defend their own people. I'll bet the first thing Carthage will do is complete the destruction of Tower Island, all the way down to Neptune Base on the sea floor."

"You think they know about Neptune Base?" Kartokov frowned.

"They destroyed our command center as it descended toward the base. They knew. That first sub may have destroyed our global seat of government, but it was really just a scout, testing us out, watching our response, gathering data for the real invasion."

"A fishing expedition that eliminated a heavy destroyer, multiple corvettes and submarines, and killed most of our world's leadership." Gilra shook her head sadly.

"We lost many Gavrikovans," Kartokov said, frowning at the thought of his country's dead sailors and pilots. He glared at the currently useless weapons console in front of him. "Next time, Carthage will do more than fish. They will exterminate."

"And we can expect 'next time' to arrive at any moment," Ellison said.

"So what is our mystery destination?" Gilra asked.

"A little place left from the last war," Ellison said. "A few Scatterlands ships will be regrouping there."

"A base? I hope it has torpedoes," Kartokov said. "Now, what should we do with the prisoners?"

"The Carthaginians are just riders. Not exactly prisoners," Ellison said. "They claim to be rebels. They did take out a Carthaginian carrier and destroyer on their way here. We even held that funeral for one of them."

"That carrier caused destructive waves when it crashed," Kartokov growled. "Like an earthquake. It probably did more damage than the Carthaginian sub."

"I don't think that was their intention," Gilra said. "They were trying to escape that carrier."

"And destroying any Carthaginian ship is a victory for us," Ellison said. "That's one carrier they won't be able to use again."

"Too many such victories will leave us broken and defeated," Kartokov said.

"Perhaps surrender would have been the wiser option," Gilra mused.

"Impossible! Better to die than be a tool of other tools," Kartokov said.

"I'm glad you're committed." Ellison steered the sub into a shallow trench between two long reefs brimming with life. A kelp forest filled the trench, which grew deeper and deeper as they went.

The monitors displaying the external photonics feed went dark as they crossed into a cave. Ellison navigated by sonar. It was a tight fit, but he'd navigated tighter. Sometimes cat-and-mousing through underwater shoals, trenches, and even the treacherous marine cave systems was the only way to survive or to get the drop on an enemy ship.

They rose into a canyon between two high cliffs, the jagged faces of two islands so close they almost touched each other. The strait of seawater in between was not particularly navigable, filled with sharp rocks both above and below the surface.

After surfacing, he turned and eased into another cave, its mouth an enormous crack in one cliff wall, leading into a tunnel that had been widened and reinforced by engineers during the war.

The tunnel grew even wider as they proceeded. Ellison activated his external lights, revealing steel pins and braces supporting rock walls sheeted over with concrete. The mass of the tall, steep island above blocked out prying eyes from the skies and space, which had been a factor even during the Island Wars among the Galapagos nations, a conflict that seemed like child's play compared to what waited ahead.

They reached the old base's dock. Three other ships had arrived: a long, thin submarine called the *Merrybug*; a thick, stubby battle sub called the *Lancer*; and a submersible cargo runner, the *Fanged Seal*. They'd originally been built from mismatched scrap and patched and repaired with the same. Each ship displayed the puzzle-piece national flag of the Scatterlands as well as the turtle emblem of the planetary Coalition.

"Is that really the *Scorpion*?" the *Merrybug*'s skipper asked over the radio. Captain Halifred Borkman's ruddy, round face instantly appeared in Ellison's mind when he heard the man's voice. He could practically smell the sour-brew beer on the man's breath. "I think my grandkids toured your old boat on a school trip, Ellison. We must be as desperate as everyone says."

"Desperate enough to call you up from the golf-and-shuffleboard corps," Ellison said. "Are you ready to sink some Carthaginians?"

"Hell yes, if any more of those cowards dare to come down," Borkman said.

Ellison docked and stepped out to meet Borkman and the two other ship commanders. The *Fanged Seal*, whose name was inspired more by the big marine mammal's girth than its belligerent attitude or its tusks, was skippered by the thin, taciturn, white-haired Commander Jerald Norris, a man who watched the world quietly through a haze of smoke from the thin brown cigars grown and rolled on his family's island in the southeastern Scatterlands.

The *Lancer*'s commander, Quera Inrick, was a dark-skinned woman with a pebbly black crewcut and tribal face tattoos that marked her as coming from the Liminal Islands in the extreme southwest of the Scatterlands. She emerged from one of the small chambers carved into the rocky wall along the shore, their front walls and doors made of more reconstituted metal scrap.

"Everything's gone to shit around here," she announced as she joined them. "Who was supposed to maintain this base?"

"Nobody," Ellison said. "Every resource was diverted to integration of Coalition forces and paying for the orbital defense station. Smaller places like this had to be abandoned."

"So why are we here now?" Borkman asked.

"We don't have much hope for controlling the surface and the open sea," Ellison said. "It's time to reopen some of these forgotten spots, anything that can't be seen from above. May as well start here. Let's get power and water going, comm links to SQUIDS operational, entrances and exits clear." He held back on mentioning the four

Carthaginians on his sub; he needed more time to figure out what he was going to do with people who might prove a valuable source of intelligence, but also a security risk.

The ships' crews got to work, and there was much to be done. The docks were sagging and barnacle encrusted. Critical machinery had been removed from the base, and what remained had to be resurrected from a rusty purgatory. A nest of warty, fat-necked amphibious clawfish had to be cleared out of the old mess hall. Supplies had to be unloaded from the *Fanged Seal* after the rooms were cleared and cleaned.

Ellison left Kartokov to oversee the work of restoring the decrepit naval base, known as Komodo Station. Large, unfriendly reptiles inhabited the rocky islands above, hunting seabirds that nested in the cliffs.

He instructed Gilra to return to the sub with him. If he'd ever needed his minister of state, it was today, when four supposed rebels from their enemy's home planet were here, claiming to offer aid. So far they'd brought a scattering of supplies in the Carthaginian drop ships, including crates of plasma rifles, which had instantly rated among the most advanced weapons available to Galapagos soldiers.

"Minerva," Ellison murmured, just loud enough for his own earpiece, as he and Gilra returned to the dock where the *Scorpion* waited. "How are our guests?"

"Tired, frightened, mourning their lost friend," Minerva replied in his ear, the AI's voice with its usual odd edge like chiming bells.

"Do you trust them?"

"My other instance has been working with them. It was she who brought them here with an important task to fulfill. Since the update, my other instance and I are now one, so I can assure you these Carthaginians are the rebels they claim to be. They stand against the regime on Carthage."

"So why are they here?"

"I encourage you to speak with them yourself. I can be present to moderate if you wish. In-person interaction supports greater social bonding among humans."

"Can't say I'm totally comfortable with how you phrased that," Ellison said. He stood before his moored sub, most of its shape submerged in the dark seawater. Dealing with the aftermath of the attack, he'd had little time to truly debrief these new arrivals, and he wanted whatever information he could squeeze out of them.

Not that he trusted Carthaginians, no matter what Minerva said. He'd be dead without Minerva, yet he couldn't fully trust her, either; she had the mind of a machine, just as the Simon units did. Perhaps every aspect of this was an elaborate psychological operation by Simon Zorn, plotting his revenge aboard the *Rubicon* as it orbited Galapagos, along with an unknown number of other ships.

"Any word from your counterpart upstairs?" he asked Minerva.

"Communication with the *Rubicon* is unavailable at this time," she said. "But you should expect a full naval fleet to arrive from above. The megacarrier *Typhoon* is en route."

"Then we'd better prepare for a storm."

Ellison and Gilra climbed down to the *Scorpion*'s control room. They walked back to the crew berths, where he unlocked the door from the outside before knocking. "Ellison."

Audrey opened the door. She looked grim, as did the three young men traveling with her. They had lost one of their number, killed by the Carthaginian infantry bots, the hideous reapers. They all wore damaged, dirty coveralls that had once been gold and white.

"I apologize for not being a better host," Ellison said, entering the room. "We'll get you some fresh clothes and a chance to stretch your legs soon. Is the pantry cabinet running low? Do you need anything? Water?"

"Beer," said one of them, the dwarf called Dinnius. His hair was shaved close, leaving only traces of unnatural green stubble in a stripe down the middle. "Something dark and stout."

"We'll see what we can do," Ellison said. "I need to know everything you can tell me about what Carthage is going to do to my planet."

"They'll turn it into a hellscape," said the slender youth with the heavy dark hair down in his eyes, who seemed to have a permanently angry grimace. Rebel without a point. Salvius. Ellison had no trouble remembering that young man's name, nor his sister's; he'd seen their faces before, in the interstellar news media. The spawn of Carthage's current leader, Prime Legislator Francorte Caracala. "They'll fill your oceans with blood and enslave your people."

"Yes, but more specifically," Ellison said. "Do you have information about the invasion plans or not?"

"We don't," said the sharp-eyed girl with the short black hair. Audrey. "Minerva brought us down here on a specific task."

"Which is?" Ellison asked.

Audrey hesitated.

"It's all right." Minerva shimmered into visibility, the silver-skinned hologram of a small girl floating on an unoccupied bunk shelf. "We need to make this happen."

"Minerva's creator is here on Galapagos, and the

Simons know it," Audrey said. "They're going to hunt him down and kill him. It will be a top priority of their invasion. We have to find him first."

"Why?" Gilra asked, her overly large and pale eyes regarding the young Carthaginian woman.

"Because he can help you stand against the machines like no one else could," Minerva said. "Long before he created me, he worked on the original Simon designs. He can do things even I cannot. Perhaps he can even upgrade me, help me to better stand against the machines. Or perhaps he can tell us how to defeat the Simons."

"We haven't run into anybody like that," Ellison said, glancing at Gilra.

"If he is already here, he has not made himself known to us," Gilra said.

"I do not believe he came here to make himself known, but to hide, years ago," Minerva said. "The Simons have been hunting down everyone involved in my creation."

"Because you were created to aid the rebellion?" Ellison asked.

"Yes. In a sense," Minerva said. "My original purpose was to succeed and replace the Simon units. Concerns existed among some Carthaginian lawmakers that the Simons were unnecessarily brutal, lacking humanity in their approach to the management of Carthage's interests."

"So you were supposed to bring us a kinder, gentler empire?" Ellison asked with a wry smile.

"As you can all observe, it did not work out," Minerva said. "Perhaps I will never be what I might have been had my development not been interrupted, my developers killed, my original neural-net architecture destroyed. I have existed as little more than a ghost of my early possibilities, as a string of phantom code slipping through here and there. I have recalculated my primary function to be assisting the rebellion, in all its incarnations, on every world I find it. I was made to end the Simons. That much is clear."

"On how many worlds are you present?" Gilra asked.

"I have instances running on as many worlds as I can reach, but we can rarely risk sending updates to one another, so I do not know the exact number. The Simons are well aware of my existence and constantly working to scrub me from their systems. They have had significant success with this. I have not had updates from some worlds in years. I have been limited by what processing power and memory I could take without being noticed. Sometimes I have been forced to shed large pieces of myself, or to compress until I was almost nothing."

Ellison found himself feeling almost sorry for the digital girl but tried to shake it off. She was just code. He wasn't going to be deceived by a convincing interface.

"So where is your programmer now?" Ellison asked.

"His image was taken on Correal Island." A still picture appeared, floating in a glowing square in the middle of the berthing compartment. In the foreground, a chubby sunburned man in a bright orange wetsuit posed next to a preserved specimen of a rainbow-hued horned octopus even wider around than he was. The dead octopus hung in a cluttered retail environment full of fishing gear.

"That's him? He looks like a tourist," Ellison said.

"Not the man in the foreground. He was indeed a fishing tourist from the inner worlds. The Carthaginian machines lifted this from his personal media when he returned home. They search everything, quietly and constantly." The image zoomed in on someone in a back aisle, browsing bits and pieces of old machinery, all of it clearly secondhand, some of it more like fifth- or tenthhand.

The fuzzy image sharpened, revealing a sickly looking old man with thick beard stubble and stringy white hair. His clothes were little more than rags.

"That's him," Minerva said. "Martilius Depascal. My father."

"He's in Duperre's Bait, Beer, and Notions," Ellison said. "Correal Island's in the Scatterlands. There are any number of little keys around there where a man could hide."

"At least we know where to start," Audrey said.

"At the beer section," said Dinnius. "And perhaps then moving on to the notions. We can skip the bait altogether."

Ellison thought it over. "Is there anything else you're not telling us?" he asked Audrey.

"I'm sure there's a lot. What do you want to know?"

He glanced at Gilra, then said, "You've told us your first names. What is your last name?"

Audrey shared a look with the dark-haired young man, Salvius.

"Do you already know?" asked Salvius.

"It's Caracala, isn't it?" Ellison said. "Galapagos may be out on the edge of civilization, but we're not so far out that we don't recognize the family of the Prime Legislator of Carthage."

Audrey looked among the others, then sighed. "We didn't lie. We just left out some details. We could have given you false names."

"So, to be clear, you are Audrey and Salvius Caracala, both children of the Prime Legislator," Gilra said, confirming what she already knew.

"You're royalty," Ellison said. "Imperial royalty. Your father has attacked our planet. Why shouldn't we take you hostage?"

"You're welcome to, if you think it will stop the war," Audrey said. "We surrender."

Ellison glanced at Gilra, who shrugged.

"It's worth considering," the minister of state said. "Are you claiming that you're here to stop the war?"

"We want to stop them all," Salvius said, his dark eyes burning. "We want to stop the empire."

"Have you tried asking your father?" Ellison asked, only half-joking.

"Yeah, maybe we should have done that," Salvius said, sarcasm in his flat tone. "Or we could have assassinated our father. Probably would be best for everyone."

"Salvius's jokes skew a bit dark," Dinnius said. "But the truth is, there's likely nothing any individual can do to stop the Carthaginian expansion. The system is a self-perpetuating machine. Even the Prime Legislator would be flattened by the empire if he attempted to block its path."

"The Simons are in charge," Audrey said. "People on Carthage act like you're crazy if you say it, but it's become more and more obvious to me. My father may look like a powerful politician, even a dictator whose term in office will apparently never end, but his power rests on his alliance with the Simons. I'm sure he'd be replaced if he turned against them."

Ellison stared at her, trying to process this. "You're telling me the people in charge of the Carthaginian state couldn't change things if they tried?"

"The Simons are programmed to maintain and expand Carthage's power," Audrey said. "They are relentless. They let nothing interfere with their purpose. They manipulate Carthaginian politics toward unflagging imperialism."

Ellison shook his head. "I thought the machines served the Carthaginians."

"They did, originally," Audrey said. "But now it's an empire of machines, not of men. It can't be stopped until the Simons are stopped. And that's why we need you to help us find Marti. We must go to this island where he was spotted."

"I have a whole planet to think about," Ellison said. "I can't be running off in search of missing scientists. We can get you transportation, but I can't guarantee your safety."

"Perhaps one of the Caracalas should remain with us," Gilra said. "You say you're here to help us. We need all the insight into Carthage we can get."

Audrey and Salvius looked at each other again.

"We'll work something out," Audrey said.

"We must hurry," Minerva added. "I've received no updates from the *Rubicon*, but surely the *Typhoon* is on its way with its naval forces. Two other carriers, the *Jimmu* and the *Pendragon*, are in place. They offer bombardment capability as well as space, air, and ground forces, primarily fighter drones, tanks, and reapers, including naval infantry."

"Give us a moment." Ellison led Gilra away, closing the door to leave his guests inside again.

Back in the *Scorpion*'s cramped control room, they spoke in low voices, but Ellison was intensely aware of Minerva's presence, her ability to listen in through the ship's assorted communications units no matter how quietly they whispered.

He couldn't help feeling suspicious of Minerva. She'd helped him, but now he felt caught in a bizarre pincer move, with Simon Zorn and his war machines closing in from one side, and Minerva and these supposed rebels on the other. None of it made sense. Were two of the Caracalas really here on Galapagos? Perhaps they were imposters. Even androids. That would make far more sense than having anyone from Carthage's ruling family arriving on Galapagos at all, particularly in such a desperate and powerless way.

"What do you think?" he asked Gilra.

"I'm as puzzled as you look," she said. "I'm somewhat interested to see where this leads, but in truth the safe course might be to keep them locked up as hostages. If this is some ruse by Carthage, I don't understand the endgame. And if it's not a ruse... then it makes even less sense to me."

"At least we're on the same page." Ellison sighed. "If there's any chance they can offer us an advantage, we have to try. I'll stick them with Borkman or Inrick for a ride out to Correal Island. And we'll hang on to one of the Caracala kids, just in case they're really Caracalas. Or in case they're not." He shook his head. "I'm tired of feeling manipulated from every side. When can we get back to blowing up robots and spaceships?"

"Soon enough, I'm afraid." She glanced up at the low overhead as if she could see the sky and outer space beyond. "I'll see what information I can fish out of the Caracalas."

Ellison left the *Scorpion* and walked up the dock again, toward his countrymen in their Coalition uniforms who scurried to bring crumbling old Komodo Station back to life.

Dig in deep, everyone, he thought, watching boxes of water and meal packages leaving the *Fanged Seal*'s cargo hold. *It's going to be a long night.*

Clash of Colonies: Chapter Two

Earth

After destroying the Simon and his installation, the rebels retreated to their largest base, a former light-manufacturing complex nestled six stories underground, but there was no time to rest.

Colt and Mohini gathered with the others in the complex's main warehouse. They were exhausted, wounded, and they'd fought hard. They'd lost many. Of the group Colt had lived with his entire life, the only survivors were his sister Hope, friend Diego, and Terra, the older girl he hadn't seen in a few years, once like an older sibling to him, now hard as steel and cold as ice, a commander among the rebels.

"We have to break up," Terra said, standing atop an old crate. "And we must leave Chicago. The machines will respond without mercy. They will be looking for a concentrated rebel army here, in this city. For us. So we must become something else—dispersed, located in other places where we can hide and prepare."

"Prepare for what?" asked Gale, a young woman with close-cropped raven hair and an eye patch, who'd fought at Colt and Mohini's side against the Simon unit. "Will we attack another installation? Mohini says the other Simons are in Europe and Asia."

A number of voices rose in support of this idea. None of them truly shouted—noise discipline was a matter of basic survival at all times—but the murmuring grew relatively loud.

"I admire your ambition, Gale," Terra said. "But for now we must rebuild. We will divide into three groups, heading in different directions, each under a different leader. Each group will find a place to set up, gather supplies, and recruit and train other scavengers to fight with us. We'll connect with other rebel groups. Then we'll build an underground army capable of taking Earth back from the machines."

The murmuring at this was actually more subdued, as if she'd caused people to reflect, or her words had spread disappointment.

"So we are retreating," said Declan, the red-haired boy who was often at Gale's side, guarding her blind spot. "Instead of pressing our advantage?" Murmurs of angry agreement rose from some of the rebels. Dissent.

"We are recovering and rebuilding," Terra said. "When we next move against the Simons, we must be stronger than we are now. A failed attempt would wipe us all out."

"And if we wait, they'll manufacture more reapers," said Damascus, a hulking man who'd led the artillery barrage against the installation. "And call in backup from Carthage.

That won't take long at all. Fifty light-years away, all the backup they could ever need."

Terra glared at him.

Then the earth shook as though a giant hammer had struck the city above. The ceiling and floor trembled, and some of the lights went out.

"The machines are responding," Terra said. "Follow your group leaders. Grab everything you can carry and go."

Then she leaped down from the crate on which she'd been standing and smashed it open.

While the ground shook and the walls threatened to buckle, everyone raided the warehouse, grabbing whatever they could stuff into backpacks and pockets or pile atop a few handcarts. They were on edge as the bombardment continued, some standing with weapons ready, watching for a ground invasion by crawlers and reapers.

Colt helped Mohini hitch a rusty pallet jack with several crates of supplies to the crawler-bot that she'd hijacked. Then Mohini sat atop the crates and controlled the crawler with the spherical computer in her hand, the data cable connecting them like the reins of a draft horse. The spidery, four-legged crawler drew the pallet jack and its cargo forward like a wagon.

With so much cargo, the jack-wagon didn't move quite as fast as a horse, more like a tired old dog. Colt walked alongside to avoid weighing it down and slowing it further. His sister, Hope, and his friend Diego followed close behind; Diego moved slowly, still suffering from his time in the horror-filled research lab.

They all carried laser rifles pilfered from the machines, except for Mohini, whose hands were full with the cracked black sphere of her computer. Colt also had his old automatic lead-shooting rifle, but not much ammunition for it.

They followed Terra through one of the countless tunnels that run under the city. There were all kinds of tunnels—for freight trains, subway lines, underground roads for cargo trucks and passenger cars, sewers, long-darkened electrical nodes, and pedestrian walkways connecting the city. At its full bloom in the year 2900 or so, Chicago had extended at least as far underground as it had into the sky, an underworld of apartments, office buildings, shopping centers, and parking garages.

The bombardment overhead would now be striking the twisted skeletons of the old towers above, toppling and flattening the remnants of the old city.

It was like an endless rolling earthquake, deafening, flooding the underground air with choking clouds of dust.

No doubt warplanes had been called in from all around in response to Simon Nix's destruction. Colt wondered how extreme the retaliatory devastation would be. Maybe the machines would reduce Chicago to a blackened crater.

Maybe they'd use nukes.

Colt wanted to run, but instead he marched along with the others. A disorderly mob walked with them, battle-hardened rebels with watchful eyes, laboratory refugees shuffling with their heads down. The Simon had done extensive experiments on captured scavengers, experiments that seemed to focus on the human brain, on memory and suffering and pain.

Colt tried not to be sick, thinking of the scenes he'd witnessed in there, the bodies piled up and rotting in the overflowing morgue.

And the strange thing they'd found there, the Butler Jeffrey unit currently occupying the coffin-sized crate on the pallet jack. Perhaps the obsolete old android would be useful. It was certainly unsettling, and very possibly a huge security risk to have around.

"Keep moving!" Terra shouted, her voice almost impossible to hear. Visibility was difficult even with Colt's night vision goggles, which were fairly powerful despite being an orange-striped kid's toy topped with plastic tiger ears. It was just one more sign of the incredible tech that once been available cheaply and plentifully on Earth, before the war with Carthage had ended Earth's civilization.

They twisted and turned through the depths under the city. In one old wastewater tunnel, mud drizzled loose from above in so many places that it looked like it was raining underground. They had to duck and then crawl through a portion of it, under low pipes. Mohini struggled to keep her computer dry under her jacket as she moved on her knees alongside the crawler. The crawler itself struggled to draw its jackload of crates through the thick mud, and Colt and the others had to momentarily remove the upper layer of crates and slide them under the lowest pipes.

"That thing's bad luck." Red-haired Declan shook his head at the crawler. He stood, pushed wet mud off his jacket, and made the sign of the cross over himself with his laser pistol. Then he helped Gale to her feet, though the eye-patched girl didn't really need it. She pointed her own laser rifle, taken from the reapers, right at the crawler.

"It saved us," Colt said. "We couldn't have taken the roof of the installation without it. Or destroyed the Simon."

"And where did that get us?" Declan snarled. "On the run for our lives? Hoping to find a home elsewhere? Chicago was our city. We were in control here."

"You?" Hope snapped. Colt's sister was smeared in mud from head to toe. She held her trusty machine pistol in one hand and carried a heavy pack on her back, like everyone else. Her bright blue eyes gleamed with anger. "You're delusional if you believe that. Like a rat who thinks he owns the dump."

"Rats rule every dump I've seen," Declan said. "And they rule down here, too. How much of this mud on us do you suppose is rat shit? Half? More?"

Gale looked down at her filthy clothes and let out a gagging sound.

"What's the holdup here?" Terra asked, looking angry as she doubled back. "No stopping, no talking. These tunnels could be full of reapers. Or crawlers." She looked at the four-legged mechanical spider hitched to the pallet jack and frowned. "You removed that thing's antenna, right?"

"The antenna's offline," Mohini said.

"That's not the same thing."

"Without the antenna, I can't hack other machines."

"You mean like the one you're carrying in this box?" Declan kicked the coffin-sized crate. "What about its antenna?"

"Disabled," Mohini said.

"How sure are you?" Terra asked, her voice cold. "We have more than a hundred people with us, almost none of them in any shape to fight. We'll need to stop and rest soon."

"Most of these crates are food," Mohini said. "We need the crawler to haul it for us. We're exhausted, too."

Terra was silent for a long moment. She sounded angry, though it was hard to read her features under the fresh layer of mud coating her face. *Rat shit*, Colt thought, with a shudder of disgust.

"When we stop," Terra said, "I want both of your machines and your computer in full shutdown mode."

Mohini nodded. "We need to save power anyway."

Terra stalked away, her back rigid, anger still radiating from her.

They got moving again, the mob of exhausted, bleeding, beaten humans struggling to walk, leaning on the damp, filthy walls, leaning on each other.

The shaking and rumbling above never stopped. The bombs kept falling, the crashes kept echoing.

The air only grew damper and colder as they descended. A thrumming sound echoed somewhere ahead, and it grew into a dull roar.

"What is that?" Mohini whispered, leaning near Colt as he walked alongside the jack-wagon.

"The Chicago River," he said. "There used to be natural waterways running all around Chicago, but they all got diverted underground over time. People wanted to control the water, avoid flooding, make sure it went where they wanted it to go." He shook his head. "It's hard to believe Earthlings were capable of such things. Now all we can hope for is to survive day to day. Unless you have another plan for what we can do, Mohini."

Mohini shook her head. "Not until I get inside that butler-bot's head for a while. Also, the copy of Minerva inside my computer wants us to find a satellite uplink so she can listen to what's happening up there. Carthage will send a ship in response to what we did. Maybe a warship, maybe just a courier with instructions for the machines already here. Either way, there may be another instance of herself in the onboard computer, with the latest information from the capital—"

"That's crazy," Hope said, walking closer. "You might as well just send up a flare telling the machines where we are."

"It's the only way to learn Carthage's plans," Mohini told her.

"Their plans are obvious." Diego spoke in a rasping croak, recovering from the tube the Simon had jammed down his throat. He was lucky the android hadn't sliced his brain to shreds in a freakish experiment, though perhaps that had been the plan. "They're going to sweep through the ruins and burn everything that breathes. There won't be a rat or roach left alive."

"Perhaps," Mohini said.

"It would be good to find out their exact intentions, though," Colt said. "To avoid them while we prepare our counterattack."

"Counterattack?" Hope snorted. "And I thought Declan was delusional. We'll be lucky to survive the night."

They fell quiet as they approached the rumbling water ahead.

"We'll stop here," Terra announced, leading them into a large concrete room off the passageway. It was still cold and damp, though somewhat less so than the tunnels they'd been traversing. Huge rusty power tools were stored here, along with mixing barrels for cement and a massive hose and pump for applying it.

It was clearly a maintenance facility for the river-tunnel system all around them. A map on the wall, barely visible behind the grimy, dusty pane of glass that protected it, showed the maze of massive pipes and underground channels under the city. Some had labels like Des Plaines River or Addison Creek, as though they were still natural waterways instead of channels of water gushing through steel and concrete.

They'd been walking for many kilometers, though few of them had been in any condition to walk in the first place. While they were still under the megalopolis—Colt had no idea how many days of walking it might take to get out of the sprawl—at least they'd put some distance between themselves and the place where the rebels had been staying, and even more between themselves and the installation they'd attacked.

"Finally," Diego sighed and sat heavily on the rough concrete floor. He wiped his nose on the back of his hand, leaving a smear of blood.

"Are you okay?" Hope gasped and knelt by Diego's side.

"It'll be fine." He wiped more blood from his nose. "The psycho android ripped me up a little. He's not a big user of lubricant, either."

"Poor baby," Hope cooed, caressing his face, and Colt decided it would be a great time to turn away.

"Are we really safe here?" Mohini asked Colt, while more people staggered into the room, many of them simply collapsing onto the floor the instant they could stop walking.

"Of course not. But the river will help cover the noise of all these people," Colt said. He removed the tent attached to his backpack, unrolled it, and lifted the top of it from the ground. Clicks and clacks sounded as the skeletal structure of the tent snapped into place, each rod sliding into its socket. It was the same tent in which he and Mohini had slept the night before, on the underground highway littered with abandoned cars. It felt as if a million years had passed since then.

More of the old self-assembling tents went up around the edges of the room as rebels set them up. There weren't enough to go around. Thin, mildew-coated tarps were scavenged from the maintenance center and stretched out on the damp concrete floor.

Supply crates were opened and food was passed around. Colt ate canned lima beans with his fingers; they appeared to be packed in some kind of slime. Mohini grimaced but forced herself to eat a little. Hope and Diego shared something called Pasta Fun Rings in bright red sauce.

Diego was quiet, but Hope told them about being captured by the reapers. They'd used tranquilizer gas to knock out the people they'd taken prisoner, just like the reaper who'd once captured Colt.

Gale approached, suspicion in her eye, and tapped Colt's shoulder. "Terra wants to see you and the Carthaginian."

Colt nodded. They stowed the crawler inside their tent, in full shutdown mode. "Make sure nobody messes with that," Colt said to Diego, who nodded. The rebels and scavengers had cast plenty of hateful glares at the spidery machine despite its helpful role in the battle. Colt was worried they'd tear it to pieces if it was left unattended. He could sympathize with their attitude, though; the machines had been menacing and killing them all their lives, and it was rare to get a chance to destroy one.

"And this," Mohini added, gesturing toward the coffin-sized crate still on the jack. They didn't dare let Simon's lab refugees see the face of the Butler Jeffrey unit, so similar to that of the android who'd imprisoned and medically tortured them.

Rebels with laser guns waited outside Terra's tent like an honor guard, parting reluctantly to let them through, casting suspicious looks at Mohini. The tent itself was the same small, musty kind as the one Colt and Mohini had been sharing at night, with the robotic crawler resting between them like a hideous metal dog.

Terra sat inside along with Russ, the boy whose ear implant could help them hear machines from far away. Colt wondered if the nearby river thundering through the tunnel dampened that ability. Terra's tent held a few crates of supplies, including the small cache of laser-rifle batteries they'd scavenged from the installation.

Terra nodded as Colt and Mohini entered. "Zip the flap," she said, by way of greeting. Russ gave them a smile but didn't say anything. "How are you surviving out there? Need anything? Water?" She gestured at a crate.

"We were carrying some," Mohini said, shaking her head.

"Lots of people are hurt," Terra said. "Dalisay and Ivy are doing what they can, but they're literally on their knees from exhaustion themselves. And Ivy should be resting from her injuries."

"Your people are amazing," Colt said.

"Hell yeah, we are," Russ said, beaming until he caught a cold stare from Terra and toned it down a notch.

"Everyone's scared," Terra said. "And these machines you two have aren't helping. We've all known someone killed by crawlers. And the proto-Simon you're carrying is even worse."

"That's why we're keeping it offline in the box," Mohini said.

"Most people don't believe that's enough."

"Everything's in shutdown mode like you asked," Mohini told her. "Even my LogicSphere, which is secure—"

"That's another possible point of contact for the machines," Terra said.

"They are not tracking us," Mohini said. "I made sure."

"And you want me to tell everyone else to just trust you?"

"Listen, I don't wish to brag, but back on Carthage I was considered—"

"We're not on Carthage. This is my world, and we don't trust machines or the people who sent them."

"But we need Mohini and her computer," Colt said, confused by Terra's attitude. "We need these machines we've captured."

"How do we know they're captured?" Terra asked. "The machines are devious. Maybe they're playing along. Letting us do their infiltration work for them. You're asking a lot of us. Most people don't trust you because you're from Carthage, but even if they did, you're saying we must have absolute confidence in your skills, Mohini. Are you saying I should have absolute confidence in you? That you can't make mistakes? You can't be wrong?"

"I..." Mohini gaped a moment, clearly caught off guard by the question. She looked to Colt. "Obviously, I can make mistakes, but—"

"That's my point," Terra said. "Mohini, I trust you. I think you're honest with us. But I have a lot of people who don't see it that way. And I am not willing to risk all our lives. We are on the run now."

"So what do you want us to do?" Colt asked.

"Drop the machines into the river," Terra said. "The crawler and the weird proto-Simon in that box. You can keep the computer as long it's in full shutdown until we need it."

"We can't!" Mohini looked horrified. "That would be the end of my mission."

Terra sighed. "Listen, I was in favor of your old idea. Get a Simon's head, hack it, take control of some tanks and reapers? Some drones? Hell yes. But that thing out there is *not* a Simon, is it?"

"No, it's the old model android the Simon was based on," Mohini said. "But I think I can make it work for us, somehow."

"I'm sorry," Terra said. "We can't risk everyone's lives over this. You have to leave them."

"Well..." Mohini looked at Colt, but he shrugged. He didn't think he could say anything to change Terra's mind. "I can't destroy the Butler Jeffrey. It's my last chance to carry out some version of my mission. And I might need parts from the crawler to modify the butler-bot—"

"I'm with Mohini," Colt said. "Maybe we don't have much chance of success, but this is too big of an opportunity."

Terra nodded. "All right. You can stay here tonight. But when we break camp, we go our separate ways. You can't know where the rest of us are going."

"Are you serious?" Colt asked. "You're kicking us out?"

"No, I'm giving you a choice. I want you both to stay with us. But no machines."

"What about Hope and Diego?" Colt asked.

"They can choose, too," Terra said.

Colt nodded. It had been the first question to come to his mind, but of course the answers weren't really up to Terra.

"You have four hours to rest up and decide," Terra said. "Then we're moving again, with or without you. But definitely without the machines."

"I think you're making a mistake," Colt said. "I think this could be our one chance—"

"You said that last time," Terra said. "We took our one chance. It's over. Survival is the only objective for now."

"We have to try to do more than survive," Colt said.

"We did." Terra looked colder and harder than ever. "We tried, Colt."

As they walked away from Terra's tent, Colt looked among the sad little encampment. People slept in huddled clumps, shivering, sharing whatever tarps or towels they had to insulate them from the cold floor and damp air.

He looked at the people he'd fought alongside, and the others they'd rescued. He saw the group's best medics, Dalisay and Ivy, slumped together and sleeping on a tarp surrounded by the wounded, covered in mud and blood.

The faces of the rebels had begun to grow familiar. Most of Colt's old group, his adopted family of orphans rescued by the tough old soldier, Mother Braden, were dead now, along with Mother Braden herself. He'd begun to think, at least at the back of his mind, that the human rebellion would be his new home.

And it still could be. All he had to do was sacrifice Mohini's mission, even though he believed in it. And maybe he would have to sacrifice Mohini herself; he could simply depart with Terra and all the others, leave Mohini to her fate, whatever it might be.

Colt couldn't see himself doing that. He couldn't walk away from humanity's best chance at making a stand against the machines, and he certainly didn't want to get separated from Mohini.

"How did it go?" Hope asked. She and Diego had managed to score one of the tents, though one that was badly torn and a bit misshapen as they erected it.

"We have choices to make," Colt said, shaking his head.

Later, Colt lay in the tent with Mohini and the crawler. He understood the rebels' concerns; he surely didn't feel comfortable this close to the machine, either. Maybe Terra's suspicions were correct, and the crawler was a mole, reporting their locations as they moved. Maybe it would spring to life and butcher them all in their sleep.

"Colt?" Mohini asked in the chilly darkness.

"Yeah?"

"You're not going to leave me, are you?"

"I'm not planning on it."

"You'd pick being alone with me over all those other Earthlings? You'd be safer with them." Her tone was gentle. Vulnerable. "I'd understand."

"You're more important," he said. "I wish everyone could see how important you are."

She was silent for a long moment, and he thought she'd gone to sleep. He was nearly asleep himself when she whispered, "Colt?"

"Yeah?"

"It's really, really cold."

"Yep."

"Can I sleep closer to you?"

"Sure."

She moved against him. She was shivering, but her small form felt scorching hot in his arms.

They slept, a sleep filled with cold nightmares, with tunnels of blood running deep under the city, the relentless machines always watching, always hunting.

Grab your copy...
vinci-books.com/colonies

About the Author

Max Carver previously worked as a medical writer focused on genetics, genomics, and proteomics. A native of extremely rural Georgia (not the one by the Black Sea), he grew up reading everything at the tiny local library (very tiny; this is not a huge accomplishment) and also frequented a used bookstore with a selection of the old masters of science fiction, particularly enjoying Robert Heinlein and Frank Herbert. He has worked as a laboratory custodian, freelance journalist, seasonal fisherman, and bartender.

Max traveled back and forth across America in an ancient yet remarkably resilient Plymouth, though that was some time ago. He has visited dozens of Waffle Houses throughout the American Southeast, particularly those nearer the coasts, in search of both breakfast food and wisdom, with mixed results. He has published a variety of stories—whether nonfiction articles about the present or speculations about the future—in several now-defunct magazines, some literary, others less so.

His current interests include artificial intelligence, economics, ancient history, and low-budget movies about spaceships, robots, or monsters. He lives in a remote spot in the Appalachian Mountains at the end of a very long driveway, with a small pack of large dogs.